D1380393

*Many of these titles are also available as abridged and unabridged audiobooks.
Order the full range of Horus Heresy novels and audiobooks from*
www.blacklibrary.com

Download the full range of Horus Heresy audio dramas from
www.blacklibrary.com

THE HORUS HERESY®

Dan Abnett

HORUS RISING

The seeds of heresy are sown

BLACK LIBRARY

For Rick Priestley, John Blanche and Alan Merrett, Architects of the Imperium.

Thanks to Graham McNeill and Ben Counter, to Nik and Lindsey, and to Geoff Davis at GW Maidstone.

A BLACK LIBRARY PUBLICATION

Paperback edition first published in Great Britain in 2006.
Hardback edition published in 2012.
This edition published in 2013 by
Black Library,
Games Workshop Ltd.,
Willow Road,
Nottingham, NG7 2WS, UK.

10 9 8 7 6 5 4 3 2 1

Cover illustration by Neil Roberts.

A CIP record for this book is available from the British Library.

UK ISBN: 978 1 84970 617 9
US ISBN: 978 1 84970 618 6

See Black Library on the internet at

www.blacklibrary.com

Find out more about Games Workshop
and the world of Warhammer 40,000 at

www.games-workshop.com

Printed and bound by CPI Group (UK) Ltd, Croydon, CR0 4YY

THE HORUS HERESY®
It is a time of legend.

Mighty heroes battle for the right to rule the galaxy.

The vast armies of the Emperor of Earth have conquered
the galaxy in a Great Crusade – the myriad alien races have
been smashed by the Emperor's elite warriors and
wiped from the face of history.

The dawn of a new age of supremacy for humanity beckons.

Gleaming citadels of marble and gold celebrate the many
victories of the Emperor. Triumphs are raised on a million
worlds to record the epic deeds of his most powerful
and deadly warriors.

First and foremost amongst these are the primarchs,
superheroic beings who have led the Emperor's armies of
Space Marines in victory after victory. They are unstoppable
and magnificent, the pinnacle of the Emperor's genetic
experimentation. The Space Marines are the mightiest
human warriors the galaxy has ever known, each capable
of besting a hundred normal men or more in combat.

Organised into vast armies of tens of thousands called
Legions, the Space Marines and their primarch leaders
conquer the galaxy in the name of the Emperor.

Chief amongst the primarchs is Horus, called the Glorious,
the Brightest Star, favourite of the Emperor, and like a son
unto him. He is the Warmaster, the commander-in-chief
of the Emperor's military might, subjugator of a thousand
thousand worlds and conqueror of the galaxy. He is a
warrior without peer, a diplomat supreme.

Horus is a star ascendant, but how much further can a star
rise before it falls?

~ DRAMATIS PERSONAE ~

The Primarchs

HORUS	First Primarch and Warmaster, Commander-in-Chief of the Luna Wolves
ROGAL DORN	Primarch of the Imperial Fists
SANGUINIUS	Primarch of the Blood Angels

The XVI Legion 'Luna Wolves'

EZEKYLE ABADDON	First Captain
TARIK TORGADDON	Captain, Second Company
IACTON QRUZE	'The Half-heard', captain, Third Company
HASTUR SEJANUS	Captain, Fourth Company
HORUS AXIMAND	'Little Horus', captain, Fifth Company
SERGHAR TARGOST	Captain, Seventh Company, Lodge Master
GARVIEL LOKEN	Captain, Tenth Company
LUC SEDIRAE	Captain, 13th Company
TYBALT MARR	'The Either', captain, 18th Company
VERULAM MOY	'The Or', captain, 19th Company
LEV GOSHEN	Captain, 25th Company
KALUS EKADDON	Captain, Catulan Reaver Squad
FALKUS KIBRE	'Widowmaker', captain, Justaerin Terminator Squad
NERO VIPUS	Sergeant, Locasta Tactical Squad
XAVYER JUBAL	Sergeant, Hellebore Tactical Squad
MALOGHURST	'The Twisted', equerry to the Warmaster

The XVII Legion 'Word Bearers'

EREBUS   First Chaplain

The VII Legion 'Imperial Fists'

SIGISMUND   First Captain

The III Legion 'Emperor's Children'

EIDOLON   Lord Commander

LUCIUS   Captain

SAUL TARVITZ   Captain

The IX Legion 'Blood Angels'

RALDORON   Chapter Master

The 63rd Imperial Expedition Fleet

BOAS COMNENUS   Master of the Fleet

HEKTOR VARVARAS   Lord Commander of the Army

ING MAE SING   Mistress of Astropaths

ERFA HINE

SWEQ CHOROGUS   High Senior of the Navis Nobilite

REGULUS   Adept, envoy of the Martian
                        Mechanicum

The 140th Imperial Expedition Fleet

MATHANUAL AUGUST   Master of the Fleet

Imperial Personae

KYRIL SINDERMANN	Primary Iterator
IGNACE KARKASY	Official remembrancer, poet
MERSADIE OLITON	Official remembrancer, documentarist
EUPHRATI KEELER	Official remembrancer, imagist
PEETER EGON MOMUS	Architect designate
AENID RATHBONE	High Administratrix

Non Imperial Personae

JEPHTA NAUD	General Commander, the armies of the interex
DIATH SHEHN	Abbrocarius
ASHEROT	Indentured kinebrach, Keeper of Devices
MITHRAS TULL	Subordinate Commander, the armies of the interex

PART ONE
THE DECEIVED

I was there, the day Horus slew the Emperor…

'Myths grow like crystals, according to their own recurrent pattern; but there must be a suitable core to start their growth.'

– attributed to the remembrancer Koestler (fl. M2)

'The difference between gods and daemons largely depends upon where one is standing at the time.'

– the Primarch Lorgar

'The new light of science shines more brightly than the old light of sorcery. Why, then, do we not seem to see as far?'

– the Sumaturan philosopher Sahlonum (fl. M29)

ONE

Blood from misunderstanding
Our brethren in ignorance
The Emperor dies

'I WAS THERE,' he would say afterwards, until afterwards became a time quite devoid of laughter. 'I was there, the day Horus slew the Emperor.' It was a delicious conceit, and his comrades would chuckle at the sheer treason of it.

The story was a good one. Torgaddon would usually be the one to cajole him into telling it, for Torgaddon was the joker, a man of mighty laughter and idiot tricks. And Loken would tell it again, a tale rehearsed through so many retellings, it almost told itself.

Loken was always careful to make sure his audience properly understood the irony in his story. It was likely that he felt some shame about his complicity in the matter itself, for it was a case of blood spilled from misunderstanding. There was a great tragedy implicit in the tale of the Emperor's murder, a tragedy that Loken always wanted his listeners to appreciate. But the death of Sejanus was usually all that fixed their attentions.

That, and the punchline.

It had been, as far as the warp-dilated horologs could attest, the two hundred and third year of the Great Crusade. Loken always set his story in its proper time and place. The commander had been Warmaster for about a year, since the triumphant conclusion of the Ullanor campaign, and he was anxious to prove his new-found status, particularly in the eyes of his brothers.

Warmaster. Such a title. The fit was still new and unnatural, not yet worn in.

It was a strange time to be abroad amongst stars. They had been doing what they had been doing for two centuries, but now it felt unfamiliar. It was a start of things. And an ending too.

The ships of the 63rd Expedition came upon the Imperium by chance. A sudden etheric storm, later declared providential by Maloghurst, forced a route alteration, and they translated into the edges of a system comprising nine worlds.

Nine worlds, circling a yellow sun.

Detecting the shoal of rugged expedition warships on station at the out-system edges, the Emperor first demanded to know their occupation and agenda. Then he painstakingly corrected what he saw as the multifarious errors in their response.

Then he demanded fealty.

He was, he explained, the Emperor of Mankind. He had stoically shepherded his people through the miserable epoch of warp storms, through the Age of Strife, staunchly maintaining the rule and law of man. This had been expected of him, he declared. He had kept the flame of human culture alight through the aching isolation of Old Night. He had sustained this precious, vital fragment, and kept it intact, until such time as the scattered diaspora of humanity re-established contact. He rejoiced that such a time was now at hand. His soul leapt to see the orphan ships returning to the heart of the Imperium. Everything was ready and waiting. Everything had been preserved. The orphans would be embraced to his bosom, and then the Great Scheme of rebuilding would begin, and the Imperium of Mankind would stretch itself out again across the stars, as was its birthright.

As soon as they showed him proper fealty. As Emperor. Of mankind.

The commander, quite entertained by all accounts, sent Hastur Sejanus to meet with the Emperor and deliver greeting.

Sejanus was the commander's favourite. Not as proud or irascible as Abaddon, nor as ruthless as Sedirae, nor even as solid and venerable as Iacton Qruze, Sejanus was the perfect captain, tempered evenly in all respects. A warrior and a diplomat in equal measure, Sejanus's martial record, second only to Abaddon's, was easily forgotten when in company with the man himself. A beautiful man, Loken would say, building his tale, a beautiful man adored by all. 'No finer figure in Mark IV plate than Hastur Sejanus. That he is remembered, and his deeds celebrated, even here amongst us, speaks of Sejanus's qualities. The noblest hero of the Great Crusade.' That was how Loken would describe him to the eager listeners. 'In future times, he will be recalled with such fondness that men will name their sons after him.'

Sejanus, with a squad of his finest warriors from the Fourth Company, travelled in-system in a gilded barge, and was received for audience by the Emperor at his palace on the third planet.

And killed.

Murdered. Hacked down on the onyx floor of the palace even as he stood before the Emperor's golden throne. Sejanus and his glory squad – Dymos, Malsandar, Gorthoi and the rest – all slaughtered by the Emperor's elite guard, the so-called Invisibles.

Apparently, Sejanus had not offered the correct fealty. Indelicately, he had suggested there might actually be *another* Emperor.

The commander's grief was absolute. He had loved Sejanus like a son. They had warred side by side to affect compliance on a hundred worlds. But the commander, always sanguine and wise in such matters, told his signal men to offer the Emperor another chance. The commander detested resorting to war, and always sought alternative paths away from violence, where such were workable. This was a mistake, he reasoned, a terrible, terrible mistake. Peace could be salvaged. This 'Emperor' could be made to understand.

It was about then, Loken liked to add, that a suggestion of quote marks began to appear around the 'Emperor's' name.

It was determined that a second embassy would be despatched. Maloghurst volunteered at once. The commander agreed, but ordered the speartip forwards into assault range. The intent was clear: one hand extended open, in peace, the other held ready as a fist. If the second embassy failed, or was similarly met with violence, then the fist would already be in position to strike. That sombre day, Loken said, the honour of the speartip had fallen, by the customary drawing of lots, to the strengths of Abaddon, Torgaddon, 'Little Horus' Aximand. And Loken himself.

At the order, battle musters began. The ships of the speartip slipped forward, running under obscurement. On board, Storm-birds were hauled onto their launch carriages. Weapons were issued and certified. Oaths of moment were sworn and witnessed. Armour was machined into place around the anointed bodies of the chosen.

In silence, tensed and ready to be unleashed, the speartip watched as the shuttle convoy bearing Maloghurst and his envoys arced down towards the third planet. Surface batteries smashed them out of the heavens. As the burning scads of debris from Maloghurst's flotilla billowed away into the atmosphere, the 'Emperor's' fleet elements rose up out of the oceans, out of the high cloud, out of the gravity wells of nearby moons. Six hundred warships, revealed and armed for war.

Abaddon broke obscurement and made a final, personal plea to the 'Emperor', beseeching him to see sense. The warships began to fire on Abaddon's speartip.

'My commander,' Abaddon relayed to the heart of the waiting fleet, 'there is no dealing here. This fool imposter will not listen.'

And the commander replied, 'Illuminate him, my son, but spare all you can. That order not withstanding, avenge the blood of my noble Sejanus. Decimate this "Emperor's" elite murderers, and bring the imposter to me.'

'And so,' Loken would sigh, 'we made war upon our brethren, so lost in ignorance.'

IT WAS LATE evening, but the sky was saturated with light. The photo-tropic towers of the High City, built to turn and follow the sun with their windows during the day, shifted uneasily at the pulsating radiance in the heavens. Spectral shapes swam high in the upper atmosphere: ships engaging in a swirling mass, charting brief, nonsensical zodiacs with the beams of their battery weapons.

At ground level, around the wide, basalt platforms that formed the skirts of the palace, gunfire streamed through the air like horizontal rain, hosing coils of tracer fire that dipped and slithered heavily like snakes, die-straight zips of energy that vanished as fast as they appeared, and flurries of bolt shells like blizzarding hail. Downed Stormbirds, many of them crippled and burning, littered twenty square kilometres of the landscape.

Black, humanoid figures paced slowly in across the limits of the palace sprawl. They were shaped like armoured men, and they trudged like men, but they were giants, each one hundred and forty metres tall. The Mechanicum had deployed a half-dozen of its Titan war engines. Around the Titans' soot-black ankles, troops flooded forward in a breaking wave three kilometres wide.

The Luna Wolves surged like the surf of the wave, thousands of gleaming white figures bobbing and running forward across the skirt platforms, detonations bursting amongst them, lifting rippling fireballs and trees of dark brown smoke. Each blast juddered the ground with a gritty thump, and showered down dirt as an after-curse. Assault craft swept in over their heads, low, between the shambling frames of the wide-spaced Titans, fanning the slowly lifting smoke clouds into sudden, energetic vortices.

Every Astartes helmet was filled with vox-chatter: snapping voices, chopping back and forth, their tonal edges roughened by the transmission quality.

It was Loken's first taste of mass war since Ullanor. Tenth Company's first taste too. There had been skirmishes and scraps, but nothing testing. Loken was glad to see that his cohort hadn't grown rusty. The unapologetic regimen of live drills and punishing exercises he'd maintained had kept them whetted as sharp and serious as the terms of the oaths of moment they had taken just hours before.

Ullanor had been glorious; a hard, unstinting slog to dislodge and overthrow a bestial empire. The greenskin had been a pernicious and resilient foe, but they had broken his back and kicked over the embers of his revel fires. The commander had won the field through the employment of his favourite, practiced strategy: the speartip thrust to tear out the throat. Ignoring the greenskin masses, which had outnumbered the crusaders five to one, the commander had struck directly at the Overlord and his command coterie, leaving the enemy headless and without direction.

The same philosophy operated here. Tear out the throat and let the body spasm and die. Loken and his men, and the war engines that supported them, were the edge of the blade unsheathed for that purpose.

But this was not like Ullanor at all. No thickets of mud and clay-built ramparts, no ramshackle fortresses of bare metal and wire, no black powder air bursts or howling ogre-foes. This was not a barbaric brawl determined by blades and upper body strength.

This was modern warfare in a civilised place. This was man against man, inside the monolithic precincts of a cultured people. The enemy possessed ordnance and firearms every bit the technological match of the Legion forces, and the skill and training to use them. Through the green imaging of his visor, Loken saw armoured men with energy weapons ranged against them in the lower courses of the palace. He saw tracked weapon carriages, automated artillery; nests of four or even eight automatic cannons shackled together on cart platforms that lumbered forward on hydraulic legs.

Not like Ullanor at all. That had been an ordeal. This would be a test. Equal against equal. Like against like.

Except that for all its martial technologies, the enemy lacked one essential quality, and that quality was locked within each and every case of Mark IV power armour: the genetically enhanced flesh and blood of the Imperial Astartes. Modified, refined, post-human, the Astartes were superior to anything they had met or would ever meet. No fighting force in the galaxy could ever hope to match the Legions, unless the stars went out, and madness ruled, and lawful sense turned upside down. For, as Sedirae had once said, 'The only thing that can beat an Astartes is another Astartes', and they had all laughed at that. The impossible was nothing to be scared of.

The enemy – their armour a polished magenta trimmed in silver, as Loken later discovered when he viewed them with his helmet off – firmly held the induction gates into the inner palace. They were big men, tall, thick through the chest and shoulders, and at the peak of fitness. Not one of them, not even the tallest, came up to the chin of one of the Luna Wolves. It was like fighting children.

Well-armed children, it had to be said.

Through the billowing smoke and the jarring detonations, Loken led the veteran First Squad up the steps at a run, the plasteel soles of their boots grating on the stone: First Squad, Tenth Company, Hellebore Tactical Squad, gleaming giants in pearl-white armour, the wolf head insignia stark black on their auto-responsive shoulder plates. Crossfire zigzagged around them from the defended gates ahead. The night air shimmered with the heat distortion of weapons discharge. Some kind of upright, automated mortar was casting a sluggish, flaccid stream of fat munition charges over their heads.

'Kill it!' Loken heard Brother-Sergeant Jubal instruct over the link. Jubal's order was given in the curt argot of Cthonia, their derivation world, a language that the Luna Wolves had preserved as their battle-tongue.

The battle-brother carrying the squad's plasma cannon obeyed without hesitation. For a dazzling half-second, a twenty-metre ribbon of light linked the muzzle of his weapon to the auto-mortar, and then the device engulfed the facade of the palace in a roasting wash of yellow flame.

Dozens of enemy soldiers were cast down by the blast. Several were thrown up into the air, landing crumpled and boneless on the flight of steps.

'Into them!' Jubal barked.

Wildfire chipped and pattered off their armour. Loken felt the distant sting of it. Brother Calends stumbled and fell, but righted himself again, almost at once.

Loken saw the enemy scatter away from their charge. He swung his bolter up. His weapon had a gash in the metal of the foregrip, the legacy of a greenskin's axe during Ullanor, a cosmetic mark Loken had told the armourers not to finish out. He began to fire, not on burst, but on single shot, feeling the weapon buck and kick against his palms. Bolter rounds were explosive penetrators. The men he hit popped like blisters, or shredded like bursting fruit. Pink mist fumed off every ruptured figure as it fell.

'Tenth Company!' Loken shouted. 'For the Warmaster!'

The war cry was still unfamiliar, just another aspect of the newness. It was the first time Loken had declaimed it in war, the first chance he'd had since the honour had been bestowed by the Emperor after Ullanor.

By the Emperor. The true Emperor.

'Lupercal! Lupercal!' the Wolves yelled back as they streamed in, choosing to answer with the old cry, the Legion's pet-name for their beloved commander. The warhorns of the Titans boomed.

They stormed the palace. Loken paused by one of the induction gates, urging his front-runners in, carefully reviewing the advance of his company main force. Hellish fire continued to rake them from the upper balconies and towers. In the far distance, a brilliant dome of light suddenly lifted into the sky, astonishingly bright and vivid. Loken's visor automatically dimmed. The ground trembled and a noise like a thunderclap reached him. A capital ship of some size, stricken and ablaze, had fallen out of the sky and impacted in the outskirts of the High City. Drawn by the flash, the phototropic towers above him fidgeted and rotated.

Reports flooded in. Aximand's force, Fifth Company, had secured the Regency and the pavilions on the ornamental lakes to the west of the High City. Torgaddon's men were driving up through the lower town, slaying the armour sent to block them.

Loken looked east. Three kilometres away, across the flat plain of the basalt platforms, across the tide of charging men and striding Titans and stitching fire, Abaddon's company, First Company, was crossing the bulwarks into the far flank of the palace. Loken magnified his view, resolving hundreds of white-armoured figures pouring through the smoke and chop-fire. At the front of them, the dark figures of First Company's foremost Terminator squad, the Justaerin. They wore polished black armour, dark as night, as if they belonged to some other, black Legion.

'Loken to First,' he sent. 'Tenth has entry.'

There was a pause, a brief distort, then Abaddon's voice answered. 'Loken, Loken… are you trying to shame me with your diligence?'

'Not for a moment, First Captain,' Loken replied. There was a strict hierarchy of respect within the Legion, and though he was a senior officer, Loken regarded the peerless First Captain with awe. All of the Mournival, in fact, though Torgaddon had always favoured Loken with genuine shows of friendship.

Now Sejanus was gone, Loken thought. The aspect of the Mournival would soon change.

'I'm playing with you, Loken,' Abaddon sent, his voice so deep that some vowel sounds were blurred by the vox. 'I'll meet you at the feet of this false Emperor. First one there gets to illuminate him.'

Loken fought back a smile. Ezekyle Abaddon had seldom sported with him before. He felt blessed, elevated. To be a chosen man was enough, but to be in with the favoured elite, that was every captain's dream.

Reloading, Loken entered the palace through the induction gate, stepping over the tangled corpses of the enemy dead. The plaster facings of the inner walls had been cracked and blown down, and loose crumbs, like dry sand, crunched under his feet. The air was full of smoke, and his visor display kept jumping from one register to another as it attempted to compensate and get a clean reading.

He moved down the inner hall, hearing the echo of gunfire from deeper in the palace compound. The body of a brother lay slumped in a doorway to his left, the large, white-armoured corpse odd and out of place amongst the smaller enemy bodies. Marjex, one of the Legion's Apothecaries, was bending over him. He glanced up as Loken approached, and shook his head.

'Who is it?' Loken asked.

'Tibor, of Second Squad,' Marjex replied. Loken frowned as he saw the devastating head wound that had stopped Tibor.

'The Emperor knows his name,' Loken said.

Marjex nodded, and reached into his narthecium to get the reductor tool. He was about to remove Tibor's precious gene-seed, so that it might be returned to the Legion banks.

Loken left the Apothecary to his work, and pushed on down the hall. In a wide colonnade ahead, the towering walls were decorated with frescoes, showing familiar scenes of a haloed Emperor upon a golden throne. How blind these people are, Loken thought, how sad this is. One day, one single day with the iterators, and they would understand. We are not the enemy. We are the same, and we bring with us a glorious message of redemption. Old Night is done. Man walks the stars again, and the might of the Astartes walks at his side to keep him safe.

In a broad, sloping tunnel of etched silver, Loken caught up with elements of Third Squad. Of all the units in his company, Third Squad – Locasta Tactical Squad – was his favourite and his favoured. Its commander, Brother-Sergeant Nero Vipus, was his oldest and truest friend.

'How's your humour, captain?' Vipus asked. His pearl-white plate was smudged with soot and streaked with blood.

'Phlegmatic, Nero. You?'

'Choleric. Red-raged, in fact. I've just lost a man, and two more of mine are injured. There's something covering the junction ahead. Something heavy. Rate of fire like you wouldn't believe.'

'Tried fragging it?'

'Two or three grenades. No effect. And there's nothing to see. Garvi, we've all heard about these so-called Invisibles. The ones that butchered Sejanus. I was wondering–'

'Leave the wondering to me,' Loken said. 'Who's down?'

Vipus shrugged. He was a little taller than Loken, and his shrug made the heavy ribbing and plates of his armour clunk together. 'Zakias.'

'Zakias? No…'

'Torn into shreds before my very eyes. Oh, I feel the hand of the ship on me, Garvi.'

The hand of the ship. An old saying. The commander's flagship was called the *Vengeful Spirit*, and in times of duress or loss, the Wolves liked to draw upon all that implied as a charm, a totem of retribution.

'In Zakias's name,' Vipus growled, 'I'll find this bastard Invisible and–'

'Sooth your choler, brother. I've no use for it,' Loken said. 'See to your wounded while I take a look.'

Vipus nodded and redirected his men. Loken pushed up past them to the disputed junction.

It was a vault-roofed crossways where four hallways met. The area read cold and still to his imaging. Fading smoke wisped up into the rafters. The ouslite floor had been chewed and peppered with thousands of impact craters. Brother Zakias, his body as yet unretrieved, lay in pieces at the centre of the crossway, a steaming pile of shattered white plasteel and bloody meat.

Vipus had been right. There was no sign of an enemy present. No heat-trace, not even a flicker of movement. But studying the area, Loken saw a heap of empty shell cases, glittering brass, that had spilled out from behind a bulkhead across from him. Was that where the killer was hiding?

Loken bent down and picked up a chunk of fallen plasterwork. He lobbed it into the open. There was a click, and then a hammering deluge of autofire raked across the junction. It lasted five seconds, and in that time over a thousand rounds were expended. Loken saw the fuming shell cases spitting out from behind the bulkhead as they were ejected.

The firing stopped. Fycelene vapour fogged the junction. The gunfire had scored a mottled gouge across the stone floor, pummelling Zakias's corpse in the process. Spots of blood and scraps of tissue had been spattered out.

Loken waited. He heard a whine and the metallic clunk of an autoloader system. He read weapon heat, fading, but no body warmth.

'Won a medal yet?' Vipus asked, approaching.

'It's just an automatic sentry gun,' Loken replied.

'Well, that's a small relief at least,' Vipus said. 'After the grenades we've pitched in that direction, I was beginning to wonder if these vaunted Invisibles might be "Invulnerables" too. I'll call up Devastator support to–'

'Just give me a light flare,' Loken said.

Vipus stripped one off his leg plate and handed it to his captain. Loken ignited it with a twist of his hand, and threw it down the hallway opposite. It bounced, fizzling, glaring white hot, past the hidden killer.

There was a grind of servos. The implacable gunfire began to roar down the corridor at the flare, kicking it and bouncing it, ripping into the floor.

'Garvi–' Vipus began.

Loken was running. He crossed the junction, thumped his back against the bulkhead. The gun was still blazing. He wheeled round the bulkhead and saw the sentry gun, built into an alcove.

A squat machine, set on four pad feet and heavily plated, it had turned its short, fat, pumping cannons away from him to fire on the distant, flickering flare.

Loken reached over and tore out a handful of its servo flexes. The guns stuttered and died.

'We're clear!' Loken called out. Locasta moved up.

'That's generally called showing off,' Vipus remarked.

Loken led Locasta up the corridor, and they entered a fine state apartment. Other apartment chambers, similarly regal, beckoned beyond. It was oddly still and quiet.

'Which way now?' Vipus asked.

'We go find this "Emperor",' Loken said.

Vipus snorted. 'Just like that?'

'The First Captain bet me I couldn't reach him first.'

'The First Captain, eh? Since when was Garviel Loken on pally terms with him?'

'Since Tenth breached the palace ahead of First. Don't worry, Nero, I'll remember you little people when I'm famous.'

Nero Vipus laughed, the sound snuffling out of his helmet mask like the cough of a consumptive bull.

What happened next didn't make either of them laugh at all.

TWO

Meeting the Invisibles
At the foot of a Golden Throne
Lupercal

'CAPTAIN LOKEN?'

He looked up from his work. 'That's me.'

'Forgive me for interrupting,' she said. 'You're busy.'

Loken set aside the segment of armour he had been polishing and rose to his feet. He was almost a metre taller than her, and naked but for a loin cloth. She sighed inwardly at the splendour of his physique. The knotted muscles, the old ridge-scars. He was handsome too, this one, fair hair almost silver, cut short, his pale skin slightly freckled, his eyes grey like rain. What a waste, she thought.

Though there was no disguising his inhumanity, especially in this bared form. Apart from the sheer mass of him, there was the overgrown gigantism of the face, that particular characteristic of the Astartes, almost equine, plus the hard, taut shell of his ribless torso, like stretched canvas.

'I don't know who you are,' he said, dropping a nub of polishing fibre into a little pot, and wiping his fingers.

She held out her hand. 'Mersadie Oliton, official remembrancer,' she said. He looked at her tiny hand and then shook it, making it seem even more tiny in comparison with his own giant fist.

'I'm sorry,' she said, laughing, 'I keep forgetting you don't do that out here. Shaking hands, I mean. Such a parochial, Terran custom.'

'I don't mind it. Have you come from Terra?'

'I left there a year ago, despatched to the crusade by permit of the Council.'

'You're a remembrancer?'

'You know what that means?'

'I'm not stupid,' Loken said.

'Of course not,' she said, hurriedly. 'I meant no offence.'

'None taken.' He eyed her. Small and frail, though possibly beautiful. Loken had very little experience of women. Perhaps they were all frail and beautiful. He knew enough to know that few were as black as her. Her skin was like burnished coal. He wondered if it were some kind of dye.

He wondered too about her skull. Her head was bald, but not shaved. It seemed polished and smooth as if it had never known hair. The cranium was enhanced somehow, extending back in a streamlined sweep that formed a broad ovoid behind her nape. It was like she had been crowned, as if her simple humanity had been made more regal.

'How can I help you?' he asked.

'I understand you have a story, a particularly entertaining one. I'd like to remember it, for posterity.'

'Which story?'

'Horus killing the Emperor.'

He stiffened. He didn't like it when non-Astartes humans called the Warmaster by his true name.

'That happened months ago,' he said dismissively. 'I'm sure I won't remember the details particularly well.'

'Actually,' she said, 'I have it on good authority you can be persuaded to tell the tale quite expertly. I've been told it's very popular amongst your battle-brothers.'

Loken frowned. Annoyingly, the woman was correct. Since the taking of the High City, he'd been required – forced would not be too strong a word – to retell his first-hand account of the events in the palace tower on dozens of occasions. He presumed it was because of Sejanus's death. The Luna Wolves needed catharsis. They needed to hear how Sejanus had been so singularly avenged.

'Someone put you up to this, Mistress Oliton?' he asked.

She shrugged. 'Captain Torgaddon, actually.'

Loken nodded. It was usually him. 'What do you want to know?'

'I understand the general situation, for I have heard it from others, but I'd love to have your personal observations. What was it like? When you got inside the palace itself, what did you find?'

Loken sighed, and looked round at the rack where his power armour was displayed. He'd only just started cleaning it. His private arming chamber was a small, shadowy vault adjoining the off-limits embarkation deck, the metal walls lacquered pale green. A cluster of glow-globes lit the room, and an Imperial eagle had been stencilled on one wall plate, beneath which copies of Loken's various oaths of moment had been pinned. The close air smelled of oils and lapping powder. It was a tranquil, introspective place, and she had invaded that tranquility.

Becoming aware of her trespass, she suggested, 'I could come back later, at a better time.'

'No, now's fine.' He sat back down on the metal stool where he had been perching when she'd entered. 'Let me see... When we got inside the palace, what we found was the Invisibles.'

'Why were they called that?' she asked.

'Because we couldn't see them,' he replied.

THE INVISIBLES WERE waiting for them, and they well deserved their sobriquet.

Just ten paces into the splendid apartments, the first brother died. There was an odd, hard bang, so hard it was painful to feel and hear, and Brother Edrius fell to his knees, then folded onto his side. He had been struck in the face by some form of energy weapon. The white plasteel/ceramite alloy of his visor and breastplate had actually deformed into a rippled crater, like heated wax that had flowed and then set again. A second bang, a quick concussive vibration of air, obliterated an ornamental table beside Nero Vipus. A third bang dropped Brother Muriad, his left leg shattered and snapped off like a reed stalk.

The science adepts of the false Imperium had mastered and harnessed some rare and wonderful form of field technology, and armed their elite guard with it. They cloaked their bodies with a passive application, twisting light to render themselves invisible. And they were able to project it in a merciless, active form that struck with mutilating force.

Despite the fact that they had been advancing combat-ready and wary, Loken and the others were taken completely off guard. The Invisibles were even hidden to their visor arrays. Several had simply been standing in the chamber, waiting to strike.

Loken began to fire, and Vipus's men did likewise. Raking the area ahead of him, splintering furniture, Loken hit something. He saw pink mist kiss the air, and something fell down with enough force to overturn a chair. Vipus scored a hit too, but not before Brother Tarregus had been struck with such power that his head was punched clean off his shoulders.

The cloak technology evidently hid its users best if they

remained still. As they moved, they became semi-visible, heat-haze suggestions of men surging to attack. Loken adapted quickly, firing at each blemish of air. He adjusted his visor gain to full contrast, almost black and white, and saw them better: hard outlines against the fuzzy background. He killed three more. In death, several lost their cloaks. Loken saw the Invisibles revealed as bloody corpses. Their armour was silver, ornately composed and machined with a remarkable detail of patterning and symbols. Tall, swathed in mantles of red silk, the Invisibles reminded Loken of the mighty Custodian Guard that warded the Imperial Palace on Terra. This was the bodyguard corps which had executed Sejanus and his glory squad at a mere nod from their master.

Nero Vipus was raging, offended by the cost to his squad. The hand of the ship was truly upon him.

He led the way, cutting a path into a towering room beyond the scene of the ambush. His fury gave Locasta the opening it needed, but it cost him his right hand, crushed by an Invisible's blast. Loken felt choler too. Like Nero, the men of Locasta were his friends. Rituals of mourning awaited him. Even in the darkness of Ullanor, victory had not been so dearly bought.

Charging past Vipus, who was down on his knees, groaning in pain as he tried to pluck the mangled gauntlet off his ruined hand, Loken entered a side chamber, shooting at the air blemishes that attempted to block him. A jolt of force tore his bolter from his hands, so he reached over his hip and drew his chainsword from its scabbard. It whined as it kicked into life. He hacked at the faint outlines jostling around him and felt the toothed blade meet resistance. There was a shrill scream. Gore drizzled out of nowhere and plastered the chamber walls and the front of Loken's suit.

'Lupercal!' he grunted, and put the full force of both arms

behind his strokes. Servos and mimetic polymers, layered between his skin and his suit's outer plating to form the musculature of his power armour, bunched and flexed. He landed a trio of two-handed blows. More blood showered into view. There was a warbled shriek as loops of pink, wet viscera suddenly became visible. A moment later, the field screening the soldier flickered and failed, and revealed his disembowelled form, stumbling away down the length of the chamber, trying to hold his guts in with both hands.

Invisible force stabbed at Loken again, scrunching the edge of his left shoulder guard and almost knocking him off his feet. He rounded and swung the chainsword. The blade struck something, and shards of metal flew out. The shape of a human figure, just out of joint with the space it occupied, as if it had been cut out of the air and nudged slightly to the left, suddenly filled in. One of the Invisibles, his charged field sparking and crackling around him as it died, became visible and swung his long, bladed lance at Loken.

The blade rebounded off Loken's helm. Loken struck low with his chainsword, ripping the lance out of the Invisible's silver gauntlets and buckling its haft. At the same time, Loken lunged, shoulder barging the warrior against the chamber wall so hard that the friable plaster of the ancient frescoes crackled and fell out.

Loken stepped back. Winded, his lungs and ribcage almost crushed flat, the Invisible made a gagging, sucking noise and fell down on his knees, his head lolling forward. Loken sawed his chainsword down and sharply up again in one fluid, practiced mercy stroke, and the Invisible's detached head bounced away.

Loken circled slowly, the humming blade raised ready in his right hand. The chamber floor was slick with blood and black scraps of meat. Shots rang out from nearby rooms. Loken walked

across the chamber and retrieved his bolter, hoisting it in his left
fist with a clatter.

Two Luna Wolves entered the chamber behind him, and Loken
briskly pointed them off into the left-hand colonnade with a
gesture of his sword.

'Form up and advance,' he snapped into his link. Voices
answered him.

'Nero?'

'I'm behind you, twenty metres.'

'How's the hand?'

'I left it behind. It was getting in the way.'

Loken prowled forward. At the end of the chamber, past the
crumpled, leaking body of the Invisible he had disembowelled,
sixteen broad marble steps led up to a stone doorway. The splendid stone frame was carved with complex linenfold motifs.

Loken ascended the steps slowly. Mottled washes of light cast
spastic flickers through the open doorway. There was a remarkable stillness. Even the din of the fight engulfing the palace all
around seemed to recede. Loken could hear the tiny taps made
by the blood dripping off his outstretched chainsword onto the
steps, a trail of red beads up the white marble.

He stepped through the doorway.

The inner walls of the tower rose up around him. He had evidently stepped through into one of the tallest and most massive
of the palace's spires. A hundred metres in diameter, a kilometre
tall.

No, more than that. He'd come out on a wide, onyx platform
that encircled the tower, one of several ring platforms arranged
at intervals up the height of the structure, but there were more
below. Peering over, Loken saw as much tower drop away into the
depths of the earth as stood proud above him.

He circled slowly, gazing around. Great windows of glass or

some other transparent substance glazed the tower from top to bottom between the ring platforms, and through them the light and fury of the war outside flared and flashed. No noise, just the flickering glow, the sudden bursts of radiance.

He followed the platform round until he found a sweep of curved stairs, flush with the tower wall, that led up to the next level. He began to ascend, platform to platform, scanning for any blurs of light that might betray the presence of more Invisibles.

Nothing. No sound, no life, no movement except the shimmer of light from outside the windows as he passed them. Five floors now, six.

Loken suddenly felt foolish. The tower was probably empty. This search and purge should have been left to others while he marshalled Tenth Company's main force.

Except… its ground-level approach had been so furiously protected. He looked up, pushing his sensors hard. A third of a kilometre above him, he fancied he caught a brief sign of movement, a partial heat-lock.

'Nero?'

A pause. 'Captain.'

'Where are you?'

'Base of a tower. Heavy fighting. We–' There was a jumble of noises, the distorted sounds of gunfire and shouting. 'Captain? Are you still there?'

'Report!'

'Heavy resistance. We're locked here! Where are–'

The link broke. Loken hadn't been about to give away his position anyway. There was something in this tower with him. At the very top, something was waiting.

The penultimate deck. From above came a soft creaking and grinding, like the sails of a giant windmill. Loken paused. At this height, through the wide panes of glass, he was afforded

a view out across the palace and the High City. A sea of luminous smoke, underlit by widespread firestorms. Some buildings
glowed pink, reflecting the light of the inferno. Weapons flashed,
and energy beams danced and jumped in the dark. Overhead,
the sky was full of fire too, a mirror of the ground. The speartip
had visited murderous destruction upon the city of the 'Emperor'.

But had it found the throat?

He mounted the last flight of steps, his grip on the weapons tight.

The uppermost ring platform formed the base of the tower's
top section, a vast cupola of crystal-glass petals, ribbed together
with steel spars that curved up to form a finial mast at the apex
high above. The entire structure creaked and slid, turning slightly
one way then another as it responded phototropically to the
blooms of light outside in the night. On one side of the platform,
its back to the great windows, sat a golden throne. It was a massive object, a heavy plinth of three golden steps rising to a vast
gilt chair with a high back and coiled arm rests.

The throne was empty.

Loken lowered his weapons. He saw that the tower top turned
so that the throne was always facing the light. Disappointed,
Loken took a step towards the throne, and then halted when he
realised he wasn't alone after all.

A solitary figure stood away to his left, hands clasped behind its
back, staring out at the spectacle of war.

The figure turned. It was an elderly man, dressed in a floor-
length mauve robe. His hair was thin and white, his face thinner
still. He stared at Loken with glittering, miserable eyes.

'I defy you,' he said, his accent thick and antique. 'I defy you,
invader.'

'Your defiance is noted,' Loken replied, 'but this fight is over. I
can see you've been watching its progress from up here. You must
know that.'

'The Imperium of Man will triumph over all its enemies,' the man replied.

'Yes,' said Loken. 'Absolutely, it will. You have my promise.'

The man faltered, as if he did not quite understand.

'Am I addressing the so-called "Emperor"?' Loken asked. He had switched off and sheathed his sword, but he kept his bolter up to cover the robed figure.

'So-called?' the man echoed. 'So-called? You cheerfully blaspheme in this royal place. The Emperor is the Emperor Undisputed, saviour and protector of the race of man. You are some imposter, some evil daemon–'

'I am a man like you.'

The other scoffed. 'You are an imposter. Made like a giant, malformed and ugly. No man would wage war upon his fellow man like this.' He gestured disparagingly at the scene outside.

'Your hostility started this,' Loken said calmly. 'You would not listen to us or believe us. You murdered our ambassadors. You brought this upon yourself. We are charged with the reunification of mankind, throughout the stars, in the name of the Emperor. We seek to establish compliance amongst all the fragmentary and disparate strands. Most greet us like the lost brothers we are. You resisted.'

'You came to us with lies!'

'We came with the truth.'

'Your truth is obscenity!'

'Sir, the truth itself is amoral. It saddens me that we believe the same words, the very same ones, but value them so differently. That difference has led directly to this bloodshed.'

The elderly man sagged, deflated. 'You could have left us alone.'

'What?' Loken asked.

'If our philosophies are so much at odds, you could have passed us by and left us to our lives, unviolated. Yet you did not.

Why? Why did you insist on bringing us to ruin? Are we such a threat to you?'

'Because the truth–' Loken began.

'–is amoral. So you said, but in serving your fine truth, invader, you make yourself immoral.'

Loken was surprised to find he didn't know quite how to answer. He took a step forward and said, 'I request you surrender to me, sir.'

'You are the commander, I take it?' the elderly man asked.

'I command Tenth Company.'

'You are not the overall commander, then? I assumed you were, as you entered this place ahead of your troops. I was waiting for the overall commander. I will submit to him, and to him alone.'

'The terms of your surrender are not negotiable.'

'Will you not even do that for me? Will you not even do me that honour? I would stay here, until your lord and master comes in person to accept my submission. Fetch him.'

Before Loken could reply, a dull wail echoed up into the tower top, gradually increasing in volume. The elderly man took a step or two backwards, fear upon his face.

The black figures rose up out of the tower's depths, ascending slowly, vertically, up through the open centre of the ring platform. Ten Astartes warriors, the blue heat of their whining jump pack burners shimmering the air behind them. Their power armour was black, trimmed with white. Catulan Reaver Squad, First Company's veteran assault pack. First in, last out.

One by one, they came in to land on the edge of the ring platform, deactivating their jump packs.

Kalus Ekaddon, Catulan's captain, glanced sidelong at Loken.

'The First Captain's compliments, Captain Loken. You beat us to it after all.'

'Where is the First Captain?' Loken asked.

'Below, mopping up,' Ekaddon replied. He set his vox to transmit. 'This is Ekaddon, Catulan. We have secured the false emperor–'

'No,' said Loken firmly.

Ekaddon looked at him again. His visor lenses were stern and unreflective jet glass set in the black metal of his helmet mask. He bowed slightly. 'My apologies, captain,' he said, archly. 'The prisoner and the honour are yours, of course.'

'That's not what I meant,' Loken replied. 'This man demands the right to surrender in person to our commander-in-chief.'

Ekaddon snorted, and several of his men laughed. 'This bastard can demand all he likes, captain,' Ekaddon said, 'but he's going to be cruelly disappointed.'

'We are dismantling an ancient empire, Captain Ekaddon,' Loken said firmly. 'Might we not display some measure of gracious respect in the execution of that act? Or are we just barbarians?'

'He murdered Sejanus!' spat one of Ekaddon's men.

'He did,' Loken agreed. 'So should we just murder him in response? Didn't the Emperor, praise be his name, teach us always to be magnanimous in victory?'

'The Emperor, praise be his name, is not with us,' Ekaddon replied.

'If he's not with us in spirit, captain,' Loken replied, 'then I pity the future of this crusade.'

Ekaddon stared at Loken for a moment, then ordered his second to transmit a signal to the fleet. Loken was quite sure Ekaddon had not backed down because he'd been convinced by any argument or fine principle. Though Ekaddon, as Captain of First Company's assault elite, had glory and favour on his side, Loken, a company captain, had superiority of rank.

'A signal has been sent to the Warmaster,' Loken told the elderly man.

'Is he coming here? Now?' the man asked eagerly.

'Arrangements will be made for you to meet him,' Ekaddon snapped.

They waited for a minute or two for a signal response. Astartes attack ships, their engines glowing, streaked past the windows. The light from huge detonations sheeted the southern skies and slowly died away. Loken watched the criss-cross shadows play across the ring platform in the dying light.

He started. He suddenly realised why the elderly man had insisted so furiously that the commander should come in person to this place. He clamped his bolter to his side and began to stride towards the empty throne.

'What are you doing?' the elderly man asked.

'Where is he?' Loken cried. 'Where is he really? Is he invisible too?'

'Get back!' the elderly man cried out, leaping forward to grapple with Loken.

There was a loud bang. The elderly man's ribcage blew out, spattering blood, tufts of burned silk and shreds of meat in all directions. He swayed, his robes shredded and on fire, and pitched over the edge of the platform.

Limbs limp, his torn garments flapping, he fell away like a stone down the open drop of the palace tower.

Ekaddon lowered his bolt pistol. 'I've never killed an emperor before,' he laughed.

'That wasn't the Emperor,' Loken yelled. 'You moron! The Emperor's been here all the time.' He was close to the empty throne now, reaching out a hand to grab at one of the golden armrests. A blemish of light, almost perfect, but not so perfect that shadows behaved correctly around it, recoiled in the seat.

This is a trap. Those four words were the next that Loken was going to utter. He never got the chance.

The golden throne trembled and broadcast a shockwave of invisible force. It was a power like that which the elite guard had wielded, but a hundred times more potent. It slammed out in all directions, casting Loken and all the Catulan off their feet like corn sheaves in a hurricane. The windows of the tower top shattered outwards in a multicoloured blizzard of glass fragments.

Most of Catulan Reaver Squad simply vanished, blown out of the tower, arms flailing, on the bow-wave of energy. One struck a steel spar on his way out. Back snapped, his body tumbled away into the night like a broken doll. Ekaddon managed to grab hold of another spar as he was launched backwards. He clung on, plasteel digits sinking into the metal for purchase, legs trailing out behind him horizontally as air and glass and gravitic energy assaulted him.

Loken, too close to the foot of the throne to be caught by the full force of the shockwave, was knocked flat. He slid across the ring platform towards the open fall, his white armour shrieking as it left deep grooves in the onyx surface. He went over the edge, over the sheer drop, but the wall of force carried him on like a leaf across the hole and slammed him hard against the far lip of the ring. He grabbed on, his arms over the lip, his legs dangling, held in place as much by the shock pressure as by the strength of his own, desperate arms.

Almost blacking out from the relentless force, he fought to hold on.

Inchoate light, green and dazzling, sputtered into being on the platform in front of his clawing hands. The teleport flare became too bright to behold, and then died, revealing a god standing on the edge of the platform.

The god was a true giant, as large again to any Astartes warrior as an Astartes was to a normal man. His armour was white gold, like the sunlight at dawn, the work of master artificers. Many symbols covered its surfaces, the chief of which was the motif of a single, staring eye fashioned across the breastplate. Robes of white cloth fluttered out behind the terrible, haloed figure.

Above the breastplate, the face was bare, grimacing, perfect in every dimension and detail, suffused in radiance. So beautiful. So very beautiful.

For a moment, the god stood there, unflinching, beset by the gale of force, but unmoving, facing it down. Then he raised the storm bolter in his right hand and fired into the tumult.

One shot.

The echo of the detonation rolled around the tower. There was a choking scream, half lost in the uproar, and then the uproar itself stilled abruptly.

The wall of force died away. The hurricane faded. Splinters of glass tinkled as they rained back down onto the platform.

No longer impelled, Ekaddon crashed back down against the blown-out sill of the window frame. His grip was secure. He clawed his way back inside and got to his feet.

'My lord!' he exclaimed, and dropped to one knee, his head bowed.

With the pressure lapsed, Loken found he could no longer support himself. Hands grappling, he began to slide back over the lip where he had been hanging. He couldn't get any purchase on the gleaming onyx.

He slipped off the edge. A strong hand grabbed him around the wrist and hauled him up onto the platform.

Loken rolled over, shaking. He looked back across the ring at the golden throne. It was a smoking ruin, its secret mechanisms exploded from within. Amidst the twisted, ruptured plates and broken workings, a smouldering corpse sat upright, teeth grinning from a blackened skull, charred, skeletal arms still braced along the throne's coiled rests.

'So will I deal with all tyrants and deceivers,' rumbled a deep voice.

Loken looked up at the god standing over him. 'Lupercal...' he murmured.

The god smiled. 'Not so formal, please, captain,' whispered Horus.

'May I ask you a question?' Mersadie Oliton said.

Loken had taken a robe down from a wall peg and was putting it on. 'Of course.'

'Could we not have just left them alone?'

'No. Ask a better question.'

'Very well. What is he like?'

'What is who like, lady?' he asked.

'Horus.'

'If you have to ask, you've not met him,' he said.

'No, I haven't yet, captain. I've been waiting for an audience. Still, I would like to know what you think of Horus–'

'I think he is Warmaster,' Loken said. His tone was stone hard. 'I think he is the master of the Luna Wolves and the chosen proxy of the Emperor, praise be his name, in all our undertakings. He is the first and foremost of all primarchs. And I think I take offence when a mortal voices his name without respect or title.'

'Oh!' she said. 'I'm sorry, captain, I meant no–'

'I'm sure you didn't, but he is *Warmaster* Horus. You're a remembrancer. Remember that.'

THREE

Replevin
Amongst the remembrancers
Raised to the four

THREE MONTHS AFTER the battle for the High City, the first of the remembrancers had joined the expedition fleet, brought directly from Terra by mass conveyance. Various chroniclers and record- ers had, of course, been accompanying Imperial forces since the commencement of the Great Crusade, two hundred sidereal years earlier. But they had been individuals, mostly volunteers or accidental witnesses, gathered up like road dust on the advanc- ing wheels of the crusader hosts, and the records they had made had been piecemeal and irregular. They had commemorated events by happenstance, sometimes inspired by their own artistic appetites, sometimes encouraged by the patronage of a particu- lar primarch or lord commander, who thought it fit to have his deeds immortalised in verse or text or image or composition.

Returning to Terra after the victory of Ullanor, the Emperor had decided it was time a more formal and authoritative celebration of mankind's reunification be undertaken. The fledgling Council of Terra evidently agreed wholeheartedly, for the bill inaugurating the foundation and sponsorship of the remembrancer order had been countersigned by no less a person than Malcador the Sigillite, First Lord of the Council. Recruited from all levels of Terran society – and from the societies of other key Imperial worlds – simply on the merit of their creative gifts, the remembrancers were quickly accredited and assigned, and despatched to join all the key expedition fleets active in the expanding Imperium.

At that time, according to War Council logs, there were four thousand two hundred and eighty-seven primary expedition fleets engaged upon the business of the crusade, as well as sixty thousand odd secondary deployment groups involved in compliance or occupation endeavours, with a further three hundred and seventy-two primary expeditions in regroup and refit, or resupplying as they awaited new tasking orders. Almost four point three million remembrancers were sent abroad in the first months following the ratification of the bill. 'Arm the bastards,' Primarch Russ had been reported as saying, 'and they might win a few bloody worlds for us in between verses.'

Russ's sour attitude reflected well the demeanor of the martial class. From primarch down to common army soldier, there was a general unease about the Emperor's decision to quit the crusade campaign and retire to the solitude of his palace on Terra. No one had questioned the choice of First Primarch Horus as Warmaster to act in his stead. They simply questioned the need for a proxy at all.

The formation of the Council of Terra had come as more unpleasant news. Since the inception of the Great Crusade, the War Council, formed principally of the Emperor and the primarchs, had been the epicentre of Imperial authority. Now, this new body supplanted it, taking up the reins of Imperial governance, a body composed of civilians instead of warriors. The War Council, left under Horus's leadership, effectively became relegated to a satellite status, its responsibilities focused on the campaign and the campaign alone.

For no crime of their own, the remembrancers, most of them eager and excited at the prospect of the work ahead, found themselves the focus of that discontent everywhere they went. They were not welcomed, and they found their commission hard to fulfil. Only later, when the eaxector tributi administrators began to visit expedition fleets, did the discontent find a better, truer target to exercise itself upon.

So, three months after the battle of the High City, the remembrancers arrived to a cold welcome. None of them had known what to expect. Most had never been off-world before. They were virgin and innocent, over-eager and gauche. It didn't take long for them to become hardened and cynical at their reception.

When they arrived, the fleet of the 63rd Expedition still encircled the capital world. The process of replevin had begun, as the Imperial forces sectioned the 'Imperium', dismantled its mechanisms, and bestowed its various properties upon the Imperial commanders chosen to oversee its dispersal.

Aid ships were flocking down from the fleet to the surface, and hosts of the Imperial Army had been deployed to effect police actions. Central resistance had collapsed almost overnight following the 'Emperor's' death, but fighting continued to spasm amongst some of the western cities, as well as on three of the other worlds in the system. Lord Commander Varvaras, an honourable, 'old school' veteran, was the commander of the army forces attached to the expedition fleet, and not for the first time he found himself organising an effort to pick up the pieces behind an Astartes speartip. 'A body often twitches as it dies,' he remarked philosophically to the Master of the Fleet. 'We're just making sure it's dead.'

The Warmaster had agreed to a state funeral for the 'Emperor'.

He declared it only right and proper, and sympathetic to the desires of a people they wished to bring to compliance rather than crush wholesale. Voices were raised in objection, particularly as the ceremonial interment of Hastur Sejanus had only just taken place, along with the formal burials of the battle-brothers lost at the High City. Several Legion officers, including Abaddon himself, refused point blank to allow his forces to attend any funeral rites for the killer of Sejanus. The Warmaster understood this, but fortunately there were other Astartes amongst the expedition who could take their place.

Primarch Dorn, escorted by two companies of his Imperial Fists, the VII Legion, had been travelling with the 63rd Expedition for eight months, while Dorn conducted talks with the Warmaster about future War Council policies.

Because the Imperial Fists had taken no part in the annexation of the planet, Rogal Dorn agreed to have his companies stand tribute at the 'Emperor's' funeral. He did this so that the Luna Wolves would not have to tarnish their honour. Gleaming in their yellow plate, the Imperial Fists silently lined the route of the 'Emperor's' cortege as it wound its way through the battered avenues of the High City to the necropolis.

By order of the Warmaster, bending to the will of the chief captains and, most especially, the Mournival, no remembrancers were permitted to attend.

IGNACE KARKASY WANDERED into the retiring room and sniffed at a decanter of wine. He made a face.

'It's fresh opened,' Keeler told him sourly.

'Yes, but local vintage,' Karkasy replied. 'This petty little empire. No wonder it fell so easily. Any culture founded upon a wine so tragic shouldn't survive long.'

'It lasted five thousand years, through the limits of Old Night,'

Keeler said. 'I doubt the quality of its wine influenced its survival.'

Karkasy poured himself a glass, sipped it and frowned. 'All I can say is that Old Night must have seemed much longer here than it actually was.'

Euphrati Keeler shook her head and turned back to her work, cleaning and refitting a hand-held picter unit of very high quality.

'And then there's the matter of sweat,' Karkasy said. He sat down on a lounger and put his feet up, settling the glass on his wide chest. He sipped again, grimacing, and rested his head back. Karkasy was a tall man, generously upholstered in flesh. His garments were expensive and well-tailored to suit his bulk. His round face was framed by a shock of black hair.

Keeler sighed and looked up from her work. 'The what?'

'The sweat, dear Euphrati, the sweat! I have been observing the Astartes. Very big, aren't they? I mean to say, very big in every measurement by which one might quantify a man.'

'They're Astartes, Ignace. What did you expect?'

'Not sweat, that's what. Not such a rank, pervasive reek. They are our immortal champions, after all. I expected them to smell rather better. Fragrant, like young gods.'

'Ignace, I have no clue how you got certified.'

Karkasy grinned. 'Because of the beauty of my lyric, my dear, because of my mastery of words. Although that might be found wanting here. How may I begin...?

'The Astartes save us from the brink, the brink,
But oh my life how they stink, they stink.'

Karkasy sniggered, pleased with himself. He waited for a response, but Keeler was too occupied with her work.

'Dammit!' Keeler complained, throwing down her delicate tools. 'Servitor? Come here.'

One of the waiting servitors stalked up to her on thin, piston legs. She held out her picter. 'This mechanism is jammed. Take it for repair. And fetch me my spare units.'

'Yes, mistress,' the servitor croaked, taking the device. It plodded away. Keeler poured herself a glass of wine from the decanter and went to lean at the rail. Below, on the sub-deck, most of the expedition's other remembrancers were assembling for luncheon. Three hundred and fifty men and women gathered around formally laid tables, servitors moving amongst them, offering drinks. A gong was sounding.

'Is that lunch already?' Karkasy asked from the lounger.

'Yes,' she said.

'And is it going to be one of the damned iterators hosting again?' he queried.

'Yes. Sindermann yet again. The topic is promulgation of the living truth.'

Karkasy settled back and tapped his glass. 'I think I'll take luncheon here,' he said.

'You're a bad man, Ignace,' Keeler laughed. 'But I think I'll join you.'

Keeler sat down on the chaise facing him, and settled back. She was tall, lean-limbed and blonde, her face pale and slender. She wore chunky army boots and fatigue breeches, with a black combat jacket open to show a white vest, like a cadet officer, but the very masculinity of her chosen garb made her feminine beauty all the more apparent.

'I could write a whole epic about you,' Karkasy said, gazing.

Keeler snorted. It had become a daily routine for him to make a pass at her.

'I've told you, I'm not interested in your wretched, pawing approaches.'

'Don't you like men?' he asked, tilting his reclined head on one side.

'Why?'

'You dress like one.'

'So do you. Do you like men?'

Karkasy made a pained expression and sat back again, fiddling with the glass on his chest. He stared up at the heroic figures painted on the roof of the mezzanine. He had no idea what they were supposed to represent. Some great act of triumph that clearly had involved a great deal of standing on the bodies of the slain with arms thrust into the sky whilst shouting.

'Is this how you expected it to be?' he asked quietly.

'What?'

'When you were selected,' he said. 'When they contacted me, I felt so…'

'So what?'

'So… proud, I suppose. I imagined so much. I thought I would set foot amongst the stars and become a part of mankind's finest moment. I thought I would be uplifted, and thus produce my finest works.'

'And you're not?' Keeler asked.

'The beloved warriors we've been sent here to glorify couldn't be less helpful if they tried.'

'I've had some success,' Keeler said. 'I was down on the assembly deck earlier, and captured some fine images. I've put in a request to be allowed transit to the surface. I want to see the war zone first-hand.'

'Good luck. They'll probably deny you. Every request for access I've made has been turned down.'

'They're warriors, Ig. They've been warriors for a long time. They resent the likes of us. We're just passengers, along for the ride, univited.'

'You got your shots,' he said.

Keeler nodded. 'They don't seem to mind me.'

'That's because you dress like a man,' he smiled.

The hatch slid open and a figure joined them in the quiet mezzanine chamber. Mersadie Oliton went directly to the table where the decanter sat, poured herself a drink, and knocked it back. Then she stood, silently, gazing out at the drifting stars beyond the barge's vast window ports.

'What's up with her now?' Karkasy ventured.

'Sadie?' Keeler asked, getting to her feet and setting her glass down. 'What happened?'

'Apparently, I just offended someone,' Oliton said quickly, pouring another drink.

'Offended? Who?' Keeler asked.

'Some haughty Space Marine bastard called Loken. Bastard!'

'You got time with Loken?' Karkasy asked, sitting up rapidly and swinging his feet to the deck. 'Loken? *Tenth Company Captain* Loken?'

'Yes,' Oliton said. 'Why?'

'I've been trying to get near him for a month now,' Karkasy said. 'Of all the captains, they say, he is the most steadfast, and he's to take Sejanus's place, according to the rumour mill. How did you get authorisation?'

'I didn't,' Oliton said. 'I was finally given credentials for a brief interview with Captain Torgaddon, which I counted as no small success in itself, given the days I've spent petitioning to meet him, but I don't think he was in the mood to talk to me. When I went to see him at the appointed time, his equerry turned up instead and told me Torgaddon was busy. Torgaddon had sent the equerry to take me to see Loken. "Loken's got a good story," he said.'

'Was it a good story?' Keeler asked.

Mersadie nodded. 'Best I've heard, but I said something he didn't like, and he turned on me. Made me feel this small.' She gestured with her hand, and then took another swig.

'Did he smell of sweat?' Karkasy asked.

'No. No, not at all. He smelled of oils. Very sweet and clean.'

'Can you get me an introduction?' asked Ignace Karkasy.

HE HEARD FOOTSTEPS, then a voice called his name. 'Garvi?'

Loken looked around from his sword drill and saw, through the bars of the cage, Nero Vipus framed in the doorway of the blade-school. Vipus was dressed in black breeches, boots and a loose vest, and his truncated arm was very evident. The missing hand had been bagged in sterile jelly, and nanotic serums injected to reform the wrist so it would accept an augmetic implant in a week or so. Loken could still see the scars where Vipus had used his chainsword to amputate his own hand.

'What?'

'Someone to see you,' Vipus said.

'If it's another damn remembrancer–' Loken began.

Vipus shook his head. 'It's not. It's Captain Torgaddon.'

Loken lowered his blade and deactivated the practice cage as Vipus drew aside. The target dummies and armature blades went dead around him, and the upper hemisphere of the cage slid into the roof space as the lower hemisphere retracted into the deck beneath the mat. Tarik Torgaddon entered the blade-school chamber, dressed in fatigues and a long coat of silver mail. His features were saturnine, his hair black. He grinned at Vipus as the latter slipped out past him. Torgaddon's grin was full of perfect white teeth.

'Thanks, Vipus. How's the hand?'

'Mending, captain. Fit to be rebonded.'

'That's good,' said Torgaddon. 'Wipe your arse with the other one for a while, all right? Carry on.'

Vipus laughed and disappeared.

Torgaddon chuckled at his own quip and climbed the short

steps to face Loken in the middle of the canvas mat. He paused
at a blade rack outside the opened cage, selected a long-handled
axe, and drew it out, hacking the air with it as he advanced.

'Hello, Garviel,' he said. 'You've heard the rumour, I suppose?'

'I've heard all sorts of rumours, sir.'

'I mean the one about you. Take a guard.'

Loken tossed his practice blade onto the deck and quickly drew
a tabar from the nearest rack. It was all-steel, blade and handle
both, and the cutting edge of the axe head had a pronounced
curve. He raised it in a hunting stance and took up position facing Torgaddon.

Torgaddon feinted, then smote in with two furious chops.
Loken deflected Torgaddon's axe head with the haft of his tabar,
and the blade-school rang with chiming echoes. The smile had
not left Torgaddon's face.

'So, this rumour…' he continued, circling.

'This rumour,' Loken nodded. 'Is it true?'

'No,' said Torgaddon. Then he grinned impishly. 'Of course it
bloody is! Or maybe it's not… No, it is.' He laughed loudly at
the mischief.

'That's funny,' said Loken.

'Oh, belt up and smile,' Torgaddon hissed, and scythed in
again, striking at Loken with two very non-standard cross-swings
that Loken had trouble dodging. He was forced to spin his body
out of the way and land with his feet wide-braced.

'Interesting work,' Loken said, circling again, his tabar low and
loose. 'Are you, may I ask, just making these moves up?'

Torgaddon grinned. 'Taught to me by the Warmaster himself,'
he said, pacing around and allowing the long axe to spin in his
fingers. The blade flashed in the glow of the downlighters aimed
on the canvas.

He halted suddenly, and aimed the head of the axe at Loken.

'Don't you want this, Garviel? Terra, I put you up for this myself.'

'I'm honoured, sir. I thank you for that.'

'And it was seconded by Ekaddon.'

Loken raised his eyebrows.

'All right, no it wasn't. Ekaddon hates your guts, my friend.'

'The feeling is mutual.'

'That's the boy,' Torgaddon roared, and lunged at Loken. Loken smashed the hack away, and counter-chopped, forcing Torgaddon to leap back onto the edges of the mat. 'Ekaddon's an arse,' Torgaddon said, 'and he feels cheated you got there first.'

'I only–' Loken began.

Torgaddon raised a finger for silence. 'You got there first,' he said quietly, not joking any more, 'and you saw the truth of it. Ekaddon can go hang, he's just smarting. Abaddon seconded you for this.'

'The First Captain?'

Torgaddon nodded. 'He was impressed. You beat him to the punch. Glory to the Tenth. And the vote was decided by the Warmaster.'

Loken lowered his guard completely. 'The Warmaster?'

'He wants you in. Told me to tell you that himself. He appreciated your work. He admired your sense of honour. "Tarik," he said to me, "if anyone's going to take Sejanus's place, it should be Loken." That's what he said.'

'Did he?'

'No.'

Loken looked up. Torgaddon was coming at him with his axe high and whirling. Loken ducked, side-stepped, and thumped the butt of his tabar's haft into Torgaddon's side, causing Torgaddon to mis-step and stumble.

Torgaddon exploded in laughter. 'Yes! Yes, he did. Terra, you're too easy, Garvi. Too easy. The look on your face!'

Loken smiled thinly. Torgaddon looked at the axe in his hand, and then tossed it aside, as if suddenly bored with the whole thing. It landed with a clatter in the shadows off the mat.

'So what do you say?' Torgaddon asked. 'What do I tell them? Are you in?'

'Sir, it would be the finest honour of my life,' Loken said.

Torgaddon nodded and smiled. 'Yes, it would,' he said, 'and here's your first lesson. You call me Tarik.'

IT WAS SAID that the iterators were selected via a process even more rigorous and scrupulous than the induction mechanisms of the Astartes. 'One man in a thousand might become a Legion warrior,' so the sentiment went, 'but only one in a hundred thousand is fit to be an iterator.'

Loken could believe that. A prospective Astartes had to be sturdy, fit, genetically receptive, and ripe for enhancement. A chassis of meat and bone upon which a warrior could be built.

But to be an iterator, a person had to have certain rare gifts that belied enhancement. Insight, articulacy, political genius, keen intelligence. The latter could be boosted, either digitally or pharmaceutically, of course, and a mind could be tutored in history, ethic-politics and rhetoric. A person could be taught what to think, and how to express that line of thought, but he couldn't be taught *how* to think.

Loken loved to watch the iterators at work. On occasions, he had delayed the withdrawal of his company so that he could follow their functionaries around conquered cities and watch as they addressed the crowds. It was like watching the sun come out across a field of wheat.

Kyril Sindermann was the finest iterator Loken had ever seen. Sindermann held the post of Primary Iterator in the 63rd Expedition, and was responsible for the shaping of the message. He had, it was well known, a deep and intimate friendship with the Warmaster, as well as the expedition master and the senior equerries. And his name was known by the Emperor himself.

Sindermann was finishing a briefing in the School of Iterators when Loken strayed into the audience hall, a long vault set deep in the belly of the *Vengeful Spirit*. Two thousand men and women, each dressed in the simple, beige robes of their office, sat in the banks of tiered seating, rapt by his every word.

'To sum up, for I've been speaking far too long,' Sindermann was saying, 'this recent episode allows us to observe genuine blood and sinew beneath the wordy skin of our philosophy. The truth we convey is the truth, because we say it is the truth. Is that enough?'

He shrugged.

'I don't believe so. "My truth is better than your truth" is a school-yard squabble, not the basis of a culture. "I am right, so you are wrong" is a syllogism that collapses as soon as one applies any of a number of fundamental ethical tools. I am right, ergo, you are wrong. We can't construct a constitution on that, and we cannot, should not, will not be persuaded to iterate on its basis. It would make us what?'

He looked out across his audience. A number of hands were raised.

'There?'

'Liars.'

Sindermann smiled. His words were being amplified by the array of vox-mics set around his podium, and his face magnified by picter onto the hololithic wall behind him. On the wall, his smile was three metres wide.

'I was thinking bullies, or demagogues, Memed, but "liars" is apt. In fact, it cuts deeper than my suggestions. Well done. *Liars*. That is the one thing we iterators can never allow ourselves to become.'

Sindermann took a sip of water before continuing. Loken, at the back of the hall, sat down in an empty seat. Sindermann was a tall man, tall for a non-Astartes at any rate, proudly upright, spare, his patrician head crowned by fine white hair. His eyebrows were black, like the chevron markings on a Luna Wolf shoulder plate. He had a commanding presence, but it was his voice that really mattered. Pitched deep, rounded, mellow, compassionate, it was the vocal tone that got every iterator candidate selected. A soft, delicious, clean voice that communicated reason and sincerity and trust. It was a voice worth searching through one hundred thousand people to find.

'Truth and lies,' Sindermann continued. 'Truth and lies. I'm on my hobby-horse now, you realise? Your supper will be delayed.'

A ripple of amusement washed across the hall.

'Great actions have shaped our society,' Sindermann said. 'The greatest of these, physically, has been the Emperor's formal and complete unification of Terra, the outward sequel to which, this Great Crusade, we are now engaged upon. But the greatest, intellectually, has been our casting off of that heavy mantle called religion. Religion damned our species for thousands of years, from the lowest superstition to the highest conclaves of spiritual faith. It drove us to madness, to war, to murder, it hung upon us like a disease, like a shackle ball. I'll tell you what religion was... No, you tell me. You, there?'

'Ignorance, sir.'

'Thank you, Khanna. Ignorance. Since the earliest times, our species has striven to understand the workings of the cosmos, and where that understanding has failed, or fallen short, we have filled in the gaps, plastered over the discrepancies, with blind faith. Why does the sun go round the sky? I don't know, so I will attribute it to the efforts of a sun god with a golden chariot. Why do people die? I can't say, but I will choose to believe it is the murky business of a reaper who carries souls to some afterworld.'

His audience laughed. Sindermann got down off his podium and walked to the front steps of the stage, beyond the range of the vox-mics. Though he dropped his voice low, its trained pitch, that practiced tool of all iterators, carried his words with perfect clarity, unenhanced, throughout the chamber.

'Religious faith. Belief in daemons, belief in spirits, belief in an afterlife and all the other trappings of a preternatural existence, simply existed to make us all more comfortable and content in the face of a measureless cosmos. They were sops, bolsters for the soul, crutches for the intellect, prayers and lucky charms to help us through the darkness. But we have witnessed the cosmos now, my friends. We have passed amongst it. We have learned and understood the fabric of reality. We have seen the stars from behind, and found they have no clockwork mechanisms, no golden chariots carrying them abroad. We have realised there is no need for god, or any gods, and by extension no use any longer for daemons or devils or spirits. The greatest thing mankind ever did was to reinvent itself as a secular culture.'

His audience applauded this wholeheartedly. There were a few cheers of approval. Iterators were not simply schooled in the art of public speaking. They were trained in both sides of the business. Seeded amongst a crowd, iterators could whip it into enthusiasm with a few well-timed responses, or equally turn a rabble against the speaker. Iterators often mingled with audiences to bolster the effectiveness of the colleague actually speaking.

Sindermann turned away, as if finished, and then swung back again as the clapping petered out, his voice even softer and even more penetrating. 'But what of faith? Faith has a quality, even when religion has gone. We still need to believe in something, don't we? Here it is. The true purpose of mankind is to bear the torch of truth aloft and shine it, even into the darkest places. To share our forensic, unforgiving, liberating understanding with the dimmest reaches of the cosmos. To emancipate those shackled in ignorance. To free ourselves and others from false gods, and take our place at the apex of sentient life. That… *that* is what we may pour faith into. *That* is what we can harness our boundless faith to.'

More cheers and clapping. He wandered back to the podium. He rested his hands on the wooden rails of the lectern. 'These last months, we have quashed an entire culture. Make no mistake… we haven't brought them to heel or rendered them compliant. We have *quashed* them. Broken their backs. Set them to flame. I know this, because I know the Warmaster unleashed his Astartes in this action. Don't be coy about what they do. They are killers, but sanctioned. I see one now, one noble warrior, seated at the back of the hall.'

Faces turned back to crane at Loken. There was a flutter of applause.

Sindermann started clapping furiously. 'Better than that. He deserves better than that!' A huge, growing peal of clapping rose to the roof of the hall. Loken stood, and took it with an embarrassed bow.

The applause died away. 'The souls we have lately conquered believed in an Imperium, a rule of man,' Sindermann said as soon as the last flutter had faded. 'Nevertheless, we killed their Emperor and forced them into submission. We burned their cities and scuppered their warships. Is all we have to say in response to their "why?" a feeble "I am right, so you are wrong"?'

He looked down, as if in thought. 'Yet we are. We *are* right. They *are* wrong. This simple, clean faith we must undertake to teach them. We *are* right. They *are* wrong. Why? Not because we say so. Because we *know* so! We will not say "I am right and you are wrong" because we have bested them in combat. We must proclaim it because we know it is the responsible truth. We cannot, should not, *will* not promulgate that idea for any other reason than we know, without hesitation, without doubt, without prejudice, that it is the truth, and upon that truth we bestow our faith. They are *wrong*. Their culture was constructed upon lies. We have brought them the keen edge of truth and enlightened them. On that basis, and that basis alone, go from here and iterate our message.'

He had to wait, smiling, until the uproar subsided. 'Your supper's getting cold. Dismissed.'

The student iterators began to file slowly out of the hall. Sindermann took another sip of water from the glass set upon his lectern and walked up the steps from the stage to where Loken was seated.

'Did you hear anything you liked?' he asked, sitting down beside Loken and smoothing the skirts of his robes.

'You sound like a showman,' Loken said, 'or a carnival peddler, advertising his wares.'

Sindermann crooked one black, black eyebrow. 'Sometimes, Garviel, that's precisely how I feel.'

Loken frowned. 'That you don't believe what you're selling?'

'Do you?'

'What am I selling?'

'Faith, through murder. Truth, through combat.'

'It's just combat. It has no meaning other than combat. The meaning has been decided long before I'm instructed to deliver it.'

'So as a warrior, you are without conscience?'

Loken shook his head. 'As a warrior, I am a man of conscience, and that conscience is directed by my faith in the Emperor. My faith in our cause, as you were just describing to the school, but as a weapon, I am without conscience. When activated for war, I set aside my personal considerations, and simply act. The value of my action has already been weighed by the greater conscience of our commander. I kill until I am told to stop, and in that period, I do not question the killing. To do so would be non-sense, and inappropriate. The commander has already made a determination for war, and all he expects of me is to prosecute it to the best of my abilities. A weapon doesn't question who it kills, or why. That isn't the point of weapons.'

Sindermann smiled. 'No it's not, and that's how it should be. I'm curious, though. I didn't think we had a tutorial scheduled for today.'

Beyond their duties as iterators, senior counsellors like Sinder-mann were expected to conduct programmes of education for the Astartes. This had been ordered by the Warmaster himself. The men of the Legion spent long periods in transit between wars, and the Warmaster insisted they use the time to develop their minds and expand their knowledge. 'Even the mightiest warriors should be schooled in areas beyond warfare,' he had ordained. 'There will come a time when war is over, and fighting done, and my warriors should prepare themselves for a life of peace. They must know of other things besides martial matters, or else find themselves obsolete.'

'There's no tutorial scheduled,' Loken said, 'but I wanted to talk with you, informally.'

'Indeed? What's on your mind?'

'A troubling thing…'

'You have been asked to join the Mournival,' Sindermann said. Loken blinked.

'How did you know? Does everyone know?'

Sindermann grinned. 'Sejanus is gone, bless his bones. The Mournival lacks. Are you surprised they came to you?'

'I am.'

'I'm not. You chase Abaddon and Sedirae with your glories, Loken. The Warmaster has his eye on you. So does Dorn.'

'Primarch Dorn? Are you sure?'

'I have been told he admires your phlegmatic humour, Garviel. That's something, coming from a person like him.'

'I'm flattered.'

'You should be. Now what's the problem?'

'Am I fit? Should I agree?'

Sindermann laughed. 'Have faith,' he said.

'There's something else,' Loken said.

'Go on.'

'A remembrancer came to me today. Annoyed me deeply, to be truthful, but there was something she said. She said, "could we not have just left them alone?"'

'Who?'

'These people. This Emperor.'

'Garviel, you know the answer to that.'

'When I was in the tower, facing that man–'

Sindermann frowned. 'The one who pretended to be the "Emperor"?'

'Yes. He said much the same thing. Quartes, from his *Quantifications*, teaches us that the galaxy is a broad space, and that much I have seen. If we encounter a person, a society in this cosmos that disagrees with us, but is sound of itself, what right do we have to destroy it? I mean… could we not just leave them be and ignore them? The galaxy is, after all, such a broad space.'

'What I've always liked about you, Garviel,' Sindermann said, 'is your humanity. This has clearly played on your mind. Why haven't you spoken to me about it before?'

'I thought it would fade,' Loken admitted.

Sindermann rose to his feet, and beckoned Loken to follow him. They walked out of the audience chamber and along one of the great spinal hallways of the flagship, an arch-roofed, buttressed canyon three decks high, like the nave of an ancient cathedral fane elongated to a length of five kilometres. It was gloomy, and the glorious banners of Legions and companies and campaigns, some faded, or damaged by old battles, hung down from the roof at intervals. Tides of personnel streamed along the hallway, their voices lifting an odd susurration into the vault, and Loken could see other flows of foot traffic in the illuminated galleries above, where the upper decks overlooked the main space.

'The first thing,' Sinderman said as they strolled along, 'is a simple bandage for your worries. You heard me essay this at length to the class and, in a way, you ventured a version of it just a moment ago when you spoke on the subject of conscience. You are a weapon, Garviel, an example of the finest instrument of destruction mankind has ever wrought. There must be no place inside you for doubt or question. You're right. Weapons should not think, they should only allow themselves to be employed, for the decision to use them is not theirs to make. That decision must be made – with great and terrible care, and ethical consideration beyond our capacity to judge – by the primarchs and the commanders. The Warmaster, like the beloved Emperor before him, does not employ you lightly. Only with a heavy heart and a certain determination does he unleash the Astartes. The Adeptus Astartes is the last resort, and is only ever used that way.'

Loken nodded.

'This is what you must remember. Just because the Imperium has the Astartes, and thus the ability to defeat and, if necessary, annihilate any foe, that's not the reason it happens. We have developed the means to annihilate... We have developed warriors like you, Garviel... because it is necessary.'

'A necessary evil?'

'A necessary instrument. Right does not follow might. Mankind has a great, empirical truth to convey, a message to bring, for the good of all. Sometimes that message falls on unwilling ears. Sometimes that message is spurned and denied, as here. Then, and only then, thank the stars that we own the might to enforce it. We are mighty because we are right, Garviel. We are not right because we are mighty. Vile the hour when that reversal becomes our credo.'

They had turned off the spinal hallway and were walking along a lateral promenade now, towards the archive annex. Servitors waddled past, their upper limbs laden with books and data-slates.

'Whether our truth is right or not, must we always enforce it upon the unwilling? As the woman said, could we not just leave them to their own destinies, unmolested?'

'You are walking along the shores of a lake,' Sindermann said. 'A boy is drowning. Do you let him drown because he was foolish enough to fall into the water before he had learned to swim? Or do you fish him out, and teach him how to swim?'

Loken shrugged. 'The latter.'

'What if he fights you off as you attempt to save him, because he is afraid of you? Because he doesn't want to learn how to swim?'

'I save him anyway.'

They had stopped walking. Sindermann pressed his hand to the key plate set into the brass frame of a huge door, and allowed his palm to be read by the scrolling light. The door opened, exhaling like a mouth, gusting out climate-controlled air and a background hint of dust.

They stepped into the vault of Archive Chamber Three. Scholars, sphragists and metaphrasts worked in silence at the reading desks, summoning servitors to select volumes from the sealed stacks.

'What interests me about your concerns,' Sindermann said, keeping his voice precisely low so that only Loken's enhanced hearing could follow it, 'is what they say about you. We have established you are a weapon, and that you don't need to think about what you do because the thinking is done for you. Yet you allow the human spark in you to worry, to fret and empathise. You retain the ability to consider the cosmos as a man would, not as an instrument might.'

'I see,' Loken replied. 'You're saying I have forgotten my place. That I have overstepped the bounds of my function.'

'Oh no,' Sindermann smiled. 'I'm saying you have *found* your place.'

'How so?' Loken asked.

Sindermann gestured to the stacks of books that rose, like towers, into the misty altitudes of the archive. High above, hovering servitors searched and retrieved ancient texts sealed in plastek carriers, swarming across the cliff-faces of the library like honey bees.

'Regard the books,' Sindermann said.

'Are there some I should read? Will you prepare a list for me?'

'Read them all. Read them again. Swallow the learning and ideas of our predecessors whole, for it can only improve you as a man, but if you do, you'll find that none of them holds an answer to still your doubts.'

Loken laughed, puzzled. Some of the metaphrasts nearby looked up from their study, annoyed at the interruption. They quickly looked down again when they saw the noise had issued from an Astartes.

'What is the Mournival, Garviel?' Sindermann whispered.

'You know very well…'

'Humour me. Is it an official body? An organ of governance, formally ratified, a Legio rank?'

'Of course not. It is an informal honour. It has no official weight. Since the earliest era of our Legion there has been a

Mournival. Four captains, those regarded by their peers to be...'

He paused.

'The best?' Sindermann asked.

'My modesty is ashamed to use that word. The most appropriate. At any time, the Legion, in an unofficial manner quite separate from the chain of command, composes a Mournival. A confraternity of four captains, preferably ones of markedly different aspects and humours, who act as the soul of the Legion.'

'And their job is to watch over the moral health of the Legion, isn't that so? To guide and shape its philosophy? And, most important of all, to stand beside the commander and be the voices he listens to before any others. To be the comrades and friends he can turn to privately, and talk out his concerns and troubles with freely, before they ever become matters of state or Council.'

'That is what the Mournival is supposed to do,' Loken agreed.

'Then it occurs to me, Garviel, that only a weapon which questions its use could be of any value in that role. To be a member of the Mournival, you need to have concerns. You need to have wit, and most certainly you need to have doubts. Do you know what a naysmith is?'

'No.'

'In early Terran history, during the dominance of the Sumaturan dynasts, naysmiths were employed by the ruling classes. Their job was to disagree. To question everything. To consider any argument or policy and find fault with it, or articulate the counter position. They were highly valued.'

'You want me to become a naysmith?' Loken asked.

Sindermann shook his head. 'I want you to be you, Garviel. The Mournival needs your common sense and clarity. Sejanus was always the voice of reason, the measured balance between Abaddon's choler and Aximand's melancholic disdain. The balance is gone, and the Warmaster needs that balance now more than ever. You came to me this morning because you wanted my blessing. You wanted to know if you should accept the honour. By your own admission, Garviel, by the merit of your own doubts, you have answered your own question.'

FOUR

Summoned
Ezekyle by name
A winning hand

SHE HAD ASKED what the planet was called, and the crew of
the shuttle had answered her 'Terra', which was hardly useful.
Mersadie Olitan had spent the first twenty-eight years of her
twenty-nine-year life on Terra, and this wasn't it.

The iterator sent to accompany her was of little better use. A
modest, olive-skinned man in his late teens, the iterator's name
was Memed, and he was possessed of a fearsome intellect and
precocious genius. But the violent sub-orbital passage of the
shuttle disagreed with his constitution, and he spent most of the
trip unable to answer her questions because he was too occupied
retching into a plastek bag.

The shuttle set down on a stretch of formal lawn between
rows of spayed and pollarded trees, eight kilometres west of the
High City. It was early evening, and stars already glimmered
in the violet smudge at the sky's edges. At high altitude, ships
passed over, their lights blinking. Mersadie stepped down the
shuttle's ramp onto the grass, breathing in the odd scents and

slightly variant atmosphere of the world.

She stopped short. The air, oxygen rich, she imagined, was making her giddy, and that giddiness was further agitated by the thought of where she was. For the first time in her life she was standing on another soil, another world. It seemed to her quite momentous, as if a ceremonial band ought to be playing. She was, as far as she knew, one of the very first of the remembrancers to be granted access to the surface of the conquered world.

She turned to look at the distant city, taking in the panorama and committing it to her memory coils. She blink-clicked her eyes to store certain views digitally, noting that smoke still rose from the cityscape, though the fight had been over months ago.

'We are calling it Sixty-Three Nineteen,' the iterator said, coming down the ramp behind her. Apparently, his queasy constitution had been stabilised by planetfall. She recoiled delicately from the stink of sick on his breath.

'Sixty-Three Nineteen?' she asked.

'It being the nineteenth world the 63rd Expedition has brought to compliance,' Memed said, 'though, of course, full compliance is not yet established here. The charter is yet to be ratified. Lord Governor Elect Rakris is having trouble forming a consenting coalition parliament, but Sixty-Three Nineteen will do. The locals call this world Terra, and we can't be having two of those, can we? As far as I see it, that was the root of the problem in the first place...'

'I see,' said Mersadie, moving away. She touched her hand against the bark of one of the pollarded trees. It felt... real. She smiled to herself and blink-clicked it. Already, the basis of her account, with visual keys, was formulating in her enhanced mind. A personal angle, that's what she'd take. She'd use the novelty and unfamiliarity of her first planetfall as a theme around which her remembrance would hang.

'It's a beautiful evening,' the iterator announced, coming to stand beside her. He'd left his sloshing bags of vomit at the foot of the ramp, as if he expected someone to dispose of them for him.

The four army troopers delegated to her protection certainly weren't about to do it. Perspiring in their heavy velvet overcoats and shakos, their rifles slung over their shoulders, they closed up around her.

'Mistress Oliton?' the officer said. 'He's waiting.'

Mersadie nodded and followed them. Her heart was beating hard. This was going to be quite an occasion. A week before, her friend and fellow remembrancer Euphrati Keeler, who had emphatically achieved more than any of the remembrancers so far, had been on hand in the eastern city of Kaentz, observing crusader operations, when Maloghurst had been found alive.

The Warmaster's equerry, believed lost when the ships of his embassy had been burned out of orbit, had survived, escaping via drop pod. Badly injured, he had been nursed and protected by the family of a farmer in the territories outside Kaentz. Keeler had been right there, by chance, to pict record the equerry's recovery from the farmstead. It had been a coup. Her picts, so beautifully composed, had been flashed around the expedition fleet, and savoured by the Imperial retinues. Suddenly, Euphrati Keeler was being talked about. Suddenly, remembrancers weren't such a bad thing after all. With a few, brilliant clicks of her picter, Euphrati had advanced the cause of the remembrancers enormously.

Now Mersadie hoped she could do the same. She had been summoned. She still couldn't quite get over that. She had been summoned to the surface. That fact alone would have been enough, but it was *who* had summoned her that really mattered. He had personally authorised her transit permit, and seen to the appointment of a bodyguard and one of Sindermann's best iterators.

She couldn't understand why. Last time they'd met, he'd been so brutal that she'd considered resigning and taking the first conveyance home.

He was standing on a gravel pathway between the tree rows, waiting for her. As she came up, the soldiers around her, she registered simple awe at the sight of him in his full plate. Gleaming white, with a trace of black around the edges. His helm, with its lateral horse-brush crest, was off, hung at his waist. He was a giant, two and a half metres tall.

She sensed the soldiers around her hesitating.

'Wait here,' she told them, and they dropped back, relieved. A soldier of the Imperial army could be as tough as old boots, but he didn't want to tangle with an Astartes. Especially not one of the Luna Wolves, the mightiest of the mighty, the deadliest of all Legions.

'You too,' she said to the iterator.

'Oh, right,' Memed said, coming to a halt.

'The summons was personal.'

'I understand,' he said.

Mersadie walked up to the Luna Wolves captain. He towered over her, so much she had to shield her eyes with her hand against the setting sun to look up at him.

'Remembrancer,' he said, his voice as deep as an oak-root.

'Captain. Before we start, I'd like to apologise for any offence I may have caused the last time we–'

'If I'd taken offence, mistress, would I have summoned you here?'

'I suppose not.'

'You suppose right. You raised my hackles with your questions last time, but I admit I was too hard on you.'

'I spoke with unnecessary temerity–'

'It was that temerity that caused me to think of you,' Loken replied. 'I can't explain further. I won't, but you should know that it was your very speaking out of turn that brought me here. Which is why I decided to have you brought here too. If that's what remembrancers do, you've done your job well.'

Mersadie wasn't sure what to say. She lowered her hand. The last rays of sunlight were in her eyes. 'Do you… do you want me to witness something? To remember something?'

'No,' he replied curtly. 'What happens now happens privately, but I wanted you to know that, in part, it is because of you. When I return, if I feel it is appropriate, I will convey certain recollections to you. If that is acceptable.'

'I'm honoured, captain. I will await your pleasure.'

Loken nodded.

'Should I come with–' Memed began.

'No,' said the Luna Wolf.

'Right,' Memed said quickly, backing off. He went away to study a tree bole.

'You asked me the right questions, and so showed me I was asking the right questions too,' Loken told Mersadie.

'Did I? Did you answer them?'

'No,' he replied. 'Wait here, please,' he said, and walked away towards a box hedge trimmed by the finest topiarists into a thick, green bastion wall. He vanished from sight under a leafy arch.

Mersadie turned to the waiting soldiers.

'Know any games?' she asked.

They shrugged.

She plucked a deck of cards from her coat pocket. 'I've got one to show you,' she grinned, and sat down on the grass to deal.

The soldiers put down their rifles and grouped around her in the lengthening blue shadows.

'Soldiers love cards,' Ignace Karkasy had said to her before she left the flagship, right before he'd grinned and handed her the deck.

BEYOND THE HIGH hedge, an ornamental water garden lay in shadowy ruin. The height of the hedge and the neighbouring trees, just now becoming spiky black shapes against the rose sky, screened out what was left of the direct sunlight. The gloom upon the gardens was almost misty.

The garden had once been composed of rectangular ouslite slabs laid like giant flagstones, surrounding a series of square, shallow basins where lilies and bright water flowers had flourished in pebbly sinks fed by some spring or water source. Frail ghost ferns and weeping trees had edged the pools.

During the assault of the High City, shells or airborne munitions had bracketed the area, felling many of the plants and shattering a great number of the blocks. Many of the ouslite slabs had been dislodged, and several of the pools greatly increased in breadth and depth by the addition of deep, gouging craters.

But the hidden spring had continued to feed the place, filling the shell holes, and pouring overflow between dislodged stones.

The whole garden was a shimmering, flat pool in the gloom, out of which tangled branches, broken root balls and asymmetric shards of rock stuck up in miniature archipelagos.

Some of the intact blocks, slabs two metres long and half a metre thick, had been rearranged, and not randomly by the blasts. They had been levered out to form a walkway into the pool area, a stone jetty sunk almost flush with the water's surface.

Loken stepped out onto the causeway and began to follow it. The air smelled damp, and he could hear the clack of amphibians and the hiss of evening flies. Water flowers, their fragile colours almost lost in the closing darkness, drifted on the still water either side of his path.

Loken felt no fear. He was not built to feel it, but he registered a trepidation, an anticipation that made his hearts beat. He was, he knew, about to pass a threshold in his life, and he held faith that what lay beyond that threshold would be provident. It also felt right that he was about to take a profound step forward in his career. His world, his life, had changed greatly of late, with the rise of the War-master and the consequent alteration of the crusade, and it was only proper that he changed with it. A new phase. A new time.

He paused and looked up at the stars that were beginning to light in the purpling sky. A new time, and a *glorious* new time at that. Like him, mankind was on a threshold, about to step for-ward into greatness.

He had gone deep into the ragged sprawl of the water garden, far beyond the lamps of the landing zone behind the hedge, far beyond the lights of the city. The sun had vanished. Blue shad-ows surrounded him.

The causeway path came to an end. Water gleamed beyond. Ahead, across thirty metres of still pond, a little bank of weeping trees rose up like an atoll, silhouetted against the sky.

He wondered if he should wait. Then he saw a flicker of light amongst the trees across the water, a flutter of yellow flame that went as quickly as it came.

Loken stepped off the causeway into the water. It was shin deep. Ripples, hard black circles, radiated out across the reflec-tive pool. He began to wade out towards the islet, hoping that his feet wouldn't suddenly encounter some unexpected depth of submerged crater and so lend comedy to this solemn moment.

He reached the bank of trees and stood in the shallows, gazing up into the tangled blackness.

'Give us your name,' a voice called out of the darkness. It spoke the words in Cthonic, his home-tongue, the battle-argot of the Luna Wolves.

'Garviel Loken is my name to give.'

'And what is your honour?'

'I am Captain of the Tenth Company of the Sixteenth Legio Astartes.'

'And who is your sworn master?'

'The Warmaster and the Emperor both.'

Silence followed, interrupted only by the splash of frogs and the noise of insects in the waterlogged thickets.

The voice spoke again. Two words. 'Illuminate him.'

There was a brief metallic scrape as the slot of a lantern was pulled open, and yellow flame-light shone out across him. Three figures stood on the tree-lined bank above him, one holding the lantern up.

Aximand. Torgaddon, lifting the lantern. Abaddon.

Like him, they wore their warrior armour, the dancing light catching bright off the curves of the plate. All were bareheaded, their crested helmets hung at their waists.

'Do you vouch that this soul is all he claims to be?' Abaddon asked. It seemed a strange question, as all three of them knew him well enough. Loken understood it was part of the ceremony.

'I so vouch,' Torgaddon said. 'Increase the light.'

Abaddon and Aximand stepped away, and began to open the slots of a dozen other lanterns hanging from the surrounding boughs. When they had finished, a golden light suffused them all. Torgaddon set his own lamp on the ground.

The trio stepped forward into the water to face Loken. Tarik Torgaddon was the tallest of them, his trickster grin never leaving his face. 'Loosen up, Garvi,' he chuckled. 'We don't bite.'

Loken flashed a smile back, but he felt unnerved. Partly, it was the high status of these three men, but he also hadn't expected the induction to be so ritualistic.

Horus Aximand, Captain of Fifth Company, was the youngest

and shortest of them, shorter than Loken. He was squat and robust, like a guard dog. His head was shaved smooth, and oiled, so that the lamp-light gleamed off it. Aximand, like many in the younger generations of the Legion, had been named in honour of the commander, but only he used the name openly. His noble face, with wide-set eyes and firm, straight nose, uncannily resembled the visage of the Warmaster, and this had earned him the affectionate name 'Little Horus'. Little Horus Aximand, the devil-dog in war, the master strategist. He nodded greeting to Loken.

Ezekyle Abaddon, First Captain of the Legion, was a towering brute. Somewhere between Loken's height and Torgaddon's, he seemed greater than both due to the cresting top-knot adorning his otherwise shaved scalp. When his helm was off, Abaddon bound his mane of black hair up in a silver sleeve that made it stand proud like a palm tree or a fetish switch on his crown. He, like Torgaddon, had been in the Mournival from its inception. He, like Torgaddon and Aximand both, shared the same aspect of straight nose and wide-spaced eyes so reminiscent of the Warmaster, though only in Aximand were the features an actual likeness. They might have been brothers, actual womb brothers, if they had been sired in the old way. As it was, they were brothers in terms of gene-source and martial fraternity.

Now Loken was to be their brother too.

There was a curious incidence in the Luna Wolves Legion of Astartes bearing a facial resemblance to their primarch. This had been put down to conformities in the gene-seed, but still, those who echoed Horus in their features were considered especially lucky, and were known by all the men as 'the Sons of Horus'. It was a mark of honour, and it often seemed the case that 'Sons' rose faster and found better favour than the rest. Certainly, Loken knew for a fact, all the previous members of the Mournival had been 'Sons of Horus'. In this respect, he was unique. Loken owed

his looks to an inheritance of the pale, craggy bloodline of Cthonia. He was the first non-'Son' to be elected to this elite inner
circle.

Though he knew it couldn't be the case, he felt as if he had
achieved this eminence through simple merit, rather than the
atavistic whim of physiognomy.

'This is a simple act,' Abaddon said, regarding Loken. 'You have
been vouched for here, and proposed by great men before that.
Our lord, and the Lord Dorn have both put your name forward.'

'As have you, sir, so I understand,' Loken said.

Abaddon smiled. 'Few match you in soldiering, Garviel. I've
had my eye on you, and you proved my interest when you took
the palace ahead of me.'

'Luck.'

'There's no such thing,' said Aximand gruffly.

'He only says that because he never has any,' Torgaddon grinned.

'I only say that because there's no such thing,' Aximand
objected. 'Science has shown us this. There is no luck. There is
only success or the lack of it.'

'Luck,' said Abaddon. 'Isn't that just a word for modesty? Garviel is too modest to say "Yes, Ezekyle, I bested you, I won the
palace, and triumphed where you did not," for he feels that
would not become him. And I admire modesty in a man, but
the truth is, Garviel, you are here because you are a warrior of
superlative talent. We welcome you.'

'Thank you, sir,' Loken said.

'A first lesson, then,' Abaddon said. 'In the Mournival, we are
equals. There is no rank. Before the men, you may refer to me as
"sir" or "First Captain", but between us, there is no ceremony. I
am Ezekyle.'

'Horus,' said Aximand.

'Tarik,' said Torgaddon.

'I understand,' Loken answered, 'Ezekyle.'

'The rules of our confraternity are simple,' Aximand said, 'and we will get to them, but there is no structure to the duties expected of you. You should prepare yourself to spend more time with the command staff, and function at the Warmaster's side. Have you a proxy in mind to oversee the Tenth in your absence?'

'Yes, Horus,' Loken said.

'Vipus?' Torgaddon smiled.

'I would,' Loken said, 'but the honour should be Jubal's. Seniority and rank.'

Aximand shook his head. 'Second lesson. Go with your heart. If you trust Vipus, make it Vipus. Never compromise. Jubal's a big boy. He'll get over it.'

'There will be other duties and obligations, special duties...' Abaddon said. 'Escorts, ceremonies, embassies, planning meetings. Are you sanguine about that? Your life will change.'

'I am sanguine,' Loken nodded.

'Then we should mark you in,' Abaddon said. He stepped past Loken and waded forward into the shallow lake, away from the light of the lamps. Aximand followed him. Torgaddon touched Loken on the arm and ushered him along as well.

They strode out into the black water and formed a ring. Abaddon bade them stand stock-still until the water ceased to lap and ripple. It became mirror-smooth. The bright reflection of the rising moon wavered on the water between them.

'The one fixture that has always witnessed an induction,' Abaddon said. 'The moon. Symbolic of our Legion name. No one has ever entered the Mournival, except by the light of a moon.'

Loken nodded.

'This seems a poor, false one,' Aximand muttered, looking up at the sky, 'but it will do. The image of the moon must also always be reflected. In the first days of the Mournival, close on two hundred years ago, it was favoured to have the chosen moon's image captured in a scrying dish or polished mirror. We make do now. Water suffices.'

Loken nodded again. His feeling of being unnerved had returned, sharp and unwelcome. This was a ritual, and it smacked dangerously of the practices of corpse-whisperers and spiritual-ists. The entire process seemed shot through with superstition and arcane worship, the sort of spiritual unreason Sindermann had taught him to rail against.

He felt he had to say something before it was too late. 'I am a man of faith,' he said softly, 'and that faith is the truth of the Imperium. I will not bow to any fane or acknowledge any spirit. I own only the empirical clarity of Imperial Truth.'

The other three looked at him.

'I told you he was straight up and down,' Torgaddon said.

Abaddon and Aximand laughed.

'There are no spirits here, Garviel,' Abaddon said, resting a hand reassuringly against Loken's arm.

'We're not trying to ensorcel you,' Aximand chuckled.

'This is just an old habit, a practice. The way it has always been done,' Torgaddon said. 'We keep it up for no other reason than it seems to make it matter. It's… pantomime, I suppose.'

'Yes, pantomime,' agreed Abaddon.

'We want this moment to be special to you, Garviel,' Aximand said. 'We want you to remember it. We believe it's important to mark an induction with a sense of ceremony and occasion, so we use the old ways. Perhaps that's just theatrical of us, but we find it reassuring.'

'I understand,' Loken said.

'Do you?' Abaddon asked. 'You're going to make a pledge to us. An oath as firm as any oath of moment you have ever under-taken. Man to man. Cold and clear and very, very secular. An oath of brothership, not some occult pact. We stand together in the light of a moon, and swear a bond that only death will break.'

'I understand,' Loken repeated. He felt foolish. 'I want to take the oath.'

Abaddon nodded. 'Let's mark you, then. Say the names of the others.'

Torgaddon bowed his head and recited nine names. Since the foundation of the Mournival, only twelve men had held the unofficial rank, and three of those were present. Loken would be the thirteenth.

'Keyshen. Minos. Berabaddon. Litus. Syrakul. Deradaeddon. Karaddon. Janipur. Sejanus.'

'Lost in glory,' Aximand and Abaddon said as one voice. 'Mourned by the Mournival. Only in death does duty end.'

A bond that only death will break. Loken thought about Abaddon's words. Death was the single expectation of each and every Astartes. Violent death. It was not an if, it was a when. In the service of the Imperium, each of them would eventually sacrifice his life. They were phlegmatic about it. It would happen, it was that simple. One day, tomorrow, next year. It would happen.

There was an irony, of course. To all intents and purposes, and by every measurement known to the gene-scientists and gerontologists, the Astartes, like the primarchs, were immortals. Age would not wither them, nor bring them down. They would live forever... five thousand years, ten thousand, beyond even that into some unimaginable millennium. Except for the scythe of war.

Immortal, but not invulnerable. Yes, they might live forever, but they would never get the chance. Immortality was a by-product of their Astartes strengths, but those strengths had been gene-built for combat. They had been born immortal only to die in war. That was the way of it. Brief, bright lives. Like Hastur Sejanus, the warrior Loken was replacing. Only the beloved Emperor, who had left the warring behind, would truly live forever.

Loken tried to imagine the future, but the image would not form. Death would wipe them all from history. Not even the great First Captain Ezekyle Abaddon would survive forever. There would be a time when Abaddon no longer waged bloody war across the territories of humanity.

Loken sighed. That would be a sad day indeed. Men would cry out for Abaddon's return, but he would never come.

He tried to picture the manner of his own death. Fabled, imaginary combats flashed through his mind. He imagined himself at the Emperor's side, fighting some great, last stand against an unknown foe. Primarch Horus would be there, of course. He had to be. It wouldn't be the same without him. Loken would battle, and die, and perhaps even Horus would die, to save the Emperor at the last.

Glory. Glory, like he'd never known. Such an hour would become so ingrained in the minds of men that it would be the cornerstone of all that came after. A great battle, upon which human culture would be based.

Then, briefly, he imagined another death. Alone, far away from his comrades and his Legion, dying from cruel wounds on some nameless rock, his passing as memorable as smoke.

Loken swallowed hard. Either way, his service was to the Emperor, and his service would be true to the end.

'The names are said,' Abaddon intoned, 'and of them, we hail Sejanus, latest to fall.'

'Hail, Sejanus!' Torgaddon and Aximand cried.

'Garviel Loken,' Abaddon said, looking at Loken. 'We ask you to take Sejanus's place. How say you?'

'I will do this thing gladly.'

'Will you swear an oath to uphold the confraternity of the Mournival?'

'I will,' said Loken.

'Will you accept our brothership and give it back as a brother?'

'I will.'

'Will you be true to the Mournival to the end of your life?'

'I will.'

'Will you serve the Luna Wolves for as long as they bear that proud name?'

'I will,' said Loken.

'Do you pledge to the commander, who is primarch over us all?' asked Aximand.

'I so pledge.'

'And to the Emperor above all primarchs, everlasting?'

'I so pledge.'

'Do you swear to uphold the truth of the Imperium of Mankind, no matter what evil may assail it?' Torgaddon asked.

'I swear,' said Loken.

'Do you swear to stand firm against all enemies, alien and domestic?'

'This I swear.'

'And in war, kill for the living and kill for the dead?'

'Kill for the living! Kill for the dead!' Abaddon and Aximand echoed.

'I swear.'

'As the moon lights us,' Abaddon said, 'will you be a true brother to your brother Astartes?'

'I will.'

'No matter the cost?'

'No matter the cost.'

'Your oath is taken, Garviel. Welcome into the Mournival. Tarik? Illuminate us.'

Torgaddon pulled a vapour flare from his belt and fired it off into the night sky. It burst in a bright umbrella of light, white and harsh.

As the sparks of it rained slowly down onto the waters, the four warriors hugged and whooped, clasping hands and slapping backs. Torgaddon, Aximand and Abaddon took turns to embrace Loken.

'You're one of us now,' Torgaddon whispered as he drew Loken close.

'I am,' said Loken.

LATER, ON THE islet, by the light of the lanterns, they branded Loken's helm above the right eye with the crescent mark of the new moon. This was his badge of office. Aximand's helm bore the brand of the half moon, Torgaddon's the gibbous, and Abaddon's the full. The four stage cycle of a moon was shared between their wargear. So the Mournival was denoted.

They sat on the islet, talking and joking, until the sun rose again.

THEY WERE PLAYING cards on the lawn by the light of chemical lanterns. The simple game Mersadie had proposed had long been eclipsed by a punitive betting game suggested by one of the soldiers. Then the iterator, Memed, had joined them, and taken great pains to teach them an old version of cups.

Memed shuffled and dealt the cards with marvellous dexterity. One of the soldiers whistled mockingly. 'A real card hand we have here,' the officer remarked.

'This is an old game,' Memed said, 'which I'm sure you will enjoy. It dates back a long way, its origins lost in the very beginnings of Old Night. I have researched it, and I understand it was popular amongst the peoples of Ancient Merica, and also the tribes of the Franc.'

He let them play a few dummy hands until they had the way of it, but Mersadie found it hard to remember what spread won over what. In the seventh turn, believing she had the game's measure at last, she discarded a hand which she believed inferior to the cards Memed was holding.

'No, no,' he smiled. 'You win.'

'But you have four of a kind again.'

He laid out her cards. 'Even so, you see?'

She shook her head. 'It's all too confusing.'

'The suits correspond,' he said, as if beginning a lecture, 'to the layers of society back then. Swords stand for the warrior aristocracy; cups, or chalices, for the ancient priesthood; diamonds, or coins, for the merchant classes; and baton clubs for the worker caste…'

Some of the soldiers grumbled.

'Stop iterating to us,' Mersadie said.

'Sorry,' Memed grinned. 'Anyway, you win. I have four alike, but you have ace, monarch, empress and knave. A mournival.'

'What did you just say?' Mersadie Oliton asked, sitting up.

'Mournival,' Memed replied, reshuffling the old, square-cut cards. 'It's the old Franc word for the four royal cards. A winning hand.'

Behind them, away beyond a high wall of hedge invisible in the still night, a flare suddenly banged off and lit the sky white.

'A winning hand,' Mersadie murmured. Coincidence, and something she privately believed in, called fate, had just opened the future up to her.

It looked very inviting indeed.

FIVE

Peeter Egon Momus
Lectitio Divinitatus
Malcontent

PEETER EGON MOMUS was doing them a great honour. Peeter Egon Momus was deigning to share with them his visions for the new High City. Peeter Egon Momus, architect designate for the 63rd Expedition, was unveiling his preparatory ideas for the transformation of the conquered city into a permanent memorial to glory and compliance.

The trouble was, Peeter Egon Momus was just a figure in the distance and largely inaudible. In the gathered audience, in the dusty heat, Ignace Karkasy shifted impatiently and craned his neck to see.

The assembly had been gathered in a city square north of the palace. It was just after midday, and the sun was at its zenith, scorching the bare basalt towers and yards of the city. Though the high walls around the square offered some shade, the air was oven dry and stiflingly hot. There was a breeze, but even that was heated like exhaust vapour, and it did nothing but stir up fine grit in the air. Powder dust, the particulate residue of the great battle, was everywhere, hazing the bright air like smoke. Karkasy's throat was as arid as a river bed in drought. Around him, people in the crowd coughed and sneezed.

The crowd, five hundred strong, had been carefully vetted. Three-quarters of them were local dignitaries; grandees, nobles, merchants, members of the overthrown government, representatives of that part of Sixty-Three Nineteen's ruling classes who had pledged compliance to the new order. They had been summoned by invitation so that they might participate, however superficially, in the renewal of their society.

The rest were remembrancers. Many of them, like Karkasy, had been granted their first transit permit to the surface, at long last, so they could attend. If this was what he had been waiting for, Karkasy thought, they could keep it. Standing in a crowded kiln while some old fart made incoherent noises in the background.

The crowd seemed to share his mood. They were hot and despondent. Karkasy saw no smiles on the faces of the invited locals, just hard, drawn looks of forbearance. The choice between compliance or death didn't make compliance any more pleasurable. They were defeated, deprived of their culture and their way of life, facing a future determined by alien minds. They were simply, wearily enduring the indignity of this period of transition into the Imperium of Man. From time to time, they clapped in a desultory manner, but only when stirred up by the iterators carefully planted in their midst.

The crowd had drawn up around the aprons of a metal stage erected for the event. Upon it were arranged hololithic screens and relief models of the city to be, as well as many of the extravagantly complex brass and steel surveying instruments Momus utilised in his work. Geared, spoked and meticulous, the instruments suggested to Karkasy's mind devices of torture.

Torture was right.

Momus, when he could be seen between the heads of the crowd, was a small, trim man with over-dainty mannerisms. As he explained his plans, the staff of iterators on stage with him aimed live picters close up at relevant areas of the relief models, the images transferring directly to the screens, along with graphic schematics. But the sunlight was too glaring for decent hololithic projection, and the images were milked-out and hard to comprehend. Something was wrong with the vox-mic Momus was using too, and what little of his speech came through served only to demonstrate the man had no gift whatsoever for public speaking.

'...always a heliolithic city, a tribute to the sun above, and we may see this afternoon, indeed, I'm sure you will have noticed, the glory of the light here. A city of light. Light out of darkness is a noble theme, by which, of course, I mean the light of truth shining upon the darkness of ignorance. I am much taken with the local phototropic technologies I have found here, and intend to incorporate them into the design...'

Karkasy sighed. He never thought he would find himself wishing for an iterator, but at least those bastards knew how to speak in public. Peeter Egon Momus should have left the talking to one of the iterators while he aimed the wretched picter wand for them.

His mind wandered. He looked up at the high walls around them, geometric slabs against the blue sky, baked pink in the sunlight, or smoke black where shadows slanted. He saw the scorch marks and dotted bolt craters that pitted the basalt like acne. Beyond the walls, the towers of the palace were in worse repair, their plasterwork hanging off like shed snakeskin, their missing windows like blinded eyes.

In a yard to the south of the gathering, a Titan of the Mechanicum stood on station, its grim humanoid form rising up over the walls. It stood perfectly still, like a piece of monumental martial statuary, instantly installed. Now that, thought Karkasy, was a far more appropriate celebration of glory and compliance.

Karkasy stared at the Titan for a little while. He'd never seen anything like it before in his life, except in picts. The awesome sight of it almost made the tedious outing worthwhile.

The more he stared at it, the more uncomfortable it made him feel. It was so huge, so threatening, and so very still. He knew it could move. He began to wish it would. He found himself yearning for it to suddenly turn its head or take a step, or otherwise rumble into animation. Its immobility was agonising.

Then he began to fear that if it did suddenly move, he would be quite unmanned, and might be forced to cry out in involuntary terror, and fall to his knees.

A burst of clapping made him jump. Momus had apparently said something apposite, and the iterators were stirring up the crowd in response. Karkasy slapped his sweaty hands together a few times obediently.

Karkasy was sick of it. He knew he couldn't bear to stand there much longer with the Titan staring at him.

He took one last look at the stage. Momus was rambling on, well into his fiftieth minute. The only other point of interest to the whole affair, as far as Karkasy was concerned, stood at the back of the podium behind Momus. Two giants in yellow plate. Two noble Astartes from the VII Legion, the Imperial Fists, the Emperor's Praetorians. They were presumably in attendance to lend Momus an appropriate air of authority. Karkasy guessed the VII had been chosen over the Luna Wolves because of their noted genius in the arts of fortification and defence. The Imperial Fists were fortress builders, warrior masons who raised such impenetrable redoubts that they could be held for eternity against any enemy. Karkasy smelled the artful handiwork of iterator propaganda: the architects of war watching over the architect of peace.

Karkasy had waited to see if either would speak, or come forward to remark upon Momus's plans, but they did not. They stood there, bolters across their broad chests, as static and unwavering as the Titan.

Karkasy turned away, and began to push his way out through the inflexible crowd. He headed towards the rear of the square.

Troopers of the Imperial army had been stationed around the hem of the crowd as a precaution. They had been required to wear full dress uniform, and they were so overheated that their sweaty cheeks were blanched a sickly green-white.

One of them noticed Karkasy moving out through the thinnest part of the audience, and came over to him.

'Where are you going, sir?' he asked.

'I'm dying of thirst,' Karkasy replied.

'There will be refreshments, I'm told, after the presentation,' the soldier said. His voice caught on the word 'refreshments' and Karkasy knew there would be none for the common soldiery.

'Well, I've had enough,' Karkasy said.

'It's not over.'

'I've had enough.'

The soldier frowned. Perspiration beaded at the bridge of his nose, just beneath the rim of his heavy fur shako. His throat and jowls were flushed pink and sheened with sweat.

'I can't allow you to wander away. Movement is supposed to be restricted to approved areas.'

Karkasy grinned wickedly. 'And I thought you were here to keep trouble out, not keep us in.'

The soldier didn't find that funny, or even ironic. 'We're here to keep you safe, sir,' he said. 'I'd like to see your permit.'

Karkasy took out his papers. They were an untidy, crumpled bundle, warm and damp from his trouser pocket. Karkasy waited, faintly embarrassed, while the soldier studied them. He had never liked barking up against authority, especially not in front of people, though the back of the crowd didn't seem to be at all interested in the exchange.

'You're a remembrancer?' the soldier asked.

'Yes. Poet,' Karkasy added before the inevitable second question got asked.

The soldier looked up from the papers into Karkasy's face, as if searching for some essential characteristic of poet-hood that might be discerned there, comparable to a Navigator's third eye or a slave-drone's serial tattoo. He'd likely never seen a poet before, which was all right, because Karkasy had never seen a Titan before.

'You should stay here, sir,' the soldier said, handing the papers back to Karkasy.

'But this is pointless,' Karkasy said. 'I have been sent to make a memorial of these events. I can't get close to anything. I can't even hear properly what that fool's got to say. Can you imagine the wrong-headedness of this? Momus isn't even history. He's just another kind of memorialist. I've been allowed here to remember his remembrance, and I can't even do that properly. I'm so far removed from the things I should be engaging with, I might as well have stayed on Terra and made do with a telescope.'

The soldier shrugged. He'd lost the thread of Karkasy's speech early on. 'You should stay here, sir. For your own safety.'

'I was told the city had been made safe,' Karkasy said. 'We're only a day or two from compliance, aren't we?'

The soldier leaned forward discreetly, so close that Karkasy could smell the stale odour of garbage the heat was infusing into his breath. 'Just between us, that's the official line, but there has been trouble. Insurgents. Loyalists. You always get it in a con-quered city, no matter how clean the victory. The back streets are not secure.'

'Really?'

'They're saying loyalists, but it's just discontent, if you ask me. These bastards have lost it all, and they're not happy about it.'

Karkasy nodded. 'Thanks for the tip,' he said, and turned back to rejoin the crowd.

Five minutes later, with Momus still droning on and Karkasy close to despair, an elderly noblewoman in the crowd fainted, and there was a small commotion. The soldiers hurried in to take charge of the situation and carry her into the shade.

When the soldier's back was turned, Karkasy took himself off out of the square and into the streets beyond.

HE WALKED FOR a while through empty courts and high-walled streets where shadows pooled like water. The day's heat was still pitiless, but moving around made it more bearable. Periodic breezes gusted down alleyways, but they were not at all relieving. Most were so full of sand and grit that Karkasy had to turn his back to them and close his eyes until they abated.

The streets were vacant, except for an occasional figure hunched in the shadows of a doorway, or half-visible behind broken shutters. He wondered if anybody would respond if he approached them, but felt reluctant to try. The silence was penetrating, and to break it would have felt as improper as disturbing a mourning vigil.

He was alone, properly alone for the first time in over a year, and master of his own actions. It felt tremendously liberating. He could go where he pleased, and quickly began to exercise that privilege, taking street turns at random, walking where his feet took him. For a while, he kept the still-unmoving Titan in sight, as a point of reference, but it was soon eclipsed by towers and high roofs, so he resigned himself to getting lost. Getting lost would be liberating too. There were always the great towers of the palace. He could follow those back to their roots if necessary.

War had ravaged many parts of the city he passed through. Buildings had toppled into white and dusty heaps of slag, or been reduced to their very basements. Others were roofless, or burned out, or wounded in their structures, or simply rendered into facades, their innards blown out, standing like the wooden flats of stage scenery.

Craters and shell holes pock-marked certain pavements, or the surfaces of metalled roads, sometimes forming strange rows and patterns, as if their arrangement was deliberate, or concealed, by some secret code, great truths of life and death. There was a smell in the dry, hot air, like burning or blood or ordure, yet none of those things. A mingled scent, an afterscent. It wasn't burning he could smell, it was things burnt. It wasn't blood, it was dry residue. It wasn't ordure, it was the seeping consequence of sewer systems broken and cracked by the bombardment.

Many streets had stacks of belongings piled up along the pavements. Furniture, bundles of clothing, kitchenware. A great deal of it was in disrepair, and had evidently been recovered from ruined dwellings. Other piles seemed more intact, the items carefully packed in trunks and coffers. People were intending to quit the city, he realised. They had piled up their possessions in readiness while they tried to procure transportation, or perhaps the relevant permission from the occupying authorities.

Almost every street and yard bore some slogan or other notice upon its walls. All were hand written, in a great variety of styles and degrees of calligraphic skill. Some were daubed in pitch, others paint or dye, others chalk or charcoal – the latter, Karkasy reasoned, marks made by the employment of burnt sticks and splinters taken from the ruins. Many were indecipherable, or unfathomable. Many were bold, angry graffiti, splenetically cursing the invaders or defiantly announcing a surviving spark of resistance. They called for death, for uprising, for revenge.

Others were lists, carefully recording the names of the citizens who had died in that place, or plaintive requests for news about the missing loved ones listed below. Others were agonised statements of lament, or minutely and delicately transcribed texts of some sacred significance.

Karkasy found himself increasingly captivated by them, by the variation and contrast of them, and the emotions they conveyed. For the first time, the first true and proper time since he'd left Terra, he felt the poet in him respond. This feeling excited him. He had begun to fear that he might have accidentally left his poetry behind on Terra in his hurry to embark, or at least that it malingered, folded and unpacked, in his quarters on the ship, like his least favourite shirt.

He felt the muse return, and it made him smile, despite the heat and the mummification of his throat. It seemed apt, after all, that it should be words that brought words back into his mind.

He took out his chapbook and his pen. He was a man of traditional inclinations, believing that no great lyric could ever be composed on the screen of a data-slate, a point of variance that had almost got him into a fist fight with Palisad Hadray, the other 'poet of note' amongst the remembrancer group. That had been near the start of their conveyance to join the expedition, during one of the informal dinners held to allow the remembrancers to get to know one another. He would have won the fight, if it had come to it. He was fairly sure of that. Even though Hadray was an especially large and fierce woman.

Karkasy favoured notebooks of thick, cream cartridge paper, and at the start of his long, feted career, had sourced a supplier in one of Terra's arctic hives, who specialised in antique methods of paper manufacture. The firm was called Bondsman, and it offered a particularly pleasing quarto chapbook of fifty leaves, bound in a case of soft, black kid, with an elasticated strap to keep it closed. The Bondsman Number 7. Karkasy, a sallow, raw-headed youth back then, had paid a significant proportion of his first royalty income for an order of two hundred. The volumes had come, packed head to toe, in a waxed box lined with tissue paper, which had smelled, to him at least, of genius and potential. He had used the books sparingly, leaving not one precious page unfilled before starting a new one. As his fame grew, and his earnings soared, he had often thought about ordering another box, but always stopped when he realised he had over half the original shipment still to use up. All his great works had been composed upon the pages of Bondsman Number 7's. His *Fanfare to Unity*, all eleven of his *Imperial Cantos*, his *Ocean Poems*, even the meritorious and much republished *Reflections and Odes*, written in his thirtieth year, which had secured his reputation and won him the Ethiopic Laureate.

The year before his selection to the role of remembrancer, after what had been, in all fairness, a decade of unproductive doldrums that had seen him living off past glories, he had decided to rejuvenate his muse by placing an order for another box. He had been dismayed to discover that Bondsman had ceased operation.

Ignace Karkasy had nine unused volumes left in his possession. He had brought them all with him on the voyage. But for an idiot scribble or two, their pages were unmarked.

On a blazing, dusty street corner in the broken city, he took the chapbook out of his coat pocket, and slid off the strap. He found his pen – an antique plunger-action fountain, for his traditionalist tastes applied as much to the means of marking as what should be marked – and began to write.

The heat had almost congealed the ink in his nib, but he wrote anyway, copying out such pieces of wall writing as affected him, sometimes attempting to duplicate the manner and form of their delineation.

He recorded one or two at first, as he moved from street to street, and then became more inclusive, and began to mark down almost every slogan he saw. It gave him satisfaction and delight to do this. He could feel, quite definitely, a lyric beginning to form, taking shape from the words he read and recorded. It would be superlative. After years of absence, the muse had flown back into his soul as if it had never been away.

He realised he had lost track of time. Though it was still stifling hot and bright, the hour was late, and the blazing sun had worked its way over, lower in the sky. He had filled almost twenty pages, almost half his chapbook.

He felt a sudden pang. What if he had only nine volumes of genius left in him? What if that box of Bondsman Number 7's, delivered so long ago, represented the creative limits of his career?

He shuddered, chilled despite the clinging heat, and put his chapbook and pen away. He was standing on a lonely, war-scabbed street-corner, persecuted by the sun, unable to fathom which direction to turn.

For the first time since escaping Peeter Egon Momus's presentation, Karkasy felt afraid. He felt that eyes were watching him from the blind ruins.

He began to retrace his steps, slouching through gritty shadow and dusty light. Only once or twice did a new graffito persuade him to stop and take out his chapbook again.

He'd been walking for some time, in circles probably, for all the streets had begun to look the same, when he found the eating house. It occupied the ground floor and basement of a large basalt tenement, and bore no sign, but the smell of cooking announced its purpose. Door-shutters had been opened onto the street, and there was a handful of tables set out. For the first time, he saw people in numbers. Locals, in dark sun cloaks and shawls, as unresponsive and indolent as the few souls he had glimpsed in doorways. They were sitting at the tables under a tattered awning, alone or in small, silent groups, drinking thimble glasses of liquor or eating food from finger bowls.

Karkasy remembered the state of his throat, and his belly remembered itself with a groan.

He walked inside, into the shade, nodding politely to the patrons. None responded.

In the cold gloom, he found a wooden bar with a dresser behind it, laden with glassware and spouted bottles. The hostel keeper, an old woman in a khaki wrap, eyed him suspiciously from behind the serving counter.

'Hello,' he said.

She frowned back.

'Do you understand me?' he asked.

She nodded slowly.

'That's good, very good. I had been told our languages were largely the same, but that there were some accent and dialect differences.' He trailed off.

The old woman said something that might have been 'What?' or might have been any number of curses or interrogatives.

'You have food?' he asked. Then he mimed eating.

She continued to stare at him.

'Food?' he asked.

She replied with a flurry of guttural words, none of which he could make out. Either she didn't have food, or was unwilling to serve him, or she didn't have any food for the likes of him.

'Something to drink then?' he asked.

No response.

He mimed drinking, and when that brought nothing, pointed at the bottles behind her.

She turned and took down one of the glass containers, selecting one as if he had indicated it directly instead of generally. It was three-quarters full of a clear, oily fluid that roiled in the gloom. She thumped it onto the counter, and then put a thimble glass beside it.

'Very good,' he smiled. 'Very, very good. Well done. Is this local? Ah ha! Of course it is, of course it is. A local speciality? You're not going to tell me, are you? Because you have no idea what I'm actually saying, have you?'

She stared blankly at him.

He picked up the bottle and poured a measure into the glass. The liquor flowed as slowly and heavily through the spout as his ink had done from his pen in the street. He put the bottle down and lifted the glass, toasting her.

'Your health,' he said brightly, 'and to the prosperity of your world. I know things are hard now, but trust me, this is all for the best. All for the very best.'

He swigged the drink. It tasted of liquorice and went down very well, heating his dry gullet and lighting a buzz in his gut.

'Excellent,' he said, and poured himself a second. 'Very good indeed. You're not going to answer me, are you? I could ask your name and your lineage and anything at all, and you would just stand there like a statue, wouldn't you? Like a Titan?'

He sank the second glass and poured a third. He felt very good about himself now, better than he had done for hours, better even than when the muse had flown back to him in the streets. In truth, drink had always been a more welcome companion to Ignace Karkasy than any muse, though he would never have been willing to admit it, or to admit the fact that his affection for drink had long weighed down his career, like rocks in a sack. Drink and his muse, both beloved of him, each pulling in opposite directions.

He drank his third glass, and tipped out a fourth. Warmth infused him, a biological warmth much more welcome than the brutal heat of the day. It made him smile. It revealed to him how extraordinary this false Terra was, how complex and intoxicating. He felt love for it, and pity, and tremendous goodwill. This world, this place, this hostelry, would not be forgotten.

Suddenly remembering something else, he apologised to the old woman, who had remained facing him across the counter like a fugued servitor, and reached into his pocket. He had currency – Imperial coin and plastek wafers. He made a pile of them on the stained and glossy bartop.

'Imperial,' he said, 'but you take that. I mean, you're obliged to. I was told that by the iterators this morning. Imperial currency is legal tender now, to replace your local coin. Terra, you don't know what I'm saying, do you? How much do I owe you?'

No answer.

He sipped his fourth drink and pushed the pile of cash towards her. 'You decide, then. You tell me. Take for the whole bottle.' He tapped his finger against the side of the flask. 'The whole bottle? How much?'

He grinned and nodded at the money. The old woman looked at the heap, reached out a bony hand and picked up a five aquila piece. She studied it for a moment, then spat on it and threw it at Karkasy. The coin bounced off his belly and fell onto the floor.

Karkasy blinked and then laughed. The laughter boomed out of him, hard and joyous, and he was quite unable to keep it in. The old woman stared at him. Her eyes widened ever so slightly.

Karkasy lifted up the bottle and the glass. 'I tell you what,' he said. 'Keep it all. All of it.'

He walked away and found an empty table in the corner of the place. He sat down and poured another drink, looking about him. Some of the silent patrons were staring at him. He nodded back, cheerfully.

They looked so human, he thought, and realised it was a ridiculous thing to think, because they were without a doubt human. But at the same time, they weren't. Their drab clothes, their drab manner, the set of their features, their way of sitting and looking and eating. They seemed a little like animals, man-shaped creatures trained to ape human behaviour, yet not quite accomplished in that art.

'Is that what five thousand years of separation does to a species?' he asked aloud. No one answered, and some of his watchers turned away.

Was that what five thousand years did to the divided branches of mankind? He took another sip. Biologically identical, but for a few strands of genetic inheritance, and yet culturally grown so far apart. These were men who lived and walked and drank and shat, just as he did. They lived in houses and raised cities, and wrote upon walls and even spoke the same language, old women not withstanding. Yet time and division had grown them along alternate paths. Karkasy saw that clearly now. They were a graft from the rootstock, grown under another sun, similar yet alien. Even the way they sat at tables and sipped at drinks.

Karkasy stood up suddenly. The muse had abruptly jostled the pleasure of drink out of the summit of his mind. He bowed to the old woman as he collected up his glass and two-thirds empty bottle, and said, 'My thanks, madam,'

Then he teetered back out into the sunlight.

HE FOUND A vacant lot a few streets away that had been levelled to rubble by bombing, and perched himself on a chunk of basalt. Setting down the bottle and the glass carefully, he took out his half-filled Bondsman Number 7 and began to write again, forming the first few stanzas of a lyric that owed much to the writings on the walls and the insight he had garnered in the hostelry. It flowed well for a while, and then dried up.

He took another drink, trying to restart his inner voice. Tiny black ant-like insects milled industriously in the rubble around him, as if trying to rebuild their own miniature lost city. He had to brush one off the open page of his chapbook. Others raced exploratively over the toe-caps of his boots in a frenetic expedition.

He stood up, imagining itches, and decided this wasn't a place to sit. He gathered up his bottle and his glass, taking another sip once he'd fished out the ant floating in it with his finger.

A building of considerable size and magnificence faced him across the damaged lot. He wondered what it was. He stumbled over the rubble towards it, almost losing his footing on the loose rocks from time to time.

What was it – a municipal hall, a library, a school? He wandered around it, admiring the fine rise of the walls and the decorated headers of the stonework. Whatever it was, the building was important. Miraculously, it had been spared the destruction visited on its neighbouring lots.

Karkasy found the entrance, a towering arch of stone filled with copper doors. They weren't locked. He pushed his way in.

The interior of the building was so profoundly and refreshingly cool it almost made him gasp. It was a single space, an arched roof raised on massive ouslite pillars, the floor dressed in cold onyx. Under the end windows, some kind of stone structure rose.

Karkasy paused. He put down his bottle beside the base of one of the pillars, and advanced down the centre of the building with his glass in his hand. He knew there was a word for a place like this. He searched for it.

Sunlight, filleted by coloured glass, slanted through the thin windows. The stone structure at the end of the chamber was a carved lectern supporting a very massive and very old book.

Karkasy touched the crinkled parchment of the book's open pages with delight. It appealed to him the same way as the pages of a Bondsman Number 7 did. The sheets were old, and faded, covered with ornate black script and hand-coloured images.

This was an altar, he realised. This place, a temple, a fane!

'Terra alive!' he declared, and then winced as his words echoed back down the cool vault. History had taught him about fanes and religious belief, but he had never before set foot inside such a place. A place of sprits and divinity. He sensed that the spirits were looking down on his intrusion with disapproval, and then laughed at his own idiocy. There were no spirits. Not anywhere in the cosmos. Imperial Truth had taught him that. The only spirits in this building were the ones in his glass and his belly.

He looked at the pages again. Here was the truth of it, the crucial mark of difference between his breed of man and the local variety. They were heathens. They continued to embrace the superstitions that the fundamental strand of mankind had set aside. Here was the promise of an afterlife, and an ethereal world. Here was the nonsense of a faith in the intangible.

Karkasy knew that there were some, many perhaps, amongst the population of the compliant Imperium, who longed for a return to those ways. God, in every incarnation and pantheon, was long perished, but still men hankered after the ineffable. Despite prosecution, new credos and budding religions were sprouting up amongst the cultures of Unified Man. Most vigorous of all was the Imperial Creed that insisted humanity adopt the Emperor as a divine being. A God-Emperor of Mankind.

The idea was ludicrous and, officially, heretical. The Emperor had always refused such adoration in the most stringent terms, denying his apotheosis. Some said it would only happen after his death, and as he was functionally immortal, that tended to cap the argument. Whatever his powers, whatever his capacity, whatever his magnificence as the finest and most gloriously total leader of the species, he was still just a man. The Emperor liked to remind mankind of this whenever he could. It was an edict that rattled around the bureaucracies of the expanding Imperium. The Emperor is the Emperor, and he is great and everlasting.

But he is not a god, and he refuses any worship offered to him.

Karkasy took a swig and put his empty thimble-glass down, at an angle on the edge of the lectern shelf. The Lectitio Divinitatus, that's what it was called. The missal of the underground wellspring that strove, in secret, to establish the Cult of the Emperor, against his will. It was said that even some of the upstanding members of the Council of Terra supported its aims.

The Emperor as god. Karkasy stifled a laugh. Five thousand years of blood, war and fire to expunge all gods from the culture, and now the man who achieved that goal supplants them as a new deity.

'How foolish is mankind?' Karkasy laughed, enjoying the way his words echoed around the empty fane. 'How desperate and flailing? Is it that we simply need a concept of god to fulfill us? Is that part of our make up?'

He fell silent, considering the point he had raised to himself. A good point, well-reasoned. He wondered where his bottle had gone.

It *was* a good point. Maybe that was mankind's ultimate weakness. Maybe it was one of humanity's basic impulses, the need to believe in another, higher order. Perhaps faith was like a vacuum, sucking up credulity in a frantic effort to fill its own void. Perhaps it was a part of mankind's genetic character to need, to hunger for, a spiritual solace.

'Perhaps we are cursed,' Karkasy told the empty fane, 'to crave something which does not exist. There are no gods, no spirits, no daemons. So we make them up, to comfort ourselves.'

The fane seemed oblivious to his ramblings. He took hold of his empty glass and wandered back to where he had left the bottle. Another drink.

He left the fane and threaded his way out into the blinding sunlight. The heat was so intense that he had to take another swig.

Karkasy wobbled down a few streets, away from the temple, and heard a rushing, roasting noise. He discovered a team of Imperial soldiers, stripped to the waist, using a flamer to erase anti-Imperial slogans from a wall. They had evidently been working their way down the street, for all the walls displayed swathes of heat burns.

'Don't do that,' he said.

The soldiers turned and looked at him, their flamer spitting. From his garments and demeanour, he was unmistakably not a local.

'Don't do that,' he said again.

'Orders, sir,' said one of the troopers.

'What are you doing out here?' asked another.

Karkasy shook his head and left them alone. He trudged through narrow alleys and open courts, sipping from the spout of the bottle.

He found another vacant lot very similar to the one he had sat down in before, and placed his rump upon a scalene block of basalt. He took out his chapbook and ran through the stanzas he had written.

They were terrible.

He groaned as he read them, then became angry and tore the precious pages out. He balled the thick, cream paper up and tossed it away into the rubble.

Karkasy suddenly became aware that eyes were staring at him

from the shadows of doorways and windows. He could barely make out their shapes, but knew full well that locals were watching him.

He got up, and quickly retrieved the balls of crumpled paper he had discarded, feeling that he had no right to add in any way to the mess. He began to hurry down the street, as thin boys emerged from hiding to lob stones and jeers after him.

He found himself, unexpectedly, in the street of the hostelry again. It was uninhabited, but he was pleased to have found it as his bottle had become unaccountably empty.

He went into the gloom. There was no one around. Even the old woman had disappeared. His pile of Imperial currency lay where he had left it on the counter.

Seeing it, he felt authorised to help himself to another bottle from behind the bar. Clutching the bottle in his hand, he very carefully sat down at one of the tables and poured another drink.

He had been sitting there for an indefinite amount of time when a voice asked him if he was all right.

Ignace Karkasy blinked and looked up. The gang of Imperial army troops who had been burning clean the walls of the city had entered the hostelry, and the old woman had reappeared to fetch them drinks and food.

The officer looked down at Karkasy as his men took their seats.

'Are you all right, sir?' he asked.

'Yes. Yes, yes, yes,' Karkasy slurred.

'You don't look all right, pardon me for saying. Should you be out in the city?'

Karkasy nodded furiously, tucking into his pocket for his permit. It wasn't there. 'I'm meant to be here,' he said, instead. 'Meant to. I was ordered to come. To hear Eater Piton Momus. Shit, no, that's wrong. To hear Peeter Egon Momus present his plans for the new city. That's why I'm here. I'm meant to be.'

The officer regarded him cautiously. 'If you say so, sir. They say Momus has drawn up a wonderful scheme for the reconstruction.'

'Oh yes, quite wonderful,' Karkasy replied, reaching for his bottle and missing. 'Quite bloody wonderful. An eternal memorial to our victory here...'

'Sir?'

'It won't last,' Karkasy said. 'No, no. It won't last. It can't. Nothing lasts. You look like a wise man to me, friend, what do you think?'

'I think you should be on your way, sir,' the officer said gently.

'No, no, no... about the city! The city! It won't last, Terra take Peeter Egon Momus. To the dust, all things return. As far as I can see, this city was pretty wonderful before we came and hobbled it.'

'Sir, I think–'

'No, you don't,' Karkasy said, shaking his head. 'You don't, and no one does. This city was supposed to last forever, but we broke it and laid it in tatters. Let Momus rebuild it, it will happen again, and again. The work of man is destined to perish. Momus said he plans a city that will celebrate mankind forever. You know what? I bet that's what the architects who built this place thought too.'

'Sir–'

'What man does comes apart, eventually. You mark my words. This city, Momus's city. The Imperium–'

'Sir, you–'

Karkasy rose to his feet, blinking and wagging a finger. 'Don't "sir" me! The Imperium will fall asunder as soon as we construct it! You mark my words! It's as inevitable as–'

Pain abruptly splintered Karkasy's face, and he fell down, bewildered. He registered a frenzy of shouting and movement, then felt boots and fists slamming into him, over and over again. Enraged by his words, the troopers had fallen upon him.

Shouting, the officer tried to pull them off.

Bones snapped. Blood spurted from Karkasy's nostrils.

'Mark my words!' he coughed. 'Nothing we build will last for-ever! You ask these bloody locals!'

A bootcap cracked into his sternum. Bloody fluid washed into his mouth.

'Get off him! Get off him!' the officer was yelling, trying to rein in his provoked and angry men.

By the time he managed to do so, Ignace Karkasy was no longer pontificating.

Or breathing.

SIX

Counsel
A question well answered
Two gods in one room

TORGADDON WAS WAITING for him in the towering ante-hall behind the strategium.

'There you are,' he grinned.

'Here I am,' Loken agreed.

'There will be a question,' Torgaddon remarked, keeping his voice low. 'It will seem a minor thing, and will not be obviously directed to you but be ready to catch it.'

'Me?'

'No, I was talking to myself. Yes, you, Garviel! Consider it a baptismal test. Come on.'

Loken didn't like the sound of Torgaddon's words, but he appreciated the warning. He followed Torgaddon down the length of the ante-hall. It was a perilously tall, narrow place, with embossed columns of wood set into the walls that soared up and branched like carved trees to support a glass roof two hundred metres above them, through which the stars could be seen. Darkwood panels cased the walls between the columns, and they were covered with millions of lines of hand-painted names and numbers, all rendered in exquisite gilt lettering. They were the names of the dead: all those of the Legions, the army, the fleet and the Divisio Militaris who had fallen since the start of the Great Crusade in actions where this flagship vessel had been present. The names of immortal heroes were limned here on the walls, grouped in columns below header legends that proclaimed the world-sites of famous actions and hallowed conquests. From this display, the ante-hall earned its particular name: the Avenue of Glory and Lament.

The walls of fully two-thirds of the ante-hall were filled up with golden names. As the two striding captains in their glossy white plate drew closer to the strategium end, the wall boards became bare, unoccupied. They passed a group of hooded necrologists hudd-led by the last, half-filled panel, who were carefully stencil-ling new names onto the dark wood with gold-dipped brushes.

The latest dead. The roll call from the High City battle.

The necrologists stopped work and bowed their heads as the two captains went by. Torgaddon didn't spare them a second glance, but Loken turned to read the half-writ names. Some of them were brothers from Locasta he would never see again.

He could smell the tangy oil suspension of the gold-leaf the necrologists were using.

'Keep up,' Torgaddon grunted.

High doors, lacquered gold and crimson, stood closed at the end of the Avenue Hall. Before them, Aximand and Abaddon were waiting. They were likewise fully armoured, their heads bare, their brush-crested helms held under their left arms. Abad-don's great white shoulder plates were draped with a black wolf-pelt.

'Garviel,' he smiled.

'It doesn't do to keep him waiting,' Aximand grumbled. Loken wasn't sure if Little Horus meant Abaddon or the commander. 'What were you two gabbing about? Like fishwives, the pair of you.'

'I was just asking him if he'd settled Vipus in,' Torgaddon said simply.

Aximand glanced at Loken, his wide-set eyes languidly half-hooded by his lids.

'And I was reassuring Tarik that I had,' Loken added. Evidently, Torgaddon's quiet heads-up had been for his ears only.

'Let's enter,' Abaddon said. He raised his gloved hand and pushed the gold and crimson doors wide.

A short processional lay before them, a twenty-metre colon-nade of ebon stone chased with a fretwork of silver wire. It was lined by forty Guardsmen of the Imperial army, members of Varvaras's own Byzant Janizars, twenty against each wall. They were splendidly appointed in full dress uniforms: long cream greatcoats with gold frogging, high-crowned chrome helms with basket visors and scarlet cockades, and matching sashes. As the Mournival came through the doors, the Janizars brandished their ornate power lances, beginning with the pair directly inside the doorway. The polished blades of the weapons whirled up into place in series, like chasing dominoes along the processional, each facing pair of weapons locking into position just before the marching captains caught up with the ripple.

The final pair came to salute, eyes-front, in perfect discipline, and the Mournival stepped past them onto the deck of the strategium.

The strategium was a great, semicircular platform that projected like a lip out above the tiered theatre of the flagship's bridge. Far below lay the principal command level, thronging with hun-dreds of uniformed personnel and burnished aide servitors, tiny as ants. To either side, the beehive sub-decks of the secondary platforms, dressed in gold and black ironwork, rose up, past the level of the projecting strategium, up into the roof itself, each storey busy with Navy staff, operators, cogitation officers and astropaths. The front section of the bridge chamber was a great, strutted window, through which the constellations and the ink of space could be witnessed. The standards of the Luna Wolves and the Imperial Fists hung from the arching roof, either side of the staring eye banner of the Warmaster himself. That great banner was marked, in golden thread, with the decree: 'I am the Emperor's Vigilance and the Eye of Terra.'

Loken remembered the award of that august symbol with pride during the great triumph after Ullanor was done.

In all his decades of service, Loken had only been on the bridge of the *Vengeful Spirit* twice before: once to formally accept his promotion to captain, and then again to mark his elevation to the captaincy of the Tenth. The scale of the place took his breath away, as it had done both times before.

The strategium deck itself was an ironwork platform which supported, at its centre, a circular dais of plain, unfinished ouslite, one metre deep and ten in diameter. The commander had always eschewed any form of throne or seat. The ironwork walk space around the dais was half-shadowed by the overhang of tiered galleries that climbed the slopes of the chamber behind it. Glancing up, Loken saw huddles of senior iterators, tacticians, ship captains of the expedition fleet and other notables gathering to view the proceedings. He looked for Sindermann, but couldn't find his face.

Several attendant figures stood quietly around the edges of the dais. Lord Commander Hektor Varvaras, marshal of the expedition's army, a tall, precise aristocrat in red robes, stood discussing the content of a data-slate with two formally uniformed army aides. Boas Comnenus, Master of the Fleet, waited, drumming

steel fingers on the edge of the ouslite plinth. He was a squat bear
of a man, his ancient, flaccid body encased in a superb silver-
and-steel exo-skeleton, further draped in robes of deep, rich, selpic
blue. Neatly machined ocular lenses whirred and exchanged in
the augmetic frame that supplanted his long-dead eyes.

Ing Mae Sing, the expedition's Mistress of Astropaths, stood to
the master's left, a gaunt, blind spectre in a hooded white gown,
and, round from her, in order, the High Senior of the Navis
Nobilite, Navigator Chorogus, the Master Companion of Vox,
the Master Companion of Lucidation, the senior tacticae, the
senior heraldists, and various gubernatorial legates.

Each one, Loken noticed, had placed a single personal item on
the edge of the dais where they stood: a glove, a cap, a wand-stave.

'We stay in the shadows,' Torgaddon told him, bringing Loken
up short under the edge of the shade cast by the balcony above.
'This is the Mournival's place, apart, yet present.'

Loken nodded, and remained with Torgaddon and Aximand in
the symbolic shadow of the overhang. Abaddon stepped forward
into the light, and took his place at the edge of the dais between
Varvarus, who nodded pleasantly to him, and Comnenus, who
didn't. Abaddon placed his helm upon the edge of the ouslite
disc.

'An item placed on the dais registers a desire to be heard and
noted,' Torgaddon told Loken. 'Ezekyle has a place by dint of his
status as first captain. For now, he will speak as first captain, not
as the Mournival.'

'Will I get the hang of this ever?' Loken asked.

'No, not at all,' Torgaddon said. Then he grinned. 'Yes, you will.
Of course, you will!'

Loken noticed another figure, removed from the main assembly. The man, if it were a man, lurked at the rail of the strategium
deck, gazing out across the chasm of the bridge. He was a

machine, it seemed, much more a machine than a man. Vague relics of flesh and muscle remained in the skeletal fabric of his mechanical body, a fabulously wrought armature of gold and steel.

'Who is that?' Loken whispered.

'Regulus,' Aximand replied curtly. 'Adept of the Mechanicum.'

So that was what a Mechanicum adept looked like, Loken thought. That was the sort of being who could command the invincible Titans into war.

'Hush now,' Torgaddon said, tapping Loken on the arm.

Plated glass doors on the other side of the platform slid open, and laughter boomed out. A huge figure came out onto the strategium, talking and laughing animatedly, along with a diminutive presence who scuttled to keep up.

Everybody dropped in a bow. Loken, going down on one knee, could hear the rustle of others bowing in the steep balconies above him. Boas Comnenus did so slowly, because his exoskeleton was ancient. Adept Regulus did so slowly, not because his machine body was stiff, but rather because he was clearly reluctant.

Warmaster Horus looked around, smiled, and then leapt up onto the dais in a single bound. He stood at the centre of the ouslite disc, and turned slowly.

'My friends,' he said. 'Honour's done. Up you get.'

Slowly, they rose and beheld him.

He was as magnificent as ever, Loken thought. Massive and limber, a demi-god manifest, wrapped in white-gold armour and pelts of fur. His head was bare. Shaven, sculptural, his face was noble, deeply tanned by multiple sunlights, his wide-spaced eyes bright, his teeth gleaming. He smiled and nodded to each and every one of them.

He had such vitality, like a force of nature – a tornado, a

tempest, an avalanche – trapped in humanoid form and distilled, the potential locked in. He rotated slowly on the dais, grinning, nodding to some, pointing out certain friends with a familiar laugh.

The primarch looked at Loken, back in the shadows of the overhang, and his smile seemed to broaden for a second.

Loken felt a shudder of fear. It was pleasant and vigorous. Only the Warmaster could make an Astartes feel that.

'Friends,' Horus said. His voice was like honey, like steel, like a whisper, like all of those things mixed as one. 'My dear friends and comrades of the 63rd Expedition, is it really that time again?'

Laughter rippled around the deck, and from the galleries above.

'Briefing time,' Horus chuckled, 'and I salute you all for coming here to bear the tedium of yet another session. I promise I'll keep you no longer than is necessary. First though…'

Horus jumped back down off the dais and stooped to place a sheltering arm around the tiny shoulders of the man who had accompanied him out of the inner chamber, like a father showing off a small child to his brothers. So embraced, the man fixed a stiff, sickly grin upon his face, more a desperate grimace than a show of pleasure.

'Before we begin,' Horus said, 'I want to talk about my good friend Peeter Egon Momus here. How I deserved… pardon me, how *humanity* deserved an architect as fine and gifted as this, I don't know. Peeter has been telling me about his designs for the new High City here, and they are wonderful. Wonderful, wonderful.'

'Really, I don't know, my lord…' Momus harrumphed, his rictus trembling. The architect designate was beginning to shake, enduring direct exposure to such supreme attention.

'Our lord the Emperor himself sent Peeter to us,' Horus told them. 'He knew his worth. You see, I don't want to conquer.

Conquest of itself is so messy, isn't it Ezekyle?'

'Yes, lord,' Abaddon murmured.

'How can we draw the lost outposts of man back into one harmonious whole if all we bring them is conquest? We are duty-bound to leave them better than we found them, enlightened by the communication of the Imperial Truth and dazzlingly made over as august provinces of our wide estate. This expedition – and all expeditions – must look to the future and be mindful that what we leave in our wake must stand as an enduring statement of our intent, especially upon worlds, as here, where we have been forced to inflict damage in the promulgation of our message. We must leave legacies behind us. Imperial cities, monuments to the new age, and fitting memorials to those who have fallen in the struggle to establish it. Peeter, my friend Peeter here, understands this. I urge you all to take the time to visit his workshops and review his marvellous schemes. And I look forward to seeing the genius of his vision gracing all the new cities we build in the course of our crusade.'

Applause broke out.

'A-all the new cities…' Momus coughed.

'Peeter is the man for the job,' Horus cried, ignoring the architect's muted gasp. 'I am at one with the way he perceives architecture as celebration. He understands, like no other, I believe, how the spirit of the crusade may be realised in steel and glass and stone. What we raise up is far more important than what we strike down. What we leave behind us, men must admire for eternity, and say "This was well done indeed. This is what the Imperium means, and without it we would be shadows". For that, Peeter's our man. Let's laud him now!'

A huge explosion of applause rang out across the vast chamber. Many officers in the command tiers below joined in. Peeter Egon Momus looked slightly glazed as he was led off the strategium by an aide.

Horus leapt back onto the dais. 'Let's begin... my worthy adept?'

Regulus stepped towards the edge of the dais and put a polished machine-cog down delicately on the lip of the ouslite. When he spoke, his voice was augmented and inhuman, like an electric wind brushing through the boughs of steel trees. 'My lord Warmaster, the Mechanicum is satisfied with this rock. We continue to study, with great interest, the technologies captured here. The gravitic and phasic weapons are being reverse-engineered in our forges. At last report, three standard template construct patterns, previously unknown to us, have been recovered.'

Horus clapped his hands together. 'Glory to our brothers of the tireless Mechanicum! Slowly, we piece together the missing parts of humanity's knowledge. The Emperor will be delighted, as will, I'm sure, your Martian lords.'

Regulus nodded, lifting up the cog and stepping back from the dais.

Horus looked around. 'Rakris? My dear Rakris?'

Lord Governor Elect Rakris, a portly man in dove-grey robes, had already placed his sceptre-wand on the edge of the dais to mark his participation. Now he fiddled with it as he made his report. Horus heard him out patiently, nodding encouragingly from time to time. Rakris droned on, at unnecessary length. Loken felt sorry for him. One of Lord Commander Varvaras's generals, Rakris had been selected to remain at Sixty-Three Nineteen as governor overseer, marshalling the occupation forces as the world transmuted into a full Imperial state. Rakris was a career soldier, and it was clear that, though he took his election as a signal honour, he was quite aghast at the prospect of being left behind. He looked pale and ill, brooding on the time, not long away, when the expedition fleet left him to manage the work alone. Rakris was Terran born, and Loken knew that once the fleet sailed on and left him to his job, Rakris would feel as abandoned as if he had been marooned. A governorship was intended to be the ultimate reward for a war-hero's service, but it seemed to Loken a quietly terrible fate: to be monarch of a world, and then cast away upon it.

Forever.

The crusade would not be back to visit conquered worlds in a hurry.

'...in truth, my commander,' Rakris was saying, 'it may be many decades until this world achieves a state of equity with the Imperium. There is great opposition.'

'How far are we from compliance?' Horus asked, looking around.

Varvaras replied. 'True compliance, lord? Decades, as my good friend Rakris says. Functional compliance? Well, that is different. There is a seed of dissidence in the southern hemisphere that we cannot quench. Until that is brought into line, this world cannot be certified.'

Horus nodded. 'So we stay here, if we must, until the job is done. We must hold over our plans to advance. Such a shame...' The primarch's smile faded for a second as he pondered. 'Unless there is another suggestion?'

He looked at Abaddon and let the words hang. Abaddon seemed to hesitate, and glanced quickly back into the shadows behind him.

Loken realised that this was the question. This was a moment of counsel when the primarch looked outside the official hierarchy of the expedition's command echelon for the informal advice of his chosen inner circle.

Torgaddon nudged Loken, but the nudge was unnecessary. Loken had already stepped forward into the light behind Abaddon.

'My lord Warmaster,' Loken said, almost startled by the sound of his own voice.

'Captain Loken,' Horus said with a delighted flash of his eyes. 'The thoughts of the Mournival are always welcome at my counsel.'

Several present, including Varvaras, made approving sounds.

'My lord, the initial phase of the war here was undertaken quickly and cleanly,' Loken said. 'A surgical strike by the speartip against the enemy's head to minimise the loss and hardship that both sides would suffer in a longer, full-scale offensive. A guerilla war against insurgents would inevitably be an arduous, drawn out, costly affair. It could last for years without resolution, erod-ing Lord Commander Varvaras's precious army resources and blighting any good beginning of the Lord Governor Elect's rule. Sixty-Three Nineteen cannot afford it, and neither can the expe-dition. I say, and if I speak out of turn, forgive me, I say that if the speartip was meant to conquer this world in one, clean blow, it has failed. The work is not yet done. Order the Legion to finish the job.'

Murmuring sprang up all around. 'You'd have me unleash the Luna Wolves again, captain?' Horus asked.

Loken shook his head. 'Not the Legion as a whole, sir. Tenth Company. We were first in, and for that we have been praised, but the praise was not deserved, for the job is not done.'

Horus nodded, as if quite taken with this. 'Varvaras?'

'The army always welcomes the support of the noble Legion. The insurgent factions might plague my men for months, as the captain rightly points out, and make a great tally of killing before they are done with. A company of Luna Wolves could crush them utterly and end their mutiny.'

'Rakris?'

'An expedient solution would be a weight off my back, sir,'

Rakris said. He smiled. 'It would be a hammer to crush a nut, perhaps, but it would be emphatic. The work would be done, and quickly.'

'First captain?'

'The Mournival speaks with one voice, lord,' Abaddon said. 'I urge for a swift conclusion to our business here, so that Sixty-Three Nineteen can get on with its life, and we can get on with the crusade.'

'So it shall be,' Horus said, smiling broadly again. 'So I make a command of it. Captain, have Tenth Company drawn ready and oathed to the moment. We will anticipate news of your success eagerly. Thank you for speaking your mind plainly, and for cutting to the quick of this thorny problem.'

There was a firm flutter of approving applause.

'Then possibilities open for us after all,' Horus said. 'We can begin to prepare for the next phase. When I signal him...' Horus looked at the blind Mistress of Astropaths, who nodded silently '...our beloved Emperor will be delighted to learn that our portion of the crusade is about to advance again. We should now discuss the options open to us. I thought to brief you on our findings concerning these myself, but there is another who positively insists he is fit to do it.'

Everyone present turned to look as the plate glass doors slid open for a second time. The primarch began to clap, and the applause gathered and swept around the galleries, as Maloghurst limped out onto the stage of the strategium. It was the equerry's first formal appearance since his recovery from the surface.

Maloghurst was a veteran Luna Wolf, and a 'Son of Horus' to boot. He had been in his time a company captain, and might even have risen to the first captaincy had he not been promoted to the office of equerry. A shrewd and experienced soul, Maloghurst's talents for intrigue and intelligence ideally served him in that role, and had long since earned him the title 'Twisted'. He took no shame in this. The Legion might protect the Warmaster physically, but he protected him politically, guiding and advising, blocking and out-playing, aware and perfectly sensitive to every nuance and current in the expedition's hierarchy. He had never been well-liked, for he was a hard man to get close to, even by the intimidating standards of the Astartes, and he had never made any particular effort to be liked. Most thought of him as a neutral power, a facilitator, loyal only to Horus himself. No one was ever foolish enough to underestimate him.

But circumstance had suddenly made him popular. Beloved almost. Believed dead, he had been found alive, and in the light of Sejanus's death, this had been taken as some compensation. The work of the remembrancer Euphrati Keeler had cemented his new role as the noble, wounded hero as the picts of his unexpected rescue had flashed around the fleet. Now the assembly welcomed him back rapturously, cheering his fortitude and resolve. He had been reinvented through misfortune into an adored hero.

Loken was quite sure Maloghurst was aware of this ironic turn, and fully prepared to make the most of it.

Maloghurst came out into the open. His injuries had been so severe that he was not yet able to clothe himself in the armour of the Legion, and wore instead a white robe with the wolf's head emblem embroidered on the back. A gold signet in the shape of the Warmaster's icon, the staring eye, formed the cloak's clasp under his throat. He limped, and walked with the aid of a metal staff. His back bulged with a kyphotic misalignment. His face, drawn thin and pale since last it had been seen, was lined with effort, and waddings of synthetic skin-gel covered gashes upon his throat and the left side of his head.

Loken was shocked to see that he was now truly twisted. The

old, mocking nickname suddenly seemed crass and indelicate.

Horus got down off the dais and threw his arms around his equerry. Varvaras and Abaddon both went over to greet him with warm embraces. Maloghurst smiled, and nodded to them, then nodded and waved up to the galleries around to acknowledge the welcome.

As the applause abated, Maloghurst leaned heavily against the side of the dais, and placed his staff upon it in the ceremonial manner. Instead of returning to his place, the Warmaster stood back, away from the circle, giving his equerry centre stage.

'I have enjoyed,' Maloghurst began, his voice hard, but brittle with effort, 'a certain luxury of relaxation in these last few days.' Laughter rattled out from all sides, and the clapping resumed for a moment.

'Bed rest,' Maloghurst went on, 'that bane of a warrior's life, has suited me well, for it has given me ample opportunity to review the intelligence gathered in these last few months by our advance scouts. However, bed rest, as a thing to be enjoyed, has its limits. I insisted that I be allowed to present this evidence to you today for, Emperor bless me, never in my dreams did I imagine I would die of inaction.'

More approving laughter. Loken smiled. Maloghurst really was making the best use of his new status amongst them. He was almost... likable.

'To review,' Maloghurst said, taking out a control wand and gesturing with it briefly. 'Three key areas are of interest to us at this juncture.' His gestures activated the underdeck hololithic projectors, and shapes of solid light came into being above the strategium, projected so that all in the galleries could see them. The first was a rotating image of the world they orbited, surrounded by graphic indicators of elliptical alignment and pre-cession. The spinning world shrank rapidly until it became part of a system arrangement, similarly draped in schematic overlays, a turning, three-dimensional orrery suspended in the air. Then that too shrank and became a small, highlighted component in a mosaic of stars.

'First,' Maloghurst said, 'this area here, itemised eight fifty-eight one-seven, the cluster adjacent to our current locale.' A particular stellar neighbourhood on the light map glowed. 'Our most obvious and accessible next port of call. Scout ships report eighteen systems of interest, twelve of which promise fundamental worth in terms of elemental resource, but no signs of life or habitation. The searches are not yet conclusive, but at this early juncture might I be so bold as to suggest that this region need not concern the expedition. Subject to certification, these systems should be added to the manifest of the colonial pioneers who follow in our footsteps.'

He waved the wand again, and a different group of stars lit up. 'This second region, estimated as... Master?'

Boas Comnenus cleared his throat and obligingly said, 'Nine weeks, standard travel time to spinward of us, equerry.'

'Nine weeks to spinward, thank you,' Maloghurst replied. 'We have barely begun to scout this district, but there are early indications that some significant culture or cultures, of interstellar capability, exist within its bounds.'

'Currently functioning?' Abaddon asked. Too often, Imperial expeditions came upon the dry traces of long perished societies in the desert of stars.

'Too early to tell, first captain,' Maloghurst said. 'Though the scouts report some discovered relics bear similarities to those we found on seven ninety-three one-five half a decade ago.'

'So, not human?' Adept Regulus asked.

'Too early to tell, sir,' Maloghurst repeated. 'The region has an itemisation code, but I believe you'll all be interested to hear that it bears an Old Terran name. Sagittarius.'

'The Dreadful Sagittary,' Horus whispered, with a delighted grin.

'Quite so, my lord. The region certainly requires further examination.' The crippled equerry moved the wand again, and brought up a third coil of suns. 'Our third option, further to spinward.'

'Eighteen weeks, standard,' Boas Comnenus supplied before he had to be asked.

'Thank you, Master. Our scouts have yet to examine it, but we have received word from the 140th Expedition, commanded by Khitas Frome of the Blood Angels, that opposition to Imperial advance has been encountered there. Reports are patchy, but war has broken out.'

'Human resistance?' Varvaras asked. 'Are we talking about lost colonies?'

'Xenos, sir,' Maloghurst said, succinctly. 'Alien foes, of some capacity. I have sent a missive to the 140th asking if they require our support at this time. It is significantly smaller than ours. No reply has yet been received. We may consider it a priority to venture forward to this region to reinforce the Imperial presence there.'

For the first time since the briefing began, the smile had left the Warmaster's face. 'I will speak with my brother Sanguinius on this matter,' he said. 'I would not see his men perish, unsupported.' He looked at Maloghurst. 'Thank you for this, equerry. We appreciate your efforts, and the brevity of your summation.'

There was a ripple of applause.

'One last thing, my lord,' Maloghurst said. 'A personal matter I wish to clear up. I have become known, so I understand, as Maloghurst the Twisted, for reasons of… character that I know are not lost on any present. I have always rejoiced in the title, though some of you might think that odd. I relish the arts politic, and make no effort to hide that. Some of my aides, as I have learned, have made efforts to have the soubriquet quashed, believing it offends my altered state. They worry that I might find it cruel. A slur. I want all here assembled to know that I do not. My body is broken, but my mind is not. I would take offence if the name was to be dropped out of politeness. I don't value sympathy much, and I don't want pity. I am twisted in body now, but I am still complex in mind. Don't think you are somehow sparing my feelings. I wish to be known as I always was.'

'Well said,' Abaddon cried, and smacked his palms together. The assembly rose in a tumult as brisk as the one that had ushered Maloghurst on to the stage.

The equerry picked up his staff from the dais and, leaning upon it, turned to the Warmaster. Horus raised both hands to restore quiet.

'Our thanks to Maloghurst for presenting these options to us. There is much to consider. I dissolve this briefing now, but I request policy suggestions and remarks to my attention in the next day, ship-time. I urge you to study all possibilities and present your assessments. We will reconvene the day after tomorrow at this time. That is all.'

The meeting broke up. As the upper galleries emptied, buzzing with chatter, the parties on the strategium deck gathered in informal conference. The Warmaster stood in quiet conversation with Maloghurst and the Mechanicum Adept.

'Nicely done,' Torgaddon whispered to Loken.

Loken breathed out. He hadn't realised what a weight of tension had built up in him since his summons to the briefing had arrived.

'Yes, finely put,' said Aximand. 'I approve your commentary, Garviel.'

'I just said what I felt. I made it up as I went along,' Loken admitted.

Aximand frowned at him as if not sure whether he was joking or not.

'Are you not cowed by these circumstances, Horus?' Loken asked.

'At first, I suppose I must have been,' Aximand replied in an off-hand way. 'You get used to it, once you've been through one or two. I found it was helpful to look at his feet.'

'His feet?'

'The Warmaster's feet. Catch his eye and you'll quite forget what you were going to say.' Aximand smiled slightly. It was the first hint of any softening towards Loken that Little Horus had shown.

'Thanks. I'll remember that.'

Abaddon joined them under the shadow of the overhang. 'I knew we'd picked right,' he said, clasping Loken's hand in his own. 'Cut to the quick, that's what the Warmaster wants of us. A clean appraisal. Good job, Garviel. Now just make sure it's a good job.'

'I will.'

'Need any help? I can lend you the Justaerin if you need them.'

'Thank you, but Tenth can do this.'

Abaddon nodded. 'I'll tell Falkus his widowmakers are super-fluous to requirements.'

'Please don't do that,' Loken snapped, alarmed at the prospect of insulting Falkus Kibre, Captain of First Company's Terminator elite. The other three quarters of the Mournival laughed out loud.

'Your face,' said Torgaddon.

'Ezekyle goads you so easily,' chuckled Aximand.

'Ezekyle knows he will develop a tough skin, soon enough,' Abaddon remarked.

'Captain Loken?' Lord Governor Elect Rakris was approaching them. Abaddon, Aximand and Torgaddon stood aside to let him through. 'Captain Loken,' Rakris said, 'I just wanted to say, sir, I just wanted to say how grateful I was. To take this matter upon yourself and your company. To speak out so very directly. Lord Varvaras's soldiers are trying their best, but they are just men. The regime here is doomed unless firm action is taken.'

'Tenth Company will deal with the problem, lord governor,' Loken said. 'You have my word as an Astartes.'

'Because the army can't hack it?' They looked around and found that the tall, princely figure of Lord Commander Varvaras had joined them too.

'I-I didn't mean to suggest...' Rakris blithered.

'No offence was intended, lord commander,' said Loken.

'And none taken,' Varvaras said, extending a hand towards Loken. 'An old custom of Terra, Captain Loken...'

Loken took his hand and shook it. 'One I have been reminded of lately,' he said.

Varvaras smiled. 'I wanted to welcome you into our inner circle, captain. And to assure you that you did not speak out of turn today. In the south, my men are being slaughtered. Day in, day out. I have, I believe, the finest army in all of the expeditions, but I know full well it is composed of men, and just men. I understand when a fighting man is needed and when an Astartes is needed. This is the latter time. Come to my war cabinet, at your convenience, and I'll be happy to brief you fully.'

'Thank you, lord commander. I will attend you this afternoon.' Varvaras nodded.

'Excuse me, lord commander,' Torgaddon said. 'The Mournival is needed. The Warmaster is withdrawing and he has called for us.'

THE MOURNIVAL FOLLOWED the Warmaster through the plated glass doors into his private sanctum, a wide, well-appointed chamber built below the well of the audience galleries on the port side of the flagship. One wall was glass, open to the stars. Maloghurst and the Warmaster bustled in ahead of them, and the Mournival drew back into the shadows, waiting to be called upon.

Loken stiffened as three figures descended the ironwork screw stair into the room from the gallery above. The first two were Astartes of the Imperial Fists, almost glowing in their yellow plate. The third was much larger. Another god.

Rogal Dorn, primarch of the Imperial Fists, brother to Horus.

Dorn greeted the Warmaster warmly, and went to sit with him and Maloghurst upon the black leather couches facing the glass wall. Servitors brought them refreshments.

Rogal Dorn was a being as great in all measure as Horus. He, and his entourage of Imperial Fists, had been travelling with the expedition for some months, though they were expected to take their leave soon. Other duties and expeditions called. Loken had been told that Primarch Dorn had come to them at Horus's behest, so that the two of them might discuss in detail the obligations and remit of the role of Warmaster. Horus had solicited the opinions and advice of all his brother primarchs on the subject since the honour had been bestowed upon him. Being named Warmaster set him abruptly apart from them, and raised him up above his brothers, and there had been some stifled objections and discontent, especially from those primarchs who felt the title should have been theirs. The primarchs were as prone to sibling rivalry and petty competition as any group of brothers.

Guided, it was likely, by Maloghurst's shrewd hand, Horus had courted his brothers, stilling fears, calming doubts, reaffirming pacts and generally securing their cooperation. He wanted none to feel slighted, or overlooked. He wanted none to think they were no longer listened to. Some, like Sanguinius, Lorgar and Fulgrim, had acclaimed Horus's election from the outset. Others, like Angron and Perturabo, had raged biliously at the new order, and it had taken masterful diplomacy on the Warmaster's part to placate their choler and jealousy. A few, like Russ and the Lion, had been cynically resolved, unsurprised by the turn of events.

But others, like Guilliman, Khan and Dorn had simply taken it in their stride, accepting the Emperor's decree as the right and obvious choice. Horus had ever been the brightest, the first and the favourite. They did not doubt his fitness for the role, for none of the primarchs had ever matched Horus's achievements, nor the intimacy of his bond with the Emperor. It was to these solid, resolved brothers that Horus turned in particular for counsel. Dorn and Guilliman both embodied the staunchest and most dedicated Imperial qualities, commanding their Legion expeditions with peerless devotion and military genius. Horus desired their approval as a young man might seek the quiescence of older, more accomplished brothers.

Rogal Dorn possessed perhaps the finest military mind of all the primarchs. It was as ordered and disciplined as Roboute Guilliman's, as courageous as the Lion's, yet still supple enough to allow for the flex of inspiration, the flash of battle zeal that had won the likes of Leman Russ and the Khan so many victory wreaths. Dorn's record in the crusade was second only to Horus's, but he was resolute where Horus was flamboyant, reserved where Horus was charismatic, and that was why Horus had been the obvious choice for Warmaster. In keeping with his patient, stony character, Dorn's Legion had become renowned for siegecraft and defensive strategies. The Warmaster had once joked that where he could storm a fortress like no other, Rogal Dorn could hold it. 'If I ever laid assault to a bastion possessed by you,' Horus had quipped at a recent banquet, 'then the war would last for all eternity, the best in attack matched by the best in defence.' The Imperial Fists were an immovable object to the Luna Wolves' unstoppable force.

Dorn had been a quiet, observing presence in his months with the 63rd Expedition. He had spent hours in close conference with the Warmaster, but Loken had seen him from time to time, watching drills and studying preparations for war. Loken had not yet spoken to him, or met him directly. This was the smallest place they had both been in at the same time.

He regarded him now, in calm discussion with the Warmaster; two mythical beings manifest in one room. Loken felt it an honour just to be in their presence, to see them talk, like men, in unguarded fashion. Maloghurst seemed a tiny form beside them.

Primarch Dorn wore a case of armour that was burnished and ornate like a tomb chest, dark red and copper-gold compared to Horus's white dazzle. Unfurled eagle wings, fashioned in metal, haloed his head and decorated his chest and shoulder plate, and aquilas and graven laurels embossed the armour sections of his limbs. A mantle of red velvet hung around his broad shoulders, trimmed in golden weave. His lean face was stern and unsmiling, even when the Warmaster raised a joke, and his hair was a shock of white, bleached like dead bones.

The two Astartes who had escorted him down from the gallery came over to wait with the Mournival. They were well known to Abaddon, Torgaddon and Aximand, but Loken had only yet seen them indirectly about the flagship. Abaddon introduced them as Sigismund, First Captain of the Imperial Fists, resplendent in black and white heraldry, and Efried, Captain of the Third Company. The Astartes made the sign of the aquila to one another in formal greeting.

'I approve of your direction,' Sigismund told Loken at once.

'I'm gratified. You were watching from the galleries?'

Sigismund nodded. 'Prosecute the foe. Get it over with. Get on. There is still so much to be done, we cannot afford delays or time wasting.'

'There are so many worlds still to be brought to compliance,' Loken agreed. 'One day, we will rest at last.'

'No,' Sigismund replied bluntly. 'The crusade will never end. Don't you know that?'

Loken shook his head, 'I wouldn't–'

'Not ever,' said Sigismund emphatically. 'The more we spread, the more we find. World after world. New worlds to conquer. Space is limitless, and so is our appetite to master it.'

'I disagree,' Loken said. 'War will end, one day. A rule of peace will be established. That is the very purpose of our efforts.'

Sigismund grinned. 'Is it? Perhaps. I believe that we have set ourselves an unending task. The nature of mankind makes it so. There will always be another goal, another prospect.'

'Surely, brother, you can conceive of a time when all worlds have been brought into one unity of Imperial rule. Isn't that the dream we strive to realise?'

Sigismund stared into Loken's face. 'Brother Loken, I have heard much about you, all of it good. I had not imagined I would discover such naivety in you. We will spend our lives fighting to secure this Imperium, and then I fear we will spend the rest of our days fighting to keep it intact. There is such involving darkness amongst the stars. Even when the Imperium is complete, there will be no peace. We will be obliged to fight on to preserve what we have fought to establish. Peace is a vain wish. Our crusade may one day adopt another name, but it will never truly end. In the far future, there will be only war.'

'I think you're wrong,' Loken said.

'How innocent you are,' Sigismund mocked, 'and I thought the Luna Wolves were supposed to be the most aggressive of us all. That's how you like the other Legions to think of you, isn't it? The most feared of mankind's warrior classes?'

'Our reputation speaks for itself, sir,' said Loken.

'As does the reputation of the Imperial Fists,' Sigismund replied. 'Are we going to scrap about it now? Argue which Legion is toughest?'

'The answer, always, is the Wolves of Fenris,' Torgaddon put in, 'because they are clinically insane.' He grinned broadly, sensing the tension, and wishing to dispel it. 'If you're comparing sane Legions, of course, the question becomes more complex. Primarch Roboute's Ultramarines make a good show, but then there are so bloody many of them. The Word Bearers, the White Scars, the Imperial Fists, oh, all have fine records. But the Luna Wolves, ah me, the Luna Wolves. Sigismund, in a straight fight? Do you really think you'd have a hope? Honestly? Your yellow ragamuffins against the best of the best?'

Sigismund laughed. 'Whatever helps you sleep, Tarik. Terra bless us all it is a paradigm that will never be tested.'

'What brother Sigismund isn't telling you, Garviel,' Torgaddon said, 'is that his Legion is going to miss all the glory. It's to be withdrawn. He's quite miffed about it.'

'Tarik is being selective with the truth,' Sigismund snorted. 'The Imperial Fists have been commanded by the Emperor to return to Terra and establish a guard around him there. We are chosen as his Praetorians. Now who's miffed, Luna Wolf?'

'Not I,' said Torgaddon. 'I'll be winning laurels in war while you grow fat and lazy minding the home fires.'

'You're quitting the crusade?' Loken asked. 'I had heard something of this.'

'The Emperor wishes us to fortify the Palace of Terra and guard its bulwarks. This was his word at the Ullanor Triumph. We have been the best part of two years tying up our business so we might comply with his desires. Yes, we're going home to Terra. Yes, we will sit out the rest of the crusade. Except that I believe there will be plenty of crusade left once we have been given leave to quit

Earth, our duty done. You won't finish this, Luna Wolves. The stars will have long forgotten your name when the Imperial Fists war abroad again.'

Torgaddon placed his hand on the hilt of his chainsword, playfully. 'Are you so keen to be slapped down by me for your insolence, Sigismund?'

'I don't know. Is he?'

Rogal Dorn suddenly towered behind them. 'Does Sigismund deserve a slap, Captain Torgaddon? Probably. In the spirit of comradeship, let him be. He bruises easily.'

All of them laughed at the primarch's words. The barest hint of a smile flickered across Rogal Dorn's lips.

'Loken,' he said, gesturing. Loken followed the massive primarch to the far corner of the chamber. Behind them, Sigismund and Efried continued to sport with the others of the Mournival, and elsewhere Horus sat in intense conference with Maloghurst.

'We are charged to return to the homeworld,' Dorn said, conversationally. His voice was low and astonishingly soft, like the lap of water on a distant beach, but there was a strength running through it, like the tension of a steel cable. 'The Emperor has asked us to fortify the Imperial stronghold, and who am I to question the Emperor's needs? I am glad he recognises the particular talents of the VII Legion.'

Dorn looked down at Loken. 'You're not used to the likes of me, are you, Loken?'

'No, lord.'

'I like that about you. Ezekyle and Tarik, men like them have been so long in the company of your lord, they think nothing of it. You, however, understand that a primarch is not like a man, or even an Astartes. I'm not talking about strength. I'm talking about the weight of responsibilty.'

'Yes, lord.'

Dorn sighed. 'The Emperor has no like, Loken. There are no gods in this hollow universe to keep him company. So he made us, demi-gods, to stand beside him. I have never quite come to terms with my status. Does that surprise you? I see what I am capable of, and what is expected of me, and I shudder. The mere fact of me frightens me sometimes. Do you think your lord Horus ever feels that way?'

'I do not, lord,' Loken said. 'Self-confidence is one of his keenest qualities.'

'I think so too, and I am glad of it. There could be no better Warmaster than Horus, but a man, even a primarch, is only as good as the counsel he receives, especially if he is utterly self-confident. He must be tempered and guided by those close to him.'

'You speak of the Mournival, sir.'

Rogal Dorn nodded. He gazed out through the armoured glass wall at the scintillating expanse of the starfield. 'You know that I've had my eye on you? That I spoke in support of your election?'

'I have been told so, lord. It baffles and flatters me.'

'My brother Horus needs an honest voice in his ear. A voice that appreciates the scale and import of our undertaking. A voice that is not blasé in the company of demi-gods. Sigismund and Efried do this for me. They keep me honest. You should do the same for your lord.'

'I will endeavour to–' Loken began.

'They wanted Luc Sedirae or Iacton Qruze. Did you know that? Both names were considered. Sedirae is a battle-hungry killer, so much like Abaddon. He would say yes to anything, if it meant war-glory. Qruze – you call him the "Half-heard" I'm told?'

'We do, lord.'

'Qruze is a sycophant. He would say yes to anything if it meant he stayed in favour. The Mournival needs a proper, dissenting opinion.'

'A naysmith,' Loken said.

Dorn flashed a real smile. 'Yes, just so, like the old dynasts did! A naysmith. Your schooling's good. My brother Horus needs a voice of reason in his ear, if he is to rein in his eagerness and act in the Emperor's stead. Our other brothers, some of them quite demented by the choice of Horus, need to see he is firmly in control. So I vouched for you, Garviel Loken. I examined your record and your character, and thought you would be the right mix in the alloy of the Mournival. Don't be insulted, but there is something very human about you, Loken, for an Astartes.'

'I fear, my lord, that my helm will no longer fit me, you have swelled my head so with your compliments.'

Dorn nodded. 'My apologies.'

'You spoke of responsibility. I feel that weight suddenly, terribly.'

'You're strong, Loken. Astartes-built. Endure it.'

'I will, lord.'

Dorn turned from the armoured port and looked down at Loken. He placed his great hands gently on Loken's shoulders. 'Be yourself. Just be yourself. Speak your mind plainly, for you have been granted the rare opportunity to do so. I can return to Terra confident that the crusade is in safe hands.'

'I wonder if your faith in me is too much, lord,' Loken said. 'As fervent as Sedirae, I have just proposed a war–'

'I heard you speak. You made the case well. That is all part of your role now. Sometimes you must advise. Sometimes you must allow the Warmaster to use you.'

'Use me?'

'You understand what Horus had you do this morning?'

'Lord?'

'He had primed the Mournival to back him, Loken. He is cultivating the air of a peacemaker, for that plays well across the worlds of the Imperium. This morning, he wanted someone other than himself to suggest unleashing the Legions for war.'

SEVEN

Oaths of moment
Keeler takes a pict
Scare tactics

'STAY CLOSE, PLEASE,' the iterator said. 'No one wander away from the group, and no one make any record beyond written notes without prior permission. Is that clear?'

They all answered yes.

'We have been granted ten minutes, and that limit will be strictly observed. This is a real privilege.'

The iterator, a sallow man in his thirties called Emont, who despite his appearance possessed what Euphrati Keeler thought was a most beautiful speaking voice, paused and offered one last piece of advice to the group. 'This is also a hazardous place. A place of war. Watch your step, and be aware of where you are.'

He turned and led them down the concourse to the massive blast hatch. The rattle of machine tools echoed out to them. This was an area of the ship the remembrancers had never previously been allowed to visit. Most of the martial areas were off limits except by strict permission, but the embarkation deck was utterly forbidden at all times.

There were six of them in the group. Keeler, another imagist called Siman Sark, a painter called Fransisko Twell, a composer of symphonic patterns called Tolemew Van Krasten, and two documentarists called Avrius Carnis and Borodin Flora. Carnis and Flora were already bickering quietly about 'themes and approaches'.

All of the remembrancers wore durable clothing appropriate for bad weather, and all carried kit bags. Keeler was fairly sure they'd all prepared in vain. The permission they hoped for would not be issued. They were lucky to get this far.

She looped her own kit bag over her shoulder, and settled her favourite picter unit around her neck on its strap. At the head of the party, Emont came to a halt before the two fully armoured Luna Wolves standing watch at the hatch, and showed them the group's credentials.

'Approved by the equerry,' she heard him say. In his beige robes, Emont was a fragile figure compared to the two armoured giants. He had to lift his head to look up at them. The Astartes studied the paperwork, made comments to one another in brief clicks of inter-suit vox, and then nodded them through.

The embarkation deck – and Keeler had to remind herself that this was just *one* embarkation deck, for the flagship possessed six – was an immense space, a long, echoing tunnel dominated by the launch ramps and delivery trackways running its length. At the far end, half a kilometre away, open space was visible through the shimmer of integrity fields.

The noise was punishing. Motorised tools hammered and ratcheted, hoists whined, loading units trundled and rattled, hatches slammed, and reactive engines whooped and flared as they were tested. There was activity everywhere: deck crews hurrying into position, fitters and artificers making final checks and adjustments, servitors unlocking fuel lines. Munition carts hummed past in long sausage-chains. The air stank of heat, oil and exhaust fumes.

Six Stormbirds sat on launch carriages before them. Heavy, armoured delivery vehicles, they were void capable, but also honed and sleek for atmospheric work. They sat in two rows of three, wings extended, like hawks waiting to be thrown to the lure. They were painted white, and showed the wolf's head icon and the eye of Horus on their hulls.

'...known as Stormbirds,' the iterator was saying as he walked them forward. 'The actual pattern type is Warhawk VI. Most expedition forces are now reliant on the smaller, standard construct Thunderhawk pattern, examples of which you can see under covers to our left in the hardstand area, but the Legion has made an effort to keep these old, heavy-duty machines in service. They have been delivering the Luna Wolves into war since the start of the Great Crusade, since before that, actually. They were manufactured on Terra by the Yndonesic Bloc for use against the Panpacific tribes during the Unification Wars. A dozen will be employed in this venture today. Six from this deck, six from Aft Embarkation 2.'

Keeler raised her picter and took several quick shots of the line of Stormbirds ahead. For the last, she crouched down to get a low, impressive angle down the row of their flared wings.

'I said no records!' Emont snapped, hurrying to her.

'I didn't think for a moment you were serious,' Keeler responded smoothly. 'We've got ten minutes. I'm an imagist. What the hell did you think I was going to do?'

Emont looked flustered. He was about to say something when he noticed that Carnis and Flora were wandering astray, locked in some petty squabble.

'Stay with the group!' Emont cried out, hurrying to shepherd them back.

'Get anything good?' Sark asked Keeler.

'*Please*, it's me,' she replied.

He laughed, and took out a picter of his own from his rucksack. 'I didn't have the balls, but you're right. What the hell are we doing here if not our job?'

He took a few shots. Keeler liked Sark. He was good company and had a decent track record of work on Terra. She doubted he would get much here. His eye for composition was fine when it came to faces, but this was very much her thing.

Both the documentarists had now cornered Emont and were grilling him with questions that he struggled to answer. Keeler wondered where Mersadie Oliton had got to. Competition amongst the remembrancers for these six places had been fierce, and Mersadie had won a slot thanks to Keeler's good word and, it was said, approval from someone high up in the Legion, but she had failed to show up on time that morning, and her place had been taken at the last minute by Borodin Flora.

Ignoring the iterator's instructions, she moved away from the group, and chased images with her picter. The Luna Wolf emblem stencilled on an erect braking flap; two servitors glistening with lubricant as they struggled to fix a faulty feed; deck crew panting and wiping sweat from their brows beside a munition trolley they had just loaded; the bare-metal snout of an underwing cannon.

'Are you trying to get me replaced?' Emont asked, catching up with her.

'No.'

'I really must ask you to keep in line, madam,' he said. 'I know you're in favour, but there is a limit. After that business on the surface…'

'What business?' she asked.

'A couple of days ago, surely you heard?'

'No.'

'Some remembrancer gave his minders the slip during a surface visit and got into a deal of trouble. Quite a scandal. It's annoyed the higher-ups. The Primary Iterator had to wrangle hard to prevent the remembrancer contingent being suspended from activity.'

'Was it that bad?'

'I don't know the details. Please, for me, stay in line.'

'You have a very lovely voice,' Keeler said. 'You could ask me to do anything. Of course I will.'

Emont blushed. 'Let's continue with the visit.'

As he turned, she took another pict, capturing the scruffy iterator, head down, against a backdrop of bustling crewmen and threatening ships.

'Iterator?' she called. 'Have we been granted permission to accompany the drop?'

'I don't believe so,' he said sadly. 'I'm sorry. I've not been told.'

A fanfare boomed out across the vast deck. Keeler heard – and felt – a beat like a heavy drum, like a warhammer striking again and again against metal.

'Come to one side. Now! To one side!' Emont called, trying to gather the group on the edge of the deck space.

The drumming grew closer and louder. It was feet. Steel-shod feet marching across decking.

Three hundred Astartes, in full armour and marching perfectly in step, advanced onto the embarkation deck between the waiting Stormbirds. At the front of them, a standard bearer carried the great banner of the Tenth Company.

Keeler gasped at the sight of them. So many, so perfect, so huge, so regimented. She raised her picter with trembling hands and began to shoot. Giants in white metal, assembling for war, uniform and identical, precise and composed.

Orders flew out, and the Astartes came to a halt with a crashing din of heels. They became statues, as equerries hurried through their files, directing and assigning men to their carriers.

Smoothly, units began to turn in fluid sequence, and filed onto the waiting vessels.

'They will have already taken their oaths of moment,' Emont was saying to the group in a hushed whisper.

'Explain,' Van Krasten requested.

Emont nodded. 'Every soldier of the Imperium is sworn to uphold his loyalty to the Emperor at the start of his commission, and the Astartes are no exception. No one doubts their continued devotion to the pledge, but before individual missions, the Astartes choose to swear an immediate oath, an "oath of moment", that binds them specifically to the matter at hand. They pledge to uphold the particular concerns of the enterprise before them. You may think of it as a reaffirmation, I suppose. It is a ritual re-pledging. The Astartes do love their rituals.'

'I don't understand,' said Van Krasten. 'They are already sworn but–'

'To uphold the truth of the Imperium and the light of the Emperor,' Emont said, 'but, as the name suggests, an oath of moment applies to an individual action. It is specific and precise.'

Van Krasten nodded.

'Who's that?' Twell asked, pointing. A senior Astartes, a captain by his cloak, was walking the lines of warriors as they streamed neatly onto the drop-ships.

'That's Loken,' Emont said.

Keeler raised her picter.

Loken's comb-crested helm was off. His fair, cropped hair framed his pale, freckled face. His grey eyes seemed immense. Mersadie had spoken to her of Loken. Quite a force now, if the rumours were true. One of the four.

She shot him speaking to a subordinate, and again, waving servitors clear of a landing ramp. He was the most extraordinary subject. She didn't have to compose around him, or shoot to crop later. He dominated every frame.

No wonder Mersadie was so taken with him. Keeler wondered again why Mersadie Oliton had missed this chance.

Now Loken turned away, his men all but boarded. He spoke with the standard bearer, and touched the hem of the banner with affection. Another fine shot. Then he swung round to face five armoured figures approaching across the suddenly empty deck.

'This is...' Emont whispered. 'This is quite something. I hope you all understand you're lucky to see this.'

'See what?' asked Sark.

'The captain takes his oath of moment last of all. It will be heard and sworn to by two of his fellow captains, but, oh my goodness, the rest of the Mournival have come to hear him pledge.'

'That's the Mournival?' Keeler asked, her picter shooting.

'First Captain Abaddon, Captain Torgaddon, Captain Aximand, and with them Captains Sedirae and Targost,' Emont breathed, afraid of raising his voice.

'Which one is Abaddon?' Keeler asked, aiming her picter.

Loken knelt. 'There was no need–' he began.

'We wanted to do this right,' Torgaddon replied. 'Luc?'

Luc Sedirae, Captain of the Thirteenth Company, took out the seal paper on which the oath of moment was written. 'I am sent to hear you,' he said.

'And I am here to witness it,' Targost said.

'And we are here to keep you cheerful,' Torgaddon added. Abaddon and Little Horus chuckled.

Neither Targost nor Sedirae were Sons of Horus. Targost, Captain of the Seventh, was a blunt-faced man with a deep scar across his brow. Luc Sedirae, champion of so many wars, was a smiling rogue, blond and handsome, his eyes blue and bright, his mouth permanently half-open as if about to bite something. Sedirae raised the scrap of parchment.

'Do you, Garviel Loken, accept your role in this? Do you promise to lead your men into the zone of war, and conduct them to glory, no matter the ferocity or ingenuity of the foe? Do you swear to crush the insurgents of Sixty-Three Nineteen, despite all they might throw at you? Do you pledge to do honour to the XVI Legion and the Emperor?'

Loken placed his hand on the bolter Targost held out.

'On this matter and by this weapon, I swear.'

Sedirae nodded and handed the oath paper to Loken.

'Kill for the living, brother,' he said, 'and kill for the dead.' He turned to walk away. Targost holstered his bolter, made the sign of the aquila, and followed him.

Loken rose to his feet, securing his oath paper to the rim of his right shoulderguard.

'Do this right, Garviel,' Abaddon said.

'I'm glad you told me that,' Loken dead-panned. 'I'd been considering making a mess of it.'

Abaddon hesitated, wrong-footed. Torgaddon and Aximand laughed.

'He's growing that thick skin already, Ezekyle,' Aximand sniggered.

'You walked into that,' Torgaddon added.

'I know, I know,' Abaddon snapped. He glared at Loken. 'Don't let the commander down.'

'Would I?' Loken replied, and walked away to his Stormbird.

'OUR TIME'S UP,' Emont said.

Keeler didn't care. That last pict had been exceptional. The

Mournival, Sedirae and Targost, all in a solemn group, Loken on his knees.

Emont conducted the remembrancers out of the embarkation deck space to an observation deck, adjacent to the launch port from which they could watch the Stormbirds deploy. They could hear the rising note of the Stormbird engines behind them, trembling the embarkation deck as they fired up in pre-launch test. The roaring dulled away as they walked down the long access tunnel, hatches closing one by one after them.

The observation deck was a long chamber, one side of which was a frame of armoured glass. The deck's internal lighting had been switched low so that they could better see into the darkness outside.

It was an impressive view. They directly overlooked the yawning maw of the embarkation deck, a colossal hatch ringing with winking guide lights. The bulk of the flagship rose away above them, like a crenellated Gothic city. Beyond, lay the void itself.

Small service craft and cargo landers flitted past, some on local business, some heading out to other ships of the expedition fleet. Five of these could be seen from the observation deck, sleek monsters at high anchor several kilometres away. They were virtual silhouettes, but the distant sun caught them obliquely, and gave them hard, golden outlines along their ribbed upper hulls.

Below lay the world they orbited. Sixty-Three Nineteen. They were above its nightside, but there was a smoky grey crescent of radiance where the terminator crept forward. In the dark mass, Keeler could make out the faint light-glow of cities speckling the sleeping surface.

Impressive though the view was, she knew shots would be a waste of time. Between the glass, the distance and the odd light sources, resolution would be poor.

She found a seat away from the others, and began to review

the picts she'd already taken, calling them up on the picter's viewscreen.

'May I see?' asked a voice.

She looked up and had to peer in the deck's gloom to identify the speaker. It was Sindermann, the Primary Iterator.

'Of course,' she said, rising to her feet and holding the picter so he could see the images as she thumbed them up one by one. He craned his head forward, curious.

'You have a wonderful eye, Mistress Keeler. Oh, that one is particularly fine! The crew working so hard. I find it striking because it is so natural, candid, I suppose. So very much of our pictorial record is arch and formally posed.'

'I like to get people when they're not aware of me.'

'This one is simply magnificent. You've captured Garviel perfectly there.'

'You know him personally, sir?'

'Why do you ask?'

'You called him by his forename, not by any honorific or rank.'

Sindermann smiled at her. 'I think Captain Loken might be considered a friend of mine. I'd like to think so, anyway. You never can tell with an Astartes. They form relationships with mortals in a curious way, but we spend time together and discuss certain matters.'

'You're his mentor?'

'His tutor. There is a great difference. I know things he does not, so I am able to expand his knowledge, but I do not presume to have influence over him. Oh, Mistress Keeler! This one is superb! The best, I should say.'

'I thought so. I was very pleased with it.'

'All of them together like that, and Garviel kneeling so humbly, and the way you've framed them against the company standard.'

'That was just happenstance,' Keeler said. 'They chose what they were standing beside.'

Sindermann placed his hand gently upon hers. He seemed genuinely grateful for the chance to review her work. 'That pict alone will become famous, I have no doubt. It will be reproduced in history texts for as long as the Imperium endures.'

'It's just a pict,' she chided.

'It is a witness. It is a perfect example of what the remembrancers can do. I have been reviewing some of the material produced by the remembrancers thus far, the material that's been added to the expedition's collective archive. Some of it is... patchy, shall I say? Ideal ammunition for those who claim the remembrancer project is a waste of time, funds and ship space, but some is outstanding, and I would class your work amongst that.'

'You're very kind.'

'I am honest, mistress. And I believe that if mankind does not properly document and witness his achievements, then only half of this undertaking has been made. Speaking of honest, come with me.'

He led her back to the main group by the window. Another figure had joined them on the observation deck, and stood talking to Van Karsten. It was the equerry, Maloghurst, and he turned as they approached.

'Kyril, do you want to tell them?'

'You engineered it, equerry. The pleasure's yours.'

Maloghurst nodded. 'After some negotiation with the expedition seniors, it has been agreed that the six of you can follow the strike force to the surface and observe the venture. You will travel down with one of the ancillary support vessels.'

The remembrancers chorused their delight.

'There's been a lot of debate about allowing remembrancers to become embedded in the layers of military activity,' Sindermann said, 'particularly concerning the issue of civilian welfare in a warzone. There is also, if I may be quite frank, some concern about what you will see. The Astartes in war is a shocking, savage sight. Many believe that such images are not for public distribution, as they might paint a negative picture of the crusade.'

'We both believe otherwise,' Maloghurst said. 'The truth can't be wrong, even if it is ugly or shocking. We need to be clear about what we are doing, and how we are doing it, and allow persons such as yourselves to respond to it. That is the honesty on which a mature culture must be based. We also need to celebrate, and how can you celebrate the courage of the Astartes if you don't see it? I believe in the strength of positive propaganda, thanks, in no small part, to Mistress Keeler here and her documenting of my own plight. There is a rallying power in images and reports of both Imperial victory and Imperial suffering. It communicates a common cause to bind and uplift our society.'

'It helps,' Sindermann put in, 'that this is a low-key action. An unusual use of the Astartes in a policing role. It should be over in a day or so, with little collateral risk. However, I wish to empha-sise that this is still dangerous. You will observe instruction at all times, and never stray from your protection detail. I am to accompany you – this was one of the stipulations made by the Warmaster. Listen to me and do as I say at all times.'

So we're still to be vetted and controlled, Keeler thought. Shown only what they choose to show us. Never mind, this is still a great opportunity. One that I can't believe Mersadie has missed.

'Look!' cried Borodin Flora.

They all turned.

The Stormbirds were launching. Like giant steel darts they shot from the deck mouth, the sunlight catching their armoured flanks. Majestically, they turned in the darkness as they fell away, burners lighting up like blue coals as they dropped in formation towards the planet.

✠ ✠ ✠

BRACING HIMSELF AGAINST the low, overhead handrails, Loken moved down the spinal aisle of the lead Stormbird. Luna Wolves, impassive behind their visors, their weapons locked and stowed, sat in the rear-facing cage-seats either side of him. The bird rocked and shuddered as it cut its steep path through the upper atmosphere.

He reached the cockpit section and wrenched open the hatch to enter. Two flight officers sat back to back, facing wall panel consoles, and beyond them two pilot servitors lay, hardwired into forward-facing helm positions in the cone. The cockpit was dark, apart from the coloured glow of the instrumentation and the sheen of light coming in through the forward slit-ports.

'Captain?' one of the flight officers said, turning and looking up.

'What's the problem with the vox?' Loken asked. 'I've had several reports of comm faults from the men. Ghosting and chatter.'

'We're getting that too, sir,' the officer said, his hands playing over his controls. 'and I'm hearing similar reports from the other birds. We think it's atmospherics.'

'Disruption?'

'Yes, sir. I've checked with the flagship, and they haven't picked up on it. It's probably an acoustic echo from the surface.'

'It seems to be getting worse,' Loken said. He adjusted his helm and tried his link again. The static hiss was still there, but now it had shapes in it, like muffled words.

'Is that language?' he asked.

The officer shook his head. 'Can't tell, sir. It's just reading as general interference. Perhaps we're bouncing up broadcasts from one of the southern cities. Or maybe even army traffic.'

'We need clean vox,' Loken said. 'Do something.'

The officer shrugged and adjusted several dials. 'I can try purging the signal. I can wash it through the signal buffers. Maybe that will tidy up the channels...'

In Loken's ears, there was a sudden, seething rush of static, and then things became quieter suddenly.

'Better,' he said. Then he paused. Now the hiss was gone, he could hear the voice. It was tiny, distant, impossibly quiet, but it was speaking proper words.

'…only name you'll hear….'

'What is that?' Loken asked. He strained to hear. The voice was so very far away, like a rustle of silk.

The flight officer craned his neck, listening to his own headphones. He made minute adjustments to his dials.

'I might be able to…' he began. A touch of his hand had suddenly cleaned the signal to audibility.

'What in the name of Terra *is* that?' he asked.

Loken listened. The voice, like a gust of dry, desert wind, said, 'Samus. That's the only name you'll hear. Samus. It means the end and the death. Samus. I am Samus. Samus is all around you. Samus is the man beside you. Samus will gnaw upon your bones. Look out! Samus is here.'

The voice faded. The channel went dead and quiet, except for the occasional echo pop.

The flight officer took off his headset and looked at Loken. His face was wide-eyed and fearful. Loken recoiled slightly. He wasn't made to deal with fear. The concept disgusted him.

'I d-don't know what that was,' the flight officer said.

'I do,' said Loken. 'Our enemy is trying to scare us.'

EIGHT

One-way war
Sindermann in grass and sand
Jubal

FOLLOWING THE 'EMPEROR'S' death and the fall of their ancient, centralised government, the insurgents had fled into the mountain massifs of the southern hemisphere, and occupied a fastness in a range of peaks, called the Whisperheads in the local language. The air was thin, for the altitude was very great. Dawn was coming up, and the mountains loomed as stern, misty steeples of pale green ice that reflected sun glare.

The Stormbirds dropped from the edge of space, out of the sky's dark blue mantle, trailing golden fire from their ablative surfaces. In the frugal habitations and villages in the foothills, the townsfolk, born into a culture of myth and superstition, saw the fiery marks in the dawn sky as an omen. Many fell to wailing and lamenting, or hurried to their village fanes.

The religious faith of Sixty-Three Nineteen, strong in the capital and the major cities, was distilled here into a more potent brew. These were impoverished backwaters, where the anachronistic beliefs of the society were heightened by a subsistence lifestyle

and poor education. The Imperial army had already struggled
to contain this primitive zealotry during its occupation. As the
streaks of fire crossed the sky, they found themselves hard-
pressed to control the mounting agitation in the villages.

The Stormbirds set down, engines screaming, on a plateau
of dry, white lava-rock five thousand metres below the caps of
the highest peaks where the rebel fastness lay. They whirled up
clouds of pumice grit from their jets as they crunched in.

The sky was white, and the peaks were white against them, and
white cloud softened the air. A series of precipitous rifts and ice
canyons dropped away behind the plateau, wreathed in smoke-
cloud, and the lower peaks gleamed in the rising light.

Tenth Company clattered out into the sparse, chilly air, weapons ready. They came to martial order, and disembarked as
smoothly as Loken could have wished.

But the vox was still disturbed. Every few minutes, 'Samus' chat-
tered again, like a sigh upon the mountain wind.

Loken called the senior squad leaders to him as soon as he
had landed: Vipus of Locasta, Jubal of Hellebore, Rassek of the
Terminator squad, Talonus of Pithraes, Kairus of Walkure, and
eight more.

All grouped around, showing deference to Xavyer Jubal.

Loken, who had always read men well as a commander, needed
none of his honed leadership skills to realise that Jubal wasn't
wearing Vipus's elevation well. As the others of the Mournival
had advised him, Loken had followed his gut and appointed
Nero Vipus his proxy-commander, to serve when matters of state
drew Loken apart from Tenth. Vipus was popular, but Jubal, as
sergeant of the first squad, felt slighted. There was no rule that
stated the sergeant of a company's first squad automatically
followed in seniority. The sequencing was simply a numerical
distinction, but there was a given order to things, and Jubal felt

aggrieved. He had told Loken so, several times.

Loken remembered Little Horus's words. *If you trust Vipus, make it Vipus. Never compromise. Jubal's a big boy. He'll get over it.*

'Let's do this, and quickly,' Loken told his officers. 'The Terminators have the lead here. Rassek?'

'My squad is ready to serve, captain,' Rassek replied curtly. Like all the men in his specialist squad, Sergeant Rassek wore the titanic armour of a Terminator, a variant only lately introduced into the arsenal of the Astartes. By dint of their primacy, and the fact that their primarch was Warmaster, the Luna Wolves had been amongst the first Legions to benefit from the issue of Terminator plate. Some entire Legions still lacked it. The armour was designed for heavy assault. Thickly plated and consequently exaggerated in its dimensions, a Terminator suit turned an Astartes warrior into a slow, cumbersome, but entirely unstoppable humanoid tank. An Astartes clad in Terminator plate gave up all his speed, dexterity, agility and range of movement. What he got in return was the ability to shrug off almost any ballistic attack.

Rassek towered over them in his armour, dwarfing them as a primarch dwarfs Astartes, or an Astartes dwarfs mortal men. Massive weapons systems were built into his shoulders, arms and gauntlets.

'Lead off to the bridges and clear the way,' Loken said. He paused. Now was a moment for gentle diplomacy. 'Jubal, I want Hellebore to follow the Terminators in as the weight of the first strike.'

Jubal nodded, evidently pleased. The scowl of displeasure he had been wearing for weeks now lifted for a moment. All the officers were bare-headed for this briefing, despite the fact that the air was unbreathably thin by human standards. Their enhanced pulmonary systems didn't even labour. Loken saw

Nero Vipus smile, and knew he understood the significance of this instruction. Loken was offering Jubal some measure of glory, to reassure him he was not forgotten.

'Let's go to it!' Loken cried. 'Lupercal!'

'Lupercal!' the officers answered. They clamped their helms into place.

Portions of the company began to move ahead towards the natural rock bridges and causeways that linked the plateau to the higher terrain.

Army regiments, swaddled in heavy coats and rebreathers against the cold, thin air, had moved up onto the plateau to meet them from the town of Kasheri in the lower gorge.

'Kasheri is at compliance, sir,' an officer told Loken, his voice muffled by his mask, his breathing pained and ragged. 'The enemy has withdrawn to the high fortress.'

Loken nodded, gazing up at the bright crags looming in the white light. 'We'll take it from here,' he said.

'They're well armed, sir,' the officer warned. 'Every time we've pushed to take the rock bridges, they've killed us with heavy cannon. We don't think they have much in the way of numerical weight, but they have the advantage of position. It's a slaughter ground, sir, and they have the cross-draw on us. We understand the insurgents are being led by an Invisible called Rykus or Ryker. We–'

'We'll take it from here,' Loken repeated. 'I don't need to know the name of the enemy before I kill him.'

He turned. 'Jubal. Vipus. Form up and move ahead!'

'Just like that?' the army officer asked sourly. 'Six weeks we've been here, slogging it out, the body toll like you wouldn't believe, and you–'

'We're Astartes,' Loken said. 'You're relieved.'

The officer shook his head with a sad laugh. He muttered something under his breath.

Loken turned back and took a step towards the man, causing him to start in alarm. No man liked to see the stern eye-slits of a Luna Wolf's impassive visor turn to regard him.

'What did you say?' Loken asked.

'I... I... nothing, sir.'

'What did you say?'

'I said... "and the place is haunted", sir.'

'If you believe this place is haunted, my friend,' Loken said, 'then you are admitting to a belief in spirits and daemons.'

'I'm not, sir! I'm really not!'

'I should think not,' Loken said. 'We're not barbarians.'

'All I mean,' said the soldier breathlessly, his face flushed and sweaty behind his breather mask, 'is that there's something about this place. These mountains. They're called the Whisperheads, and I've spoken to some of the locals in Katheri. The name's old, sir. Really old. The locals believe that a man might hear voices out here, calling to him, when there's no one around. It's an old tale.'

'Superstition. We know this world has temples and fanes. They are dark-age in their beliefs. Bringing light to that ignorance is part of why we're here.'

'So what are the voices, sir?'

'What?'

'Since we've been here, fighting our way up the valley, we've all heard them. I've heard them. Whispers. In the night, and sometimes in the bold brightness of day when there's no one about, and on the vox too. Samus has been talking.'

Loken stared at the man. The oath of moment fixed to his shoulder plate fluttered in the mountain wind. 'Who is Samus?'

'Damned if I know,' the officer shrugged. 'All I know for certain is the whole vox-net has been loopy these past few days. Voices on the line, all saying the same thing. A threat.'

'They're trying to scare us,' Loken said.

'Well, it worked then, didn't it?'

LOKEN WALKED OUT across the plateau in the biting wind, between the parked Stormbirds. Samus was muttering again, his voice a dry crackle in the background of Loken's open link.

'Samus. That's the only name you'll hear. I'm Samus. Samus is all around you. Samus is the man beside you. Samus will gnaw upon your bones.'

Loken was forced to admit the enemy propaganda was good. It was unsettling in its mystery and its whisper. It had probably been highly effective in the past against other nations and cultures on Sixty-Three Nineteen. The 'Emperor' had most likely come to global power on the basis of malignant whispers and invisible warriors.

The Astartes of the true Emperor would not be gulled and unmanned by such simple tools.

Some of the Luna Wolves around him were standing still, listening to the mutter in their helm sets.

'Ignore it,' Loken told them. 'It's just a game. Let's move in.'

Rassek's lumbering Terminators approached the rock bridges, arches of granite and lava that linked the plateau to the fierce verticality of the peaks. These were natural spans left behind by the action of ancient glaciers.

Corpses, some of them reduced to desiccated mummies by the altitude, littered the plateau shelf and the rock bridges. The officer had not been lying. Hundreds of army troopers had been cut down in the various attempts to storm the high fortresses. The field of fire had been so intense, their comrades had not been able even to retrieve their bodies.

'Advance!' Loken ordered.

Raising their storm bolters, the Terminator squad began to

crunch out across the rock bridges, dislodging white bone and rotten tunics with their immense feet. Gunfire greeted them immediately, blistering down from invisible positions up in the crags. The shots spanked and whined off the specialised armour. Heads set, the Terminators walked into it, shrugging it away, like men walking into a gale wind. What had kept the army at bay for weeks, and cost them dearly, merely tickled the Legion warriors.

This would be over quickly, Loken realised. He regretted the loyal blood that had been wasted needlessly. This had always been a job for the Astartes.

The front ranks of the Terminator squad, halfway across the bridges, began to fire. Bolters and inbuilt heavy weapon systems unloaded across the abyss, blitzing las shots and storms of explosive munitions at the upper slopes. Hidden positions and fortifications exploded, and limp, tangled bodies tumbled away into the chasm below in flurries of rock and ice.

'Samus' began his worrying again. 'Samus. That's the only name you'll hear. Samus. It means the end and the death. Samus. I am Samus. Samus is all around you. Samus is the man beside you. Samus will gnaw upon your bones. Look out! Samus is here.'

'Advance!' Loken cried, 'and please, someone, shut that bastard up!'

'AND WHO'S SAMUS?' Borodin Flora asked.

The remembrancers, with an escort of army troopers and servitors, had just disembarked from their lander into the bitter cold of a township called Kasheri. The cold mountains swooped up beyond them into the mist.

The area had been securely occupied by Varvaras's troopers and war machines. The party stepped into the light, all of them giddy and breathless from the altitude. Keeler was calibrating her picter against the harsh glare, trying to slow her desperate breath-rate.

She was annoyed. They'd set down in a safe zone, a long way back from the actual fighting area. There was nothing to see. They were being handled.

The town was a bleak outcrop of longhouses in a lower gorge below the peaks. It looked like it hadn't changed much in centuries. There were opportunities for shots of rustic dwellings or parked army war machines, but nothing significant. The glaring light had a pure quality, though. There was a thin rain in it. Some of the servitors had been instructed to carry the remembrancers' bags, but the rest were fighting to keep parasol canopies upright over the heads of the party in the crosswind. Keeler felt they all looked like some idle gang of aristos on a grand tour, exposing themselves not to risk but to some vague, stage-managed version of danger.

'Where are the Astartes?' she asked. 'When do we approach the war zone?'

'Never mind that,' Flora interrupted. 'Who is Samus?'

'Samus?' Sindermann asked, puzzled. He had walked a short distance away from the group beside the lander into a scrubby stretch of white grass and sand, from where he could overlook the misty depth of the rainswept gorge. He looked small, as if he was about to address the canyon as an audience.

'I keep hearing it,' Flora insisted, following him. He was having trouble catching a breath. Flora wore an earplug so he could listen in to the military's vox traffic.

'I heard it too,' said one of the protection squad soldiers from behind his fogged rebreather.

'The vox has been playing up,' said another.

'All the way down to the surface,' said the officer in charge. 'Ignore it. Interference.'

'I've been told it's been happening for days here,' Van Krasten said.

'It's nothing,' said Sindermann. He looked pale and fragile, as if he might be about to faint from the airlessness.

'The captain says it's scare tactics,' said one of the troopers.

'The captain is surely right,' said Sindermann. He took out his data-slate, and connected it to the fleet archive base. As an after-thought, he uncoupled his rebreather mask and set it to his face, sucking in oxygen from the compact tank strapped to his hip.

After a few moments' consultation, he said, 'Oh, that's interesting.'

'What is?' asked Keeler.

'Nothing. It's nothing. The captain is right. Spread yourselves out, please, and look around. The soldiers here will be happy to answer any questions. Feel free to inspect the war machines.'

The remembrancers glanced at one another and began to disperse. Each one was followed by an obedient servitor with a parasol and a couple of grumpy soldiers.

'We might as well not have come,' Keeler said.

'The mountains are splendid,' Sark said.

'Bugger the mountains. Other worlds have mountains. Listen.'

They listened. A deep, distant booming rolled down the gorge to them. The sound of a war happening somewhere else.

Keeler nodded in the direction of the noise. 'That's where we ought to be. I'm going to ask the iterator why we're stuck here.'

'Best of luck,' said Sark.

Sindermann had walked away from the group to stand under the eaves of one of the mountain town's crude longhouse dwell-ings. He continued to study his slate. The mountain wind nodded the tusks of dry grass sprouting from the white sand around his feet. Rain pattered down.

Keeler went over to him. Two soldiers and a servitor with a parasol began to follow her. She turned to face them.

'Don't bother,' she said. They stopped in their tracks and allowed her to walk away, alone. By the time she reached the iterator, she was sucking on her own oxygen supply. Sindermann was entirely occupied with his data-slate. She held off with her complaint for a moment, curious.

'There's something wrong, isn't there?' she asked quietly.

'No, not at all,' Sindermann said.

'You've found out what Samus is, haven't you?'

He looked at her and smiled. 'Yes. You're very tenacious, Euphrati.'

'Born that way. What is it, sir?'

Sindermann shrugged. 'It's silly,' he said, showing her the screen of the data-slate. 'The background history we've already been able to absorb from this world features the name Samus, and the Whisper-heads. It seems this is a sacred place to the people of Sixty-Three Nineteen. A holy, haunted place, where the alleged barrier between reality and the spirit world is at its most permeable. This is intriguing. I am endlessly fascinated by the belief systems and superstitions of primitive worlds.'

'What does your slate tell you, sir?' Keeler asked.

'It says... this is quite funny. I suppose it would be scary, if one actually believed in such things. It says that the Whisperheads are the one place on this world where the spirits walk and speak. It mentions Samus as chief of those spirits. Local, and very ancient, legend, tells how one of the emperors battled and restrained a nightmarish force of devilry here. The devil was called Samus. It is here in their myths, you see? We had one of our own, in the very antique days, called Seytan, or Tearmat. Samus is the equivalent.'

'Samus is a spirit, then?' Keeler whispered, feeling unpleasantly light-headed.

'Yes. Why do you ask?'

'Because,' said Keeler, 'I've heard him hissing at me since the moment we touched down. And I don't have a vox.'

✠ ✠ ✠

BEYOND THE ROCK bridges, the insurgents had raised shield walls of stone and metal. They had heavy cannons covering the gully approaches to their fortress, wired munition charges in the narrow defiles, electrified razor wire, bolted storm-doors, barricades of rockcrete blocks and heavy iron poles. They had a few automated sentry devices, and the advantage of the sheer drop and unscalable ice all around. They had faith and their god on their side.

They had held off Varvaras's regiments for six weeks.

They had no chance whatsoever.

Nothing they did even delayed the advance of the Luna Wolves. Shrugging off cannon rounds and the backwash of explosives, the Terminators wrenched their way through the shield walls, and blasted down the storm-doors. They crushed the spark of electric life out of the sentry drones with their mighty claws, and pushed down the heaped barricades with their shoulders. The company flooded in behind them, firing their weapons into the rising smoke.

The fortress itself had been built into the mountain peak. Some sections of roof and battlement were visible from outside, but most of the structure lay within, thickly armoured by hundreds of metres of rock. The Luna Wolves poured in through the fortified gates. Assault squads rose up the mountain face on their jump packs and settled like flocks of white birds on the exposed roofs, ripping them apart to gain entry and drop in from above. Explosions ripped out the interior chambers of the fortress, opening them to the air, and sending rafts of dislodged ice and rock crashing down into the gorge.

The interior was a maze of wet-black rock tunnels and old tile work, through which the wind funnelled so sharply it seemed to be hyperventilating. The bodies of the slain lay everywhere, slumped and twisted, sprawled and broken. Stepping over them, Loken pitied them. Their culture had deceived them into this resistance, and the resistance had brought down the wrath of the Astartes on their heads. They had all but invited a catastrophic doom.

Terrible human screams echoed down the windy rock tunnels, punctuated by the door-slam bangs of bolter fire. Loken hadn't even bothered to keep a tally of his kills. There was little glory in this, just duty. A surgical strike by the Emperor's martial instruments.

Gunfire pinked off his armour, and he turned, without really thinking, and cut down his assailants. Two desperate men in mail shirts disintegrated under his fire and spattered across a wall. He couldn't understand why they were still fighting. If they'd ventured a surrender, he would have accepted it.

'That way,' he ordered, and a squad moved up past him into the next series of chambers. As he followed them, a body on the floor at his feet stirred and moaned. The insurgent, smeared in his own blood and gravely wounded, looked up at Loken with glassy eyes. He whispered something.

Loken knelt down and cradled his enemy's head in one massive hand. 'What did you say?'

'Bless me...' the man whispered.

'I can't.'

'Please, say a prayer and commend me to the gods.'

'I can't. There are no gods.'

'Please... the otherworld will shun me if I die without a prayer.'

'I'm sorry,' Loken said. 'You're dying. That's all there is.'

'Help me...' the man gasped.

'Of course,' Loken said. He drew his combat blade, the standard-issue short, stabbing sword, and activated the power cell. The grey blade glowed with force. Loken cut down and sharply back up again in the mercy stroke, and gently set the man's detached head on the ground.

The next chamber was vast and irregular. Meltwater trickled down from the black ceiling, and formed spurs of glistening mineral, like silver whiskers, on the rocks it ran over. A pool had been cut in the centre of the chamber floor to collect the meltwater, probably as one of the fortress's primary water reserves. The squad he had sent on had come to a halt around its lip.

'Report,' he said.

One of the Wolves looked round. 'What is this, captain?' he asked.

Loken stepped forward to join them and saw that a great number of bottles and glass flasks had been set around the pool, many of them in the path of the trickling feed from above. At first, he assumed they were there to collect the water, but there were other items too: coins, brooches, strange doll-like figures of clay and the head bones of small mammals and lizards. The spattering water fell across them, and had evidently done so for some time, for Loken could see that many of the bottles and other items were gleaming and distorted with mineral deposits. On the overhang of rock above the pool, ancient, eroded script had been chiselled. Loken couldn't read the words, and realised he didn't want to. There were symbols there that made him feel curiously uneasy.

'It's a fane,' he said simply. 'You know what these locals are like. They believe in spirits, and these are offerings.'

The men glanced at one another, not really understanding.

'They believe in things that aren't real?' asked one.

'They've been deceived,' Loken said. 'That's why we're here. Destroy this,' he instructed, and turned away.

THE ASSAULT LASTED sixty-eight minutes, start to finish. By the end, the fastness was a smoking ruin, many sections of it blown wide to the fierce sunlight and mountain air. Not a single Luna Wolf had been lost. Not a single insurgent had survived.

'How many?' Loken asked Rassek.

'They're still counting bodies, captain,' Rassek replied. 'As it stands, nine hundred and seventy-two.'

In the course of the assault, something in the region of thirty meltwater fanes had been discovered in the labyrinthine fortress, pools surrounded by offerings. Loken ordered them all expunged.

'They were guarding the last outpost of their faith,' Nero Vipus remarked.

'I suppose so,' Loken replied.

'You don't like it, do you, Garvi?' Vipus asked.

'I hate to see men die for no reason. I hate to see men give their lives like this, for nothing. For a belief in nothing. It sickens me. This is what we were once, Nero. Zealots, spiritualists, believers in lies we'd made up ourselves. The Emperor showed us the path out of that madness.'

'So be of good humour that we've taken it,' Vipus said. 'And, though we spill their blood, be phlegmatic that we're at last bringing truth to our lost brothers here.'

Loken nodded. 'I feel sorry for them,' he said. 'They must be so scared.'

'Of us?'

'Yes, of course, but that's not what I mean. Scared of the truth we bring. We're trying to teach them that there are no greater forces at work in the galaxy than light, gravity and human will. No wonder they cling to their gods and spirits. We're removing every last crutch of their ignorance. They felt safe until we came. Safe in the custody of the spirits that they believed watched over them. Safe in the ideal that there was an afterlife, an otherworld. They thought they would be immortal, beyond flesh.'

'Now they have met real immortals,' Vipus quipped. 'It's a hard lesson, but they'll be better for it in the long run.'

Loken shrugged. 'I just empathise, I suppose. Their lives were comforted by mysteries, and we've taken that comfort away. All we can show them is a hard and unforgiving reality in which their lives are brief and without higher purpose.'

'Speaking of higher purpose,' Vipus said, 'you should signal the fleet and tell them we're done. The iterators have voxed us. They request permission to bring the observers up to the site here.'

'Grant it. I'll signal the fleet and give them the good news.'

Vipus turned away, then halted. 'At least that voice shut up,' he said.

Loken nodded. 'Samus' had quit his maudlin ramblings half an hour since, though the assault had failed to identify any vox system or broadcast device.

Loken's intervox crackled.

'Captain?'

'Jubal? Go ahead.'

'Captain, I'm…'

'What? You're what? Say again, Jubal.'

'Sorry, captain. I need you to see this. I'm… I mean, I need you to see this. It's Samus.'

'What? Jubal, where are you?'

'Follow my locator. I've found something. I'm… I've found something. Samus. It means the end and the death.'

'What have you found, Jubal?'

'I'm… I've found… Captain, Samus is here.'

LOKEN LEFT VIPUS to orchestrate the clean-up, and descended into the bowels of the fastness with Seventh Squad, following the pip of Jubal's locator. Seventh Squad, Brakespur Tactical Squad, was commanded by Sergeant Udon, one of Loken's most reliable warriors.

The locator led them down to a massive stone well in the very

basement of the fortress, deep in the heart of the mountain. They
gained access to it via a corroded iron gate built into a niche in
the dark stone. The dank chamber beyond the gate was a natural,
vertical split in the mountain rock, a slanting cavern that overlooked a deep fault where only blackness could be detected. A
pier of old stone steps arced out over the abyss, which dropped
away into the very bottom of the mountain. Meltwater sprinkled
down the glistening walls of the cavern well.

The wind whined through invisible fissures and vents.

Xavyer Jubal was alone at the edge of the drop. As Loken and
Seventh Squad approached, Loken wondered where the rest of
Helle-bore had gone.

'Xavyer?' Loken called.

Jubal looked around. 'Captain,' he said. 'I've found something
wonderful.'

'What?'

'See?' Jubal said. 'See the words?'

Loken stared where Jubal was pointing. All he saw was water
streaming down a calcified buttress of rock.

'No. What words?'

'There! There!'

'I see only water,' Loken said. 'Falling water.'

'Yes, yes! It's written in the water! In the falling water! There
and gone, there and gone, You see? It makes words and they
stream away, but the words come back.'

'Xavyer? Are you well? I'm concerned that–'

'Look, Garviel! Look at the words! Can't you hear the water
speaking?'

'Speaking?'

'Drip drip drop. One name. Samus. That's the only name you'll
hear.'

'Samus?'

'Samus. It means the end and the death. I'm...'

Loken looked at Udon and the men. 'Restrain him,' he said quietly.

Udon nodded. He and four of his men slung their bolters and stepped forward.

'What are you doing?' Jubal laughed. 'Are you threatening me? For Terra's sake, Garviel, can't you see? Samus is all around you!'

'Where's Hellebore, Jubal?' Loken snapped. 'Where's the rest of your squad?'

Jubal shrugged. 'They didn't see it either,' he said, and glanced towards the edge of the precipice. 'They couldn't see, I suppose. It's so clear to me. Samus is the man beside you.'

'Udon,' Loken nodded. Udon moved towards Jubal. 'Let's go, brother,' he said, kindly.

Jubal's bolter came up very suddenly. There was no warning. He shot Udon in the face, blowing gore and pulverised skull fragments out through the back of Udon's exploded helm. Udon fell on his face. Two of his men lunged forward, and the bolter roared again, punching holes in their chestplates and throwing them over onto their backs.

Jubal's visor swung to look at Loken. 'I'm Samus,' he said, chuckling. 'Look out! Samus is here.'

NINE

The unthinkable
Spirits of the Whisperheads
Compatible minds

TWO DAYS BEFORE the Legion's assault on the Whisperheads, Loken had consented to another private interview with the remembrancer Mersadie Oliton. It was the third such interview he had granted since his election to the Mournival, at which time his attitude towards her seemed to have substantially altered. Though the subject had not been mentioned formally, Mersadie had begun to feel that Loken had chosen her to be his particular memorialist. He had told her on the night of his election that he might choose to share his recollections with her, but she was now secretly astonished at the extent of his eagerness to do so. She had already recorded almost six hours of reminiscence – accounts of battles and tactics, descriptions of especially demanding military operations, reflections on the qualities of certain types of weapon, celebrations of notable deeds and triumphs accomplished by his comrades. In the time between interviews, she took herself to her room and processed the material, composing it into the skeleton of a long, fluid account. She hoped eventually to have a complete history of the expedition, and a more general record of the Great Crusade as witnessed by Loken during the other expeditions that had preceded the 63rd.

Indeed, the weight of anecdotal fact she was gathering was huge, but one thing was lacking, and that was Loken himself. In the latest interview, she tried once again to draw out some spark of the man.

'As I understand it,' she said, 'you have nothing in you that we ordinary mortals might know as fear?'

Loken paused and frowned. He had been lapping a plate section of his armour. This seemed to be his favourite diversion when in her company. He would call her to his private arming chamber and sit there, scrupulously polishing his war harness while he spoke and she listened. To Mersadie, the particular smell of the lapping powder had become synonymous with the sound of his voice and the matter of his tales. He had well over a century of stories to tell.

'A curious question,' he said.

'And how curious is the answer?'

Loken shrugged lightly. 'The Astartes have no fear. It is unthinkable to us.'

'Because you have trained yourself to master it?' Mersadie asked.

'No, we are trained for discipline, but the capacity for fear is bred out of us. We are immune to its touch.'

Mersadie made a mental note to edit this last comment later. To her, it seemed to leach away some of the heroic mystique of the Astartes. To deny fear was the very character of a hero, but there was nothing courageous about being insensible to the emotion. She wondered too if it was possible to simply remove an entire emotion from what was essentially a human mind. Did that not leave a void? Were other emotions compromised by its lack?

Could fear even be removed cleanly, or did its excision tear out shreds of other qualities along with it? It certainly might explain why the Astartes seemed larger than life in almost every aspect except their own personalities.

'Well, let us continue,' she said. 'At our last meeting, you were going to tell me about the war against the overseers. That was twenty years ago, wasn't it?'

He was still looking at her, eyes slightly narrowed. 'What?' he asked.

'I'm sorry?'

'What is it? You didn't like my answer just then.'

Mersadie cleared her throat. 'No, not at all. It wasn't that. I had just been…'

'What?'

'May I be candid?'

'Of course,' he said, patiently rubbing a nub of polishing fibre around the edges of a pot.

'I had been hoping to get something a little more personal. You have given me a great deal, sir, authentic details and points of fact that would make any history text authoritative. Posterity will know with precision, for instance, which hand Iacton Qruze carried his sword in, the colour of the sky over the Monastery Cities of Nabatae, the methodology of the White Scars' favoured pincer assault, the number of studs on the shoulder plate of a Luna Wolf, the number of axe blows, and from which angles, it took to fell the last of the Omakkad Princes…' She looked at him squarely, 'but nothing about you, sir. I know what you saw, but not what you felt.'

'What I felt? Why would anyone be interested in that?'

'Humanity is a sensible race, sir. Future generations, those that our remembrances are intended for, will learn more from any factual record if those facts are couched in an emotional context.

They will care less for the details of the battles at Ullanor, for instance, than they will for a sense of what it felt like to be there.'

'Are you saying that I'm boring?' Loken asked.

'No, not at all,' she began, and then realised he was smiling. 'Some of the things you have told me sound like wonders, yet you do not yourself seem to wonder at them. If you know no fear, do you also not know awe? Surprise? Majesty? Have you not seen things so bizarre they left you speechless? Shocked you? Unnerved you even?'

'I have,' he said. 'Many times the sheer oddity of the cosmos has left me bemused or startled.'

'So tell me of those things.'

He pursed his lips and thought about it. 'Giant hats,' he began.

'I beg your pardon?'

'On Sarosel, after compliance, the citizens held a great carnival of celebration. Compliance had been bloodless and willing. The carnival ran for eight weeks. The dancers in the streets wore giant hats of ribbon and cane and paper, each one fashioned into some gaudy form: a ship, a sword and fist, a dragon, a sun. They were as broad across as my span.' Loken spread his arms wide. 'I do not know how they balanced them, or suffered their weight, but day and night they danced along the inner streets of the main city, these garish forms weaving and bobbing and circling, as if carried along on a slow flood, quite obscuring the human figures beneath. It was an odd sight.'

'I believe you.'

'It made us laugh. It made Horus laugh to see it.'

'Was that the strangest thing you ever knew?'

'No, no. Let's see... the method of war on Keylek gave us all pause. This was eighty years ago. The keylekid were a grosteque alien kind, of a manner you might describe as reptilian. They were greatly skilled in the arts of combat, and rose against us angrily

the moment we made contact. Their world was a harsh place. I
remember crimson rock and indigo water. The commander – this
was long before he was made Warmaster – expected a prolonged
and brutal struggle, for the keylekid were large and strong creatures. Even the least of their warriors took three or four bolt
rounds to bring down. We drew forth upon their world to make
war, but they would not fight us.'

'How so?'

'We did not comprehend the rules they fought by. As we
learned later, the keylekid considered war to be the most abhor-
rent activity a sentient race could indulge in, so they set upon it
tight controls and restrictions. There were large structures upon
the surface of their world, rectangular fields many kilometres in
dimension, covered with high, flat roofs and open at the sides.
We named them "slaughter-houses", and there was one every
few hundred kilometres. The keylekid would only fight at these
prescribed places. The sites were reserved for combat. War was
forbidden on any other part of their world's surface. They were
waiting for us to meet them at a slaughter-house and decide the
matter.'

'How bizarre! What was done about it?'

'We destroyed the keylekid,' he said, matter of factly.

'Oh,' she replied, with a tilt of her abnormally long head.

'It was suggested that we might meet them and fight them by
the terms of their rules,' Loken said. 'There may have been some
honour in that, but Maloghurst, I think it was, reasoned that we
had rules of our own which the enemy chose not to recognise.
Besides, they were formidable. Had we not acted decisively, they
would have remained a threat, and how long would it have taken
them to learn new rules or abandon old ones?'

'Is an image of them recorded?' Mersadie asked.

'Many, I believe. The preserved cadaver of one of their warriors is displayed in this ship's Museum of Conquest, and since you ask what I feel, sometimes it is sadness. You mentioned the over-seers, a story I was going to tell. That was a long campaign, and one which filled me with misery.'

As he told the story, she sat back, occasionally blink-clicking to store his image. He was concentrating on the preparation of his armour, but she could see sadness behind that concern. The over-seers, he explained, were a machine race and, as artificial sentients, quite beyond the limits of Imperial law. Machine life untempered by organic components had long been outlawed by both the Imperial Council and the Mechanicum. The overseers, commanded by a senior machine called the Archdroid, inhab-ited a series of derelict, crumbling cities on the world of Dahinta. These were cities of fine mosaics, which had once been very beautiful indeed, but extreme age and decay had faded them. The overseers scuttled amongst the mouldering piles, fighting a losing battle of repair and refurbishment in a single-minded obsession to keep the neglected cities intact.

The machines had eventually been destroyed after a lasting and brutal war in which the skills of the Mechanicum had proved invaluable. Only then was the sad secret found.

'The overseers were the product of human ingenuity,' Loken said.

'Humans made them?'

'Yes, thousands of years ago, perhaps even during the last Age of Technology. Dahinta had been a human colony, home to a lost branch of our race, where they had raised a great and mar-vellous culture of magnificent cities, with thinking machines to serve them. At some time, and in a manner unknown to us, the humans had become extinct. They left behind their ancient cit-ies, empty but for the deathless guardians they had made. It was most melancholy, and passing strange.'

'Did the machines not recognise men?' she asked.

'All they saw was the Astartes, lady, and we did not look like the men they had called master.'

She hesitated for a moment, then said, 'I wonder if I shall witness so many marvels as we make this expedition.'

'I trust you will, and I hope that many will fill you with joy and amazement rather than distress. I should tell you sometime of the Great Triumph after Ullanor. That was an event that should be remembered.'

'I look forward to hearing it.'

'There is no time now. I have duties to attend to.'

'One last story, then? A short one, perhaps? Something that filled you with awe.'

He sat back and thought. 'There was a thing. No more than ten years ago. We found a dead world where life had once been. A species had lived there once, and either died out or moved to another world. They had left behind them a honeycomb of subterranean habitats, dry and dead. We searched them carefully, every last cave and tunnel, and found just one thing of note. It was buried deepest of all, in a stone bunker ten kilometres under the planet's crust. A map. A great chart, in fact, fully twenty metres in diameter, showing the geophysical relief of an entire world in extraordinary detail. We did not at first recognise it, but the Emperor, beloved of all, knew what it was.'

'What?' she asked.

'It was Terra. It was a complete and full map of Terra, perfect in every detail. But it was a map of Terra from an age long gone, before the rise of the hives or the molestation of war, with coastlines and oceans and mountains of an aspect long since erased or covered over.'

'That is… amazing,' she said.

He nodded. 'So many unanswerable questions, locked into

one forgotten chamber. Who had made the map, and why? What business had brought them to Terra so long ago? What had caused them to carry the chart across half the galaxy, and then hide it away, like their most precious treasure, in the depths of their world? It was unthinkable. I cannot feel fear, Mistress Olitan, but if I could I would have felt it then. I cannot imagine anything ever unsettling my soul the way that thing did.'

UNTHINKABLE.

Time had slowed to a pinprick point on which it seemed all the gravity in the cosmos was pressing. Loken felt lead-heavy, slow, out of joint, unable to frame a lucid response, or even begin to deal with what he was seeing.

Was this fear? Was he tasting it now, after all? Was this how terror cowed a mortal man?

Sergeant Udon, his helm a deformed ring of bloody ceramite, lay dead at his feet. Beside him sprawled two other battle-brothers, shot point-blank through the hearts, if not dead then fatally damaged.

Before him stood Jubal, the bolter in his hand.

This was madness. This could not be. Astartes had turned upon Astartes. A Luna Wolf had murdered his own kind. Every law of fraternity and honour that Loken understood and trusted had just been torn as easily as a cobweb. The insanity of this crime would echo forever.

'Jubal? What have you done?'

'Not Jubal. Samus. I am Samus. Samus is all around you. Samus is the man beside you.'

Jubal's voice had a catch to it, a dry giggle. Loken knew he was about to fire again. The rest of Udon's squad, quite as aghast as Loken, stumbled forward, but none raised their bolters. Even in the stark light of what Jubal had just done, not one of them could break the sworn code of the Astartes and fire upon one of their own.

Loken knew he certainly couldn't. He threw his bolter aside and leapt at Jubal.

Xavyer Jubal, commander of Hellebore squad and one of the finest file officers in the company, had already begun to fire. Bolt rounds screeched out across the chamber and struck into the hesitating squad. Another helmet exploded in a welter of blood, bone chips and armour fragments, and another battle-brother crashed to the cave floor. Two more were knocked down beside him as bolt rounds detonated against their torso armour.

Loken smashed into Jubal, and staggered him backwards, trying to pin his arms. Jubal thrashed, sudden fury in his limbs.

'Samus!' he yelled. 'It means the end and the death! Samus will gnaw upon your bones!'

They crashed against a rock wall together with numbing force, splintering stone. Jubal would not relinquish his grip on the murder weapon. Loken drove him backwards against the rock, the drizzle of meltwater spraying down across them both.

'Jubal!'

Loken threw a punch that would have decapitated a mortal man. His fist cracked against Jubal's helm and he repeated the action, driving his fist four or five times against the other's face and chest. The ceramite visor chipped. Another punch, his full weight behind it, and Jubal stumbled. Each stroke of Loken's fist resounded like a smith's hammer in the echoing chamber, steel against steel.

As Jubal stumbled, Loken grabbed his bolter and tore it out of his hand. He hurled it away across the deep stone well.

But Jubal was not yet done. He seized Loken and slammed him sideways into the rock wall. Lumps of stone flew out from the jarring impact. Jubal slammed him again, swinging Loken bodily into the rock, like a man swinging a heavy sack. Pain flared through Loken's head and he tasted blood in his mouth. He tried to pull away, but Jubal was throwing punches that ploughed into Loken's visor and bounced the back of his head off the wall repeatedly.

The other men were upon them, shouting and grappling to separate them.

'Hold him!' Loken yelled. 'Hold him down!'

They were Astartes, as strong as young gods in their power armour, but they could not do as Loken ordered. Jubal lashed out with a free fist and knocked one of them clean off his feet. Two of the remaining three clung to his back like wrestlers, like human cloaks, trying to pull him down, but he hoisted them up and twisted, throwing them off him.

Such strength. Such unthinkable strength that could shrug off Astartes like target dummies in a practice cage.

Jubal turned on the remaining brother, who launched himself forward to tackle the madman.

'Look out!' Jubal screamed with a cackle. 'Samus is here!'

His lancing right hand met the brother head on. Jubal struck with an open hand, fingers extended, and those fingers drove clean in through the battle-brother's gorget as surely as any speartip. Blood squirted out from the man's throat, through the puncture in the armour. Jubal ripped his hand out, and the brother fell to his knees, choking and gurgling, blood pumping in profuse, pulsing surges from his ruptured throat.

Beyond any thought of reason now, Loken hurled himself at Jubal, but the berserker turned and smacked him away with a mighty back-hand slap.

The power of the blow was stupendous, far beyond anything even an Astartes should have been able to wield. The force was so great that the armour of Jubal's gauntlet fractured, as did the plating of Loken's shoulder, which took the brunt. Loken blacked out for a split-second, then was aware that he was flying. Jubal had struck him so hard that he was sailing across the stone well and out over the abyssal fault.

Loken struck the arching pier of stone steps. He almost bounced off it, but he managed to grab on, his fingers gouging the ancient stone, his feet swinging above the drop. Meltwater poured down in a thin rain across him, making the steps slick and oily with mineral wash. Loken's fingers began to slide. He remembered dangling in a similar fashion over the tower lip in the 'Emperor's' palace, and snarled in frustrated rage.

Fury pulled him up. Fury, and an intense passion that he would not fail the Warmaster. Not in this. Not in the face of this terrible wrong.

He hauled himself upright on to the pier. It was narrow, no wider than a single path where men could not pass if they met. The gulf, black as the outer void, yawned below him. His limbs were shaking with effort.

He saw Jubal. He was charging forward across the cavern to the foot of the steps, drawing his combat blade. The sword glowed as it powered into life.

Loken wrenched out his own sword. Falling meltwater hissed and sparked as it touched the active metal of the short, stabbing blade.

Jubal bounded up the steps to meet him, slashing with his sword. He was raving still, in a voice that was in no way his own any longer. He struck wildly at Loken, who hopped back up the steps, and then began to deflect the strikes with his own weapon. Sparks flashed, and the blades struck one another like the tolling of a discordant bell. Height was not an advantage in this fight, as Loken had to hunch low to maintain his guard.

Combat swords were not duelling weapons. Short and

double-edged, they were made for stabbing, for battlefield onslaught. They had no reach or subtlety. Jubal hacked with his like an axe, forcing Loken to defend. Their blades cut falling water as they scythed, sizz-ling and billowing steam into the air.

Loken prided himself on maintaining a masterful discipline and practice of all weapons. He regularly clocked six or eight hours at a time in the flagship's practice cages. He expected all of the men in his command to do likewise. Xavyer Jubal, he knew, was foremost a master with daggers and sparring axes, but no slouch with the sword.

Except today. Jubal had discarded all his skill, or had forgotten it in the flush of madness that had engulfed his mind. He attacked Loken like a maniac, in a frenzy of savage cuts and blows. Loken was likewise forced to dispense with much of his skill in an effort to block and parry. Three times, Loken managed to drive Jubal back down the pier a few steps, but always the other man retaliated and forced Loken higher up the arch. Once, Loken had to leap to avoid a low slice, and barely regained his footing as he landed. In the silver downpour, the steps were treacherous, and it was as much a fight to keep balance as to resist Jubal's constant assault.

It ended suddenly, like a jolt. Jubal passed Loken's guard and sunk the full edge of his blade into Loken's left shoulder plate.

'Samus is here!' he cried in delight, but his blade, flaring with power, was wedged fast.

'Samus is done,' Loken replied, and drove the tip of his sword into Jubal's exposed chest. The sword punched clean through, and the tip emerged through Jubal's back.

Jubal wavered, letting go of his own weapon, which remained transfixed through Loken's shoulder guard. With half-open, shuddering hands, he reached at Loken's face, not violently, but gently, as if imploring some mercy or even aid. Water splashed off them and streamed down their white plating.

'Samus...' he gasped. Loken wrenched his sword out.

Jubal staggered and swayed, the blood leaking out of the gash in his chestplate, diluting as soon as it appeared and mixing with the drizzle, covering his belly plate and thigh armour with a pink stain.

He toppled backwards, crashing over and over down the steps in a windmill of heavy, loose limbs. Five metres from the base of the pier, his headlong career bounced him half-off the steps, and he came to a halt, legs dangling, partly hanging over the chasm, gradually sliding backwards under his own weight. Loken heard the slow squeal of armour scraping against slick stone.

He leapt down the flight to reach Jubal's side. He got there just moments before Jubal slid away into oblivion. Loken grabbed Jubal by the edge of his left shoulder plate and slowly began to heave him back onto the pier. It was almost impossible. Jubal seemed to weigh a billion tonnes.

The three surviving members of Brakespur squad stood at the foot of the steps, watching him struggle.

'Help me!' Loken yelled.

'To save him?' one asked.

'Why?' asked another. 'Why would you want to?'

'Help me!' Loken snarled again. They didn't move. In desperation, Loken raised his sword and stabbed it down, spearing Jubal's right shoulder to the steps. So pinned, his slide was arrested. Loken hauled his body back onto the pier.

Panting, Loken dragged off his battered helm and spat out a mouthful of blood.

'Get Vipus,' he ordered. 'Get him now.'

BY THE TIME they were conducted up to the plateau, there wasn't much to see and the light was failing. Euphrati took a few random picts of the parked Stormbirds and the cone of smoke lifting off the broken crag, but she didn't expect much from any of them. It all seemed drab and lifeless up there. Even the vista of the mountains around them was insipid.

'Can we see the combat area?' she asked Sindermann.

'We've been told to wait.'

'Is there a problem?'

He shook his head. It was an 'I don't know' kind of shake. Like all of them, he was strapped into his rebreather, but he looked frail and tired.

It was eerily quiet. Groups of Luna Wolves were trudging back to the Stormbirds from the fastness, and army troops had secured the plateau itself. The remembrancers had been told that a solid victory had been achieved, but there was no sign of jubilation.

'Oh, it's a mechanical thing,' Sindermann said when Euphrati questioned him. 'This is just a routine exercise for the Legion. A low-key action, as I said before we set out. I'm sorry if you're disappointed.'

'I'm not,' she said, but in truth there was a sense of anticlimax about it all. She wasn't sure what she had been expecting, but the rush of the drop, and the strange circumstance at Kasheri had begun to thrill her. Now everything was done, and she'd seen nothing.

'Carnis wants to interview some of the returning warriors,' Siman Sark said, 'and he's asked me to pict them while he does. Would that be permissible?'

'I should think so,' Sindermann sighed. He called out for an army officer to guide Carnis and Sark to the Astartes.

'I think,' said Tolemew Van Krasten aloud, 'that a tone poem would be most appropriate. Full symphonic composition would overwhelm the atmosphere, I feel.'

Euphrati nodded, not really understanding.

'A minor key, I think. E, or A perhaps. I'm taken with the title "The Spirits of the Whisperheads", or perhaps, "The Voice of Samus". What do you think?'

She stared at him.

'I'm joking,' he said with a sad smile. 'I have no idea what I am supposed to respond to here, or how. It all seems so dour.'

Euphrati Keeler had supposed Van Krasten to be a pompous type, but now she warmed to him. As he turned away and gazed mournfully up at the smoking peak, she was seized by a thought and raised her picter.

'Did you just take my likeness?' he asked.

She nodded. 'Do you mind? You looking at the peak like that seemed to sum up how we all feel.'

'But I'm a remembrancer,' he said. 'Should I be in your record?'

'We're all in this. Witnesses or not, we're all here,' she replied. 'I take what I see. Who knows? Maybe you can return the favour? A little refrain of flutes in your next overture that represents Euphrati Keeler?'

They both laughed.

A Luna Wolf was approaching the huddle of them.

'Nero Vipus,' he said, making the sign of the aquila. 'Captain Loken presents his respects and wishes the attention of Master Sindermann at once.'

'I'm Sindermann,' the elderly man replied. 'Is there some problem, sir?'

'I've been asked to conduct you to the captain,' Vipus replied. 'This way, please.'

The pair of them moved away, Sindermann scurrying to keep up with Vipus's great strides.

'What is going on?' Van Krasten asked, his voice hushed.

'I don't know. Let's find out,' Keeler replied.

'Follow them? Oh, I don't think so.'

'I'm game,' said Borodin Flora. 'We haven't actually been told to stay here.'

They looked round. Twell had sat himself down beside the prow landing strut of a Stormbird and was beginning to sketch with charcoal sticks on a small pad. Carnis and Sark were busy elsewhere.

'Come on,' said Euphrati Keeler.

VIPUS LED SINDERMANN up into the ruined fastness. The wind moaned and whistled through the grim tunnels and chambers. Army troopers were clearing the dead from the entry halls and casting them into the gorge, but still Vipus had to steer the iterator past many crumpled, exploded corpses. He kept saying such things as, 'I'm sorry you had to see that, sir,' and, 'Look away to spare your sensibilities.'

Sindermann could not look away. He had iterated loyally for many years, but this was the first time he had walked across a fresh battlefield. The sights appalled him and burned themselves into his memory. The stench of blood and ordure assailed him. He saw human forms burst and brutalised, and burned beyond any measure he had imagined possible. He saw walls sticky with blood and brain-matter, fragments of exploded bone weeping marrow, body parts littering the blood-soaked floors.

'Terra,' he breathed, over and again. This was what the Astartes did. This was the reality of the Emperor's crusade. Mortal hurt on a scale that passed belief.

'Terra,' he whispered to himself. By the time he was brought to Loken, who awaited him in one of the fortress's upper chambers, the word had become 'terror' without him realising it.

Loken was standing in a wide, dark chamber beside some sort of pool. Water gurgled down one of the black-wet walls and the air smelled of damp and oxides. A dozen solemn Luna Wolves attended Loken, including one giant fellow in glowering Terminator armour, but Loken himself was bareheaded. His face was smudged with bruises. He'd removed his left shoulder guard, which lay beside him on the ground, stuck through with a short sword.

'You have done such a thing,' Sindermann said, his voice small. 'I don't think I'd quite understood what you Astartes were capable of, but now I–'

'Quiet,' Loken said bluntly. He looked at the Luna Wolves around him and dismissed them with a nod. They filed out past Sindermann, ignoring him.

'Stay close, Nero,' Loken called. Stepping out through the chamber door, Vipus nodded.

Now the room was almost empty, Sindermann could see that a body lay beside the pool. It was the body of a Luna Wolf, limp and dead, his helm off, his white armour mottled with blood. His arms had been lashed to his trunk with climbing cable.

'I don't...' Sindermann began. 'I don't understand, captain. I was told there had been no losses.'

Loken nodded slowly. 'That's what we're going to say. That will be the official line. The Tenth took this fortress in a clean strike, with no losses, and that's true enough. None of the insurgents scored any kills. Not even a wounding. We took a thousand of them to their deaths.'

'But this man...?'

Loken looked at Sindermann. His face was troubled, more troubled than the iterator had ever seen before. 'What is it, Garviel?' he asked.

'Something has happened,' Loken said. 'Something so... so unthinkable that I...'

He paused, and looked at Jubal's bound corpse. 'I have to make a report, but I don't know what to say. I have no frame of reference. I'm glad you are here, Kyril, you of all people. You have steered me well over the years.'

'I like to think that…'

'I need your counsel now.'

Sindermann stepped forward and placed his hand on the giant warrior's arm. 'You may trust me with any matter, Garviel. I'm here to serve.'

Loken looked down at him. 'This is confidential. Utterly confidential.'

'I understand.'

'There have been deaths today. Six brothers of Brakespur squad, including Udon. Another barely clinging to life. And Hellebore… Hellebore has vanished, and I fear they are dead too.'

'This can't be. The insurgents couldn't have–'

'They did nothing. This is Xavyer Jubal,' Loken said, pointing towards the body on the floor. 'He killed the men,' he said simply.

Sindermann rocked back as if slapped. He blinked. 'He what? I'm sorry, Garviel, I thought for a moment you said he–'

'He killed the men. Jubal killed the men. He took his bolter and his fists and he killed six of Brakespur right in front of my eyes, and he would have killed me too, if I hadn't run him through.'

Sindermann felt his legs tremble. He found a nearby rock and sat down abruptly. 'Terra,' he gasped.

'Terror is right. Astartes do not fight Astartes. Astartes do not kill their own. It is against all the rules of nature and man. It is counter to the very gene-code the Emperor fused into us when he wrought us.'

'There must be some mistake,' Sindermann said.

'No mistake. I saw him do it. He was a madman. He was possessed.'

'What? Steady, now. You look to old terms, Garviel. Possession is a spiritualist word that–'

'He was possessed. He claimed he was Samus.'

'Oh.'

'You've heard the name, then?'

'I've heard the whisper. That was just enemy propaganda, wasn't it? We were told to dismiss it as scare tactics.'

Loken touched the bruises on his face, feeling the ache of them. 'So I thought. Iterator, I'm going to ask you this once. Are spirits real?'

'No, sir. Absolutely not.'

'So we are taught and thus we are liberated, but could they exist? This world is lousy with superstition and temple-fanes. Could they exist here?'

'No,' Sindermann replied more firmly. 'There are no spirits, no daemons, no ghosts in the dark edges of the cosmos. Truth has shown us this.'

'I've studied the archive, Kyril,' Loken replied. 'Samus was the name the people of this world gave to their arch-fiend. He was imprisoned in these mountains, so their legends say.'

'Legends, Garviel. Only legends. Myths. We have learned much during our time amongst the stars, and the most pertinent of those things is that there is always a rational explanation, even for the most mysterious events.'

'An Astartes draws his weapon and kills his own, whilst claiming to be a daemon from hell? Rationalise *that*, sir.'

Sinderman rose. 'Calm yourself, Garviel, and I will.'

Loken didn't reply. Sindermann walked over to Jubal's body and stared at it. Jubal's open, staring eyes were rolled back in his skull and utterly bloodshot. The flesh of his face was drawn and shrivelled, as if he had aged ten thousand years. Strange patterns, like clusters of blemishes or moles, were visible on the painfully stretched skin.

'These marks,' said Sindermann. 'These vile signs of wasting. Could they be the traces of disease or infection?'

'What?' Loken asked.

'A virus, perhaps? A reaction to toxicity? A plague?'

'Astartes are resistant,' Loken said.

'To most things, but not to everything. I think this could be some contagion. Something so virulent that it destroyed Jubal's mind along with his body. Plagues can drive men insane, and corrupt their flesh.'

'Then why only him?' asked Loken.

Sindermann shrugged. 'Perhaps some tiny flaw in his gene-code?'

'But he behaved as if possessed,' Loken said, repeating the word with brutal emphasis.

'We've all been exposed to the enemy's propaganda. If Jubal's mind was deranged by fever, he might simply have been repeating the words he'd heard.'

Loken thought for a moment. 'You speak a lot of sense, Kyril,' he said.

'Always.'

'A plague,' Loken nodded. 'It's a sound explanation.'

'You've suffered a tragedy today, Garviel, but spirits and daemons played no part in it. Now get to work. You need to lock down this area in quarantine and get a medicae task force here. There may yet be further outbreaks. Non-Astartes, such as myself, might be less resistant, and poor Jubal's corpse may yet be a vector for disease.'

Sindermann looked back down at the body. 'Great Terra,' he said. 'He has been so ravaged. I weep to see this waste.'

With a creak of dried sinew, Jubal raised his head and stared up at Sindermann with blood-red eyes.

'Look out,' he wheezed.

Euphrati Keeler had stopped taking picts. She stowed away her picter. The things they were seeing in the narrow tunnels of the fortress went beyond all decency to record. She had never imagined that human forms could be dismantled so grievously, so totally. The stench of blood in the close, cold air made her gag, despite her rebreather.

'I want to go back now,' Van Krasten said. He was shaking and upset. 'There is no music here. I am sick to my stomach.'

Euphrati was inclined to agree.

'No,' said Borodin Flora in a muffled, steely voice. 'We must see it all. We are chosen remembrancers. This is our duty.'

Euphrati was quite sure Flora was making an effort not to throw up, but she warmed to the sentiment. This was their duty. This was the very reason they had been summoned. To record and commemorate the Crusade of Man. Whatever it looked like.

She tugged her picter back out of its carry-bag and took a few, tentative shots. Not of the dead, for that would be indecent, but of the blood on the walls, the smoke fuming in the wind along the narrow tunnels, the piles of scattered, spent shell cases littering the black-flecked ground.

Teams of army troopers moved past them, lugging bodies away for disposal. Some looked at the three of them curiously.

'Are you lost?' one asked.

'Not at all. We're allowed to be here,' Flora said.

'Why would you want to be?' the man wondered.

Euphrati took a series of long shots of troopers, almost in silhouette, gathering up body parts at a tunnel junction. It chilled her to see it, and she hoped her picts would have the same effect on her audience.

'I want to go back,' Van Krasten said again.

'Don't stray, or you'll get lost,' Euphrati warned.

'I think I might be sick,' Van Krasten admitted.

He was about to retch when a shrill, harrowing scream echoed down the tunnels.

'What the hell was that?' Euphrati whispered.

✠ ✠ ✠

Jubal rose. The ropes binding him sheared and split, releasing his arms. He screamed, and then screamed again. His frantic wails soared and echoed around the chamber.

Sindermann stumbled backwards in total panic. Loken ran forward and tried to restrain the reanimating madman.

Jubal struck out with one thrashing fist and caught Loken in the chest. Loken flew backwards into the pool with a crash of water.

Jubal turned, hunched. Saliva dangled from his slack mouth, and his bloodshot eyes spun like compasses at true north.

'Please, oh please…' Sindermann gabbled, backing away.

'Look. Out.' The words crawled sluggishly out of Jubal's drooling mouth. He lumbered forward. Something was happening to him, something malign and catastrophic. He was bulging, expanding so furiously that his armour began to crack and shatter. Sections of broken plate split and fell away from him, exposing thick arms swollen with gangrene and fibrous growths. His taut flesh was pallid and blue. His face was distorted, puffy and livid, and his tongue flopped out of his rotting mouth, long and serpentine.

He raised his meaty, distended hands triumphantly, exposing finger-nails grown into dark hooks and psoriatic claws.

'Samus is here,' he drawled.

Sindermann fell on his knees before the misshapen brute. Jubal reeked of corruption and sore wounds. He shambled forward. His form flickered and danced with blurry yellow light, as if he was not quite in phase with the present.

A bolter round struck him in the right shoulder and detonated against the rindy integument his skin had become. Shreds of meat and gobbets of pus sprayed in all directions. In the chamber doorway, Nero Vipus took aim again.

The thing that had once been Xavyer Jubal grabbed Sindermann and threw him at Vipus. The pair of them crashed backwards against the wall, Vipus dropping his weapon in an effort to catch and cushion Sindermann and spare the frail bones of the elderly iterator.

The Jubal-thing shuffled past them into the tunnel, leaving a noxious trail of dripped blood and wretched, discoloured fluid in its wake.

EUPHRATI SAW THE thing coming for them and tried to decide whether to scream or raise her picter. In the end, she did both. Van Krasten lost control of his bodily functions, and fell to the floor in a puddle of his own manufacture. Borodin Flora just backed away, his mouth moving silently.

The Jubal-thing advanced down the tunnel towards them. It was gross and distorted, its skin stretched by humps and swellings. It had become so gigantic that what little remained of its pearl-white armour dragged behind it like metal rags. Strange puncta and moles marked its flesh. Jubal's face had contorted into a dog snout, wherein his human teeth stuck out like stray ivory markers, displaced by the thin, transparent crop of needle fangs that now invested his mouth. There were so many fangs that his mouth could no longer close. His eyes were blood pools. Jerky, spasmodic flashes of yellow light surrounded him, making vague shapes and patterns. They caused Jubal's movements to seem wrong, as if he was a pict-feed image, badly cut and running slightly too fast.

He snatched up Tolemew Van Krasten and dashed him like a toy against the walls of the tunnel, back and forth, with huge, slamming, splattering effect, so that when he let go, little of Tolemew still existed above the sternum.

'Oh Terra!' Keeler cried, retching violently. Borodin Flora stepped past her to confront the monster, and made the defiant sign of the aquila.

'Begone!' he cried out. 'Begone!'

The Jubal-thing leaned forward, opened its mouth to a hith-erto unimaginable width, revealing an unguessable number of needle teeth, and bit off Borodin Flora's head and upper body. The remainder of his form crumpled to the floor, ejecting blood like a pressure hose.

Euphrati Keeler sank to her knees. Terror had rendered her powerless to run. She accepted her fate, largely because she had no idea what it was to be. In the final moments of her life, she reassured herself that at least she hadn't added to brutal death the indignity of wetting herself in the face of such incomprehen-sible horror.

TEN

The Warmaster and his son
No matter the ferocity or ingenuity of the foe
Official denial

'YOU KILLED IT?'

'Yes,' said Loken, gazing at the dirt floor, his mind somewhere else.

'You're sure?'

Loken looked up out of his reverie. 'What?'

'I need you to be sure,' Abaddon said. 'You killed it?'

'Yes.' Loken was sitting on a crude hardwood stool in one of the longhouses in Kasheri. Night had fallen outside, bringing with it a keening, malevolent wind that shrieked around the gorge and the Whisperhead peaks. A dozen oil lamps lit the place with a feeble ochre glow. 'We killed it. Nero and I together, with our bolters. It took ninety rounds at full auto. It burst and burned, and we used a flamer to cremate all that remained.'

Abaddon nodded. 'How many people know?'

'About that last act? Myself, Nero, Sindermann and the remembrancer, Keeler. We cut the thing down just before it bit her in half. Everyone else who saw it is dead.'

'What have you said?'

'Nothing, Ezekyle.'

'That's good.'

'I've said nothing because I don't know what to say.'

Abaddon scooped up another stool and brought it over to sit down facing Loken. Both were in full plate, their helms removed. Abaddon hunched his head low to catch Loken's eyes.

'I'm proud of you, Garviel. You hear me? You dealt with this well.'

'What did I deal with?' Loken asked sombrely.

'The situation. Tell me, before Jubal rose again, who knew of the murders?'

'More. Those of Brakespur that survived. All of my officers. I wanted their advice.'

'I'll speak to them,' Abaddon muttered. 'This mustn't get out. Our line will be as you set it. Victory, splendid but unexceptional. The Tenth crushed the insurgents, though losses were taken in two squads. But that is war. We expect casualties. The insurgents fought bitterly and formidably to the last. Hellebore and Brakespur bore the brunt of their rage, but Sixty-Three Nineteen is advanced to full compliance. Glory the Tenth, and the Luna Wolves, glory the Warmaster. The rest will remain a matter of confidence within the inner circle. Can Sindermann be trusted to keep this close?'

'Of course, though he is very shaken.'

'And the remembrancer? Keener, was it?'

'Keeler. Euphrati Keeler. She's in shock. I don't know her. I don't know what she'll do, but she has no idea what it was that attacked her. I told her it was a wild beast. She didn't see Jubal… change. She doesn't know it was him.'

'Well, that's something. I'll place an injunction on her, if necessary. Perhaps a word will be sufficient. I'll repeat the wild beast story, and tell her we're keeping the matter confidential for morale's sake. The remembrancers must be kept away from this.'

'Two of them died.'

Abaddon got up. 'A tragic mishap during deployment. A landing accident. They knew the risks they were taking. It will be just a footnote blemish to an otherwise exemplary undertaking.'

Loken looked up at the first captain. 'Are we trying to forget this even happened, Ezekyle? For I cannot. And I will not.'

'I'm saying this is a military incident and will remain restricted. It's a matter of security and morale, Garviel. You are disturbed, I can see that plainly. Think what needless trauma this would cause if it got out. It would ruin confidence, break the spirit of the expedition, tarnish the entire crusade, not to mention the unimpeachable reputation of the Legion.'

The longhouse door banged open and the gale squealed in for a moment before the door closed again. Loken didn't look up. He was expecting Vipus back at any time with the muster reports.

'Leave us, Ezekyle,' a voice said.

It wasn't Vipus.

Horus was not wearing his armour. He was dressed in simple foul-weather clothes, a mail shirt and a cloak of furs. Abaddon bowed his head and quickly left the longhouse.

Loken had risen to his feet.

'Sit, Garviel,' Horus said softly. 'Sit down. Make no ceremony to me.'

Loken slowly sat back down and the Warmaster knelt beside him. He was so immensely made that kneeling, his head was on a level with Loken's. He plucked off his black leather gloves and placed his bare left hand on Loken's shoulder.

'I want you to let go of your troubles, my son,' he said.

'I try, sir, but they will not leave me alone.'

Horus nodded. 'I understand.'

'I have made a failure of this undertaking, sir,' Loken said. 'Eze-kyle says we will put a brave face on it for appearance sake, but even if these events remain secret, I will bear the shame of failing you.'

'And how did you do that?'

'Men died. A brother turned upon his own. Such a manifest sin. Such a crime. You charged me to take this seat of resistance, and I have made such a mess of it that you have been forced to come here in person to–'

'Hush,' Horus whispered. He reached out and unfixed Loken's tattered oath of moment from his shoulder plate.

'Do you, Garviel Loken, accept your role in this?' The Warmas-ter read out. 'Do you promise to lead your men into the zone of war, and conduct them to glory, no matter the ferocity or ingenu-ity of the foe? Do you swear to crush the insurgents of Sixty-Three Nineteen, despite all they might throw at you? Do you pledge to do honour to the XVI Legion and the Emperor?'

'Fine words,' Loken said.

'They are indeed. I wrote them. Well, did you, Garviel?'

'Did I what, sir?'

'Did you crush the insurgents of Sixty-Three Nineteen, despite all they threw at you?'

'Well, yes–'

'And did you lead your men into the zone of war, and conduct them to glory, no matter the ferocity or ingenuity of the foe?'

'Yes…'

'Then I can't see how you've failed in any way, my son. Consider that last phrase particularly. "No matter the ferocity or ingenuity of the foe". When poor Jubal turned, did you give up? Did you flee? Did you cast away your courage? Or did you fight against his insanity and his crime, despite your wonder at it?'

'I fought, sir,' Loken said.

'Throne of Earth, yes, you did. Yes, you did, Loken! You fought. Cast shame out. I will not have it. You served me well today, my son, and I am only sorry that the extent of your service cannot be more widely proclaimed.'

Loken started to reply, but fell silent instead. Horus rose to his feet and began to pace about the room. He found a bottle of wine amongst the clutter on a wall dresser and poured himself a glass.

'I spoke to Kyril Sindermann,' he said, and took a sip of the wine. He nodded to himself before continuing, as if surprised at its quality. 'Poor Kyril. Such a terrible thing to endure. He's even speaking of spirits, you know? Sindermann, the arch prophet of secular truth, speaking of spirits. I put him right, naturally. He mentioned spirits were a concern of yours too.'

'Kyril convinced me it was a plague, at first, but I saw a spirit… a daemon… take hold of Xavyer Jubal and remake his flesh into the form of a monster. I saw a daemon take hold of Jubal's soul and turn him against his own kind.'

'No, you didn't,' Horus said.

'Sir?'

Horus smiled. 'Allow me to illuminate you. I'll tell you what you saw, Garviel. It is a secret thing, known to a very few, though the Emperor, beloved of all, knows more than any of us. A secret, Garviel, more than any other secret we are keeping today. Can you keep it? I'll share it, for it will soothe your mind, but I need you to keep it solemnly.'

'I will,' Loken said.

The Warmaster took another sip. 'It was the warp, Garviel.'

'The… warp?'

'Of course it was. We know the power of the warp and the chaos it contains. We've seen it change men. We've seen the wretched things that infest its dark dimensions. I know you have. On

Erridas. On Syrinx. On the bloody coast of Tassilon. There are entities in the warp that we might easily mistake for daemons.'

'Sir, I...' Loken began. 'I have been trained in the study of the warp. I am well-prepared to face its horrors. I have fought the foul things that pour forth from the gates of the empyrean, and yes, the warp can seep into a man and transmute him. I have seen this happen, but only in psykers. It is the risk they take. Not in Astartes.'

'Do you understand the full mechanism of the warp, Garviel?' Horus asked. He raised the glass to the nearest light to examine the colour of the wine.

'No, sir. I don't pretend to.'

'Neither do I, my son. Neither does the Emperor, beloved by all. Not entirely. It pains me to admit that, but it is the truth, and we deal in truths above all else. The warp is a vital tool to us, a means of communication and transport. Without it, there would be no Imperium of Man, for there would be no quick bridges between the stars. We use it, and we harness it, but we have no absolute control over it. It is a wild thing that tolerates our presence, but brooks no mastery. There is power in the warp, fundamental power, not good, nor evil, but elemental and anathema to us. It is a tool we use at our own risk.'

The Warmaster finished his glass and set it down. 'Spirits. Daemons. Those words imply a greater power, a fiendish intellect and a purpose. An evil archetype with cosmic schemes and stratagems. They imply a god, or gods, at work behind the scenes. They imply the very supernatural state that we have taken great pains, through the light of science, to shake off. They imply sorcery and a palpable evil.'

He looked across at Loken. 'Spirits. Daemons. The supernatural. Sorcery. These are words we have allowed to fall out of use, for we dislike the connotations, but they are just words. What you saw today... call it a spirit. Call it a daemon. The words serve well enough. Using them does not deny the clinical truth of the universe as man understands it. There can be daemons in a secular cosmos, Garviel. Just so long as we understand the use of the word.'

'Meaning the warp?'

'Meaning the warp. Why coin new terms for its horrors when we have a bounty of old words that might suit us just as well? We use the words "alien" and "xenos" to describe the inhuman filth we encounter in some locales. The creatures of the warp are just "aliens" too, but they are not life forms as we understand the term. They are not organic. They are extra-dimensional, and they influence our reality in ways that seem sorcerous to us. Supernatural, if you will. So let's use all those lost words for them... daemons, spirits, possessors, changelings. All we need to remember is that there are no gods out there, in the darkness, no great daemons and ministers of evil. There is no fundamental, immutable evil in the cosmos. It is too large and sterile for such melodrama. There are simply inhuman things that oppose us, things we were created to battle and destroy. Orks. Gykon. Tushepta. Keylekid. Eldar. Jokaero... and the creatures of the warp, which are stranger than all for they exhibit powers that are bizarre to us because of the otherness of their nature.'

Loken rose to his feet. He looked around the lamp-lit room and heard the moaning of the mountain wind outside. 'I have seen psykers taken by the warp, sir,' he said. 'I have seen them change and bloat in corruption, but I have never seen a sound man taken. I have never seen an Astartes so abused.'

'It happens,' Horus replied. He grinned. 'Does that shock you? I'm sorry. We keep it quiet. The warp can get into anything, if it so pleases. Today was a particular triumph for its ways. These mountains are not haunted, as the myths report, but the warp is close to the surface here. That fact alone has given rise to the myths. Men have always found techniques to control the warp, and the folk here have done precisely that. They let the warp loose upon you today, and brave Jubal paid the price.'

'Why him?'

'Why not him? He was angry at you for overlooking him, and his anger made him vulnerable. The tendrils of the warp are always eager to exploit such chinks in the mind. I imagine the insurgents hoped that scores of your men would fall under the power they had let loose, but Tenth Company had more resolve than that. Samus was just a voice from the Chaotic realm that briefly anchored itself to Jubal's flesh. You dealt with it well. It could have been far worse.'

'You're sure of this, sir?'

Horus grinned again. The sight of that grin filled Loken with sudden warmth. 'Ing Mae Sing, Mistress of Astropaths, informed me of a rapid warp spike in this region just after you disembarked. The data is solid and substantive. The locals used their limited know-ledge of the warp, which they probably understood as magic, to unleash the horror of the empyrean upon you as a weapon.'

'Why have we been told so little about the warp, sir?' Loken asked. He looked directly into Horus's wide-set eyes as he asked the question.

'Because so little is known,' the Warmaster replied. 'Do you know why I am Warmaster, my son?'

'Because you are the most worthy, sir?'

Horus laughed and, pouring another glass of wine, shook his head. 'I am Warmaster, Garviel, because the Emperor is busy. He has not retired to Terra because he is weary of the crusade. He has gone there because he has more important work to do.'

'More important than the crusade?' Loken asked.

Horus nodded. 'So he said to me. After Ullanor, he believed the time had come when he could leave the crusading work in the hands of the primarchs so that he might be freed to undertake a still higher calling.'

'Which is?' Loken waited for an answer, expecting some transcendent truth.

What the Warmaster said was, 'I don't know. He didn't tell me. He hasn't told anyone.'

Horus paused. For what seemed like an age, the wind banged against the longhouse shutters. 'Not even me,' Horus whispered. Loken sensed a terrible hurt in his commander, a wounded pride that he, even he, had not been worthy enough to know this secret.

In a second, the Warmaster was smiling at Loken again, his dark mood forgotten. 'He didn't want to burden me,' he said briskly, 'but I'm not a fool. I can speculate. As I said, the Imperium would not exist but for the warp. We are obliged to use it, but we know perilously little about it. I believe that I am Warmaster because the Emperor is occupied in unlocking its secrets. He has committed his great mind to the ultimate mastery of the warp, for the good of mankind. He has realised that without final and full understanding of the immaterium, we will founder and fall, no matter how many worlds we conquer.'

'What if he fails?' Loken asked.

'He won't,' the Warmaster replied bluntly.

'What if we fail?'

'We won't,' Horus said, 'because we are his true servants and sons. Because we cannot fail him.' He looked at his half-drunk glass and put it aside. 'I came here looking for spirits,' he joked, 'and all I find is wine. There's a lesson for you.'

TRUDGING, UNSPEAKING, the warriors of Tenth Company clambered from the cooling Stormbirds and streamed away across the

embarkation deck towards their barracks. There was no sound
save for the clink of their armour and the clank of their feet.

In their midst, brothers carried the biers on which the dead of
Brakespur lay, shrouded in Legion banners. Four of them carried
Flora and Van Krasten too, though no formal flags draped the
coffins of the dead remembrancers. The Bell of Return rang out
across the vast deck. The men made the sign of the aquila and
pulled off their helms.

Loken wandered away towards his arming chamber, calling for
the service of his artificers. He carried his left shoulder guard in
his hands, Jubal's sword still stuck fast through it.

Entering the chamber, he was about to hurl the miserable
memento away into a corner, but he pulled up short, realising
he was not alone.

Mersadie Oliton stood in the shadows.

'Mistress,' he said, setting the broken guard down.

'Captain, I'm sorry. I didn't mean to intrude. Your equerry let
me wait here, knowing you were about to return. I wanted to see
you. I wanted to apologise.'

'For what?' Loken asked, hooking his battered helm on the top
strut of his armour rack.

She stepped forward, the light glowing off her black skin and
her long, augmented cranium. 'For missing the opportunity you
gave me. You were kind enough to suggest me as a candidate to
accompany the undertaking, and I did not attend in time.'

'Be grateful for that,' he said.

She frowned. 'I... there was a problem, you see. A friend of
mine, a fellow remembrancer. The poet Ignace Karkasy. He finds
himself in a deal of trouble, and I was taken up trying to assist
him. It so detained me, I missed the appointment.'

'You didn't miss anything, mistress,' Loken said as he began to
strip off his armour.

'I would like to speak with you about Ignace's plight. I hesitate
to ask, but I believe someone of your influence might help him.'

'I'm listening,' Loken said.

'So am I, sir,' Mersadie said. She stepped forward and placed a
tiny hand on his arm to restrain him slightly. He had been throwing off his armour with such vigorous, angry motions.

'I am a remembrancer, sir,' she said. 'Your remembrancer, if it is
not too bold to say so. Do you want to tell me what happened
on the surface? Is there any memory you would like to share with
me?'

Loken looked down at her. His eyes were the colour of rain. He
pulled away from her touch.

'No,' he said.

PART TWO
BROTHERHOOD IN SPIDERLAND

ONE

Loathe and love
This world is Murder
A hunger for glory

EVEN AFTER HE'D slain a fair number of them, Saul Tarvitz was still unable to say with any certainty where the biology of the megarachnid stopped and their technology began. They were the most seamless things, a perfect fusion of artifice and organism. They did not wear their armour or carry their weapons. Their armour was an integument bonded to their arthropod shells, and they possessed weapons as naturally as a man might own fingers or a mouth.

Tarvitz loathed them, and loved them too. He loathed them for their abominable want of human perfection. He loved them because they were genuinely testing foes, and in mastering them, the Emperor's Children would take another stride closer to attaining their full potential. 'We always need a rival,' his lord Eidolon had once said, and the words had stuck forever in Tarvitz's mind, 'a true rival, of considerable strength and fortitude. Only against such a rival can our prowess be properly measured.'

There was more at stake here than the Legion's prowess,

however, and Tarvitz understood that solemnly. Brother Astartes were in trouble, and this was a mission – though no one had dared actually use the term – of rescue. It was thoroughly improper to openly suggest that the Blood Angels needed rescuing.

Reinforcement. That was the word they had been told to use, but it was hard to reinforce what you could not find. They had been on the surface of Murder for sixty-six hours, and had found no sign of the 140th Expedition forces.

Or even, for the most part, of each other.

Lord Commander Eidolon had committed the entire company to the surface drop. The descent had been foul, worse than the warnings they had been given prior to the drop, and the warnings had been grim enough. Nightmarish atmospherics had scattered their drop pods like chaff, casting them wildly astray from their projected landing vectors. Tarvitz knew it was likely many pods hadn't even made it to the ground intact. He found himself one of two captains in charge of just over thirty men, around one-third of the company force, and all that had been able to regroup after planetfall. Due to the storm-cover, they couldn't raise the fleet in orbit, nor could they raise Eidolon or any other part of the landing force.

Presuming Eidolon and any other part of the landing force had survived.

The whole situation smacked of abject failure, and failure was not a concept the Emperor's Children cared to entertain. To turn failure into something else, there was little choice but to get on with the remit of the undertaking, so they spread out in a search pattern to find the brothers they had come to help. On the way, perhaps, they might reunite with other elements of their scattered force, or even find some geographical frame of reference.

The dropsite environs was disconcerting. Under an enamel-white sky, fizzling and blemished by the megarachnid shield-storms, the land was an undulating plain of ferrous red dust from which a sea of gigantic grass stalks grew, grey-white like dirty ice. Each stalk, as thick as a man's plated thigh, rose up straight to a height of twenty metres: tough, dry and bristly. They swished gently in the radio-active wind, but such was their size, at ground level, the air was filled with the creaking, moaning sound of their structures in motion. The Astartes moved through the groaning forest of stalks like lice in a wheatfield.

There was precious little lateral visibility. High above their heads, the nodding vertical shoots soared upwards and pointed incriminatingly at the curdled glare of the sky. Around them, the stalks had grown so close together that a man could see only a few metres in any direction.

The bases of most of the grass stalks were thick with swollen, black larvae: sack-things the size of a man's head, clustered tumorously to the metre or so of stalk closest to the ground. The larvae did nothing but cling and, presumably, drink. As they did so, they made a weird hissing, whistling noise that added to the eerie acoustics of the forest floor.

Bulle had suggested that the larvae might be infant forms of the enemy, and for the first few hours, they had systematically destroyed all they'd found with flamers and blades, but the work was wearying and unending. There were larvae everywhere, and eventually they had chosen to forget it and ignore the hissing sacks. Besides, the foetid ichor that burst from the larvae when they were struck was damaging the edges of their weapons and scarring their armour where it splashed.

Lucius, Tarvitz's fellow captain, had found the first tree, and called them all close to inspect it. It was a curious thing, apparently made of a calcified white stone, and it dwarfed the surrounding sea of stalks. It was shaped like a wide-capped mushroom: a fifty-metre dome supported on a thick, squat trunk ten metres broad. The dome was an intricate hemisphere of sharp, bone-white thorns, tangled and sharply pointed, the barbs some two or three metres in length.

'What is it for?' Tarvitz wondered.

'It's not for anything,' Lucius replied. 'It's a tree. It has no purpose.'

In that, Lucius was wrong.

Lucius was younger than Tarvitz, though they were both old enough to have seen many wonders in their lives. They were friends, except that the balance of their friendship was steeply and invisibly weighted in one direction. Saul and Lucius represented the bi-polar aspect of their Legion. Like all of the Emperor's Children, they devoted themselves to the pursuit of martial perfection, but Saul was diligently grounded where Lucius was ambitious.

Saul Tarvitz had long since realised that Lucius would one day outstrip him in honour and rank. Lucius would perhaps become a lord commander in due course, part of the aloof inner circle at the Legion's traditionally hierarchical core. Tarvitz didn't care. He was a file officer, born to the line, and had no desire for elevation. He was content to glorify the primarch and the Emperor, beloved of all, by knowing his place, and keeping it with unstinting devotion.

Lucius mocked him playfully sometimes, claiming Tarvitz courted the common ranks because he couldn't win the respect of the officers. Tarvitz always laughed that off, because he knew Lucius didn't properly understand. Saul Tarvitz followed the code exactly, and took pride in that. He knew his perfect destiny was as a file officer. To crave more would have been overweening and imperfect. Tarvitz had standards, and despised anyone who cast their own standards aside in the hunt for inappropriate goals.

It was all about purity, not superiority. That's what the other Legions always failed to understand.

Barely fifteen minutes after the discovery of the tree – the first of many they would find scattered throughout the creaking grasslands – they had their first dealings with the megarachnid.

The enemy's arrival had been announced by three signs: the larvae nearby had suddenly stopped hissing; the towering grass stalks had begun an abrupt shivering vibration, as if electrified; then the Astartes had heard a strange, chittering noise, coming closer.

Tarvitz barely saw the enemy warriors during that first clash. They had come, thrilling and clattering, out of the grass forest, moving so fast they were silver blurs. The fight lasted twelve chaotic seconds, a period filled to capacity with gunshots and shouts, and odd, weighty impacts. Then the enemy had vanished again, as fast as they had come, the stalks had stilled, and the larvae had resumed their hissing.

'Did you see them?' asked Kercort, reloading his bolter.

'I saw something…' Tarvitz admitted, doing the same.

'Durellen's dead. So is Martius,' Lucius announced casually, approaching them with something in his hand.

Tarvitz couldn't quite believe what he had been told. 'They're dead? Just… dead?' he asked Lucius. The fight surely hadn't lasted long enough to have included the passing of two veteran Astartes.

'Dead,' nodded Lucius. 'You can look upon their cadavers if you wish. They're over there. They were too slow.'

Weapon raised, Tarvitz pushed through the swaying stalks, some of them broken and snapped over by frantic bolter fire. He saw the two bodies, tangled amid fallen white shoots on the red earth, their beautiful purple and gold armour sawn apart and running with blood.

Dismayed, he looked away from the butchery. 'Find Varras,' he told Kercort, and the man went off to locate the Apothecary.

'Did we kill anything?' Bulle asked.

'I hit something,' Lucius said proudly, 'but I cannot find the body. It left this behind.' He held out the thing in his hand.

It was a limb, or part of a limb. Long, slender, hard. The main part of it, a metre long, was a gently curved blade, apparently made of brushed zinc or galvanised iron. It came to an astonishingly sharp point. It was thin, no thicker than a grown man's wrist. The long blade ended in a widening joint, which attached it to a thicker limb section. This part was also armoured with mottled grey metal, but came to an abrupt end where Lucius's shot had blown it off. The broken end, in cross-section, revealed a skin of metal surrounding a sleeve of natural, arthropoid chitin around an inner mass of pink, wet meat.

'Is it an arm?' Bulle asked.

'It's a sword,' Katz corrected.

'A sword with a joint?' Bulle snorted. 'And meat inside?'

Lucius grasped the limb, just above the joint, and brandished it like a sabre. He swung it at the nearest stalk, and it went clean through. With a lingering crash, the massive dry shoot toppled over, tearing into others as it fell.

Lucius started laughing, then he cried out in pain and dropped the limb. Even the base part of the limb, above the joint, had an edge, and it was so sharp that the force of his grip had bitten through his gauntlet.

'It has cut me,' Lucius complained, poking at his ruptured glove.

Tarvitz looked down at the limb, bent and still on the red soil. 'Little wonder they can slice us to ribbons.'

Half an hour later, when the stalks shivered again, Tarvitz met his first megarachnid face to face. He killed it, but it was a close-run thing, over in a couple of seconds.

From that encounter, Saul Tarvitz began to understand why Khitas Frome had named the world Murder.

THE GREAT WARSHIP exploded like a breaching whale from the smudge of un-light that was its retranslation point, and returned to the silent, physical cosmos of real space again with a shivering impact. It had translated twelve weeks earlier, by the ship-board clocks, and had made a journey that ought to have taken eighteen weeks. Great powers had been put into play to expedite the transit, powers that only a Warmaster could call upon.

It coasted for about six million kilometres, trailing the last, luminous tendrils of plasmic flare from its immense bulk, like remorae, until strobing flashes of un-light to stern announced the belated arrival of its consorts: ten light cruisers and five mass conveyance troop ships. The stragglers lit their real space engines and hurried wearily to join formation with the huge flagship. As they approached, like a school of pups swimming close to their mighty parent, the flagship ignited its own drives and led them in.

Towards One Forty Twenty. Towards Murder.

Forward arrayed detectors pinged as they tasted the magnetic and energetic profiles of other ships at high anchor around the system's fourth planet, eighty million kilometres ahead. The local sun was yellow and hot, and billowed with loud, charged particles.

As it advanced at the head of the trailing flotilla, the flagship broadcast its standard greeting document, in vox, vox-supplemented pict, War Council code, and astrotelepathic forms.

'This is the *Vengeful Spirit*, of the 63rd Expedition. This vessel approaches with peaceful intent, as an ambassador of the Imperium of Man. House your guns and stand to. Make acknowledgement.'

On the bridge of the *Vengeful Spirit*, Master Comnenus sat at his station and waited. Given its great size and number of personnel, the bridge around him was curiously quiet. There was just a murmur of low voices and the whir of instrumentation. The ship itself was protesting loudly. Undignified creaks and seismic moans issued from its immense hull and layered decks as the superstructure relaxed and settled from the horrendous torsion stresses of warp translation.

Boas Comnenus knew most of the sounds like old friends, and could almost anticipate them. He'd been part of the ship for a long time, and knew it as intimately as a lover's body. He waited, braced, for erroneous creaks, for the sudden chime of defect alarms.

So far, all was well. He glanced at the Master Companion of Vox, who shook his head. He switched his gaze to Ing Mae Sing who, though blind, knew full well he was looking at her.

'No response, master,' she said.

'Repeat,' he ordered. He wanted that signal response, but more particularly, he was waiting for the fix. It was taking too long. Comnenus drummed his steel fingers on the edge of his master console, and deck officers all around him stiffened. They knew, and feared, that sign of impatience.

Finally, an adjutant hurried over from the navigation pit with the wafer slip. The adjutant might have been about to apologise for the delay, but Comnenus glanced up at him with a whir of augmetic lenses. The whir said, 'I do not expect you to speak.' The adjutant simply held the wafer out for inspection.

Comnenus read it, nodded, and handed it back.

'Make it known and recorded,' he said. The adjutant paused long enough for another deck officer to copy the wafer for the principal transit log, then hurried up the rear staircase of the bridge to the strategium deck. There, with a salute, he handed it to the duty master, who took it, turned, and walked twenty paces to the plated glass doors of the sanctum, where he handed it in turn to the master bodyguard. The master bodyguard, a massive Astartes in gold custodes armour, read the wafer quickly, nodded, and opened the doors. He passed the wafer to the solemn, robed figure of Maloghurst, who was waiting just inside.

Maloghurst read the wafer too, nodded in turn, and shut the doors again.

'Location is confirmed and entered into the log,' Maloghurst announced to the sanctum. 'One Forty Twenty.'

Seated in a high-backed chair that had been drawn up close to the window ports to afford a better view of the starfield outside, the Warmaster took a deep, steady breath. 'Determination of passage so noted,' he replied. 'Let my acknowledgement be a matter of record.' The twenty waiting scribes around him scratched the details down in their manifests, bowed and withdrew.

'Maloghurst?' The Warmaster turned his head to look at his equerry. 'Send Boas my compliments, please.'

'Yes, lord.'

The Warmaster rose to his feet. He was dressed in full ceremonial wargear, gleaming gold and frost white, with a vast mantle of purple scale-skin draped across his shoulders. The eye of Terra stared from his breastplate. He turned to face the ten Astartes officers gathered in the centre of the room, and each one of them felt that the eye was regarding him with particular, unblinking scrutiny.

'We await your orders, lord,' said Abaddon. Like the other nine, he was wearing battle plate with a floor-length cloak, his crested helm carried in the crook of his left arm.

'And we're where we're supposed to be,' said Torgaddon, 'and alive, which is always a good start.'

A broad smile crossed the Warmaster's face. 'Indeed it is, Tarik.'

He looked into the eyes of each officer in turn. 'My friends, it seems we have an alien war to contest. This pleases me. Proud as I am of our accomplishments on Sixty-Three Nineteen, that was a painful fight to prosecute. I can't derive satisfaction from a victory over our own kind, no matter how wrong-headed and stubborn their philosophies. It limits the soldier in me, and inhibits my relish of war, and we are all warriors, you and I. Made for combat. Bred, trained and disciplined. Except you pair,' Horus smirked, nodding at Abaddon and Luc Sedirae. 'You kill until I have to tell you to stop.'

'And even then you have to raise your voice,' added Torgaddon. Most of them laughed.

'So an alien war is a delight to me,' the Warmaster continued, still smiling. 'A clear and simple foe. An opportunity to wage war without restraint, regret or remorse. Let us go and be warriors for a while, pure and undiluted.'

'Hear, hear!' cried the ancient Iacton Qruze, businesslike and sober, clearly bothered by Torgaddon's constant levity. The other nine were more modest in their assent.

Horus led them out of the sanctum onto the strategium deck, the four captains of the Mournival and the company commanders: Sedirae of the Thirteenth, Qruze of the Third, Targost of the Seventh, Marr of the Eighteenth, Moy of the Nineteenth, and Goshen of the Twenty-Fifth.

'Let's have tactical,' the Warmaster said.

Maloghurst was waiting, ready. As he motioned with his control wand, detailed hololithic images shimmered into place above the dais. They showed a general profile of the system, with orbital paths delineated, and the position and motion of tracked vessels. Horus gazed up at the hololithic graphics and reached out. Actuator sensors built into the fingertips of his gauntlets allowed him to rotate the hololithic display and bring certain segments into magnification. 'Twenty-nine craft,' he said. 'I thought the 140th was eighteen vessels strong?'

'So we were told, lord,' Maloghurst replied. As soon as they had stepped out of the sanctum, they had started conversing in Cthonic, so as to preserve tactical confidence whilst in earshot of the bridge personnel. Though Horus had not been raised on Cthonia – uncommonly, for a primarch, he had not matured on the cradle-world of his Legion – he spoke it fluently. In fact, he spoke it with the particular hard palatal edge and rough vowels of a Western Hemispheric ganger, the commonest and roughest of Cthonia's feral castes. It had always amused Loken to hear that accent. Early on, he had assumed it was because that's how the Warmaster had learned it, from just such a speaker, but he doubted that now. Horus never did anything by accident. Loken believed that the Warmaster's rough Cthonic accent was a deliberate affectation so that he would seem, to the men, as honest and low-born as any of them.

Maloghurst had consulted a data-slate provided by a waiting deck officer. 'I confirm the 140th Expedition was given a complement of eighteen vessels.'

'Then what are these others?' asked Aximand. 'Enemy ships?'

'We're awaiting sensor profile analysis, captain,' Maloghurst replied, 'and there has been no response to our signals as yet.'

'Tell Master Comnenus to be… more emphatic,' the Warmaster told his equerry.

'Should I instruct him to form our components into a battle line, lord?' Maloghurst asked.

'I'll consider it,' the Warmaster said. Maloghurst limped away down the platform steps onto the main bridge to speak to Boas Comnenus.

'Should we form a battle line?' Horus asked his commanders.

'Could the additional profiles be alien vessels?' Qruze wondered.

'It doesn't look like a battle spread, Iacton,' Aximand replied, 'and Frome said nothing about enemy vessels.'

'They're ours,' said Loken.

The Warmaster looked over at him. 'You think so, Garviel?'

'It seems evident to me, sir. The hits show a spread of ships at high anchor. Imperial anchorage formation. Others must have responded to the call for assistance...' Loken trailed off, and suddenly fought back an embarrassed smile. 'You knew that all along, of course, my lord.'

'I was just wondering who else might have been sharp enough to recognise the pattern,' Horus smiled. Qruze shook his head with a grin, sheepish at his own mistake.

The Warmaster nodded towards the display. 'So, what's this big fellow here? That's a barge.'

'The *Misericord*?' suggested Qruze.

'No, no, *that's* the *Misericord*. And what's *this* about?' Horus leaned forwards, and ran his fingers across the hard light display. 'It looks like... music. Something like music. Who's transmitting music?'

'Outstation relays,' Abaddon said, studying his own data-slate. 'Beacons. The 140th reported thirty beacons in the system grid. Xenos. Their broadcasts are repeating and untranslatable.'

'Really? They have no ships, but they have outstation beacons?' Horus reached out and changed the display to a close breakdown of scatter patterns. 'This is untranslatable?'

'So the 140th said,' said Abaddon.

'Have we taken their word for that?' asked the Warmaster.

'I imagine we have,' said Abaddon.

'There's sense in this,' Horus decided, peering at the luminous graphics. 'I want this run. I want us to run it. Start with standard numeric blocks. With respect to the 140th, I don't intend to take their word for anything. Cursed awful job they've done here so far.'

Abaddon nodded, and stepped aside to speak to one of the waiting deck officers and have the order enacted.

'You said it looks like music,' Loken said.

'What?'

'You said it looks like music, sir,' Loken repeated. 'An interesting word to choose.'

The Warmaster shrugged. 'It's mathematical, but there's a sequential rhythm to it. It's not random. Music and maths, Garviel. Two sides of a coin. This is deliberately structured. Lord knows which idiot in the 140th Fleet decided this was untranslatable.'

Loken nodded. 'You see that, just by looking at it?' he asked.

'Isn't it obvious?' Horus replied.

Maloghurst returned. 'Master Comnenus confirms all contacts are Imperial,' he said, holding out another wafer slip of print out. 'Other units have been arriving these last few weeks, in response to the calls for aid. Most of them are Imperial army conveyances en route to Carollis Star, but the big vessel is the *Proudheart*. Third Legion, the Emperor's Children. A full company, under the command privilege of Lord Commander Eidolon.'

'So, they beat us to it. How are they doing?'

Maloghurst shrugged. 'It would seem… not well, lord,' he said.

THE PLANET'S OFFICIAL designation in the Imperial Registry was One Hundred and Forty Twenty, it being the twentieth world subjected to compliance by the fleet of the 140th Expedition. But that was inaccurate, as clearly the 140th had not achieved anything like compliance. Still, the Emperor's Children had used the number to begin with, for to do otherwise would have been an insult to the honour of the Blood Angels.

Prior to arrival, Lord Commander Eidolon had briefed his Astartes comprehensively. The initial transmissions of the 140th

Expedition had been clear and succinct. Khitas Frome, captain of the three Blood Angels companies that formed the marrow of the 140th, had reported xenos hostilities a few days after his forces had touched down on the world's surface. He had described 'very capable things, like upright beetles, but made of, or shod in, metal. Each one is twice the height of a man and very belligerent. Assistance may be required if their numbers increase.'

After that, his relayed communiqués had been somewhat patchy and intermittent. Fighting had 'grown thicker and more savage' and the xenos forms 'appeared not to lack in numbers'. A week later, and his transmissions were more urgent. 'There is a race here that resists us, and which we cannot easily overcome. They refuse to admit communication with us, or any parlay. They spill from their lairs. I find myself admiring their mettle, though they are not made as we are. Their martial schooling is fine indeed. A worthy foe, one that might be written about in our annals.'

A week after that, the expedition's messages had become rather more simple, sent by the Master of the Fleet instead of Frome. 'The enemy here is formidable, and quite outweighs us. To take this world, the full force of the Legio is required. We humbly submit a request for reinforcement at this time.'

Frome's last message, relayed from the surface a fortnight later by the expedition fleet, had been a tinny rasp of generally indecipherable noise. All the articulacy and purpose of his words had been torn apart by the feral distortion. The only cogent thing that had come through was his final utterance. Each word had seemed to be spoken with inhuman effort.

'This. World. Is. Murder.'

And so they had named it.

The task force of the Emperor's Children was comparatively small in size: just a company of the Legion's main strength, conveyed by the battle-barge *Proudheart*, under the command of Lord Eidolon. After a brief, peace-keeping tour of newly compliant worlds in the Satyr Lanxus Belt, they had been en route to rejoin their primarch and brethren companies at Carollis Star to begin a mass advance into the Lesser Bifold Cluster. However, during their transit, the 140th Expedition had begun its requests for assistance. The task force had been the closest Imperial unit fit to respond. Lord Eidolon had requested immediate permission from his primarch to alter course and go to the expedition's aid.

Fulgrim had given his authority at once. The Emperor's Children would never leave their Astartes brothers in jeopardy. Eidolon had been given his primarch's instant, unreserved blessing to reroute and support the beleaguered expedition. Other forces were rushing to assist. It was said a detachment of Blood Angels was on its way, as was a heavyweight response from the Warmaster himself, despatched from the 63rd Expedition.

At best, the closest of them was still many days off. Lord Eidolon's task force was the interim measure: critical response, the first to the scene.

Eidolon's battle-barge had joined with the operational vessels of the 140th Expedition at high anchor above One Forty Twenty. The 140th Expedition was a small, compact force of eighteen carriers, mass conveyances and escorts supporting the noble battle-barge *Misericord*. Its martial composition was three companies of Blood Angels under Captain Frome, and four thousand men of the Imperial army, with allied armour, but no Mechanicum force.

Mathanual August, Master of the 140th Fleet, had welcomed Eidolon and his commanders aboard the barge. Tall and slender, with a forked white beard, August was fretful and nervous. 'I am gratified at your quick response, lord,' he'd told Eidolon.

'Where is Frome?' Eidolon had asked bluntly.

August had shrugged, helplessly.

'Where is the commander of the army divisions?'

A second pitiful shrug. 'They are all down there.'

Down there. On Murder. The world was a hazy, grey orb, mottled with storm patterning in the atmosphere. Drawn to the lonely system by the curious, untranslatable broadcasts of the outstation beacons, a clear and manifest trace of sentient life, the 140th Expedition had focussed its attentions on the fourth planet, the only orb in the star's orbit with an atmosphere. Sensor sweeps had detected abundant vital traces, though nothing had answered their signals.

Fifty Blood Angels had dropped first, in landers, and had simply disappeared. Previously calm weather cycles had mutated into violent tempests the moment the landers had entered the atmosphere, like an allergic reaction, and swallowed them up. Due to the suddenly volatile climate, communication with the surface was impossible. Another fifty had followed, and had similarly vanished.

That was when Frome and the fleet officers had begun to suspect that the life forms of One Forty Twenty somehow commanded their own weather systems as a defence. The immense storm fronts, later dubbed 'shield-storms', that had risen up to meet the surface-bound landers, had probably obliterated them. After that, Frome had used drop pods, the only vehicles that seemed to survive the descent. Frome had led the third wave himself, and only partial messages had been received from him subsequently, even though he'd taken an astrotelepath with him to counter the climatic vox-interference.

It was a grim story. Section by section, August had committed the Astartes and army forces in his expedition to surface drops in a vain attempt to respond to Frome's broken pleas for support. They had either been destroyed by the storms or lost in the impenetrable maelstrom below. The shield-storms, once roused, would not die away. There were no clean surface picts, no decent topographic scans, no uplinks or viable communication lines. One Forty Twenty was an abyss from which no one returned.

'We'll be going in blind,' Eidolon had told his officers. 'Drop pod descent.'

'Perhaps you should wait, lord,' August had suggested. 'We have word that a Blood Angels force is en route to relieve Captain Frome, and the Luna Wolves are but four days away. Combined, perhaps, you might better–'

That had decided it. Tarvitz knew Lord Eidolon had no intention of sharing any glory with the Warmaster's elite. His lord was relishing the prospect of demonstrating the excellence of his company, by rescuing the cohorts of a rival Legion… whether the word 'rescuing' was used or not. The nature of the deed, and the comparisons that it made, would speak for themselves.

Eidolon had sanctioned the drop immediately.

TWO

The nature of the enemy
A trace
The purpose of trees

THE MEGARACHNID WARRIORS were three metres tall, and possessed eight limbs. They ambulated, with dazzling speed, on their four hindmost limbs, and used the other four as weapons. Their bodies, one third again as weighty and massive as a human's, were segmented like an insect's: a small, compact abdomen hung between the four, wide-spread, slender walking limbs; a massive, armoured thorax from which all eight limbs depended; and a squat, wide, wedge-shaped head, equipped with short, rattling mouthparts that issued the characteristic chittering noise, a heavy, ctenoid comb of brow armour, and no discernible eyes. The four upper limbs matched the trophy Lucius had taken in the first round: metal-cased blades over a metre in length beyond the joint. Every part of the megarachnid appeared to be thickly plated with mottled, almost fibrous grey armour, except the head crests, which seemed to be natural, chitinous growths, rough, bony and ivory.

As the fighting wore on, Tarvitz thought he identified a status in those crests. The fuller the chitin growths, the more senior – and larger – the warrior.

Tarvitz made his first kill with his bolter. The megarachnid lunged out of the suddenly vibrating stalks in front of them, and decapitated Kercort with a flick of its upper left blade. Even stationary, it was a hyperactive blur, as if its metabolism, its very life, moved at some rate far faster than that of the enhanced gene-seed warriors of Chemos. Tarvitz had opened fire, denting the centre line of the megarachnid's thorax armour with three shots, before his fourth obliterated the thing's head in a shower of white paste and ivory crest shards. Its legs stumbled and scrabbled, its blade arms waved, and then it fell, but just before it did, there was another crash.

The crash was the sound of Kercort's headless body finally hitting the red dust, arterial spray jetting from his severed neck.

That was how fast the encounter had passed. From first strike to clean kill, poor Kercort had only had time to fall down.

A second megarachnid appeared behind the first. Its flickering limbs had torn Tarvitz's bolter out of his hands, and set a deep gouge across the facing of his breastplate, right across the palatine aquila displayed there. That was a great crime. Alone amongst the Legions, only the Emperor's Children had been permitted, by the grace of the Emperor himself, to wear that symbol upon their chestplates. Backing away, hearing bolter fire and yells from the shivering thickets all around him, Tarvitz had felt stung by genuine insult, and had unslung his broadsword, powered it, and struck downwards with a two-handed cut. His long, heavy blade had glanced off the alien's headcrest, chipping off flecks of yellowish bone, and Tarvitz had been forced to dance back out of the reach of the four, slicing limb-blades.

His second strike had been better. His sword missed the bone crest and instead hacked deeply into the megarachnid's neck, at the joint where the head connected to the upper thorax. He had split the thorax wide open to the centre, squirting out a gush of glistening white ichor. The megarachnid had trembled, fidgeting, slowly understanding its own death as Tarvitz wrenched his blade back out. It took a moment to die. It reached out with its quivering blade-limbs, and touched the tips of them against Tarvitz's recoiling face, two on either side of the visor. The touch was almost gentle. As it fell, the four points made a shrieking sound as they dragged backwards across the sides of his visor, leaving bare metal scratches in the purple gloss.

Someone was screaming. A bolter was firing on full auto, and debris from exploded grass stalks was spilling up into the air.

A third hostile flickered at Tarvitz, but his blood was up. He swung at it, turning his body right around, and cut clean through the mid line of the thorax, between upper arms and lower legs.

Pale liquid spattered into the air, and the top of the alien fell away. The abdomen, and the half-thorax remaining, pumping milky fluid, continued to scurry on its four legs for a moment before it collided with a grass stalk and toppled over.

And that was the fight done. The stalks ceased their shivering, and the wretched grubs started to whistle and buzz again.

WHEN THEY HAD been on the ground for ninety hours, and had engaged with the megarachnid twenty-eight times in the dense thickets of the grass forests, seven of their meagre party were dead and gone. The process of advance became mechanical, almost trance-like. There was no guiding narrative, no strategic detail. They had established no contact with the Blood Angels, or their lord, or any segments of other sections of their company. They moved forwards, and every few kilometres fighting broke out.

This was an almost perfect war, Saul Tarvitz decided. Simple and engrossing, testing their combat skills and physical prowess to destruction. It was like a training regime made lethal. Only days afterwards did he appreciate how truly focussed he had become during the undertaking. His instincts had grown as sharp as the enemy limb-blades. He was on guard at all times, with no opportunity to slacken or lose concentration, for the mega-rachnid ambushes were sudden and ferocious, and came out of nowhere. The party moved, then fought, moved, then fought, without space for rest or reflection. Tarvitz had never known, and would never know again, such pure martial perfection, utterly uncomplicated by politics or beliefs. He and his fellows were weapons of the Emperor, and the megarachnid were the unqualified quintessence of the hostile cosmos that stood in man's way.

Almost all of the gradually dwindling Astartes had switched to their blades. It took too many bolter rounds to bring a megarachnid down. A blade was surer, provided one was quick enough to get the first stroke in, and strong enough to ensure that stroke was a killing blow.

It was with some surprise that Tarvitz discovered his fellow captain, Lucius, thought differently. As they pushed on, Lucius boasted that he was playing the enemy.

'It's like duelling with four swordsmen at once,' Lucius crowed. Lucius was a bladesman. To Tarvitz's knowledge, Lucius had never been bested in swordplay. Where Tarvitz, and men like him, rotated through weapon drills to extend perfection in all forms and manners, Lucius had made a single art of the sword. Frustratingly, his firearms skill was such that he never seemed to need to hone it on the ranges. It was Lucius's proudest claim to have 'personally worn out' four practice cages. Sometimes, the Legion's other sword-masters, warriors like Ekhelon and Brazenor, sparred with Lucius to improve their technique. It was said, Eidolon himself often chose Lucius as a training partner.

Lucius carried an antique long sword, a relic of the Unification

Wars, forged in the smithies of the Urals by artisans of the Ter-
rawatt Clan. It was a masterpiece of perfect balance and temper.
Usually, he fought with it in the old style, with a combat shield
locked to his left arm. The sword's wire-wound handle was unusually long, enabling him to change from a single to a double
grip, to spin the blade one-handed like a baton, and to slide the
pressure of his grip back and forth: back for a looping swing,
forwards for a taut, focussed thrust.

He had his shield strapped across his back, and carried the
megarachnid blade-limb in his left hand as a secondary sword.
He had bound the base of the severed limb with strips of steel
paper from the liner of his shield to prevent the edge from further harming his grip. Head low, he paced forwards through the
endless avenues of stalks, hungry for any opportunity to deal
death.

During the twelfth attack, Tarvitz witnessed Lucius at work for
the first time. Lucius met a megarachnid head on, and set up a
flurry of dazzling, ringing blows, his two blades against the creature's four. Tarvitz saw three opportunities for straight kill strokes
that Lucius didn't so much miss as choose not to take. He was
enjoying himself so much that he didn't want the game to end
too soon.

'We will take one or two alive later,' he told Tarvitz after the
fight, without a hint of irony. 'I will chain them in the practice
cages. They will be useful for sparring.'

'They are xenos,' Tarvitz scolded.

'If I am going to improve at all, I need decent practice. Practice
that will test me. Do you know of a man who could push me?'

'They are xenos,' Tarvitz said again.

'Perhaps it is the Emperor's will,' Lucius suggested. 'Perhaps
these things have been placed in the cosmos to improve our war
skills.'

Tarvitz was proud that he didn't even begin to understand how xenos minds worked, but he was also confident that the purpose of the megarachnid, if they had some higher, ineffable purpose, was more than to give mankind a demanding training partner. He wondered, briefly, if they had language, or culture, culture as a man might recognise it. Art? Science? Emotion? Or were those things as seamlessly and exotically bonded into them as their technologies, so that mortal man might not differentiate or identify them?

Were they driven by some emotive cause to attack the Emperor's Children, or were they simply responding to trespass, like a mound of drone insects prodded with a stick? It occurred to him that the megarachnid might be attacking because, to them, the humans were hideous and xenos.

It was a terrible thought. Surely the megarachnid could see the superiority of the human design compared with their own? Maybe they fought because of jealousy?

Lucius was busy droning on, delightedly explaining some new finesse of wrist-turn that fighting the megarachnid had already taught him. He was demonstrating the technique against the bole of a stalk.

'See? A lift and turn. Lift and turn. The blow comes down and in. It would be of no purpose against a man, but here it is essential. I think I will compose a treatise on it. The move should be called "the Lucius", don't you think? How fine does that sound?'

'Very fine,' Tarvitz replied.

'Here is something!' a voice exclaimed over the vox. It was Sakian. They hurried to him. He had found a sudden and surprising clearing in the grass forest. The stalks had stopped, exposing a broad field of bare, red earth many kilometres square.

'What is this?' asked Bulle.

Tarvitz wondered if the space had been deliberately cleared, but there was no sign that stalks had ever sprouted there. The tall, swishing forest surrounded the area on all sides.

One by one, the Astartes stepped out into the open. It was unsettling. Moving through the grass forest, there had been precious little sense of going anywhere, because everywhere looked the same. This gap was suddenly a landmark. A disconcerting difference.

'Look here,' Sakian called. He was twenty metres out in the barren plain, kneeling to examine something. Tarvitz realised he had called out because of something more specific than the change in environs.

'What is it?' Tarvitz asked, trudging forwards to join Sakian.

'I think I know, captain,' Sakian replied, 'but I don't like to say it. I saw it here on the ground.'

Sakian held the object out so that Tarvitz could inspect it.

It was a vaguely triangular, vaguely concave piece of tinted glass, with rounded corners, roughly nine centimetres on its longest side. Its edges were lipped, and machine formed. Tarvitz knew what it was at once, because he was staring at it through two similar objects.

It was a visor lens from an Astartes helmet. What manner of force could have popped it out of its ceramite frame?

'It's what you think it is,' Tarvitz told Sakian.

'Not one of ours.'

'No. I don't think so. The shape is wrong. This is Mark III.'

'The Blood Angels, then?'

'Yes. The Blood Angels.' The first physical proof that anyone had been here before them.

'Look around!' Tarvitz ordered to the others. 'Search the dirt!'

The troop spent ten minutes searching. Nothing else was discovered. Overhead, an especially fierce shield-storm had begun to close in, as if drawn to them. Furious ripples of lightning striated the heavy clouds. The light grew yellow, and the storm's distortions whined and shrieked intrusively into their vox-links.

'We're exposed out here,' Bulle muttered. 'Let's get back into the forest.'

Tarvitz was amused. Bulle made it sound as if the stalk thickets were safe ground.

Giant forks of lightning, savage and yellow-white phosphorescent, were searing down into the open space, explosively scorching the earth. Though each fork only existed for a nanosecond, they seemed solid and real, like fundamental, physical structures, like upturned, thorny trees. Three Astartes, including Lucius, were struck. Secure in their Mark IV plate, they shrugged off the massive, detonating impacts and laughed as aftershock electrical blooms crackled like garlands of blue wire around their armour for a few seconds.

'Bulle's right,' Lucius said, his vox signal temporarily mauled by the discharge dissipating from his suit. 'I want to go back into the forest. I want to hunt. I haven't killed anything in twenty minutes.'

Several of the men around roared their approval at Lucius's wilfully belligerent pronouncement. They slapped their fists against their shields.

Tarvitz had been trying to contact Lord Eidolon again, or anyone else, but the storm was still blocking him. He was concerned that the few of them still remaining should not separate, but Lucius's bravado had annoyed him.

'Do as you see fit, captain. I want to find out what that is,' he said to Lucius, petulantly. He pointed. On the far side of the cleared space, three or four kilometres away, he could make out large white blobs in the far thickets.

'More trees,' Lucius said.

'Yes, but–'

'Oh, very well,' Lucius conceded.

There were now just twenty-two warriors in the group led by Lucius and Tarvitz. They spread out in a loose line and began to cross the open space. The clearing, at least, afforded them time to see any megarachnid approach.

The storm above grew still more ferocious. Five more men were struck. One of them, Ulzoras, was actually knocked off his feet. They saw fused, glassy craters in the ground where lightning had earthed with the force of penetrator missiles. The shield-storm seemed to be pressing down on them, like a lid across the sky, pressurising the air, and squeezing them in an atmospheric vice.

When the megarachnid appeared, they showed themselves in ones or twos at first. Katz saw them initially, and called out. The grey things were milling in and out of the edges of the stalk forest. Then they began to emerge en masse and move across the open ground towards the Astartes war party.

'Terra!' Lucius clucked. '*Now* we have a battle.'

There were more than a hundred of the aliens. Chittering, they closed on the Astartes from all sides, an accelerating ring of onrushing grey, closing faster and faster, a blur of scurrying limbs.

'Form a ring,' Tarvitz instructed calmly. 'Bolters.' He stuck his broadsword, tip down, into the red earth beside him and unslung his firearm. Others did likewise. Tarvitz noticed that Lucius kept his grip on his paired blades.

The flood of megarachnid swallowed up the ground, and closed in a concentric ring around the circle of the Emperor's Children.

'Ready yourselves,' Tarvitz called. Lucius, his swords raised by his sides, was evidently happy for Tarvitz to command the action.

They could hear the dry, febrile chittering as it came closer. The drumming of four hundred rapid legs.

Tarvitz nodded to Bulle, who was the best marksman in the

troop. 'The order is yours,' he said.

'Thank you, sir.' Bulle raised his bolter and yelled, 'At ten metres! Shoot till you're dry!'

'Then blades!' Tarvitz bellowed.

When the tightening wave of megarachnid warriors was ten and a half metres away, Bulle yelled, 'Fire!' and the firm circle of Astartes opened up.

Their weapons made a huge, rolling noise, despite the storm. All around them, the front ranks of the enemy buckled and toppled, some splintering apart, some bursting. Pieces of thorny, zinc-grey metal spun away into the air.

As Bulle had instructed, the Astartes fired until their weapons were spent, and then hefted their blades up in time to meet the onrushing foe. The megarachnid broke around them like a wave around a rock. There was a flurried, multiplied din of metal-on-metal impacts as human and alien blades clashed. Tarvitz saw Lucius rush forwards at the last minute, swords swinging, meeting the megarachnid host head on, severing and hacking.

The battle lasted for three minutes. Its intensity should have been spread out across an hour or two. Five more Astartes died. Dozens of megarachnid things fell, broken and rent, onto the red earth. Reflecting upon the encounter later, Tarvitz found he could not remember any single detail of the fight. He'd dropped his bolter and raised his broadsword, and then it had all become a smear of bewildering moments. He found himself, standing there, his limbs aching from effort, his sword and armour dripping with stringy, white matter. The megarachnid were falling back, pouring back, as rapidly as they had advanced.

'Regroup! Reload!' Tarvitz heard himself yelling.

'Look!' Katz called out. Tarvitz looked.

There was something in the sky, objects sweeping down out of the molten, fracturing air above them.

The megarachnid had more than one biological form.

The flying things descended on long, glassy wings that beat so furiously they were just flickering blurs that made a strident thrumming noise. Their bodies were glossy black, their abdomens much fuller and longer than those of their land-bound cousins. Their slender black legs were pulled up beneath them, like wrought-iron undercarriages.

The winged clades took men from the air, dropping sharply and seizing armoured forms in the hooked embrace of their dark limbs. Men fought back, struggled, fired their weapons, but within seconds four or five warriors had been snatched up and borne away into the tumultuous sky, writhing and shouting.

Unit cohesion broke. The men scattered, trying to evade the things swooping out of the air. Tarvitz yelled for order, but knew it was futile. He was forced to duck as a winged shape rushed over him, making a reverberative, chopping drone. He caught a glimpse of a head crest formed into a long, dark, malevolent hook.

Another passed close by. Boltguns were pumping. Tarvitz lashed out with his sword, striking high, trying to drive the creature back. The thrumming of its wings was distressingly loud and made his diaphragm quiver. He jabbed and thrust with his blade, and the thing bobbed backwards across the soil, effortless and light. With a sharp, sudden movement, it turned away, took hold of another man, and lifted him into the sky.

Another of the winged things had seized Lucius. It had him by the back and was taking him off the ground. Lucius, twisting like a maniac, was trying to stab his swords up behind himself, to no avail.

Tarvitz sprang forwards and grabbed hold of Lucius as he left the ground. Tarvitz thrust up past him with his broadsword, but a hooked black leg struck him, and his broadsword tumbled away out of his hand. He held on to Lucius.

'Drop! Drop!' Lucius yelled.

Tarvitz could see that the thing held Lucius by the shield strapped to his back. Swinging, he wrenched out his combat knife, and hacked at the straps. They sheared away, and Lucius and Tarvitz fell from the thing's clutches, plummeting ten metres onto the red dust.

The flying clades made off, taking nine of the Astartes with them. They were heading in the direction of the white blobs in the far thickets. Tarvitz didn't need to give an order. The remaining warriors took off across the ground as fast as they could, chasing after the retreating dots.

They caught up with them at the far edge of the clearing. The white blobs had indeed been more trees, three of them, and now Lucius discovered they had a purpose after all.

The bodies of the taken Astartes were impaled upon the thorns of the trees, rammed onto the stone spikes, their armoured shapes skewered into place, allowing the winged megarachnid to feed upon them. The creatures, their wings now stilled and quiet and extended, long and slender, out behind their bodies like bars of stained glass, were crawling over the stone trees, gnawing and biting, using their hooked head crests to break open thorn-pinned armour to get at the meat within.

Tarvitz and the others came to a halt and watched in sick dismay. Blood was dripping from the white thorns and streaming down the squat, chalky trunks.

Their brothers were not alone amongst the thorns. Other cadavers hung there, rotten and rendered down to bone and dry gristle. Pieces of red armour plate hung from the reduced bodies, or littered the ground at the foot of the trees.

At last, they had found out what had happened to the Blood
Angels.

THREE

During the voyage
Bad poetry
Secrets

DURING THE TWELVE-WEEK voyage between Sixty-Three Nineteen and One Forty Twenty, Loken had come to the conclusion that Sindermann was avoiding him.

He finally located him in the endless stacks of Archive Chamber Three. The iterator was sitting in a stilt-chair, examining ancient texts secured on one of the high shelves of the archive's gloomiest back annexes. There was no bustle of activity back here, no hurrying servitors laden with requested books. Loken presumed that the material catalogued in this area was of little interest to the average scholar.

Sindermann didn't hear him approach. He was intently studying a fragile old manuscript, the stilt-chair's reading lamp tilted over his left shoulder to illuminate the pages.

'Hello?' Loken hissed.

Sindermann looked down and saw Loken. He started slightly, as if woken from a deep sleep.

'Garviel,' he whispered. 'One moment.' Sindermann put the

manuscript back on the shelf, but several other books were piled up in the chair's basket rack. As he re-shelved the manuscript, Sindermann's hands seemed to tremble. He pulled a brass lever on the chair's armrest and the stilt legs telescoped down with a breathy hiss until he was at ground level.

Loken reached out to steady the iterator as he stepped out of the chair.

'Thank you, Garviel.'

'What are you doing back here?' Loken asked.

'Oh, you know. Reading.'

'Reading what?'

Sindermann cast what Loken judged to be a slightly guilty look at the books in his chair's rack. Guilty, or embarrassed. 'I confess,' Sindermann said, 'I have been seeking solace in some old and terribly unfashionable material. Pre-Unification fiction, and some poetry. Just desolate scraps, for so little remains, but I find some comfort in it.'

'May I?' Loken asked, gesturing to the basket.

'Of course,' said Sindermann.

Loken sat down in the brass chair, which creaked under his weight, and took some of the old books out of the side basket to examine them. They were frayed and foxed, even though some of them had evidently been rebound or sleeved from earlier bindings prior to archiving.

'*The Golden Age of Sumaturan Poetry*?' Loken said. '*Folk Tales of Old Muscovy*? What's this? *The Chronicles of Ursh*?'

'Boisterous fictions and bloody histories, with the occasional smattering of fine lyric verse.'

Loken took out another, heavy book. '*Tyranny of the Panpacific*,' he read, and flipped open the cover to see the title page. '"An Epic Poem in Nine Cantos, Exalting the Rule of Narthan Dume"... it sounds rather dry.'

'It's raw-headed and robust, and quite bawdy in parts. The work of over-excited poets trying to turn the matter of their own, wretched times into myth. I'm rather fond of it. I used to read such things as a child. Fairy tales from another time.'

'A better time?'

Sindermann baulked. 'Oh, Terra, no! An awful time, a murderous, rancorous age when we were sliding into species doom, not knowing that the Emperor would come and apply the brakes to our cultural plummet.'

'But they comfort you?'

'They remind me of my boyhood. That comforts me.'

'Do you need comforting?' Loken asked, putting the books back in the basket and looking up at the old man. 'I've barely seen you since–'

'Since the mountains,' Sindermann finished, with a sad smile.

'Indeed. I've been to the school on several occasions to hear you brief the iterators, but always there's someone standing in for you. How are you?'

Sindermann shrugged. 'I confess, I've been better.'

'Your injuries still–'

'I've healed in body, Garviel, but...' Sindermann tapped his temple with a gnarled finger. 'I'm unsettled. I haven't felt much like speaking. The fire's not in me just now. It will return. I've kept my own company, and I'm on the mend.'

Loken stared at the old iterator. He seemed so frail, like a baby bird, pale and skinny necked. It had been nine weeks since the bloodshed at the Whisperheads, and most of that time they had spent in warp transit. Loken felt he had begun to come to terms with things himself, but seeing Sindermann, he realised how close to the surface the hurt lay. He could block it out. He was Astartes. But Sindermann was a mortal man, and nothing like as resilient.

'I wish I could–'

Sindermann held up a hand. 'Please. The Warmaster himself was kind enough to speak with me about it, privately. I understand what happened, and I am a wiser man for it.'

Loken got out of the chair and allowed Sindermann to take his place. The iterator sat down, gratefully.

'He keeps me close,' Loken said.

'Who does?'

'The Warmaster. He brought me and the Tenth with him on this undertaking, just to keep me by him. So he could watch me.'

'Because?'

'Because I've seen what few have seen. Because I've seen what the warp can do if we're not careful.'

'Then our beloved commander is very wise, Garviel. Not only has he given you something to occupy your mind with, he's offering you the chance to reforge your courage in battle. He still needs you.'

Sindermann got to his feet again and limped along the book stacks for a moment, tracing his thin hand across the spines. From his gait, Loken knew he hadn't healed anything like as well as he'd claimed. He seemed occupied with the books once more.

Loken waited for a moment. 'I should go,' he said. 'I have duties to attend to.'

Sindermann smiled and waved Loken on his way with eyelash blinks of his fingers.

'I've enjoyed talking with you again,' Loken said. 'It's been too long.'

'It has.'

'I'll come back soon. A day or two. Hear you brief, perhaps?'

'I might be up to that.'

Loken took a book out of the basket. 'These comfort you, you say?'

'Yes.'

'May I borrow one?'

'If you bring it back. What have you there?' Sindermann shuffled over and took the volume from Loken. 'Sumaturan poetry? I don't think that's you. Try this–'

He took one of the other books out of the chair's rack. '*The Chronicles of Ursh*. Forty chapters, detailing the savage reign of Kalagann. You'll enjoy that. Very bloody, with a high body count. Leave the poetry to me.'

Loken scanned the old book and then put it under his arm. 'Thanks for the recommendation. If you like poetry, I have some for you.'

'Really?'

'One of the remembrancers–'

'Oh yes,' Sindermann nodded. 'Karkasy. I was told you'd vouched for him.'

'It was a favour, to a friend.'

'And by friend, you mean Mersadie Oliton?'

Loken laughed. 'You told me you'd kept your own company these last few months, yet you still know everything about everything.'

'That's my job. The juniors keep me up to speed. I understand you've indulged her a little. As your own remembrancer.'

'Is that wrong?'

'Not at all!' Sindermann smiled. 'That's the way it's supposed to work. Use her, Garviel. Let her use you. One day, perhaps, there will be far finer books in the Imperial archives than these poor relics.'

'Karkasy was going to be sent away. I arranged probation, and part of that was for him to submit all his work to me. I can't make head nor tail of it. Poetry. I don't do poetry. Can I give it to you?'

'Of course.'

Loken turned to leave. 'What was the book you put back?' he asked.

'What?'

'When I arrived, you had volumes in your basket there, but you were also studying one, intently, it seemed to me. You put it back on the shelves. What was it?'

'Bad poetry,' said Sindermann.

THE FLEET HAD embarked for Murder less than a week after the Whisperheads incident. The transmitted requests for assistance had become so insistent that any debate as to what the 63rd Expedition undertook next became academic. The Warmaster had ordered the immediate departure of ten companies under his personal command, leaving Varvaras behind with the bulk of the fleet to oversee the general withdrawal from Sixty-Three Nineteen.

Once Tenth Company had been chosen as part of the relief force, Loken had found himself too occupied with the hectic preparations for transit to let his mind dwell on the incident. It was a relief to be busy. There were squad formations to be reassigned, and replacements to be selected from the Legion's novitiate and Scout auxiliaries. He had to find men to fill the gaps in Hellebore and Brakespur, and that meant screening young candidates and making decisions that would change lives forever. Who were the best? Who should be given the chance to advance to full Astartes status?

Torgaddon and Aximand assisted Loken in this solemn task, and he was thankful for their contributions. Little Horus, in particular, seemed to have extraordinary insight regarding candidates. He saw true strengths in some that Loken would have dismissed, and flaws in others that Loken liked the look of. Loken began to appreciate that Aximand's place in the Mournival had been earned by his astonishing analytical precision.

Loken had elected to clear out the dormitory cells of the dead men himself.

'Vipus and I can do that,' Torgaddon said. 'Don't bother yourself.'

'I want to do it,' Loken replied. 'I should do it.'

'Let him, Tarik,' said Aximand. 'He's right. He should.' Loken found himself truly warming to Little Horus for the first time. He had not imagined they would ever be close, but what had at first seemed to be quiet, reserved and stern in Little Horus Aximand was proving to be plain-spoken, empathic and wise.

When he came to clean out the modest, spartan cells, Loken made a discovery. The warriors had little in the way of personal effects: some clothing, some select trophies, and little, tightly bound scrolls of oath papers, usually stored in canvas cargo sacks beneath their crude cots. Amongst Xavyer Jubal's meagre effects, Loken found a small, silver medal, unmounted on any chain or cord. It was the size of a coin, a wolf's head set against a crescent moon.

'What is this?' Loken asked Nero Vipus, who had come along with him.

'I can't say, Garvi.'

'I think I know what it is,' Loken said, a little annoyed at his friend's blank response, 'and I think you do too.'

'I really can't say.'

'Then guess,' Loken snapped. Vipus suddenly seemed very caught up in examining the way the flesh of his wrist was healing around the augmetic implant he had been fitted with.

'Nero…'

'It could be a lodge medal, Garvi,' Vipus replied dismissively. 'I can't say for sure.'

'That's what I thought,' Loken said. He turned the silver medal over in his palm. 'Jubal was a lodge member, then, eh?'

'So what if he was?'

'You know my feelings on the subject,' Loken replied.

Officially, there were no warrior lodges, or any other kind of fraternities, within the Adeptus Astartes. It was common knowledge that the Emperor frowned on such institutions, claiming they were dangerously close to cults, and only a step away from the Imperial creed, the Lectitio Divinitatus, that supported the notion of the Emperor, beloved by all, as a god.

But fraternal lodges did exist within the Astartes, occult and private. According to rumours, they had been active in the XVI Legion for a long time. Some six decades earlier, the Luna Wolves, in collaboration with the XVII Legion, the Word Bearers, had undertaken the compliance of a world called Davin. A feral place, Davin had been controlled by a remarkable warrior caste, whose savage nobility had won the respect of the Astartes sent to pacify their warring feuds. The Davinite warriors had ruled their world through a complex structure of warrior lodges, quasi-religious societies that had venerated various local predators. By cultural osmosis, the lodge practices had been quietly absorbed by the Legions.

Loken had once asked his mentor, Sindermann, about them. 'They're harmless enough,' the iterator had told him. 'Warriors always seek the brotherhood of their kind. As I understand it, they seek to promote fellowship across the hierarchies of command, irrespective of rank or position. A kind of internal bond, a ribwork of loyalty that operates, as it were, perpendicular to the official chain of command.'

Loken had never been sure what something that operated perpendicular to the chain of command might look like, but it sounded wrong to him. Wrong, if nothing else, in that it was deliberately secret and thus deceitful. Wrong, in that the

Emperor, beloved by all, disapproved of them.

'Of course,' Sindermann had added, 'I can't actually say if they exist.'

Real or not, Loken had made it plain that any Astartes intending to serve under his captaincy should have nothing to do with them.

There had never been any sign that anyone in the Tenth was involved in lodge activities. Now the medal had turned up. A lodge medal, belonging to the man who had turned into a daemon and killed his own.

Loken was greatly troubled by the discovery. He told Vipus that he wanted it made known that any man in his command who had information concerning the existence of lodges should come forwards and speak with him, privately if necessary. The next day, when Loken came to sort through the personal effects he had gathered, one last time, he found the medal had disappeared.

In the last few days before departure, Mersadie Oliton had come to him several times, pleading Karkasy's case. Loken remembered her talking to him about it on his return from the Whisperheads, but he had been too distracted then. He cared little about the fate of a remembrancer, especially one foolish enough to anger the expedition authorities.

But it was another distraction, and he needed as many as he could get. After consulting with Maloghurst, he told her he would intervene.

Ignace Karkasy was a poet and, it appeared, an idiot. He didn't know when to shut up. On a surface visit to Sixty-Three Nineteen, he had wandered away from the legitimate areas of visit, got drunk, and then shot his mouth off to such an extent he had received a near-fatal beating from a crew of army troopers.

'He is going to be sent away,' Mersadie said. 'Back to Terra, in disgrace, his certification stripped away. It's wrong, captain. Ignace is a good man...'

'Really?'

'No, all right. He's a lousy man. Uncouth. Stubborn. Annoying. But he is a great poet, and he speaks the truth, no matter how unpalatable that is. Ignace didn't get beaten up for lying.'

Recovered enough from his beating to have been transferred from the flagship's infirmary to a holding cell, Ignace Karkasy was a dishevelled, unedifying prospect.

He rose as Loken walked in and the stab lights came on.

'Captain, sir,' he began. 'I am gratified you take an interest in my pathetic affairs.'

'You have persuasive friends,' Loken said. 'Oliton, and Keeler too.'

'Captain Loken, I had no idea I had persuasive friends. In point of fact, I had little notion I had friends at all. Mersadie is kind, as I'm sure you've realised. Euphrati... I heard there was some trouble she was caught up in.'

'There was.'

'Is she well? Was she hurt?'

'She's fine,' Loken replied, although he had no idea what state Keeler was in. He hadn't seen her. She'd sent him a note, requesting his intervention in Karkasy's case. Loken suspected Mersadie Oliton's influence.

Ignace Karkasy was a big man, but he had suffered a severe assault. His face was still puffy and swollen, and the bruises had discoloured his skin yellow like jaundice. Blood vessels had burst in his hang-dog eyes. Every movement he made seemed to give him pain.

'I understand you're outspoken,' Loken said. 'Something of an iconoclast?'

'Yes, yes,' Karkasy said, shaking his head, 'but I'll grow out of it, I promise you.'

'They want rid of you. They want to send you home,' said

Loken. 'The senior remembrancers believe you're giving the order a bad name.'

'Captain, I could give someone a bad name just by standing next to them.'

That made Loken smile. He was beginning to like the man.

'I've spoken with the Warmaster's equerry about you, Karkasy,' Loken said. 'There is a potential for probation here. If a senior Astartes, such as myself, vouches for you, then you could stay with the expedition.'

'There'd be conditions?' Karkasy asked.

'Of course there would, but first of all I have to hear you tell me that you want to stay.'

'I want to stay. Great Terra, captain, I made a mistake, but I want to stay. I want to be part of this.'

Loken nodded. 'Mersadie says you should. The equerry, too, has a soft spot for you. I think Maloghurst likes an underdog.'

'Sir, never has a dog been so much under.'

'Here are the conditions,' Loken said. 'Stick to them, or I will withdraw my sponsorship of you entirely, and you'll be spending a cold forty months lugging your arse back to Terra. First, you reform your habits.'

'I will, sir. Absolutely.'

'Second, you report to me every three days, my duties permitting, and copy me with everything you write. Everything, do you understand? Work intended for publication and idle scribbles. Nothing goes past me. You will show me your soul on a regular basis.'

'I promise, captain, though I warn you it's an ugly, cross-eyed, crook-backed, club-footed soul.'

'I've seen ugly,' Loken assured him. 'The third condition. A question, really. Do you lie?'

'No, sir, I don't.'

'This is what I've heard. You tell the truth, unvarnished and unretouched. You are judged a scoundrel for this. You say things others dare not.'

Karkasy shrugged – with a groan brought about by sore shoulders. 'I'm confused, captain. Is saying yes to that going to spoil my chances?'

'Answer anyway.'

'Captain Loken, I always, always tell the truth as I see it, though it gets me beaten to a pulp in army bars. And, with my heart, I denounce those who lie or deliberately blur the whole truth.'

Loken nodded. 'What did you say, remembrancer? What did you say that provoked honest troopers so far they took their fists to you?'

Karkasy cleared his throat and winced. 'I said... I said the Imperium would not endure. I said that nothing lasts forever, no matter how surely it has been built. I said that we will be fighting forever, just to keep ourselves alive.'

Loken did not reply.

Karkasy rose to his feet. 'Was that the right answer, sir?'

'Are there any right answers, sir?' Loken replied. 'I know this... a warrior-officer of the Imperial Fists said much the same thing to me not long ago. He didn't use the same words, but the meaning was identical. He was not sent home.' Loken laughed to himself. 'Actually, as I think of it now, he was, but not for that reason.'

Loken looked across the cell at Karkasy.

'The third condition, then. I will vouch for you, and stand in recognisance for you. In return, you must continue to tell the truth.'

'Really? Are you sure about that?'

'Truth is all we have, Karkasy. Truth is what separates us from the xenos-breeds and the traitors. How will history judge us fairly if it doesn't have the truth to read? I was told that was what the remembrancer order was for. You keep telling the truth, ugly and unpalatable as it might be, and I'll keep sponsoring you.'

FOLLOWING HIS STRANGE and disconcerting conversation with Kyril Sindermann in the archives, Loken walked along to the gallery chamber in the flagship's midships where the remembrancers had taken to gathering.

As usual, Karkasy was waiting for him under the high arch of the chamber's entrance. It was their regular, agreed meeting place. From the broad chamber beyond the arch floated sounds of laughter, conversation and music. Figures, mostly remembrancers, but also some crew personnel and military aides, bustled in and out through the archway, many in noisy, chattering groups.

The gallery chamber, one of many aboard the massive flagship designed for large assembly meetings, addresses and military ceremonies, had been given over to the remembrancers' use once it had been recognised that they could not be dissuaded from social gathering and conviviality. It was most undignified and undisciplined, as if a small carnival had been permitted to pitch in the austere halls of the grand warship. All across the Imperium, warships were making similar accommodations as they adjusted to the uncomfortable novelty of carrying large communities of artists and freethinkers with them. By their very nature, the remembrancers could not be regimented or controlled the way the military complements of the ship could. They had an unquenchable desire to meet and debate and carouse. By giving them a space for their own use, the masters of the expedition could at least ring-fence their boisterous activities.

The chamber had become known as the Retreat, and it had

acquired a grubby reputation. Loken had no wish to go inside, and always arranged to meet Karkasy at the entrance. It felt so odd to hear unrestrained laughter and jaunty music in the solemn depths of the *Vengeful Spirit*.

Karkasy nodded respectfully as the captain approached him. Seven weeks of voyage time had seen his injuries heal well, and the bruises on his flesh were all but gone. He presented Loken with a printed sheaf of his latest work. Other remembrancers, passing by in little social cliques, eyed the Astartes captain with curiosity and surprise.

'My most recent work,' Karkasy said. 'As agreed.'

'Thank you. I'll see you here in three days.'

'There's something else, captain,' Karkasy said, and handed Loken a data-slate. He thumbed it to life. Picts appeared on the screen, beautifully composed picts of him and Tenth Company, assembling for embarkation. The banner. The files. Here he was swearing his oath of moment to Targost and Sedirae. The Mournival.

'Euphrati asked me to give you this,' Karkasy said.

'Where is she?' Loken asked.

'I don't know, captain,' Karkasy said. 'No one's seen her about much. She has become reclusive since…'

'Since?'

'The Whisperheads.'

'What has she told you about that?'

'Nothing, sir. She says there's nothing to tell. She says the first captain told her there was nothing to tell.'

'She's right about that. These are fine images. Thank you, Ignace. Thank Keeler for me. I will treasure these.'

Kakasy bowed and began to walk back into the Retreat.

'Karkasy?'

'Sir?'

'Look after Keeler, please. For me. You and Oliton. Make sure she's not alone too often.'

'Yes, captain. I will.'

SIX WEEKS INTO the voyage, while Loken was drilling his new recruits, Aximand came to him.

'*The Chronicles of Ursh?*' he muttered, noticing the volume Loken had left open beside the training mat.

'It pleases me,' Loken replied.

'I enjoyed it as a child,' Aximand replied. 'Vulgar, though.'

'I think that's why I like it,' Loken replied. 'What can I do for you?'

'I wanted to speak to you,' Aximand said, 'on a private matter.'

Loken frowned. Aximand opened his hand and revealed a silver lodge medal.

'I WOULD LIKE you to give this a fair hearing,' Aximand said, once they had withdrawn to the privacy of Loken's arming chamber. 'As a favour to me.'

'You know how I feel about lodge activities?'

'It's been made known to me. I admire your purity, but there's no hidden malice in the lodge. You have my word, and I hope, by now, that's worth something.'

'It is. Who told you of my interest?'

'I can't say. Garviel, there is a lodge meeting tonight, and I would like you to attend it as my guest. We would like to embrace you to our fraternity.'

'I'm not sure I want to be embraced.'

Aximand nodded his head. 'I understand. There would be no duress. Come, attend, see for yourself and decide for yourself. If you don't like what you find, then you're free to leave and disassociate yourself.'

Loken made no response.

'It is simply a band of brothers,' Aximand said. 'A fraternity of warriors, bi-partisan and without rank.'

'So I've heard.'

'Since the Whisperheads, we have had a vacancy. We'd like you to fill it.'

'A vacancy?' Loken said. 'You mean Jubal? I saw his medal.'

'Will you come with me?' asked Aximand.

'I will. Because it's you who's asking me,' said Loken.

FOUR

Felling the Murder trees
Megarachnid industry
Pleased to know you

THEIR BROTHERS ON the tree were already dead, past saving, but Tarvitz could not leave them skewered and unavenged. The ruination of their proud, perfect forms insulted his eyes and the honour of his Legion.

He gathered all the explosives carried by the remaining men, and moved forwards towards the trees with Bulle and Sakian.

Lucius stayed with the others. 'You're a fool to do that,' he told Tarvitz. 'We might yet need those charges.'

'What for?' Tarvitz asked.

Lucius shrugged. 'We've a war to win here.'

That almost made Saul Tarvitz laugh. He wanted to say that they were already dead. Murder had swallowed the companies of Blood Angels and now, thanks to Eidolon's zeal for glory, it had swallowed them too. There was no way out. Tarvitz didn't know how many of the company were still alive on the surface, but if the other groups had suffered losses commensurate to their own, the full number could be little higher than fifty.

Fifty men, fifty Astartes even, against a world of numberless hostiles. This was not a war to win; this was just a last stand, wherein, by the Emperor's grace, they might take as many of the foe with them as they could before they fell.

He did not say this to Lucius, but only because others were in earshot. Lucius's brand of courage admitted no reality, and if Tarvitz had been plain about their situation, it would have led to an argument. The last thing the men needed now was to see their officers quarrelling.

'I'll not suffer those trees to stand,' Tarvitz said.

With Bulle and Sakian, he approached the white stone trees, running low until they were in under the shadows of their grim, rigid canopies. The winged megarachnid up among the thorns ignored them. They could hear the cracking, clicking noises of the insects' feeding, and occasional trickles of black blood spattered down around them.

They divided the charges into three equal amounts, and secured them to the boles of the trees. Bulle set a forty-second timer.

They began to run back towards the edge of the stalk forest where Lucius and the rest of the troop lay in cover.

'Move it, Saul,' Lucius's voice crackled over the vox.

Tarvitz didn't reply.

'Move it, Saul. Hurry. Don't look back.'

Still running, Tarvitz looked behind him. Two of the winged clades had disengaged themselves from the feeding group and had taken to the air. Their beating wings were glass-blurs in the yellow light, and the lightning flash glinted off their polished black bodies. They circled up away from the thorn trees and came on in the direction of the three figures, wings throcking the air like the buzz of a gnat slowed and amplified to gargantuan, bass volumes.

'Run!' said Tarvitz.

Sakian glanced back. He lost his footing and fell. Tarvitz skidded to a halt and turned back, dragging Sakian to his feet. Bulle had run on. 'Twelve seconds!' he yelled, turning and drawing his bolter. He kept backing away, but trained his weapon at the oncoming forms.

'Come on!' he yelled. Then he started to fire and shouted 'Drop! Drop!'

Sakian pushed them both down, and he and Tarvitz sprawled onto the red dirt as the first winged clade went over them, so low the downdraft of its whirring wings raised dust.

It rose past them and headed straight for Bulle, but veered away as he struck it twice with bolter rounds.

Tarvitz looked up and saw the second megarachnid drop straight towards him in a near stall, the kind of pounce-dive that had snared so many of his comrades earlier.

He tried to roll aside. The black thing filled the entire sky.

A bolter roared. Sakian had cleared his weapon and was firing upwards, point blank. The shots tore through the winged clade's thorax in a violent puff of smoke and chitin shards, and the thing fell, crushing them both beneath its weight.

It twitched and spasmed on top of them, and Tarvitz heard Sakian cry out in pain. Tarvitz scrabbled to heave it away, his hands sticky with its ichor.

The charges went off.

The shockwave of flame rushed out across the red dirt in all directions. It scorched and demolished the nearby edge of the stalk forest, and lifted Tarvitz, Sakian and the thing pinning them, into the air. It blew Bulle off his feet, throwing him backwards. It caught the flying thing, tore off its wings, and hurled it into the thickets.

The blast levelled the three stone trees. They collapsed like buildings, like demolished towers, fracturing into brittle splinters and white dust as they fell into the fireball. Two or three of the winged clades feeding on the trees took off, but they were on fire, and the heat-suck of the explosion tumbled them back into the flames.

Tarvitz got up. The trees had been reduced to a heap of white slag, burning furiously. A thick pall of ash-white dust and smoke rolled off the blast zone. Burning, smouldering scads, like volcanic out-throw, drizzled down over him.

He hauled Sakian upright. The creature's impact on them had broken Sakian's right upper arm, and that break had been made worse when they had been thrown by the blast. Sakian was unsteady, but his genhanced metabolism was already compensating.

Bulle, unhurt, was getting up by himself.

The vox stirred. It was Lucius. 'Happy now?' he asked.

BEYOND REVENGE AND honour, Tarvitz's action had two unexpected consequences. The second did not become evident for some time, but the first was apparent in less than thirty minutes.

Where the vox had failed to link the scattered forces on the surface, the blast succeeded. Two other troops, one commanded by Captain Anteus, the other by Lord Eidolon himself, detected the considerable detonation, and followed the smoke plume to its source. United, they had almost fifty Astartes between them.

'Make report to me,' Eidolon said. They had taken up position at the edge of the clearing, some half a kilometre from the destroyed trees, near the hem of the stalk forest. The open ground afforded them ample warning of the approach of the megarachnid scurrier-clades, and if the winged forms reappeared, they could retreat swiftly into the cover of the thickets and mount a defence.

Tarvitz outlined all that had befallen his troop since landfall as quickly and clearly as possible. Lord Eidolon was one of the primarch's most senior commanders, the first chosen to such a role, and brooked no familiarity, even from senior line officers like Tarvitz. Saul could tell from his manner that Eidolon was seething with anger. The undertaking had not gone at all to his liking. Tarvitz wondered if Eidolon might ever admit he was wrong to have ordered the drop. He doubted it. Eidolon, like all the elite hierarchy of the Emperor's Children, somehow made pride a virtue.

'Repeat what you said about the trees,' Eidolon prompted.

'The winged forms use them to secure prey for feeding, lord,' Tarvitz said.

'I understand that,' Eidolon snapped. 'I've lost men to the winged things, and I've seen the thorn trees, but you say there were other bodies?'

'The corpses of Blood Angels, lord,' Tarvitz nodded, 'and men of the Imperial army force too.'

'We've not seen that,' Captain Anteus remarked.

'It might explain what happened to them,' Eidolon replied. Anteus was one of Eidolon's chosen circle and enjoyed a far more cordial relationship with his lord than Tarvitz did.

'Have you proof?' Anteus asked Tarvitz.

'I destroyed the trees, as you know, sir,' Tarvitz said.

'So you don't have proof?'

'My word is proof,' said Tarvitz.

'And good enough for me,' Anteus nodded courteously. 'I meant no offence, brother.'

'And I took none, sir.'

'You used all your charges?' Eidolon asked.

'Yes, lord.'

'A waste.'

Tarvitz began to reply, but stifled the words before he could say them. If it hadn't been for his use of the explosives, they wouldn't have reunited. If it hadn't been for his use of the explosives, the ragged corpses of fine Emperor's Children would have hung from stone gibbets in ignominious disarray.

'I told him so, lord,' Lucius remarked.

'Told him what?'

'That using all our charges was a waste.'

'What's that in your hand, captain?' Eidolon asked.

Lucius held up the limb-blade.

'You taint us,' Anteus said. 'Shame on you. Using an enemy's claw like a sword…'

'Throw it away, captain,' Eidolon said. 'I'm surprised at you.'

'Yes, lord.'

'Tarvitz?'

'Yes, my lord?'

'The Blood Angels will require some proof of their fallen. Some relic they can honour. You say shreds of armour hung from those trees. Go and retrieve some. Lucius can help you.'

'My lord, should we not secure this–'

'I gave you an order, captain. Execute it please, or does the honour of our brethren Legion mean nothing to you?'

'I only thought to–'

'Did I ask for your counsel? Are you a lord commander, and privy to the higher links of command?'

'No, lord.'

'Then get to it, captain. You too, Lucius. You men, assist them.'

THE LOCAL SHIELD-STORM had blown out. The sky over the wide clearing was surprisingly clear and pale, as if night was finally falling. Tarvitz had no idea of Murder's diurnal cycle. Since they had made planetfall, night and day periods must surely have passed, but in the stalk forests, lit by the storm flare, such changes had been imperceptible.

Now it seemed cooler, stiller. The sky was a washed-out beige, with filaments of darkness threading through it. There was no wind, and the flicker of sheet lightning came from many kilometres away. Tarvitz thought he could even glimpse stars up there, in the darker patches of the open sky.

He led his party out to the ruins of the trees. Lucius was grumbling, as if it was all Tarvitz's fault.

'Shut up,' Tarvitz told him on a closed channel. 'Consider this ample payback for your kiss-arse display to the lord commander.'

'What are you talking about?' Lucius asked.

'I told him it was a waste, lord,' Tarvitz answered, mimicking Lucius's words in an unflattering voice.

'I did tell you!'

'Yes, you did, but there's such a thing as solidarity. I thought we were friends.'

'We are friends,' Lucius said, hurt.

'And that was the act of a friend?'

'We are the Emperor's Children,' Lucius said solemnly. 'We seek perfection, we don't hide our mistakes. You made a mistake. Acknowledging our failures is another step on the road to perfection. Isn't that what our primarch teaches?'

Tarvitz frowned. Lucius was right. Primarch Fulgrim taught that only by imperfection could they fail the Emperor, and only by recognising those failures could they eradicate them. Tarvitz wished someone would remind Eidolon of that key tenet of their Legion's philosophy.

'I made a mistake,' Lucius admitted. 'I used that blade thing. I relished it. It was xenos. Lord Eidolon was right to reprimand me.'

'I told you it was xenos. Twice.'

'Yes, you did. I owe you an apology for that. You were right, Saul. I'm sorry.'

'Never mind.'

Lucius put his hand on Tarvitz's plated arm and stopped him.

'No, it's not. I'm a fine one to talk. You are always so grounded, Saul. I know I mock you for that. I'm sorry. I hope we're still friends.'

'Of course.'

'Your steadfast manner is a true virtue,' Lucius said. 'I become obsessive sometimes, in the heat of things. It is an imperfection of my character. Perhaps you can help me overcome it. Perhaps I can learn from you.' His voice had that childlike tone in it that had made Tarvitz like him in the first place. 'Besides,' Lucius added, 'you saved my life. I haven't thanked you for that.'

'No, you haven't, but there's no need, brother.'

'Then let's get this done, eh?'

The other men had waited while Tarvitz and Lucius conducted their private, vox-to-vox conversation. The pair hurried over to rejoin them.

The men Eidolon had picked to go with them were Bulle, Pherost, Lodoroton and Tykus, all men from Tarvitz's squad. Eidolon was so clearly punishing the troop, it wasn't funny. Tarvitz hated the fact that his men suffered because he was not in favour.

And Tarvitz had a feeling they weren't being punished for wasting charges. They were suffering Eidolon's opprobrium because they had achieved more of significance than either of the other groups since the drop.

They reached the ruined trees and crunched up the slopes of smouldering white slag. Remnants of stone thorns stuck out of the heap, like the antlers of bull deer, some blackened with charred scraps of flesh.

'What do we do?' asked Tykus.

Tarvitz sighed, and knelt down in the white spoil. He began to sift aside the chalky debris with his gloved hands. 'This,' he said.

✠ ✠ ✠

THEY WORKED FOR an hour or two. Some kind of night began to fall, and the air temperature dropped sharply as the light drained out of the sky. Stars came out, properly, and distant lightning played across the endless grass forests ringing the clearing.

Immense heat was issuing from the heart of the slag heap, and it made the cold air around them shimmer. They sifted the dusty slag piece by piece, and retrieved two battered shoulder plates, both Blood Angels issue, and an Imperial army cap.

'Is that enough?' asked Lodoroton.

'Keep going,' replied Tarvitz. He looked out across the dim clearing to where Eidolon's force was dug in. 'Another hour, maybe, and we'll stop.'

Lucius found a Blood Angels helmet. Part of the skull was still inside it. Tykus found a breastplate belonging to one of the lost Emperor's Children.

'Bring that too,' Tarvitz said.

Then Pherost found something that almost killed him.

It was one of the winged clades, burned and buried, but still alive. As Pherost pulled the calcified cinders away, the crumpled black thing, wingless and ruptured, reared up and stabbed at him with its hooked headcrest.

Pherost stumbled, fell, and slithered down the slag slope on his back. The clade struggled after him, dragging its damaged body, its broken wing bases vibrating pointlessly.

Tarvitz leapt over and slew it with his broadsword. It was so near death and dried out that its body crumpled like paper under his blade, and only a residual ichor, thick like glue, oozed out.

'All right?' Tarvitz asked.

'Just took me by surprise,' Pherost replied, laughing it off.

'Watch how you go,' Tarvitz warned the others.

'Do you hear that?' asked Lucius.

It had become very still and dark, like a true and proper night

fall. Amping their helmet acoustics, they could all hear the chittering noise Lucius had detected. In the edges of the thickets,
starlight flashed off busy metallic forms.

'They're back,' said Lucius, looking round at Tarvitz.

'Tarvitz to main party,' Tarvitz voxed. 'Hostile contact in the
edges of the forest.'

'We see it, captain,' Eidolon responded immediately. 'Hold your
position until we–'

The link cut off abruptly, like it was being jammed.

'We should go back,' Lucius said.

'Yes,' Tarvitz agreed.

A sudden light and noise made them all start. The main party,
half a kilometre away, had opened fire. Across the distance, they
heard and saw bolters drumming and flashing in the darkness.
Distant zinc-grey forms danced and jittered in the strobing light
of the gunfire.

Eidolon's position had been attacked.

'Come on!' Lucius cried.

'And do what?' Tarvitz asked. 'Wait! Look!'

The six of them scrambled down into cover on one side of the
spoil heap. Megarachnid were approaching from the edges of the
forest, their marching grey forms almost invisible except where
they caught the starlight and the distant blink of lightning. They
were streaming towards the tree mound in their hundreds, in
neat, ordered lines. Amongst them, there were other shapes, big-
ger shapes, massive megarachnid forms. Another clade variant.

Tarvitz's party slid down the chalky rubble and backed away
into the open, the expanse of the clearing behind them, keeping
low. To their right, Lord Eidolon's position was engulfed in loud,
furious combat.

'What are they doing?' asked Bulle.

'Look,' said Tarvitz.

The columns of megarachnid ascended the heap of rubble. Warrior forms, equipped with quad-blades, took station around the base, on guard. Others mounted the slopes and began to sort the spoil, clearing it with inhuman speed and efficiency. Tarvitz saw warrior forms doing this work, and also clades of a similar design, but which possessed spatulate shovel limbs in place of blades. With minute precision, the megarachnid began to disassemble the rubble heap, and carry the loose debris away into the thickets. They formed long, mechanical work gangs to do this. The more massive forms, the clades Tarvitz had not seen before, came forwards. They were superheavy monsters with short, thick legs and gigantic abdomens. They moved ponderously, and began to gnaw and suck on the loose rubble with ghastly, oversized mouth-parts. The smaller clades scurried around their hefty forms, pulling skeins of white matter from their abdominal spinnerets with curiously dainty, weaving motions of their upper limbs. The smaller clades carried this fibrous, stiffening matter back into the increasingly cleared site and began to plaster it together.

'They're rebuilding the trees,' Bulle whispered.

It was an extraordinary sight. The massive clades, weavers, were consuming the broken scraps of the trees Tarvitz had felled, and turning them into fresh new material, like gelling concrete. The smaller clades, busy and scurrying, were taking the material and forming new bases with it in the space that others of their kind had cleared.

In less than ten minutes, much of the area had been picked clean, and the trunks of three new trees were being formed. The scurrying builders brought limb-loads of wet, milk white matter to the bases, and then regurgitated fluid onto them so as to mix them as cement. Their limbs whirred and shaped like the trowels of master builders.

Still, the battle behind them roared. Lucius kept glancing in the direction of the fight.

'We should go back,' he whispered. 'Lord Eidolon needs us.'

'If he can't win without the six of us,' Tarvitz said, 'he can't win. I felled these trees. I'll not see them built again. Who's with me?'

Bulle answered 'Aye.' So did Pherost, Lodoroton and Tykus.

'Very well,' said Lucius. 'What do we do?'

But Tarvitz had already drawn his broadsword and was charging the megarachnid workers.

THE FIGHT THAT followed was simple insanity. The six Astartes, blades out, bolters ready, rushed the megarachnid work gangs and made war upon them in the cold night air. Picket clades, warrior forms drawn up as sentinels around the edge of the site, alerted to them first and rushed out in defence. Lucius and Bulle met them and slaughtered them, and Tarvitz and Tykus ploughed on into the main site to confront the industrious builder forms. Pherost and Lodoroton followed them, firing wide to fend off flank strikes.

Tarvitz attacked one of the monster 'weaver' forms, one of the builder clades, and split its massive belly wide open with his sword. Molten cement poured out like pus, and it began to claw at the sky with its short, heavy limbs. Warrior forms leapt over its stricken mass to attack the Imperials. Tykus shot two out of the air and then decapitated a third as it pounced on him. The megarachnid were everywhere, milling like ants.

Lodoroton had slain eight of them, including another monster clade, when a warrior form bit off his head. As if unsatisfied with that, the warrior form proceeded to flense Lodoroton's body apart with its four limb-blades. Blood and meat particles spumed into the cold air. Bulle shot the warrior clade dead with a single bolt round. It dropped on its face.

Lucius hacked his way through the outer guards, which were closing on him in ever increasing numbers. He swung his sword, no longer playing, no longer toying. This was test enough.

He'd killed sixteen megarachnid by the time they got him. A clade with spatulate limbs, bearing a cargo of wet milky cement, fell apart under his sword strokes, and dying, dumped its payload on him. Lucius fell, his arms and legs glued together by the wet load. He tried to break free, but the organic mulch began to thicken and solidify. A warrior clade pounced on him and made to skewer him with its four blade arms.

Tarvitz shot it in the side of the body and knocked it away. He stood over Lucius to protect him from the xenos scum. Bulle came to his side, shooting and chopping. Pherost fought his way to join them, but fell as a limb-blade punched clean through his torso from behind. Tykus backed up close. The three remaining Emperor's Children blazed and sliced away at the enclosing foe. At their feet, Lucius struggled to free himself and get up.

'Get this off me, Saul!' he yelled.

Tarvitz wanted to. He wanted to be able to turn and hack free his stricken friend, but there was no space. No time. The megarachnid warrior clades were all over them now, chittering and slashing. If he broke off even for a moment, he would be dead.

Thunder boomed in the clear night sky. Caught up in the fierce warfare, Tarvitz paid it no heed. Just the shield-storm returning.

But it wasn't.

Meteors were dropping out of the sky into the clearing around them, impacting hard and super-hot in the red dirt, like lightning strikes. Two, four, a dozen, twenty.

Drop pods.

The noise of fresh fire rang out above the din of the fight. Bolters boomed. Plasma weapons shrieked. The drop pods kept falling like bombs.

'Look!' Bulle cried out. 'Look!'

The megarachnid were swarming over them. Tarvitz had lost his bolter and could barely swing his broadsword, such was the density of enemies upon him. He felt himself slowly being borne over by sheer weight of numbers.

'–hear me?' The vox squealed suddenly.

'W-what? Say again!'

'I said, we are Imperial! Do we have brothers in there?'

'Yes, in the name of Terra–'

An explosion. A series of rapid gunshots. A shockwave rocked through the enemy masses.

'Follow me in,' a voice was yelling, commanding and deep. 'Follow me in and drive them back!'

More searing explosions. Grey bodies blew apart in gouts of flame, spinning broken limbs into the air like matchwood. One whizzing limb smacked into Tarvitz's visor and knocked him onto his back. The world, scarlet and concussed, spun for a second.

A hand reached down towards Tarvitz. It swam into his field of view. It was an Astartes gauntlet. White, with black edging.

'Up you come, brother.'

Tarvitz grabbed at it and felt himself hauled upright.

'My thanks,' he yelled, mayhem still raging all around him. 'Who are you?'

'My name is Tarik, brother,' said his saviour. 'Pleased to meet you.'

FIVE

Informal formalities
The war dogs' rebuke
I can't say

IT WAS A little cruel, in Loken's opinion. Someone, somewhere – and Loken suspected the scheming of Maloghurst – had omitted to tell the officers of the 140th Expedition Fleet exactly who they were about to welcome on board.

The *Vengeful Spirit*, and its attendant fleet consorts, had drawn up majestically into high anchorage alongside the vessels of the 140th and the other ships that had come to the expedition's aid, and an armoured heavy shuttle had transferred from the flagship to the battle-barge *Misericord*.

Mathanual August and his coterie of commanders, including Eidolon's equerry Eshkerrus, had assembled on one of the *Misericord's* main embarkation decks to greet the shuttle. They knew it was bearing the commanders of the relief task force from the 63rd Expedition, and that inevitably meant officers of the XVI Legion. With the possible exception of Eshkerrus, they were all nervous. The arrival of the Luna Wolves, the most famed and feared of all Astartes divisions, was enough to tension any man's nerve strings.

DAN ABNETT

When the shuttle's landing ramp extended and ten Luna Wolves descended through the clearing vapour, there had been silence, and that silence had turned to stifled gasps when it became apparent these were not the ten brothers of a captain's ceremonial detail, but ten captains themselves in full, formal wargear.

The first captain led the party, and made the sign of the aquila to Mathanual August.

'I am–' he began.

'I know who you are, lord,' August said, and bowed deeply, trembling. There were few in the Imperium who didn't recognise or fear First Captain Abaddon. 'I welcome you and–'

'Hush, master,' Abaddon said. 'We're not there yet.'

August looked up, not really understanding. Abaddon stepped back into his place, and the ten, cloaked captains, five on each side of the landing ramp, formed an honour guard and snapped to attention, visors front and hands on the pommels of their sheathed swords.

The Warmaster emerged from the shuttle. Everyone, apart from the ten captains and Mathanual August, immediately prostrated themselves on the deck.

The Warmaster stepped slowly down the ramp. His very presence was enough to inspire total and unreserved attention, but he was, quite calculatedly, doing the one thing that made matters even worse. He wasn't smiling.

August stood before him, his eyes wide open, his mouth opening and closing wordlessly, like a beached fish.

Eshkerrus, who had himself gone quite green, glanced up and yanked at the hem of August's robes. 'Abase yourself, fool!' he hissed.

August couldn't. Loken doubted the veteran fleet master could have even recalled his own name at that moment. Horus came to a halt, towering over him.

'Sir, will you not bow?' Horus inquired.

When August finally replied, his voice was a tiny, embryonic thing. 'I can't,' he said. 'I can't remember how.'

Then, once again, the Warmaster showed his limitless genius for leadership. He sank to one knee and bowed to Mathanual August.

'I have come, as fast as I was able, to help you, sir,' he said. He clasped August in an embrace. The Warmaster was smiling now. 'I like a man who's proud enough not to bend his knees to me,' he said.

'I would have bent them if I had been able, my lord,' August said. Already August was calmer, gratefully put at his ease by the War-master's informality.

'Forgive me, Mathanual... may I call you Mathanual? *Master* is so stiff. Forgive me for not informing you that I was coming in person. I detest pomp and ceremony, and if you'd known I was coming, you'd have gone to unnecessary lengths. Soldiers in dress regs, ceremonial bands, bunting. I particularly despise bunting.'

Mathanual August laughed. Horus rose to his feet and looked around at the prone figures covering the wide deck. 'Rise, please. Please. Get to your feet. A cheer or a round of applause will do me, not this futile grovelling.'

The fleet officers rose, cheering *and* applauding. He'd won them over. Just like that, thought Loken, he'd won them over. They were his now, forever.

Horus moved forwards to greet the officers and commanders individually. Loken noticed Eshkerrus, in his purple and gold robes and half-armour, taking his greeting with a bow. There was something sour about the equerry, Loken thought. Something definitely put out.

'Helms!' Abaddon ordered, and the company commanders

removed their helmets. They moved forwards, more casually now, to escort their commander through the press of applauding figures.

Horus whispered an aside to Abaddon as he took greeting kisses and bows from the assembly. Abaddon nodded. He touched his link, activating the privy channel, and spoke, in Cthonic, to the other three members of the Mournival. 'War council in thirty minutes. Be ready to play your parts.'

The other three knew what that meant. They followed Abaddon into the greeting crowd.

THEY ASSEMBLED FOR council in the strategium of the *Misericord*, a massive rotunda situated behind the barge's main bridge. The Warmaster took the seat at the head of the long table, and the Mournival sat down with him, along with August, Eshkerrus and nine senior ship commanders and army officers. The other Luna Wolf captains sat amongst the crowds of lesser fleet officers filling the tiered seating in the panelled galleries above them.

Master August called up hololithic displays to illuminate his succinct recap of the situation. Horus regarded each one in turn, twice asking August to go back so he could study details again.

'So you poured everything you had into this death trap?' Torgaddon began bluntly, once August had finished.

August recoiled, as if slapped. 'Sir, I did as–'

The Warmaster raised his hand. 'Tarik, too much, too stern. Master August was simply doing as Captain Frome told him.'

'My apologies, lord,' Torgaddon said. 'I withdraw the comment.'

'I don't believe Tarik should have to,' Abaddon cut in. 'This was a monumental misuse of manpower. Three companies? Not to mention the army units...'

'It wouldn't have happened under my watch,' murmured Torgaddon. August blinked his eyes very fast. He looked like he was attempting not to tear up.

'It's unforgivable,' said Aximand. 'Simply unforgivable.'

'We will forgive him, even so,' Horus said.

'Should we, lord?' asked Loken.

'I've shot men for less,' said Abaddon.

'Please,' August said, pale, rising to his feet. 'I deserve punishment. I implore you to—'

'He's not worth the bolt,' muttered Aximand.

'Enough,' Horus smoothed. 'Mathanual made a mistake, a command mistake. Didn't you, Mathanual?'

'I believe I did, sir.'

'He drip-fed his expedition's forces into a danger zone until they were all gone,' said Horus. 'It's tragic. It happens sometimes. We're here now, that's all that matters. Here to rectify the problem.'

'What of the Emperor's Children?' Loken put in. 'Did they not even consider waiting?'

'For what, exactly?' asked Eshkerrus.

'For us,' smiled Aximand.

'An entire expedition was in jeopardy,' replied Eshkerrus, his eyes narrowing. 'We were first on scene. A critical response. We owed it to our Blood Angels brothers to—'

'To what? Die too?' Torgaddon asked.

'Three companies of Blood Angels were—' Eshkerrus exclaimed.

'Probably dead already,' Aximand interrupted. 'They'd showed you the trap was there. Did you just think you'd walk into it too?'

'We—' Eshkerrus began.

'Or was Lord Eidolon simply hungry for glory?' asked Torgaddon.

Eshkerrus rose to his feet. He glared across the table at Torgaddon. 'Captain, you offend the honour of the Emperor's Children.'

'That may indeed be what I'm doing, yes,' Torgaddon replied.

'Then, sir, you are a base and low-born—'

'Equerry Eshkerrus,' Loken said. 'None of us like Torgaddon

much, except when he is speaking the truth. Right now, I like
him a great deal.'

'That's enough, Garviel,' Horus said quietly. 'Enough, all of you.
Sit down, equerry. My Luna Wolves speak harshly because they
are dismayed at this situation. An Imperial defeat. Companies
lost. An implacable foe. This saddens me, and it will sadden the
Emperor too, when he hears of it.'

Horus rose. 'My report to him will say this. Captain Frome was
right to assault this world, for it is clearly a nest of xenos filth.
We applaud his courage. Master August was right to support the
captain, even though it meant he spent the bulk of his military
formation. Lord Commander Eidolon was right to engage, without support, for to do otherwise would have been cowardly when
lives were at stake. I would also like to thank all those commanders who rerouted here to offer assistance. From this point on, we
will handle it.'

'How will you handle it, lord?' Eshkerrus asked boldly.

'Will you attack?' asked August.

'We will consider our options and inform you presently. That's
all.'

The officers filed out of the strategium, along with Sedirae,
Marr, Moy, Goshen, Targost and Qruze, leaving the Warmaster
alone with the Mournival.

Once they were alone, Horus looked at the four of them.
'Thank you, friends. Well played.'

Loken was fast learning both how the Warmaster liked to
employ the Mournival as a political weapon, and what a masterful political animal the Warmaster was. Aximand had quietly
briefed Loken on what would be required of him just before they
boarded the shuttle on the *Vengeful Spirit*. 'The situation here is
a mess, and the commander believes that mess has in part been
caused by incompetence and mistakes at command level. He

wants all the officers reprimanded, rebuked so hard they smart with shame, but… if he's going to pull the 140th Expedition back together again and make it viable, he needs their admiration, their respect and their unswerving loyalty. None of which he will have if he marches in and starts throwing his weight around.'

'So the Mournival does the rebuking for him?'

'Just so,' Aximand had smiled. 'The Luna Wolves are feared anyway, so let them fear us. Let them hate us. We'll be the mouthpiece of discontent and rancour. All accusations must come from us. Play the part, speak as bluntly and critically as you like. Make them squirm in discomfort. They'll get the message, but at the same time, the Warmaster will be seen as a benign conciliator.'

'We're his war dogs?'

'So he doesn't have to growl himself. Exactly. He wants us to give them hell, a dressing down they'll remember and learn from. That allows him to seem the peacemaker. To remain beloved, adored, a voice of reason and calm. By the end, if we do things properly, they'll all feel suitably admonished, and simultaneously they'll all love the Warmaster for showing mercy and calling us off. Everyone thinks the Warmaster's keenest talent is as a warrior. No one expects him to be a consummate politician. Watch him and learn, Garvi. Learn why the Emperor chose him as his proxy.'

'Well played indeed,' Horus said to the Mournival with a smile. 'Garviel, that last comment was deliciously barbed. Eshkerrus was quite incandescent.'

Loken nodded. 'From the moment I laid eyes on him, he struck me as man eager to cover his arse. He knew mistakes had been made.'

'Yes, he did,' Horus said. 'Just don't expect to find many friends amongst the Emperor's Children for a while. They are a proud bunch.'

Loken shrugged. 'I have all the friends I need, sir,' he said.

'August, Eshkerrus and a dozen others may, of course, be formally cautioned and charged with incompetence once this is done,' Horus said lightly, 'but only once this is done. Now, morale is crucial. Now we have a war to design.'

IT WAS ABOUT half an hour later when August summoned them to the bridge. A sudden and unexpected hole had appeared in the shield-storms of One Forty Twenty, an abrupt break in the fury, and quite close to the supposed landing vectors of the Emperor's Children.

'At last,' said August, 'a gap in that storm.'

'Would that I had Astartes to drop into it,' Eshkerrus muttered to himself.

'But you don't, do you?' Aximand remarked snidely. Eshkerrus glowered at Little Horus.

'Let's go in,' Torgaddon urged the Warmaster. 'Another hole might be a long time coming.'

'The storm might close in again,' Horus said, pointing to the radiating cyclonics on the lith.

'You want this world, don't you?' said Torgaddon. 'Let me take the speartip down.' The lots had already been drawn. The spear-tip was to be Torgaddon's company, along with the companies of Sedirae, Moy and Targost.

'Orbital bombardment,' Horus said, repeating what had already been decided as the best course of action.

'Men might yet live,' Torgaddon said.

The Warmaster stepped aside, and spoke quietly, in Cthonic, to the Mournival.

'If I authorise this, I echo August and Eidolon, and I've just had you take them to task for that very brand of rash mistake.'

'This is different,' Torgaddon replied. 'They went in blind, wave after wave. I'd not advocate duplicating that stupidity, but that break in the weather... it's the first they've detected in months.'

'If there are brothers still alive down there,' Little Horus said, 'they deserve one last chance to be found.'

'I'll go in,' said Torgaddon. 'See what I can find. Any sign that the weather is changing, I'll pull the speartip straight back out and we can open up the fleet batteries.'

'I still wonder about the music,' the Warmaster said. 'Anything on that?'

'The translators are still working,' Abaddon replied.

Horus looked at Torgaddon. 'I admire your compassion, Tarik, but the answer is a firm no. I'm not going to repeat the errors that have already been made and pour men into–'

'Lord?' August had come over to them again, and held out a data-slate.

Horus took it and read it.

'Is this confirmed?'

'Yes, Warmaster.'

Horus regarded the Mournival. 'The Master of Vox has detected trace vox traffic on the surface, in the area of the storm break. It does not respond or recognise our signals, but it is active. Imperial. It looks like squad to squad, or brother to brother transmissions.'

'There are men still alive,' said Abaddon. He seemed genuinely relieved. 'Great Terra and the Emperor! There are men still alive down there.'

Torgaddon stared at the Warmaster steadily and said nothing. He'd already said it.

'Very well,' said Horus to Torgaddon. 'Go.'

THE DROP PODS were arranged down the length of the *Vengeful Spirit*'s fifth embarkation deck in their launch racks, and the warriors of the speartip were locking themselves into place. Lid doors, like armoured petals, were closing around them, so the drop-pods resembled toughened, black seed cases ready for autumn. Klaxons sounded, and the firing coils of the launchers were beginning to charge. They made a harsh, rising whine and a stink of ozone smouldered like incense in the deck air.

The Warmaster stood at the side of the vast deck space, watching the hurried preparations, his arms folded across his chest.

'Climate update?' he snapped.

'No change in the weather break, my lord,' Maloghurst replied, consulting his slate.

'How long's it been now?' Horus asked.

'Eighty-nine minutes.'

'They've done a good job pulling this together in such a short time,' Horus said. 'Ezekyle, commend the unit officers, please. Make it known I'm proud of them.'

Abaddon nodded. He held the papers of four oaths of moment in his armoured hands. 'Aximand?' he suggested.

Little Horus stepped forwards.

'Ezekyle?' Loken said. 'Could I?'

'You want to?'

'Luc and Serghar heard and witnessed mine before the Whisperheads. And Tarik is my friend.'

Abaddon looked sidelong at the Warmaster, who gave an almost imperceptible nod. Abaddon handed the parchments to Loken.

Loken strode out across the deck, Aximand at his side, and heard the four captains take their oaths. Little Horus held out the bolter on which the oaths were sworn.

When it was done, Loken handed the oath papers to each of them.

'Be well,' he said to them, 'and commend your unit commanders. The Warmaster personally admired their work today.'

Verulam Moy made the sign of the aquila. 'My thanks, Captain Loken,' he said, and walked away towards his pod, shouting for his unit seconds.

Serghar Targost smiled at Loken, and clasped his fist, thumb around thumb. By his side, Luc Sedirae grinned with his ever half-open mouth, his eyes a murderous blue, eager for war.

'If I don't see you next on this deck...' Sedirae began.

'...let it be at the Emperor's side,' Loken finished.

Sedirae laughed and ran, whooping, towards his pod. Targost locked on his helm and strode away in the opposite direction.

'Luc's blood is up,' Loken said to Torgaddon. 'How's yours?'

'My humours are all where they should be,' Torgaddon replied. He hugged Loken, with a clatter of plate, and then did the same to Aximand.

'Lupercal!' he bellowed, punching the air with his fist, and turned away, running to his waiting drop pod.

'Lupercal!' Loken and Aximand shouted after him.

The pair turned and walked back to join Abaddon, Maloghurst and the Warmaster.

'I'm always a little jealous,' Little Horus muttered to Loken as they crossed the deck.

'Me too.'

'I always want it to be me.'

'I know.'

'Going into something like that.'

'I know. And I'm always just a little afraid.'

'Of what, Garviel?'

'That we won't see them again.'

'We will.'

'How can you be so sure, Horus?' Loken wondered.

'I can't say,' replied Aximand, with a deliberate irony that made Loken laugh.

The observing party withdrew behind the blast shields. A sudden, volatile pressure change announced the opening of the deck's void fields. The firing coils accelerated to maximum charge, shrieking with pent up energy.

'The word is given,' Abaddon instructed above the uproar.

One by one, each with a concussive bang, the drop pods fired down through the deck slots like bullets. It was like the ripple of a full broadside firing. The embarkation deck shuddered as the drop pods ejected free.

Then they were all gone, and the deck was suddenly quiet, and tiny armoured pellets, cocooned in teardrops of blue fire, sank away towards the planet's surface.

I CAN'T SAY.

The phrase had haunted Loken since the sixth week of the voyage to Murder. Since he had gone with Little Horus to the lodge meeting.

The meeting place had been one of the aft holds of the flagship, a lonely, forgotten pocket of the ship's superstructure. Down in the dark, the way had been lit by tapers.

Loken had come in simple robes, as Aximand had instructed him. They'd met on the fourth midships deck, and taken the rail carriage back to the aft quarters before descending via dark service stairwells.

'Relax,' Aximand kept telling him.

Loken couldn't. He'd never liked the idea of the lodges, and the discovery that Jubal had been a member had increased his disquiet.

'This isn't what you think it is,' Aximand had said.

And what did he think it was? A forbidden conclave. A cult of the Lectitio Divinitatus. Or worse. A terrible assembly. A worm in the bud. A cancer at the heart of the Legion.

As he walked down the dim, metal deckways, part of him hoped that what awaited him would be infernal. A coven. Proof that Jubal had already been tainted by some manufacture of the warp before the Whisperheads. Proof that would reveal a source of evil to Loken that he could finally strike back at in open retribution, but the greater part of him willed it to be otherwise. Little Horus Aximand was party to this meeting. If it was tainted, then Aximand's presence meant that taint ran profoundly deep. Loken didn't want to have to go head to head with Aximand. If what he feared was true, then in the next few minutes he might have to fight and kill his Mournival brother.

'Who approaches?' asked a voice from the darkness. Loken saw a figure, evidently an Astartes by his build, shrouded in a hooded cloak.

'Two souls,' Aximand replied.

'What are your names?' the figure asked.

'I can't say.'

'Pass, friends.'

They entered the aft hold. Loken hesitated. The vast, scaffold-framed area was eerily lit by candles and a vigorous fire in a metal canister. Dozens of hooded figures stood around. The dancing light made weird shadows of the deep hold's structural architecture.

'A new friend comes,' Aximand announced.

The hooded figures turned. 'Let him show the sign,' said one of them in a voice that seemed familiar.

'Show it,' Aximand whispered to Loken.

Loken slowly held out the medal Aximand had given him. It glinted in the fire light. Inside his robe, his other hand clasped the grip of the combat knife he had concealed.

'Let him be revealed,' a voice said.

Aximand reached over and drew Loken's hood down.

'Welcome, brother warrior,' the others said as one.

Aximand pulled down his own hood. 'I speak for him,' he said.

'Your voice is noted. Is he come of his own free will?'

'He is come because I invited him.'

'No more secrecy,' the voice said.

The figures removed their hoods and showed their faces in the glow of the candles. Loken blinked.

There was Torgaddon, Luc Sedirae, Nero Vipus, Kalus Ekaddon, Verulam Moy and two dozen other senior and junior Astartes.

And Serghar Targost, the hidden voice. Evidently the lodge master.

'You'll not need the blade,' Targost said gently, stepping forwards and holding out his hand for it. 'You are free to leave at any time, unmolested. May I take it from you? Weapons are not permitted within the bounds of our meetings.'

Loken took out the combat knife and passed it to Targost. The lodge master placed it on a wall strut, out of the way.

Loken continued to look from one face to another. This wasn't like anything he had expected.

'Tarik?'

'We'll answer any question, Garviel,' Torgaddon said. 'That's why we brought you here.'

'We'd like you to join us,' said Aximand, 'but if you choose not to, we will respect that too. All we ask, either way, is that you say nothing about what and who you see here to anyone outside.'

Loken hesitated. 'Or... '

'It's not a threat,' said Aximand. 'Nor even a condition. Simply a request that you respect our privacy.'

'We've known for a long time,' Targost said, 'that you have no interest in the warrior lodge.'

'I'd perhaps have put it more strongly than that,' said Loken.

Targost shrugged. 'We understand the nature of your opposition.

You're far from being the only Astartes to feel that way. That is why we've never made any attempt to induct you.'

'What's changed?' asked Loken.

'You have,' said Aximand. 'You're not just a company officer now, but a Mournival lord. And the fact of the lodge has come to your attention.'

'Jubal's medal…' said Loken.

'Jubal's medal,' nodded Aximand. 'Jubal's death was a terrible thing, which we all mourn, but it affected you more than anyone. We see how you strive to make amends, to whip your company into tighter and finer form, as you blame yourself. When the medal turned up, we were concerned that you might start to make waves. That you might start asking open questions about the lodge.'

'So this is self-interest?' Loken asked. 'You thought you'd gang up on me and force me into silence?'

'Garviel,' said Luc Sedirae, 'the last thing the Luna Wolves need is an honest and respected captain, a member of the Mournival no less, campaigning to expose the lodge. It would damage the entire Legion.'

'Really?'

'Of course,' said Sedirae. 'The agitations of a man like you would force the Warmaster to act.'

'And he doesn't want to do that,' Torgaddon said.

'He… knows?' Loken asked.

'You seemed shocked,' said Aximand. 'Wouldn't you be more shocked to learn the Warmaster *didn't* know about the quiet order within his Legion? He knows. He's always known, and he turns a blind eye, provided we remain closed and confidential in our activities.'

'I don't understand…' Loken said.

'That's why you're here,' said Moy. 'You speak out against us because you don't understand. If you wish to oppose what we do, then at least do so from an informed position.'

'I've heard enough,' said Loken, turning away. 'I'll leave now. Don't worry, I'll say nothing. I'll make no waves, but I'm disappointed in you all. Someone can return my blade to me tomorrow.'

'Please,' Aximand began.

'No, Horus! You meet in secret, and secrecy is the enemy of truth. So we are taught! Truth is everything we have! You hide yourselves, you conceal your identities... for what? Because you are ashamed? Hell's teeth, you should be! The Emperor himself, beloved by all, has ruled on this. He does not sanction this kind of activity!'

'Because he doesn't understand!' Torgaddon exclaimed.

Loken turned back and strode across the chamber until he was nose to nose with Torgaddon. 'I can hardly believe I heard you say that,' he snarled.

'It's true,' said Torgaddon, not backing down. 'The Emperor isn't a god, but he might as well be. He's so far removed from the rest of mankind. Unique. Singular. Who does he call brother? No one! Even the blessed primarchs are only sons to him. The Emperor is wise beyond all measure, and we love him and would follow him until the crack of doom, but he doesn't understand brotherhood, and that is *all* we meet for.'

There was silence for a moment. Loken turned away from Torgaddon, unwilling to look upon his face. The others stood in a ring around them.

'We are warriors,' said Targost. 'That is all we know and all we do. Duty and war, war and duty. Thus it has been since we were created. The only bond we have that is not prescribed by duty is that of brotherhood.'

'That is the purpose of the lodge,' said Sedirae. 'To be a place where we are free to meet and converse and confide, outside the strictures of rank and martial order. There is only one qualification a man needs to be a part of our quiet order. He must be a warrior.'

'In this company,' said Targost, 'a man of any rank can meet and speak openly of his troubles, his doubts, his ideas, his dreams, without fear of scorn, or monition from a commanding officer. This is a sanctuary for our spirit as men.'

'Look around,' Aximand invited, stepping forwards, gesturing with his hands. 'Look at these faces, Garviel. Company captains, sergeants, file warriors. Where else could such a mix of men meet as equals? We leave our ranks at the door when we come in. Here, a senior commander can talk with a junior initiate, man to man. Here, knowledge and experience is passed on, ideas are circulated, commonalities discovered. Serghar holds the office of lodge master only so that a function of order may be maintained.'

Targost nodded. 'Horus is right. Garviel, do you know how old the quiet order is?'

'Decades…'

'No, older. Perhaps thousands of years older. There have been lodges in the Legions since their inception, and allied orders in the army and all other branches of the martial divisions. The lodge can be traced back into antiquity, before even the Unification Wars. It's not a cult, nor a religious obscenity. Just a fraternity of warriors. Some Legions do not practise the habit. Some do. Ours always has done. It lends us strength.'

'How?' asked Loken.

'By connecting warriors otherwise divorced by rank or station. It makes bonds between men who would otherwise not even know one another's name. We thrive, like all Legions, from our firm hierarchy of formal authority, the loyalty that flows down from a commander through to his lowest soldier. Loyal to a squad, to a section, to a company. The lodge reinforces complementary links *across* that structure, from squad to squad, company to company. It could be said to be our secret weapon. It is the true strength of the Luna Wolves, strapping us together, side to side, where we are already bound up top to toe.'

'You have a dozen spears to carry into war,' said Torgaddon quietly. 'You gather them, shaft to shaft, as a bundle, so they are easier to bear. How much easier is that bundle to carry if it is tied together around the shafts?'

'If that was a metaphor,' Loken said, 'it was lousy.'

'Let me speak,' said another man. It was Kalus Ekaddon. He stepped forwards to face Loken.

'There's been bad blood between us, Loken,' he said bluntly.

'There has.'

'A little matter of rivalry on the field. I admit it. After the High City fight, I hated your guts. So, in the field, though we served the same master and followed the same standard, there'd always be friction between us. Competition. Am I right?'

'I suppose…'

'I've never spoken to you,' Ekaddon said. 'Never, informally. We don't meet or mix. But I tell you this much: I've heard you tonight, in this place, amongst friends. I've heard you stand up for your beliefs and your point of view, and I've learned respect for you. You speak your mind. You have principles. Tomorrow, Loken, no matter what you decide tonight, I'll see you in a new light. You'll not get any grief from me any more, because I know you now. I've seen you as the man you are.' He laughed, raw and loud. 'Terra, it's a crude example, Loken, for I'm a crude fellow, but it shows what the lodge can do.'

He held out his hand. After a moment, Loken took it.

'There's a thing at least,' said Ekaddon. 'Now get on, if you're going. We've talking and drinking to do.'

'Or will you stay?' asked Torgaddon.

'For now, perhaps,' said Loken.

THE MEETING LASTED for two hours. Torgaddon had brought wine, and Sedirae produced some meat and bread from the flagship's commissary. There were no crude rituals or daemonic practices to observe. The men – the brothers – sat around and talked in small groups, then listened as Aximand recounted the details of a xenos war that he had participated in, which he hoped might give them insight into the fight ahead. Afterwards, Torgaddon told some jokes, most of them bad.

As Torgaddon rambled on with a particularly involved and vulgar tale, Aximand came over to Loken.

'Where do you suppose,' he began quietly, 'the notion of the Mournival came from?'

'From this?' Loken asked.

Aximand nodded. 'The Mournival has no legitimate standing or powers. It's simply an informal organ, but the Warmaster would not be without it. It was created originally as a visible extension of the invisible lodge, though that link has long since gone. They're both informal bodies interlaced into the very formal structures of our lives. For the benefit of all, I believe.'

'I imagined so many horrors about the lodge,' said Loken.

'I know. All part of that straight up and down thing you do so well, Garvi. It's why we love you. And the lodge would like to embrace you.'

'Will there be formal vows? All the theatrical rigmarole of the Mournival?'

Aximand laughed. 'No! If you're in, you're in. There are only very simple rules. You don't talk about what passes between us here to any not of the lodge. This is downtime. Free time. The men, especially the junior ranks, need to be confident they can speak freely without any comeback. You should hear what some of them say.'

'I think I might like to.'

'That's good. You'll be given a medal to carry, just as a token. And if anyone asks you about any lodge confidence, the answer is "I can't say". There's nothing else really.'

'I've misjudged this thing,' Loken said. 'I made it quite a daemon in my head, imagining the worst.'

'I understand. Particularly given the matter of poor Jubal. And given your own staunch character.'

'Am I… to replace Jubal?'

'It's not a matter of replacement,' Little Horus said, 'and anyway, no. Jubal was a member, though he hadn't attended any meetings in years. That's why we forgot to palm away his medal before your inspection. There's your danger sign, Garvi. Not that Jubal was a member, but that he was a member and had seldom attended. We didn't know what was going on in his head. If he'd come to us and shared, we might have pre-empted the horror you endured at the Whisperheads.'

'But you told me I was to replace someone,' Loken said.

'Yes. Udon. We miss him.'

'Udon was a lodge member?'

Aximand nodded. 'A long-time brother, and, by the way, go easy on Vipus.'

Loken went over to where Nero Vipus was sitting, beside the canister fire. The lively yellow flames jumped into the dark air and sent stray sparks oscillating away into the black. Vipus looked uncomfortable, toying with the heal-seam of his new hand.

'Nero?'

'Garviel. I was bracing myself for this.'

'Why?'

'Because you... because you didn't want anyone in your command to...'

'As I understand it,' Loken said, 'and forgive me if I'm wrong, because I'm new to this, but as I understand it, the lodge is a place for free speech and openness. Not discomfort.'

Nero smiled and nodded. 'I was a member of the lodge long before I came into your command. I respected your wishes, but I couldn't leave the brotherhood. I kept it hidden. Sometimes, I thought about asking you to join, but I knew you'd hate me for it.'

'You're the best friend I have,' Loken said. 'I couldn't hate you for anything.'

'The medal though. Jubal's medal. When you found it, you wouldn't let the matter go.'

'And all you said was "I can't say". Spoken like a true lodge member.'

Nero sniggered.

'By the way,' Loken said. 'It was you, wasn't it?'

'What?'

'Who took Jubal's medal.'

'I told Captain Aximand about your interest, just so he knew, but no, Garvi. I didn't take the medal.'

WHEN THE MEETING closed, Loken walked away along one of the vast service tunnels that ran the length of the ship's bilges. Water dripped from the rusted roof, and oil rainbows shone on the dirty lakes across the deck.

Torgaddon ran to catch up with him.

'Well?' he asked.

'I was surprised to see you there,' said Loken.

'I was surprised to see you there,' Torgaddon replied. 'A starch-arse like you?'

Loken laughed. Torgaddon ran ahead and leapt up to slap his palm against a pipe high overhead. He landed with a splash.

Loken chuckled, shook his head, and did the same, slapping higher than Torgaddon had managed.

The pipe clang echoed away from them down the tunnel.

'Under the engineerium,' Torgaddon said, 'the ducts are twice as high, but I can touch them.'

'You lie.'

'I'll prove it.'

'We'll see.'

They walked on for a while. Torgaddon whistled the Legion March loudly and tunelessly.

'Nothing to say?' he asked at length.

'About what?'

'Well, about that.'

'I was misinformed. I understand better now.'

'And?'

Loken stopped and looked at Torgaddon. 'I have only one worry,' he said. 'The lodge meets in secret, so, logically, it is good at keeping itself secret. I have a problem with secrets.'

'Which is?'

'If you get good at keeping them, who knows what kind you'll end up keeping.'

Torgaddon maintained a straight face for as long as possible and then exploded in laughter. 'No good,' he spluttered. 'I can't help it. You're so straight up and down.'

Loken smiled, but his voice was serious. 'So you keep telling me, but I mean it, Tarik. The lodge hides itself so well. It's become used to hiding things. Imagine what it could hide if it wanted to.'

'The fact that you're a starch-arse?' Torgaddon asked.

'I think that's common knowledge.'

'It is. It so is!' Torgaddon chuckled. He paused. 'So... will you attend again?'

'I can't say,' Loken replied.

SIX

Chosen instrument
Rare picts
The Emperor protects

FOUR FULL COMPANIES of the Luna Wolves had dropped into the clearing, and the megarachnid forces had perished beneath their rapacious onslaught, those that had not fled back into the shivering forests. A block of smoke, as black and vast as a mountainside, hung over the battlefield in the cold night air. Xenos bodies covered the ground, curled and shrivelled like metal shavings.

'Captain Torgaddon,' the Luna Wolf said, introducing himself formally and making the sign of the aquila.

'Captain Tarvitz,' Tarvitz responded. 'My thanks and respect for your intervention.'

'The honour's mine, Tarvitz,' Torgaddon said. He glanced around the smouldering field. 'Did you really assault here with only six men?'

'It was the only workable option in the circumstances,' Tarvitz replied.

Nearby, Bulle was freeing Lucius from the wad of megarachnid cement.

'Are you alive?' Torgaddon asked, looking over.

Lucius nodded sullenly, and set himself apart while he picked the scabs of cement off his perfect armour. Torgaddon regarded him for a moment, then turned his attention to the vox intel.

'How many with you?' Tarvitz asked.

'A speartip,' said Torgaddon. 'Four companies. A moment, please. Second Company, form up on me! Luc, secure the perimeter. Bring up the heavies. Serghar, cover the left flank! Verulam... I'm waiting! Front up the right wing.'

The vox crackled back.

'Who's the commander here?' a voice demanded.

'I am,' said Torgaddon, swinging round. Flanked by a dozen of the Emperor's Children, the tall, proud figure of Lord Eidolon crunched towards them across the fuming white slag.

'I am Eidolon,' he said, facing Torgaddon.

'Torgaddon.'

'Under the circumstances,' Eidolon said, 'I'll understand if you don't bow.'

'I can't for the life of me imagine any circumstances in which I would,' Torgaddon replied.

Eidolon's bodyguards wrenched out their combat blades.

'What did you say?' demanded one.

'I said you boys should put those pig sticks away before I hurt somebody with them.'

Eidolon raised his hand and the men sheathed their swords. 'I appreciate your intervention, Torgaddon, for the situation was grave. Also, I understand that the Luna Wolves are not bred like proper men, with proper manners. So I'll overlook your comment.'

'That's *Captain* Torgaddon,' Torgaddon replied. 'If I insulted you, in any way, let me assure you, I meant to.'

'Face to face with me,' Eidolon growled, and tore off his helm, forcing his genhanced biology to cope with the atmosphere and the radioactive wind. Torgaddon did the same. They stared into each other's eyes.

Tarvitz watched the confrontation in mounting disbelief. He'd never seen anyone stand up to Lord Eidolon.

The pair were chestplate to chestplate, Eidolon slightly taller. Torgaddon seemed to be smirking.

'How would you like this to go, Eidolon?' Torgaddon inquired. 'Would you, perhaps, like to go home with your head stuck up your arse?'

'You are a base-born cur,' Eidolon hissed.

'Just so you know,' replied Torgaddon, 'you'll have to do an awful lot better than that. I'm a base-born cur and proud of it. You know what that is?'

He pointed up at one of the stars above them.

'A star?' asked Eidolon, momentarily wrong-footed.

'Yes, probably. I haven't the faintest idea. The point is, I'm the designated commander of the Luna Wolves speartip, come to rescue your sorry backsides. I do this by warrant of the Warmaster himself. He's up there, in one of those stars, and right now he thinks you're a cretin. And he'll tell Fulgrim so, next time he meets him.'

'Do not speak my primarch's name so irreverently, you bastard. Horus will–'

'There you go again,' Torgaddon sighed, pushing Eidolon away from him with a two-handed shove to the lord's breastplate. 'He's the Warmaster.' Another shove. 'The Warmaster. *Your* Warmaster. Show some cursed respect.'

Eidolon hesitated. 'I, of course, recognise the majesty of the Warmaster.'

'Do you? Do you, Eidolon? Well, that's good, because I'm *it*. I'm his chosen instrument here. You'll address me as if I were the

Warmaster. You'll show me some respect too! Warmaster Horus believes you've made some shit-awful mistakes in your prosecution of this theatre. How many brothers did you drop here? A company? How many left? Serghar? Head count?'

'Thirty-nine live ones, Tarik,' the vox answered. 'There may be more. Lots of body piles to dig through.'

'Thirty-nine. You were so hungry for glory you wasted more than half a company. If I was… *Primarch* Fulgrim, I'd have your head on a pole. The Warmaster may yet decide to do just that. So, *Lord* Eidolon, are we clear?'

'We…' Eidolon replied slowly, '… are clear, captain.'

'Perhaps you'd like to go and undertake a review of your forces?' Torgaddon suggested. 'The enemy will be back soon, I'm sure, and in greater numbers.'

Eidolon gazed venomously at Torgaddon for a few seconds and then replaced his helm. 'I will not forget this insult, captain,' he said.

'Then it was worth the trip,' Torgaddon replied, clamping on his own helmet.

Eidolon crunched away, calling to his scattered troops. Torgaddon turned and found Tarvitz looking at him.

'What's on your mind, Tarvitz?' he asked.

I've been wanting to say that for a long time, Tarvitz wished to say. Out loud, he said, 'What do you need me to do?'

'Gather up your squad and stand ready. When the shit comes down next, I'd like to know you're with me.'

Tarvitz made the sign of the aquila across his chest. 'You can count on it. How did you know where to drop?'

Torgaddon pointed at the calm sky. 'We came in where the storm had gone out,' he said.

TARVITZ HOISTED LUCIUS to his feet. Lucius was still picking at his ruined armour.

'That Torgaddon is an odious rogue,' he said. Lucius had over-heard the entire confrontation.

'I rather like him.'

'The way he spoke to our lord? He's a dog.'

'I like dogs,' Tarvitz said.

'I believe I will kill him for his insolence.'

'Don't,' Tarvitz said. 'That would be wrong, and I'd have to hurt you if you did.'

Lucius laughed, as if Tarvitz had said something funny.

'I mean it,' Tarvitz said.

Lucius laughed even more.

IT TOOK A little under an hour to assemble their forces in the clearing. Torgaddon established contact with the fleet via the astrotelepath he had brought with him. The shield-storms raged with dreadful fury over the surrounding stalk forests, but the sky directly above the clearing remained calm.

As he marshalled the remains of his force, Tarvitz observed Torgaddon and his fellow captains conducting a further angry debate with Eidolon and Anteus. There were apparently some differences of opinion as to what their course of action should be.

After a while, Torgaddon walked away from the argument. Tarvitz guessed he was recusing himself from the quarrel before he said something else to infuriate Eidolon.

Torgaddon walked the line of the picket, stopping to talk to some of his men, and finally arrived at Tarvitz's position.

'You seem like a decent sort, Tarvitz,' he remarked. 'How do you stand that lord of yours?'

'It is my duty to stand him,' Tarvitz replied. 'It is my duty to serve. He is my lord commander. His combat record is glorious.'

'I doubt he'll be adding this endeavour to his triumph roll,'

Torgaddon said. 'Tell me, did you agree with his decision to drop here?'

'I neither agreed nor disagreed,' Tarvitz replied. 'I obeyed. He is my lord commander.'

'I know that.' Torgaddon sighed. 'All right, just between you and me, Tarvitz. Brother to brother. Did you like the decision?'

'I really–'

'Oh, come on. I just saved your life. Answer me candidly and we'll call it quits.'

Tarvitz hesitated. 'I thought it a little reckless,' he admitted. 'I thought it was prompted by ambitious notions that had little to do with the safety of our company or the salvation of the missing forces.'

'Thank you for speaking honestly.'

'May I speak honestly a little more?' Tarvitz asked.

'Of course.'

'I admire you, sir,' Tarvitz said. 'For both your courage and your plain speaking. But please, remember that we are the Emperor's Children, and we are very proud. We do not like to be shown up, or belittled, nor do we like others... even other Astartes of the most noble Legions... diminishing us.'

'When you say "we" you mean Eidolon?'

'No, I mean we.'

'Very diplomatic,' said Torgaddon. 'In the early days of the crusade, the Emperor's Children fought alongside us for a time, before you had grown enough in numbers to operate autonomously.'

'I know, sir. I was there, but I was just a file trooper back then.'

'Then you'll know the esteem with which the Luna Wolves regarded your Legion. I was a junior officer back then too, but I remember distinctly that Horus said... what was it? That the Emperor's Children were the living embodiment of the Adeptus

Astartes. Horus enjoys a special bond with your primarch. The Luna Wolves have cooperated militarily with just about every other Legion during this great war. We still regard yours as about the best we've ever had the honour of serving with.'

'It pleases me to hear you say so, sir,' Tarvitz replied.

'Then... how have you changed so?' Torgaddon asked. 'Is Eidolon typical of the command echelon that rules you now? His arrogance astounds me. So damned superior...'

'Our ethos is not about superiority, captain,' Tarvitz answered. 'It is about purity. But one is often mistaken for the other. We model ourselves on the Emperor, beloved by all, and in seeking to be like him, we can seem aloof and haughty.'

'Did you ever think,' asked Torgaddon, 'that while it's laudable to emulate the Emperor as much as possible, the one thing that you cannot and should not aspire to is his supremacy? He is the Emperor. He is singular. Strive to be like him in all ways, by all means, but do not presume to be on his level. No one belongs there. No one is alike to him.'

'My Legion understands that,' Tarvitz said. 'Sometimes, though, it doesn't translate well to others.'

'There's no purity in pride,' Torgaddon said. 'Nothing pure or admirable in arrogance or over-confidence.'

'My lord Eidolon knows this.'

'He should show he knows it. He led you into a disaster, and he won't even apologise for it.'

'I'm sure, in due course, my lord will formally acknowledge your efforts in relieving us and–'

'I don't want any credit,' Torgaddon said. 'You were brothers in trouble, and we came to help. That's the start and finish of it. But I had to face down the Warmaster to get permission to drop, because he believed it was insanity to send any more men to their deaths in an unknowable place against an unknowable foe. That's what Eidolon did. In the name, I imagine, of honour and pride.'

'How did you convince the Warmaster?' Tarvitz wondered.

'I didn't,' said Torgaddon. 'You did. The storm had gone out over this area, and we detected your vox scatter. You proved you were still alive down here, and the Warmaster immediately sanctioned the speartip to come and pull you out.'

Torgaddon looked up at the misty stars. 'The storms are their best weapon,' he mused. 'If we're going to wrestle this world to compliance, we'll have to find a way to beat them. Eidolon suggested the trees might be key. That they might act as generators or amplifiers for the storm. He said that once he'd destroyed the trees, the storm in this locality collapsed.'

Tarvitz paused. 'My Lord Eidolon said that?'

'Only piece of sense I've heard out of him. He said that as soon as he set charges to the trees and demolished them, the storm went out. It's an interesting theory. The Warmaster wants me to use the storm-break to pull everyone here out, but Eidolon is dead set on finding more trees and levelling them, in the hope that we can break a hole in the enemy's cover. What do you think?'

'I think... my Lord Eidolon is wise,' said Tarvitz.

Bulle had been stationed nearby, and had overheard the exchange. He could not contain himself any longer.

'Permission to speak, captain,' he said.

'Not now, Bulle,' Tarvitz said.

'Sir, I–'

'You heard him, Bulle,' Lucius cut in, walking up to them.

'What's your name, brother?' Torgaddon asked.

'Bulle, sir.'

'What did you want to say?'

'It's not important,' Lucius snorted. 'Brother Bulle speaks out of turn.'

'You are Lucius, right?' Torgaddon asked.

'Captain Lucius.'

'And Bulle was one of the men who stood over you and fought to keep you alive?'

'He did. I am honoured by his service.'

'Maybe you could let him talk, then?' Torgaddon suggested.

'It would be inappropriate,' said Lucius.

'Tell you what,' Torgaddon said. 'As commander of the speartip, I believe I have authority here. I'll decide who talks and who doesn't. Bulle? Let's hear you, brother.'

Bulle looked awkwardly at Lucius and Tarvitz.

'That was an order,' said Torgaddon.

'My Lord Eidolon did not destroy the trees, sir. Captain Tarvitz did it. He insisted. My Lord Eidolon then chastised him for the act, claiming it was a waste of charges.'

'Is this true?' Torgaddon asked.

'Yes,' said Tarvitz.

'Why did you do it?'

'Because it didn't seem right for the bodies of our dead to hang in such ignominy,' Tarvitz said.

'And you'd let Eidolon take the credit and not say anything?'

'He is my lord.'

'Thank you, brother,' Torgaddon said to Bulle. He glanced at Lucius. 'Reprimand him or punish him in any way for speaking out and I'll have the Warmaster himself personally deprive you of your rank.'

Torgaddon turned to Tarvitz. 'It's a funny thing. It shouldn't matter, but it does. Now I know you felled the trees, I feel better about pursuing that line of action. Eidolon clearly knows a good idea when someone else has it. Let's go cut down a few more trees, Tarvitz. You can show me how it's done.'

Torgaddon walked away, shouting out orders for muster and

movement. Tarvitz and Lucius exchanged long looks, and then
Lucius turned and walked away.

THE ARMED FORCE moved away from the clearing and back into the
thickets of the stalk forest. They passed back into the embrace of
the storm cover. Torgaddon had his Terminator squads lead the
way. The man-tanks, under the command of Trice Rokus, ignited
their heavy blades, and cut a path, felling the stalks to clear a
wide avenue into the forest swathe.

They pressed on beneath the wild storms for twenty kilometres.
Twice, megarachnid skirmish parties assaulted their lines, but
the speartip drew its phalanxes close and, with the advantage
of range created by the cleared avenue, slaughtered the attackers
with their bolters.

The landscape began to change. They were apparently reaching
the edge of a vast plateau, and the ground began to slope away
steeply before them. The stalk growth became more patchy and
sparse, clinging to the rocky, ferrous soil of the descent. A wide
basin spread out below them, a rift valley. Here, the spongy,
marshy ground was covered with thousands of small, coned
trees, rising some ten metres high, which dotted the terrain like
fungal growths. The trees, hard and stony and composed of the
same milky cement from which the murder trees had been built,
peppered the depression like armour studs.

As they descended onto it, the Astartes found the land at the
base of the rift swampy and slick, decorated with long, thin lakes
of water stained orange by the iron content of the soil. The flash
of the overhead storms scintillated in reflection from the long,
slender pools. They looked like claw wounds in the earth.

The air was busy with fibrous grey bugs that milled and swirled
interminably in the stagnant atmosphere. Larger flying things,
flitting like bats, hunted the bugs in quick, sharp swoops.

At the mouth of the rift, they discovered six more thorn trees arranged in a silent grove. Reduced cadavers and residual meat and armour adorned their barbs. Blood Angels, and Imperial army. There was no sign of the winged clades, though fifty kilometres away, over the stalk forests, black shapes could be seen, circling madly in the lightning-washed sky.

'Lay them low,' Torgaddon ordered. Moy nodded and began to gather munitions. 'Find Captain Tarvitz,' Torgaddon called. 'He'll show you how to do it.'

LOKEN REMAINED ON the strategium for the first three hours after the drop, long enough to celebrate Torgaddon's signal from the surface. The speartip had secured the dropsite, and formed up with the residue of Lord Eidolon's company. After that, the atmosphere had become, strangely, more tense. They were waiting to hear Torgaddon's field decision. Abaddon, cautious and closed, had already ordered Stormbirds prepped for extraction flights. Aximand paced, silently. The Warmaster had withdrawn into his sanctum with Maloghurst.

Loken leant at the strategium rail for a while, overlooking the bustle of the vast bridge below, and discussed tactics with Tybalt Marr. Marr and Moy were both Sons of Horus, cast in his image so firmly that they looked like identical twins. At some point in the Legion's history, they had earned the nicknames 'the Either' and the 'the Or', referring to the fact that they were almost interchangeable. It was often hard to distinguish between them, they were so alike. One might do as well as the other.

Both were competent field officers, with a rack of victories each that would make any captain proud, though neither had attained the glories of Sedirae or Abaddon. They were precise, efficient and workmanlike in their leadership, but they were Luna Wolves, and what was workmanlike to that fratery was exemplary to any other regiment.

As Marr spoke, it became clear to Loken that he was envious of his 'twin's' selection to the undertaking. It was Horus's habit to send both or neither. They worked well together, complementing one another, as if somehow anticipating one another's decisions, but the ballot for the speartip had been democratic and fair. Moy had won a place. Marr had not.

Marr rattled on to Loken, evidently sublimating his worries about his brother's fate. After a while, Qruze came over to join them at the rail.

Iacton Qruze was an anachronism. Ancient and rather tiresome, he had been a captain in the Legion since its inception, his prominence entirely eclipsed once Horus had been repatriated and given command by the Emperor. He was the product of another era, a throwback to the years of the Unification Wars and the bad old times, stubborn and slightly cantankerous, a vestigial trace of the way the Legion had gone about things in antiquity.

'Brothers,' he greeted them as he came up. Qruze still had a habit, perhaps unconscious, of making the salute of the single clenched fist against his breast, the old pre-Unity symbol, rather than the double-handed eagle. He had a long, tanned face, deeply lined with creases and folds, and his hair was white. He spoke softly, expecting others to make the effort to listen, and believed that it was his quiet tone that had, over the years, earned him the nickname 'the Half-heard'.

Loken knew this wasn't so. Qruze's wits were not as sharp as they'd once been, and he often appeared tired or inappropriate in his commentary or advice. He was known as 'the Half-heard' because his pronouncements were best not listened to too closely.

Qruze believed he stood as a wise father-figure to the Legion, and no one had the spite to inform him otherwise. There had been several quiet attempts to deprive him of company command, just as Qruze had made several attempts to become elected to the first captaincy.

By duration of service, he should have been so long since. Loken believed that the Warmaster regarded Qruze with some pity and couldn't abide the idea of retiring him. Qruze was an irksome relic, regarded by the rest of them with equal measures of affection and frustration, who could not accept that the Legion had matured and advanced without him.

'We will be out of this in a day,' he announced categorically to Loken and Marr. 'You mark my words, young men. A day, and the commander will order extraction.'

'Tarik is doing well,' Loken began.

'The boy Torgaddon has been lucky, but he cannot press this to a conclusion. You mark my words. In and out, in a day.'

'I wish I was down there,' Marr said.

'Foolish thoughts,' Qruze decided. 'It's only a rescue run. I cannot for the life of me imagine what the Emperor's Children thought they were doing, going into this hell. I served with them, in the early days, you know? Fine fellows. Very proper. They taught the Wolves a thing or two about decorum, thank you very much! Model soldiers. Put us to shame on the Eastern Fringe, so they did, but that was back then.'

'It certainly was,' said Loken.

'It most certainly was,' agreed Qruze, missing the irony entirely. 'I can't imagine what they thought they were doing here.'

'Prosecuting a war?' Loken suggested.

Qruze looked at him diffidently. 'Are you mocking me, Garviel?'

'Never, sir. I would never do that.'

'I hope we're deployed,' Marr grumbled, 'and soon.'

'We won't be,' Qruze declared. He rubbed the patchy grey

goatee that decorated his long, lined face. He was most certainly not a Son of Horus.

'I've business to attend to,' Loken said, excusing himself. 'I'll take my leave, brothers.'

Marr glared at Loken, annoyed to be left alone with the Half-heard. Loken winked and wandered off, hearing Qruze embark on one of his long and tortuous 'stories' to Marr.

Loken went downship to the barrack decks of Tenth Company. His men were waiting, half-armoured, weapons and kit spread out for fitting. Apprenta and servitors manned portable lathes and forge carts, making final, precise adjustments to plate segments. This was just displacement activity: the men had been battle-ready for weeks.

Loken took the time to appraise Vipus and the other squad leaders of the situation, and then spoke briefly to some of the new blood warriors they'd raised to company service during the voyage. These men were especially tense. One Forty Twenty might see their baptism as full Astartes.

In the solitude of his arming chamber, Loken sat for a while, running through certain mental exercises designed to promote clarity and concentration. When he grew bored of them, he took up the book Sindermann had loaned him.

He'd read a good deal less of *The Chronicles of Ursh* during the voyage than he'd intended. The commander had kept him busy. He folded the heavy, yellowed pages open with ungloved hands and found his place.

The *Chronicles* were as raw and brutal as Sindermann had promised. Long-forgotten cities were routinely sacked, or burned, or simply evaporated in nuclear storms. Seas were regularly stained with blood, skies with ash, and landscapes were often carpeted with the bleached and numberless bones of the conquered. When armies marched, they marched a billion strong, the ragged banners of a million standards swaying above their heads in the atomic winds. The battles were stupendous maelstroms of blades and spiked black helms and baying horns, lit by the fires of cannons and burners. Page after page celebrated the cruel practices and equally cruel character of the despot Kalagann.

It amused Loken, for the most part. Fanciful logic abounded, as did an air of strained realism. Feats of arms were described that no pre-Unity warriors could have accomplished. These, after all, were the feral hosts of techno-barbarians that the proto-Astartes, in their crude thunder armour, had been created to bring to heel. Kalagann's great generals, Lurtois and Sheng Khal and, later, Quallodon, were described in language more appropriate to primarchs. They carved, for Kalagann, an impossibly vast domain during the latter part of the Age of Strife.

Loken had skipped ahead once or twice, and saw that later parts of the work recounted the fall of Kalagann, and described the apocalyptic conquest of Ursh by the forces of Unity. He saw passages referring to enemy warriors bearing the thunderbolt and lightning emblem, which had been the personal device of the Emperor before the eagle of the Imperium was formalised. These men saluted with the fist of unity, as Qruze still did, and were clearly arrayed in thunder armour. Loken wondered if the Emperor himself would be mentioned, and in what terms, and wanted to look to see if he could recognise the names of any of the proto-Astartes warriors.

But he felt he owed it to Kyril Sindermann to read the thing thoroughly, and returned to his original place and order. He quickly became absorbed by a sequence detailing Shang Khal's campaigns against the Nordafrik Conclaves. Shang Khal had assembled a significant horde of irregular levies from the southern client states of Ursh, and used them to support his main armed strengths, including the infamous Tupelov Lancers and the Red Engines, during the invasion.

The Nordafrik technogogues had preserved a great deal more high technology for the good of their conclaves than Ursh possessed, and sheer envy, more than anything, motivated the war. Kalagann was hungry for the fine instruments and mechanisms the conclaves owned.

Eight epic battles marked Shang Khal's advance into the Nordafrik zones, the greatest of them being Xozer. Over a period of nine days and nights, the war machines of the Red Engines blasted their way across the cultivated agroponic pastures and reduced them back to the desert, from which they had originally been irrigated and nurtured. They cut through the laserthorn hedges and the jewelled walls of the outer conclave, and unleashed dirty atomics into the heart of the ruling zone, before the Lancers led a tidal wave of screaming berserkers through the breach into the earthly paradise of the gardens at Xozer, the last fragment of Eden on a corrupted planet.

Which they, of course, trampled underfoot.

Loken felt himself skipping ahead again, as the account bogged down in interminable lists of battle glories and honour rolls. Then his eyes alighted on a strange phrase, and he read back. At the heart of the ruling zone, a ninth, minor battle had marked the conquest, almost as an afterthought. One bastion had remained, the *murengon*, or walled sanctuary, where the last hierophants of the conclaves held out, practising, so the text said, their 'sciomancy by the flame lyght of their burning realm'.

Shang Khal, wishing swift resolution to the conquest, had sent Anult Keyser to crush the sanctuary. Keyser was lord martial of the Tupelov Lancers and, by various bonds of honour, could call freely upon the services of the Roma, a squadron of mercenary fliers whose richly decorated interceptors, legend said, never landed or touched the earth, but lived eternally in the scope of

the air. During the advance on the murengon, Keyser's oneirocriticks – and by that word, Loken understood the text meant
'interpreters of dreams' – had warned of the hierophants' sciomancy, and their phantasmagorian ways.

When the battle began, just as the oneirocriticks had warned,
majiks were unleashed. Plagues of insects, as thick as monsoon
rain and so vast in their swirling masses that they blacked out
the sun, fell upon Keyser's forces, choking air intakes, weapon
ports, visors, ears, mouths and throats. Water boiled without
fire. Engines overheated or burned out. Men turned to stone, or
their bones turned to paste, or their flesh succumbed to boils
and buboes and flaked off their limbs. Others went mad. Some
became daemons and turned upon their own.

Loken stopped reading and went back over the sentences again.
'…and where the plagueing ynsects did nott crawle, or madness
lye, so men did blister and recompose them ownselves ynto the
terrible likeness of daimons, such foule pests as the afreet and
the d'genny that persist in the silent desert places. In such visage,
they turned uponn theyr kin and gnawed then upon their bloody
bones…'

Some became daemons and turned upon their own.

Anult Keyser himself was slain by one such daemon, which
had, just hours previously, been his loyal lieutenant, Wilhym
Mardol.

When Shang Khal heard the news, he flew into a fury, and went
at once to the scene, bringing with him what the text described as
his 'wrathsingers', who appeared to be magi of some sort. Their
leader, or master, was a man called Mafeo Orde, and somehow,
Orde drew the wrathsingers into a kind of remote warfare with
the hierophants. The text was annoyingly vague about exactly
what occurred next, almost as if it was beyond the understanding
of the writer. Words such as 'sorcery' and 'majik' were employed

frequently, without qualification, and there were invocations to dark, primordial gods that the writer clearly thought his audience would have some prior knowledge of. Since the start of the text, Loken had seen references to Kalagann's 'sorcerous' powers, and the 'invisibles artes' that formed a key part of Ursh's power, but he had taken them to be hyperbole. This was the first time sorcery had appeared on the page, as a kind of fact.

The earth trembled, as if afraid. The sky tore like silk. Many in the Urshite force heard the voices of the dead whispering to them. Men caught fire, and walked around, bathed in lambent flames that did not consume them, pleading for help. The remote war between the wrathsingers and the hierophants lasted for six days, and when it ended, the ancient desert was thick with snow, and the skies had turned blood red. The air formations of the Roma had been forced to flee, lest their craft be torn from the heavens by screaming angels and dashed down upon the ground.

At the end of it, all the wrathsingers were dead, except Orde himself. The murengon was a smoking hole in the ground, its stone walls so hideously melted by heat they had become slips of glass. And the hierophants were extinct.

The chapter ended. Loken looked up. He had been so enthralled, he wondered if he had missed an alert or a summons. The arming chamber was quiet. No signal runes blinked on the wall panel.

He began to read the next part, but the narrative had switched to a sequence concerning some northern war against the nomadic caterpillar cities of the Taiga. He skipped a few pages, hunting for further mention of Orde or sorcery, but could detect none. Frustrated, he set the book aside.

Sindermann... had he given Loken this work deliberately? To what end? A joke? Some veiled message? Loken resolved to study it, section by section, and take his questions to his mentor.

But he'd had enough of it for the time being. His mind was

clouded and he wanted it clear for combat. He walked to the vox-plate beside the chamber door and activated it.

'Officer of the watch. How can I serve, captain?'

'Any word from the speartip?'

'I'll check, sir. No, nothing routed to you.'

'Thank you. Keep me appraised.'

'Sir.'

Loken clicked the vox off. He walked back to where he had left the book, picked it up, and marked his page. He was using a thin sliver of parchment torn from the edge of one of his oath papers as a marker. He closed the book, and went to put it away in the battered metal crate where he kept his belongings. There were precious few items in there, little to show for such a long life. It reminded him of Jubal's meagre effects. If I die, Loken thought, who will clean this out? What will they preserve? Most of the bric-a-brac was worthless trophies, stuff that only meant something to him: the handle of a combat knife he'd broken off in the gullet of a greenskin warboss; long feathers, now musty and threadbare, from the hatchet-beak that had almost killed him on Balthasar, decades earlier; a piece of dirty, rusted wire, knotted at each end, which he'd used to garrote a nameless eldar champion when all other weapons had been lost to him.

That had been a fight. A real test. He decided he ought to tell Oliton about it, sometime. How long ago was it? Ages past, though the memory was as fresh and heavy as if it had been yesterday. Two warriors, deprived of their common arsenals by the circumstance of war, stalking one another through the fluttering leaves of a wind-lashed forest. Such skill and tenacity. Loken had almost wept in admiration for the opponent he had slain.

All that was left was the wire and the memory, and when Loken passed, only the wire would remain. Whoever came here after his death would likely throw it out, assuming it to be a twist of rusty wire and nothing more.

His rummaging hands turned up something that would not be cast away. The data-slate Karkasy had given him. The data-slate from Keeler.

Loken sat back and switched it on, flicking through the picts again. Rare picts. Tenth Company, assembled on the embarkation deck for war. The company banner. Loken himself, framed against the bold colour of the flag. Loken taking his oath of moment. The Mournival group: Abaddon, Aximand, Torgaddon and himself, with Targost and Sedirae.

He loved the picts. They were the most precious material gift he'd ever received, and the most unexpected. Loken hoped that, through Oliton, he might leave some sort of useful legacy. He doubted it would be anything like as significant as these images.

He scrolled the picts back into their file, and was about to de-activate the slate when he saw, for the first time, there was another file lodged in the memory. It was stored, perhaps deliberately, in an annex to the slate's main data folder, hidden from cursory view. Only a tiny icon digit '2' betrayed that the slate was loaded with more than one file of material.

It took him a moment to find the annex and open it. It looked like a folder of deleted or discarded images, but there was a tag caption attached to it that read 'IN CONFIDENCE'.

Loken cued it. The first pict washed into colour on the slate's small screen. He stared at it, puzzled. It was dark, unbalanced in colour or contrast, almost unreadable. He thumbed up the next, and the next.

And stared in horrid fascination.

He was looking at Jubal, or rather the thing that Jubal had become in the final moments. A rabid, insane mass, ploughing down a dark hallway towards the viewer.

There were more shots. The light, the sheen of them, seemed

unnatural, as if the picter unit that had captured them had found difficulty reading the image. There were clear, sharp-focused droplets of gore and sweat frozen in the air as they splashed out in the foreground. The thing behind them, the thing that had shaken the droplets out, was fuzzy and imprecise, but never less than abominable.

Loken switched the slate off and began to strip off his armour as quickly as he could. When he was down to the thick, mimetic polymers of his sub-suit bodyglove, he stopped, and pulled on a long, hooded robe of brown hemp. He took up the slate, and a vox-cuff, and went outside.

'Nero!'

Vipus appeared, fully plated except for his helm. He frowned in confusion at the sight of Loken's attire.

'Garvi? Where's your armour? What's going on?'

'I've an errand to run,' Loken replied quickly, clasping on the vox-cuff. 'You have command here in my absence.'

'I do?'

'I'll return shortly.' Loken held up the cuff, and allowed it to auto-sync channels with Vipus's vox system. Small notice lights on the cuff and the collar of Vipus's armour flashed rapidly and then glowed in unison.

'If the situation changes, if we're called forwards, vox me immediately. I'll not be derelict of my duties. But there's something I must do.'

'Like what?'

'I can't say,' Loken said.

Nero Vipus paused and nodded. 'Just as you say, brother. I'll cover for you and alert you of any changes.' He stood watching as his captain, hooded and hurrying, slipped away down an access tunnel and was swallowed by the shadows.

✠ ✠ ✠

THE GAME WAS going so badly against him that Ignace Karkasy decided it was high time he got his fellow players drunk. Six of them, with a fairly disinterested crowd of onlookers, occupied a table booth at the forward end of the Retreat, under the gilded arches. Beyond them, remembrancers and off-duty soldiers, along with ship personnel relaxing between shifts, and a few iterators (one could never tell if an iterator was on duty or off) mingled in the long, crowded chamber, drinking, eating, gaming and talking. There was a busy chatter, laughter, the clink of glasses. Someone was playing a viol. The Retreat had become quite the social focus of the flagship.

Just a week or two before, a sozzled second engineer had explained to Karkasy that there had never been any gleeful society aboard the *Vengeful Spirit*, nor on any other line ship in his experience. Just quiet after-shift drinking and sullen gambling schools. The remembrancers had brought their bohemian habits to the warship, and the crewmen and soldiery had been drawn to its light.

The iterators, and some senior ship officers, had clucked disapprovingly at the growing, casual conviviality, but the mingling was permitted. When Comnenus had voiced his objections to the unlicensed carousing the *Vengeful Spirit* was now host to, someone – and Karkasy suspected the commander himself – had reminded him that the purpose of the remembrancers was to meet and fraternise. Soldiers and Navy adepts flocked to the Retreat, hoping to find some poor poet or chronicler who would record their thoughts and experiences for posterity. Though mostly, they came to get a skinful, play cards and meet girls.

It was, in Karkasy's opinion, the finest achievement of the remembrancer programme to date: to remind the expedition warriors they were human, and to offer them some fun.

And to win rudely from them at cards.

The game was *targe main*, and they were playing with a pack of square-cut cards that Karkasy had once lent to Mersadie Oliton. There were two other remembrancers at the table, along with a junior deck officer, a sergeant-at-arms and a gunnery oberst. They were using, as bidding tokens, scurfs of gilt that someone had cheerfully scraped off one of the stateroom's golden columns. Karkasy had to admit that the remembrancers had abused their facilities terribly. Not only had the columns been half-stripped to the ironwork, the murals had been written on and painted over. Verses had been inscribed in patches of sky between the shoulders of ancient heroes, and those ancient heroes found themselves facing eternity wearing comical beards and eye patches. In places, walls and ceilings had been whitewashed, or lined with gum-paper, and entire tracts of new composition inscribed upon them.

'I'll sit this hand out,' Karkasy announced, and pushed back his chair, scooping up the meagre handful of scraped gilt flecks he still owned. 'I'll find us all some drinks.'

The other players murmured approval as the sergeant-at-arms dealt the next hand. The junior deck officer, his head sunk low and his eyes hooded, thumped the heels of his hands together in mock applause, his elbows on the table top, his hands fixed high above his lolling head.

Karkasy moved off through the crowd to find Zinkman. Zinkman, a sculptor, had drink, an apparently bottomless reserve of it, though where he sourced it from was anyone's guess. Someone had suggested Zinkman had a private arrangement with a crewman in climate control who distilled the stuff. Zinkman owed Karkasy at least one bottle, from an unfinished game of *merci merci* two nights earlier.

He asked for Zinkman at two or three tables, and also made inquiries with various groups standing about the place. The viol music had stopped for the moment, and some around were clapping as Carnegi, the composer, clambered up onto a table. Carnegi owned a half-decent baritone voice, and most nights he could be prevailed upon to sing popular opera or take requests.

Karkasy had one.

A squall of laughter burst from nearby, where a small, lively group had gathered on stools and recliners to hear a remembrancer give a reading from his latest work. In one of the wall booths formed by the once golden colonnade, Karkasy saw Ameri Sechloss carefully inscribing her latest remembrance in red ink over a wall she'd washed white with stolen hull paint. She'd masked out an image of the Emperor triumphant at Cyclonis. Someone would complain about that. Parts of the Emperor, beloved by all, poked out from around the corners of her white splash.

'Zinkman? Anyone? Zinkman?' he asked.

'I think he's over there,' one of the remembrancers watching Sechloss suggested.

Karkasy turned, and stood on tiptoe to peer across the press. The Retreat was crowded tonight. A figure had just walked in through the chamber's main entrance. Karkasy frowned. He didn't need to be on tiptoe to spot this newcomer. Robed and hooded, the figure towered over the rest of the crowd, by far and away the tallest person in the busy room. Not a human's build at all. The general noise level did not drop, but it was clear the newcomer was attracting attention. People were whispering, and casting sly looks in his direction.

Karkasy edged his way through the crowd, the only person in the chamber bold enough to approach the visitor. The hooded figure was standing just inside the entrance arch, scanning the crowd in search of someone.

'Captain?' Karkasy asked, coming forwards and peering up

under the cowl. 'Captain Loken?'

'Karkasy.' Loken seemed very uncomfortable.

'Were you looking for me, sir? I didn't think we were due to meet until tomorrow.'

'I was… I was looking for Keeler. Is she here?'

'Here? Oh no. She doesn't come here. Please, captain, come with me. You don't want to be in here.'

'Don't I?'

'I can read the discomfort in your manner, and when we meet, you never step inside the archway. Come on.'

They went back out through the arched entranceway into the cool, gloomy quiet of the corridor outside. A few people passed them by, heading into the Retreat.

'It must be important,' Karkasy said, 'for you to set foot in there.'

'It is,' Loken replied. He kept the hood of his robe up, and his manner remained stiff and guarded. 'I need to find Keeler.'

'She doesn't much frequent the common spaces. She's probably in her quarters.'

'Where's that?'

'You could have asked the watch officer for her billet reference.'

'I'm asking you, Ignace.'

'That important, and that private,' Karkasy remarked. Loken made no reply. Karkasy shrugged. 'Come with me and I'll show you.'

Karkasy led the captain down into the warren of the residential deck where the remembrancers were billeted. The echoing metal companionways were cold, the walls brushed steel and marked with patches of damp. This area had once been a billet for army officers but, like the Retreat, it had ceased to feel anything like the interior of a military vessel. Music echoed from some chambers, often through half-open hatches. The sound of hysterical laughter came from one room, and from another the din of a man

and a woman having a ferocious quarrel. Paper notices had been
pasted to the walls: slogans and verses and essays on the nature
of man and war. Murals had also been daubed in places, some
of them magnificent, some of them crude. There was litter on the
deck, an odd shoe, an empty bottle, scraps of paper.

'Here,' said Karkasy. The shutter of Keeler's billet was closed.
'Would you like me to…?' Karkasy asked, gesturing to the door.

'Yes.'

Karkasy rapped his fist against the shutter and listened. After a
moment, he rapped again, harder. 'Euphrati? Euphrati, are you
there?'

The shutter slid open, and the scent of body warmth spilled out
into the cool corridor. Karkasy was face to face with a lean young
man, naked but for a pair of half-buttoned army fatigue pants.
The man was sinewy and tough, hard-bodied and hard-faced.
He had numerical tattoos on his upper arms, and metal tags on
a chain around his neck.

'What?' he snapped at Karkasy.

'I want to see Euphrati.'

'Piss off,' the soldier replied. 'She doesn't want to see you.'

Karkasy backed away a step. The soldier was physically
intimidating.

'Cool down,' said Loken, looming behind Karkasy and lowering
his hood. He stared down at the soldier. 'Cool down, and I won't
ask your name and unit.'

The soldier looked up at Loken with wide eyes. 'She… she's not
here,' he said.

Loken pushed past him. The soldier tried to block him, but
Loken caught his right wrist in one hand and turned it neatly so
that the man suddenly found himself contorted in a disabling
lock.

'Don't do that again,' Loken advised, and released his hold, adding a tiny shove that dropped the soldier onto his hands and knees.

The room was quite small, and very cluttered. Discarded clothes and rumpled bedding littered the floor space, and the shelves and low table were covered with bottles and unwashed plates.

Keeler stood on the far side of the room, beside the unmade cot. She had pulled a sheet around her slim, naked body and stared at Loken with disdain. She looked weary, unhealthy. Her hair was tangled and there were dark shadows under her eyes.

'It's all right, Leef,' she told the soldier. 'I'll see you later.'

Still wary, the soldier pulled on his vest and boots, snatched up his jacket, and left, casting one last murderous look at Loken.

'He's a good man,' Keeler said. 'He cares for me.'

'Army?'

'Yes. It's called fraternisation. Does Ignace have to be here for this?'

Karkasy was hovering in the doorway. Loken turned. 'Thank you for your help,' he said. 'I'll see you tomorrow.'

Karkasy nodded. 'All right,' he said. Reluctantly, he walked away. Loken closed the shutter. He looked back at Keeler. She was pouring clear liquor from a flask into a shot glass.

'Can I interest you?' she asked, gesturing with the flask. 'In the spirit of hospitality?'

He shook his head.

'Ah. I suppose you Astartes don't drink. Another biological flaw ironed out of you.'

'We drink well enough, under certain circumstances.'

'And this isn't one, I suppose?' Keeler put the flask down and took up her glass. She walked back to the cot, holding the sheet around her with one hand and sipping from the glass held in the other. Holding her drink out steady, she settled herself down on the cot, drawing her legs up and folding the sheet modestly over herself.

'I can imagine why you're here, captain,' she said. 'I'm just amazed. I expected you weeks ago.'

'I apologise. I only found the second file tonight. I obviously hadn't looked carefully enough.'

'What do you think of my work?'

'Astonishing. I'm flattered by the picts you shot on the embarkation deck. I meant to send you a note, thanking you for copying them to me. Again, I apologise. The second file, however, is…'

'Problematic?' she suggested.

'At the very least,' he said.

'Why don't you sit down?' she asked. Loken shrugged off his robe and sat carefully on a metal stool beside the cluttered table.

'I wasn't aware any picts existed of that incident,' Loken said.

'I didn't know I'd shot them,' Keeler replied, taking another sip. 'I'd forgotten, I think. When the first captain asked me at the time, I said no, I hadn't taken anything. I found them later. I was surprised.'

'Why did you send them to me?' he asked.

She shrugged. 'I don't really know. You have to understand, sir, that I was… traumatised. For a while, I was in a very bad way. The shock of it all. I was a mess, but I got through it. I'm content now, stable, centred. My friends helped me through it. Ignace, Sadie, some others. They were kind to me. They stopped me from hurting myself.'

'Hurting yourself?'

She fiddled with her glass, her eyes focused on the floor. 'Nightmares, Captain Loken. Terrible visions, when I was asleep and when I was awake. I found myself crying for no reason. I drank too much. I acquired a small pistol, and spent long hours wondering if I had the strength to use it.'

She looked up at him. 'It was in that… that pit of despair that I sent you those picts. It was a cry for help, I suppose. I don't know.

I can't remember. Like I said, I'm past that now. I'm fine, and feel a little foolish for bothering you, especially as my efforts took so long to reach you. You wasted a visit.'

'I'm glad you feel better,' Loken said, 'but I haven't wasted anything. We need to talk about those images. Who's seen them?'

'No one. You and me. No one else.'

'Did you not think it wise to inform the first captain of their existence?'

Keeler shook her head. 'No. No, not at all. Not back then. If I'd gone to the authorities, they'd have confiscated them... destroyed them, probably, and told me the same story about a wild beast. The first captain was very certain it was a wild beast, some xenos creature, and he was very certain I should keep my mouth shut. For the sake of morale. The picts were a lifeline for me, back then. They proved I wasn't going mad. That's why I sent them to you.'

'Am I not part of the authorities?'

She laughed. 'You were there, Loken. You were there. You saw it. I took a chance. I thought you might respond and–'

'And what?'

'Tell me the truth of it.'

Loken hesitated.

'Oh, don't worry,' she admonished, rising to refill her glass. 'I don't want to know the truth now. A wild beast. A wild beast. I've got over it. This late in the day, captain, I don't expect you to break loyalty and tell me something you're sworn not to tell. It was a foolish notion, which I now regret. My turn to apologise to you.'

She looked over at him, tugging up the edge of the sheet to cover her bosom. 'I've deleted my copies. All of them. You have my word. The only ones that exist are the ones I sent to you.'

Loken took out the data-slate and placed it on the table. He had to push dirty crockery aside to make a space for it. Keeler looked at the slate for a long while, and then knocked back her glass and refilled it.

'Imagine that,' she said, her hand trembling as it lifted the flask. 'I'm terrified even to have them back in the room.'

'I don't think you're as over it as you like to pretend,' Loken said.

'Really?' she sneered. She put down her glass and ran the fingers of her free hand through her short blonde hair. 'Hell with it, then, since you're here. Hell with it.'

She walked over and snatched up the slate. 'Wild beast, eh? Wild beast?'

'Some form of vicious predator indigenous to the mountain region that–'

'Forgive me, that's so much shit,' she said. She snapped the slate into the reader slot of a compact edit engine on the far side of the room. Some of her picters and spare lenses littered the bench beside it. The engine whirred into life, and the screen lit up, cold and white. 'What did you make of the discrepancies?'

'Discrepancies?' Loken asked.

'Yes.' She expertly tapped commands into the engine's controls, and selected the file. With a stab of her index finger, she opened the first image. It bloomed on the screen.

'Terra, I can't look at it,' she said, turning away.

'Switch it off, Keeler.'

'No, you look at it. Look at the visual distortion there. Surely you noticed that? It's like it's there and yet not there. Like it's phasing in and out of reality.'

'A signal error. The conditions and the poor light foxed your picter's sensors and–'

'I know how to use a picter, captain, and I know how to recognise poor exposure, lens flare, and digital malformance. That's not it. Look.'

She punched up the second pict, and half-looked at it, gesturing with her hand. 'Look at the background. And the droplets of blood in the foreground there. Perfect pict capture. But the thing itself. I've never seen anything create that effect on a high-gain instrument. That "wild beast" is out of sync with the physical continuity around it. Which is, captain, exactly as I saw it. You've studied these closely, no doubt?'

'No,' said Loken.

Keeler pulled up another image. She stared at it fully this time, and then looked away. 'There, you see? The afterimage? It's on all of them, but this is the clearest.'

'I don't see...'

'I'll boost the contrast and lose a little of the motion blurring.' She fiddled with the engine's controls. 'There. See now?'

Loken stared. What had at first seemed to be a frothy, milky ghost blurring across the image of the nightmare thing had resolved clearly thanks to her manipulation. Superimposed on the fuzzy abomination was a semi-human shape, echoing the pose and posture of the creature. Though it was faint, there was no mistaking the shrieking face and wracked body of Xavyer Jubal.

'Know him?' she asked. 'I don't, but I recognise the physiognomy and build of an Astartes when I see it. Why would my picter register that, unless...'

Loken didn't reply.

Keeler switched the screen off, popped out the slate and tossed it back to Loken. He caught it neatly. She went back over to the cot and flopped down.

'That's what I wanted you to explain to me,' she said. 'That's why I sent you the picts. When I was in my deepest, darkest pits of madness, that's what I was hoping you'd come and explain to me, but don't worry. I'm past that now. I'm fine. A wild beast, that's all it was. A wild beast.'

Loken gazed at the slate in his hand. He could barely imagine what Keeler had been through. It had been bad enough for the rest of them, but he and Nero and Sindermann had all enjoyed the benefit of proper closure. They'd been told the truth. Keeler hadn't. She was smart and bright and clever, and she'd seen the holes in the story, the awful inconsistencies that proved there had been more to the event than the first captain's explanation. And she'd managed with that knowledge, coped with it, alone.

'What did you think it was?' he asked.

'Something awful that we should never know about,' she replied. 'Throne, Loken. Please don't take pity on me now. Please don't decide to tell me.'

'I won't,' he said. 'I can't. It was a wild beast. Euphrati, how did you deal with it?'

'What do you mean?'

'You say you're fine now. How are you fine?'

'My friends helped me through. I told you.'

Loken got up, picked up the flask, and went over to the cot. He sat down on the end of the mattress and refilled the glass she held out.

'Thank you,' she said. 'I've found strength. I've found–'

For a moment, Loken was certain she had been about to say 'faith'.

'What?'

'Trust. Trust in the Imperium. In the Emperor. In you.'

'In me?'

'Not you, personally. In the Astartes, in the Imperial army, in every branch of mankind's warrior force that is dedicated to the protection of us mere mortals.' She took a sip and sniggered. 'The Emperor, you see, protects.'

'Of course he does,' said Loken.

'No, no, you misunderstand,' said Keeler, folding her arms

around her raised, sheet-covered knees. 'He actually does. He protects mankind, through the Legions, through the martial corps, through the war machines of the Mechanicum. He understands the dangers. The inconsistencies. He uses you, and all the instruments like you, to protect us from harm. To protect our physical bodies from murder and damage, to protect our minds from madness, to protect our souls. This is what I now understand. This is what this trauma has taught me, and I am thankful for it. There are insane dangers in the cosmos, dangers that mankind is fundamentally unable to comprehend, let alone survive. So he protects us. There are truths out there that would drive us mad by one fleeting glimpse of them. So he chooses not to share them with us. That's why he made you.'

'That's a glorious concept,' Loken admitted.

'In the Whisperheads, that day... You saved me, didn't you? You shot that thing apart. Now you save me again, by keeping the truth to yourself. Does it hurt?'

'Does what hurt?'

'The truth you keep hidden?'

'Sometimes,' he said.

'Remember, Garviel. The Emperor is our truth and our light. If we trust in him, he will protect.'

'Where did you get that from?' Loken asked.

'A friend. Garviel, I have only one concern. A lingering thing that will not quit my mind. You Astartes are loyal, through and through. You keep to your own, and never break confidence.'

'And?'

'Tonight, I really believe you would have told me something, but for the loyalty you keep with your brothers. I admire that, but answer me this. How far does your loyalty go? Whatever it was happened to us in the Whisperheads, I believe an Astartes brother was part of it. But you close ranks. What has to happen before you forsake your loyalty to the Legion and recognise your loyalty to the rest of us?'

'I don't know what you mean,' he said.

'Yes, you do. If a brother turns on his brothers again, will you cover that up too? How many have to turn before you act? One? A squad? A company? How long will you keep your secrets? What will it take for you to cast aside the fraternal bonds of the Legion and cry out "This is wrong!"?'

'You're suggesting an impossible–'

'No, I'm not. You, of all people, know I'm not. If it can happen to one, it can happen to others. You're all so drilled and perfect and identical. You march to the same beat and do whatever is asked of you. Loken, do you know of any Astartes who would break step? Would you?'

'I…'

'Would you? If you saw the rot, a hint of corruption, would you step out of your regimented life and stand against it? For the greater good of mankind, I mean?'

'It's not going to happen,' Loken said. 'That would never happen. You're suggesting civil disunity. Civil war. That is against every fibre of the Imperium as the Emperor has created it. With Horus as Warmaster, as our guiding light, such a possibility is beyond countenance. The Imperium is firm and strong, and of one purpose. There are inconsistencies, Euphrati, just like there are wars and plagues and famines. They hurt us, but they do not kill us. We rise above them and move onwards.'

'It rather depends,' she remarked, 'where those inconsistencies occur.'

Loken's vox-cuff suddenly began to bleat. Loken raised his wrist, and thumbed the call stud. 'I'm on my way,' he said. He looked back at her.

'Let's talk again, Euphrati,' he said.

She nodded. He leant forwards and kissed her on the forehead. 'Be well. Be better. Look to your friends.'

'Are you my friend?' she asked.

'Know it,' he said. He got up and retrieved his robe from the floor.

'Garviel,' she called from the cot.

'Yes?'

'Delete those images, please. For me. They don't need to exist.'

He nodded, opened the shutter, and stepped out into the chill of the hall.

Once the shutter had closed, Keeler got up off the cot and let the sheet fall from her. Naked, she padded over to a cupboard, knelt and opened its doors. From inside, she took out two candles and a small figurine of the Emperor. She placed them on the top of the cupboard, and lit the candles with an igniter. Then she rummaged in the cupboard and pulled out the dog-eared pamphlet that Leef had given her. It was a cheap, crude thing, badly pressed from a mechanical bulk-printer. There were ink soils along its edges, and rather a lot of spelling mistakes in the text.

Keeler didn't care. She opened the first page and, bowed before the makeshift shrine, she began to read.

'The Emperor of Mankind is the Light and the Way, and all his actions are for the benefit of mankind, which is his people. The Emperor is God and God is the Emperor, so it is taught in the Lectitio Divinitatus, and above all things, the Emperor will protect...'

LOKEN RAN DOWN the companionways of the remembrancers' billet wing, his cloak billowing out behind him. Sirens were sounding. Men and women peered out of doorways to look at him as he passed by.

He raised his cuff to his mouth. 'Nero. Report! Is it Tarik? Has something happened?'

The vox crackled and Vipus's voice issued tinnily from the cuff speaker. 'Something's happened all right, Garvi. Get back here.'

'What? What's happened?'

'A ship, that's what. A battle-barge has just translated in-system behind us. It's Sanguinius. Sanguinius himself has come.'

SEVEN

Lord of the Angels
Brotherhood in Spiderland
Interdiction

JUST A WEEK or so earlier, during one of their regular, private interviews, Loken had finally told Mersadie Oliton about the Great Triumph after Ullanor.

'You cannot imagine it,' he said.

'I can try.'

Loken smiled. 'The Mechanicum had planed smooth an entire continent as a stage for the event.'

'Planed smooth? What?'

'With industrial meltas and geoformer engines. Mountains were erased and their matter used to infill valleys. The surface was left smooth and endless, a vast table of dry, polished rock chippings. It took months to accomplish.'

'It ought to have taken centuries!'

'You underestimate the industry of the Mechanicum. They sent four labour fleets to undertake the work. They made a stage worthy of an Emperor, so broad it could know midnight at one end and midday at the other.'

'You exaggerate!' she cried, with a delighted snort.

'Maybe I do. Have you known me do that before?'

Oliton shook her head.

'You have to understand, this was a singular event. It was a Triumph to mark the turn of an era, and the Emperor, beloved of
all, knew it. He knew it had to be remembered. It was the end
of the Ullanor campaign, the end of the crusade, the coronation
of the Warmaster. It was a chance for the Astartes to say farewell
to the Emperor before his departure to Terra, after two centuries
of personal leadership. We wept as he announced his retirement
from the field. Can you picture that, Mersadie? A hundred thousand warriors, weeping?'

She nodded. 'I think it was a shame no remembrancers were
there to witness it. It was a moment that comes only once every
epoch.'

'It was a private affair.'

She laughed again. 'A hundred thousand present, a continent
levelled for the event, and it was a private affair?'

Loken looked at her. 'Even now, you don't understand us, do
you? You still think on a very human scale.'

'I stand corrected,' she replied.

'I meant no offence,' he said, noticing her expression, 'but it was
a private affair. A ceremony. A hundred thousand Astartes. Eight
million army regulars. Legions of Titan war machines, like forests
of steel. Armour units by the hundred, formations of tanks, thousands upon thousands. Warships filling the low orbit, eclipsed by
the squadrons of aircraft flying over in unending echelons. Banners and standards, so many banners and standards.'

He fell silent for a moment, remembering. 'The Mechanicum
had made a roadway. Half a kilometre wide, and five hundred
kilometres long, a straight line across the stage they had levelled.
On each side of this road, every five metres, was an iron post

topped with the skull of a greenskin, trophies of the Ullanor war. Beyond the roadway, to either hand, promethium fires burned in rockcrete basins. For five hundred kilometres. The heat was intense. We marched along the roadway in review, passing below the dais on which the Emperor stood, beneath a steel-scale canopy. The dais was the only raised structure the Mechanicum had left, the root of an old mountain. We marched in review, and then assembled on the wide plain below the dais.'

'Who marched?'

'All of us. Fourteen Legions were represented, either in total or by a company. The others were engaged in wars too remote to allow them to attend. The Luna Wolves were there en mass, of course. Nine primarchs were there, Mersadie. Nine. Horus, Dorn, Angron, Fulgrim, Lorgar, Mortarion, Sanguinius, Magnus, the Khan. The rest had sent ambassadors. Such a spectacle. You cannot imagine.'

'I'm still trying.'

Loken shook his head. 'I'm still trying to believe I was there.'

'What were they like?'

'You think I met them? I was just another brother-warrior marching in the file. In my life, lady, I have seen almost all of the primarchs at one time or another, but mostly from a distance. I've personally spoken to two of them. Until my election to the Mournival, I didn't move in such elevated circles. I know the primarchs as distant figures. At the Triumph, I could barely believe so many were present.'

'But still, you had impressions?'

'Indelible impressions. Each one, so mighty, so huge and so proud. They seemed to embody human characteristics. Angron, red and angry; Dorn solid and implacable; Magnus, veiled in mystery, and Sanguinius, of course. So perfect. So charismatic.'

'I've heard this of him.'

'Then you've heard the truth.'

HIS LONG BLACK hair was pressed down by the weight of the shawl of gold chain he wore across his head. The edges of it framed his solemn features. He had marked his cheeks with grey ash in mourning.

An attendant stood by with ink pot and brush to paint the ritual tears of grief on his cheeks, but Primarch Sanguinius shook his head, making the chain shawl clink. 'I have real tears,' he said.

He turned, not to his brother Horus, but to Torgaddon.

'Show me, Tarik,' he said.

Torgaddon nodded. The wind moaned around the still figures assembled on the lonely hillside, and rain pattered off their armour plate. Torgaddon gestured, and Tarvitz, Bulle and Lucius stepped forwards, holding out the dirty relics.

'These men, my lord,' Torgaddon said, his voice unusually shaky, 'these Children of the Emperor, recovered these remains selflessly, and it is fit they offer them to you themselves.'

'You did this honour?' Sanguinius asked Tarvitz.

'I did, my lord.'

Sanguinius took the battered Astartes helm from Tarvitz's hands and studied it. He towered over the captain, his golden plate badged with rubies and bright jewels, and marked, like the armour of the Warmaster, with the unblinking eye of Terra. Sanguinius's vast wings, like the pinions of a giant eagle, were furled against his back, and hung with silver bands and loops of pearls.

Sanguinius turned the helm over in his hands, and regarded the armourer's mark inside the rim.

'Eight knight leopard,' he said.

At his side, Chapter Master Raldoron began to inspect the manifest.

'Don't trouble yourself, Ral,' Sanguinius told him. 'I know the mark. Captain Thoros. He will be missed.'

Sanguinius handed the helm to Raldoron and nodded to Tarvitz. 'Thank you for this kindness, captain,' he said. He looked across at Eidolon. 'And to you, sir, my gratitude that you came to Frome's help so urgently.'

Eidolon bowed, and seemed to ignore the dark glare the Warmaster was casting in his direction.

Sanguinius turned to Torgaddon. 'And to you, Tarik, most of all. For breaking this nightmare open.'

'I do only what my Warmaster instructs me,' Torgaddon replied.

Sanguinius looked over at Horus. 'Is that right?'

'Tarik had some latitude,' Horus smiled. He stepped forwards and embraced Sanguinius to his breast. No two primarchs were as close as the Warmaster and the Angel. They had barely been out of each other's company since Sanguinius's arrival.

The majestic Lord of the Blood Angels, the IX Legion Astartes, stepped back, and looked out across the forlorn landscape. Around the base of the ragged hill, hundreds of armoured figures waited in silence. The vast majority wore either the hard white of the Luna Wolves or the arterial red of the Angels, save for the remnants of the detachment of Emperor's Children, a small knot of purple and gold. Behind the Astartes, the war machines waited in the rain, silent and black, ringing the gathering like spectral mourners. Beyond them, the hosts of the Imperial army stood in observance, banners flapping sluggishly in the cold breeze. Their armoured vehicles and troop carriers were drawn up in echelon, and many of the soldiers had clambered up to stand on the hulls to get a better view of the proceedings.

Torgaddon's speartip had razed a large sector of the landscape, demolishing stone trees wherever they could be found, and thus taming the formidable weather in this part of Murder. The sky had faded to a mottled powder-grey, run through with thin white bars of cloud, and rain fell softly and persistently, reducing visibility in the distances to a foggy blur. At the Warmaster's command, the main force of the assembled Imperial ships had made planetfall in the comparative safety of the storm-free zone.

'In the old philosophies of Terra,' Sanguinius said, 'so I have read, vengeance was seen as a weak motive and a flaw of the spirit. It is hard for me to feel so noble today. I would cleanse this rock in the memory of my lost brothers, and their kin who died trying to save them.'

The Angel looked at his primarch brother. 'But that is not necessary. Vengeance is not necessary. There is xenos here, implacable alien menace that rejects any civilised intercourse with mankind, and has greeted us with murder and murder alone. That suffices. As the Emperor, beloved by all, has taught us, since the start of our crusade, what is anathema to mankind must be dealt with directly to ensure the continued survival of the Imperium. Will you stand with me?'

'We will murder Murder together,' Horus replied.

ONCE THOSE WORDS were spoken, the Astartes went to war for six months. Supported by the army and the devices of the Mechanicum, they assaulted the bleak, shivering latitudes of the world called Murder, and laid waste the megarachnid.

It was a glorious war, in many ways, and not an easy one. No matter how many of them were slaughtered, the megarachnid did not cower or turn in retreat. It seemed as if they had no will, nor any spirit, to be broken. They came on and on, issuing forth from cracks and crevasses in the ruddy land, day after day, set for further dispute. At times, it felt as if there was an endless reserve of them, as if unimaginably vast nests of them infested the mantle of the planet, or as if ceaseless subterranean factories manufactured more and yet more of them every day to replace the losses delivered by the Imperial forces. For their own part, no matter how many of them they slaughtered, the warriors of the Imperium did not come to underestimate the megarachnid. They were lethal and tough, and so numerous as to put a man out of countenance. 'The fiftieth beast I killed,' Little Horus remarked at one stage, 'was as hard to overcome as the first.'

Loken, like many of the Luna Wolves present, personally rejoiced in the circumstances of the conflict, for it was the first time since his election as Warmaster that the commander had led them on the field. Early on, in the command habitent one rainy evening, the Mournival had gently tried to dissuade Horus from field operations. Abaddon had attempted, deftly, to portray the Warmaster's role and importance as a thing of a much higher consequence than martial engagement.

'Am I not fit for it?' Horus had scowled, the rain drumming on the canopy overhead.

'I mean you are too precious for it, lord,' Abaddon had countered. 'This is one world, one field of war. The Emperor has charged you with the concerns of all worlds and all fields. Your scope is–'

'Ezekyle...' The Warmaster's tone had betrayed a warning note, and he had switched to Cthonic, a clear sign his mind was on war and nothing else, '...do not presume to instruct me on my duties.'

'Lord, I would not!' Abaddon exclaimed immediately, with a respectful bow.

'Precious is the word,' Aximand had put in quickly, coming to Abaddon's aid. 'If you were to be wounded, to fall even, it would–'

Horus rose, glaring. 'Now you deride my abilities as a warrior, little one? Have you grown soft since my ascendance?'

'No, my lord, no...'

Only Torgaddon, it seemed, had noticed the glimmer of amusement behind the Warmaster's pantomime of anger.

'We're only afraid you won't leave any glory for us,' he said.

Horus began to laugh. Realising he had been playing with
them, the members of the Mournival began to laugh too. Horus
cuffed Abaddon across the shoulder and pinched Aximand's
cheek.

'We'll war this together, my sons,' he said. 'That is how I was
made. If I had suspected, back at Ullanor, that the rank of
Warmaster would require me to relinquish the glories of the field
forever, I would not have accepted it. Someone else could have
taken the honour. Guilleman or the Lion, perhaps. They ache for
it, after all.'

More loud amusement followed. The laughter of Cthonians is
dark and hard, but the laughter of Luna Wolves is a harder thing
altogether.

Afterwards, Loken wondered if the Warmaster had not been
using his sly political skills yet again. He had avoided the central
issue entirely, and deflected their concerns with good humour
and an appeal to their code as warriors. It was his way of telling
them that, for all their good counsel, there were some matters
on which his mind would not be swayed. Loken was sure that
Sanguinius was the reason. Horus could not bring himself to
stand by and watch his dearest brother go to war. Horus could
not resist the temptation of fighting shoulder to shoulder with
Sanguinius, as they had done in the old days.

Horus would not let himself be outshone, even by the one he
loved most dearly.

To see them together on the battlefield was a heart-stopping
thing. Two gods of war, raging at the head of a tide of red and
white. Dozens of times, they accomplished victories in part-
nership on Murder that should, had what followed been any

different, become deeds as lauded and immortal as Ullanor or any other great triumph.

Indeed the war as a whole produced many extraordinary feats that posterity ought to have celebrated, especially now the remembrancers were amongst them.

Like all her kind, Mersadie Oliton was not permitted to descend to the surface with the fighting echelons, but she absorbed every detail transmitted back from the surface, the daily ebb and flow of the brutal warfare, the losses and the gains. When, periodically, Loken returned with his company to the flagship to rest, repair and re-arm, she quizzed him furiously, and made him describe all he had seen. Horus and Sanguinius, side by side, was what interested her the most, but she was captivated by all his accounts.

Many battles had been vast, pitched affairs, where thousands of Astartes led tens of thousands of army troopers against endless files of the megarachnid. Loken struggled to find the language to describe it, and sometimes felt himself, foolishly, borrowing lurid turns of phrase he had picked up from *The Chronicles of Ursh*. He told her of the great things he had witnessed, the particular moments. How Luc Sedirae had led his company against a formation of megarachnid twenty-five deep and one hundred across, and splintered it in under half an hour. How Sacrus Carminus, Captain of the Blood Angels Third Company, had held the line against a buzzing host of winged clades through one long, hideous afternoon. How Iacton Qruze, despite his stubborn, tiresome ways, had broken the back of a surprise megarachnid assault, and proved there was mettle in him still. How Tybalt Marr, 'the Either', had taken the low mountains in two days and elevated himself at last into the ranks of the exceptional. How the megarachnid had revealed more, and yet more nightmarish biological variations, including massive clades that strode forwards like armoured war machines, and how the Titans of the Mechanicum, led at the van by the *Dies Irae* of the Legio Mortis, smote them apart and trampled their blackened wing cases underfoot. How Saul Tarvitz, fighting at Torgaddon's side rather than in the cohort of his arrogant lord Eidolon, renewed the Luna Wolves' respect for the Emperor's Children through several feats of arms.

Tarvitz and Torgaddon had achieved a brotherhood during the war and eased the discontent between the two Legions. Loken had heard rumours that Eidolon was initially displeased with Tarvitz's deportment, until he recognised how simple brotherhood and effort was redeeming his mistake. Eidolon, though he would never admit it, realised full well he was out of favour with the Warmaster, but as time passed, he found he was at least tolerated within the bounds of the commander's war-tent, and consulted along with the other officers.

Sanguinius had also smoothed the way. He knew his brother Horus was keen to rebuke Fulgrim for the high-handed qualities his Astartes had lately displayed. Horus and Fulgrim were close, almost as close as Sanguinius and the Warmaster. It dismayed the Lord of Angels to see a potential rift in the making.

'You cannot afford dissent,' Sanguinius had said. 'As Warmaster, you must have the undivided respect of the primarchs, just as the Emperor had. Moreover, you and Fulgrim are too long bound as brothers for you to fall to bickering.'

The conversation had taken place during a brief hiatus in the fighting, during the sixth week, when Raldoron and Sedirae were leading the main force west into a series of valleys and narrow defiles along the foothills of a great bank of mountains. The two primarchs had rested for a day in a command camp some leagues behind the advance. Loken remembered it well. He and the others of the Mournival had been present in the main war-tent when

Sanguinius brought the matter up.

'I don't bicker,' Horus said, as his armourers removed his heavy, mud-flecked wargear and bathed his limbs. 'The Emperor's Children have always been proud, but that pride is becoming insolence. Brother or not, Fulgrim must know his place. I have trouble enough with Angron's bloody rages and Perturabo's damn petulence. I'll not brook disrespect from such a close ally.'

'Was it Fulgrim's error, or his man Eidolon's?' Sanguinius asked.

'Fulgrim made Eidolon lord commander. He favours his merits, and evidently trusts him, and approves of his manner. If Eidolon embodies the character of the III Legion, then I have issue with it. Not just here. I need to know I can rely upon the Emperor's Children.'

'And why do you think you can't?'

Horus paused while an attendant washed his face, then spat sidelong into a bowl held ready by another. 'Because they're too damn proud of themselves.'

'Are not all Astartes proud of their own cohort?' Sanguinius took a sip of wine. He looked over at the Mournival. 'Are you not proud, Ezekyle?'

'To the ends of creation, my lord,' Abaddon replied.

'If I may, sir,' said Torgaddon, 'there is a difference. There is a man's natural pride and loyalty to his own Legion. That may be a boastful pride, and the source of rivalry between Astartes. But the Emperor's Children seem particularly haughty, as if above the likes of us. Not all of them, I hasten to add.'

Listening, Loken knew Torgaddon was referring to Tarvitz and the other friends he had made amongst Tarvitz's unit.

Sanguinius nodded. 'It is their mindset. It has always been so. They seek perfection, to be the best they can, to echo the perfection of the Emperor himself. It is not superiority. Fulgrim has explained this to me himself.'

'And Fulgrim may believe so,' Horus said, 'but superiority is how it manifests amongst some of his men. There was once mutual respect, but now they sneer and condescend. I fear it is my new rank that they resent. I'll not have it.'

'They don't resent you,' Sanguinius said.

'Maybe, but they resent the role my rank invests upon my Legion. The Luna Wolves have always been seen as rude barbarians. The flint of Cthonia is in their hearts, and the smudge of its dirt upon their skins. The Children regard the Luna Wolves as peers only by dint of my Legion's record in war. The Wolves sport no finery or elegant manners. We are cheerfully raw where they are regal.'

'Then maybe it is time to consider doing what the Emperor suggested,' Sanguinius said.

Horus shook his head emphatically. 'I refused that on Ullanor, honour though it was. I'll not contemplate it again.'

'Things change. You are Warmaster now. All the Legions Astartes must recognise the preeminence of the XVI Legion. Perhaps some need to be reminded.'

Horus snorted. 'I don't see Russ trying to clean up his berserk horde and rebrand them to court respect.'

'Leman Russ is not Warmaster,' said Sanguinius. 'Your title changed, brother, at the Emperor's command, so that all the rest of us would be in no mistake as to the power you wield and the trust the Emperor placed in you. Perhaps the same thing must happen to your Legion.'

Later, as they trudged west through the drizzle, following the plodding Titans across red mudflats and skeins of surface water, Loken asked Abaddon what the Lord of Angels had meant.

'At Ullanor,' the first captain answered, 'the beloved Emperor advised our commander to rename the XVI Legion, so there might be no mistake as to the power of our authority.'

'What name did he wish us to take?' Loken asked.

'The Sons of Horus,' Abaddon replied.

THE SIXTH MONTH of the campaign was drawing to a close when the strangers arrived.

Over the period of a few days, the vessels of the expedition, high in orbit, became aware of curious signals and etheric displacements that suggested the activity of starships nearby, and various attempts were made to locate the source. Advised of the situation, the Warmaster presumed that other reinforcements were on the verge of arrival, perhaps even additional units from the Emperor's Children. Patrolling scout ships, sent out by Master Comnenus, and cruisers on picket control, could find no concrete trace of any vessels, but many reported spectral readings, like the precursor field elevations that announced an imminent translation. The expedition fleet left high anchor and took station on a battle-ready grid, with the *Vengeful Spirit* and the *Proudheart* in the vanguard, and the *Misericord* and the *Red Tear*, Sanguinius's flagship, on the trailing flank.

When the strangers finally appeared, they came in rapidly and confidently, gunning in from a translation point at the system edges: three massive capital ships, of a build pattern and drive signature unknown to Imperial records.

As they came closer, they began to broadcast what seemed to be challenge signals. The nature of these signals was remarkably similar to the repeat of the outstation beacons, untranslatable and, according to the Warmaster, akin to music.

The ships were big. Visual relay showed them to be bright, sleek and silver-white, shaped like royal sceptres, with heavy prows, long, lean hulls and splayed drive sections. The largest of them was twice the keel length of the *Vengeful Spirit*.

General alert was sounded throughout the fleet, shields raised and weapons unshrouded. The Warmaster made immediate preparations to quit the surface and return to his flagship. Engagements with the megarachnid were hastily broken off, and the ground forces recalled into a single host. Horus ordered Comnenus to make hail, and hold fire unless fired upon. There seemed a high probability that these vessels belonged to the megarachnid, come from other worlds in support of the nests on Murder.

The ships did not respond directly to the hails, but continued to broadcast their own, curious signals. They prowled in close, and halted within firing distance of the expedition formation.

Then they spoke. Not with one voice, but with a chorus of voices, uttering the same words, overlaid with more of the curious musical transmissions. The message was received cleanly by the Imperial vox, and also by the astrotelepaths, conveyed with such force and authority, Ing Mae Sing and her adepts winced.

They spoke in the language of mankind. 'Did you not see the warnings we left?' they said. 'What have you done here?'

PART THREE
THE DREADFUL SAGITTARY

ONE

Make no mistakes
Cousins far removed
Other ways

AS AN UNEXPECTED sequel to the war on Murder, they became the guests of the interex, and right from the start of their sojourn, voices had begun to call for war.

Eidolon was one, and a vociferous one at that, but Eidolon was out of favour and easy to dismiss. Maloghurst was another, and so too were Sedirae and Targost, and Goshen, and Raldoron of the Blood Angels. Such men were not so easy to ignore.

Sanguinius kept his counsel, waiting for the Warmaster's decision, understanding that Horus needed his brother primarch's unequivocal support.

The argument, best summarised by Maloghurst, ran as follows: the people of the interex are of our blood and we descend from common ancestry, so they are lost kin. But they differ from us in fundamental ways, and these are so profound, so inescapable, that they are cause for legitimate war. They contradict absolutely the essential tenets of Imperial culture as expressed by the Emperor, and such contradictions cannot be tolerated.

For the while, Horus tolerated them well enough. Loken could understand why. The warriors of the interex were easy to admire, easy to like. They were gracious and noble, and once the misunderstanding had been explained, utterly without hostility.

It took a strange incident for Loken to learn the truth behind the Warmaster's thinking. It took place during the voyage, the nine-week voyage from Murder to the nearest outpost world of the interex, the mingled ships of the expedition and its hangers-on trailing the sleek vessels of the interex flotilla.

The Mournival had come to Horus's private staterooms, and a bitter row had erupted. Abaddon had been swayed by the arguments for war. Both Maloghurst and Sedirae had been whispering in his ear. He was convinced enough to face the Warmaster and not back down. Voices had been raised. Loken had watched in growing amazement as Abaddon and the Warmaster bellowed at each other. Loken had seen Abaddon wrathful before, in the heat of combat, but he had never seen the commander so ill-tempered. Horus's fury startled him a little, almost scared him.

As ever, Torgaddon was trying to diffuse the confrontation with levity. Loken could see that even Tarik was dismayed by the anger on show.

'You have no choice!' Abaddon snarled. 'We have seen enough already to know that their ways are in opposition to ours! You must–'

'Must?' Horus roared. 'Must I? You are Mournival, Abaddon! You advise and you counsel, and that is your place! Do not imagine you can tell me what to do!'

'I don't have to! There is no choice, and you know what must be done!'

'Get out!'

'You know it in your heart!'

'Get out!' Horus yelled, and cast aside his drinking cup with such force it shattered on the steel deck. He glared at Abaddon, teeth clenched. 'Get out, Ezekyle, before I look to find another first captain!'

Abaddon glowered back for a moment, spat on the floor and stormed from the chamber. The others stood in stunned silence.

Horus turned, his head bowed. 'Torgaddon?' he said quietly.

'Lord, yes?'

'Go after him, please. Calm him down. Tell him if he craves my forgiveness in an hour or two, I might soften enough to hear him, but he'd better be on his knees when he does it, and his voice had better not rise above a whisper.'

Torgaddon bowed and left the chamber immediately. Loken and Aximand glanced at one another, made an awkward salute, and turned to follow him out.

'You two stay,' Horus growled.

They stopped in their tracks. When they turned back, they saw the Warmaster was shaking his head, wiping a hand across his mouth. A kind of smile informed his wide-set eyes. 'Throne, my sons. How the molten core of Cthonia burns in us sometimes.'

Horus sat down on one of the long, cushioned couches, and waved to them with a casual flick of his hand. 'Hard as a rock, Cthonia, hot as hell in the heart. Volcanic. We've all known the heat of the deep mines. We all know how the lava spurts up sometimes, without warning. It's in us all, and it wrought us all. Hard as rock with a burning heart. Sit, sit. Take wine. Forgive my outburst. I'd have you close. Half a Mournival is better than nothing.'

They sat on the couch facing him. Horus took up a fresh cup, and poured wine from a silver ewer. 'The wise one and the quiet one,' he said. Loken wasn't sure which the Warmaster thought he was. 'Counsel me, then. You were both entirely too silent during that debate.'

Aximand cleared his throat. 'Ezekyle had… a point,' he began. He stiffened as he saw the Warmaster raise his eyebrows.

'Go on, little one.'

'We… that is to say… we prosecute this crusade according to certain doctrines. For two centuries, we have done so. Laws of life, laws on which the Imperium is founded. They are not arbitrary. They were given to us, to uphold, by the Emperor himself.'

'Beloved of all,' Horus said.

'The Emperor's doctrines have guided us since the start. We have never disobeyed them.' Aximand paused, then added, 'Before.'

'You think this is disobedience, little one?' Horus asked. Aximand shrugged. 'What about you, Garviel?' Horus asked. 'Are you with Aximand on this?'

Loken looked back into the Warmaster's eyes. 'I know why we ought to make war upon the interex, sir,' he said. 'What interests me is why you think we shouldn't.'

Horus smiled. 'At last, a thinking man.' He rose to his feet and, carrying his cup carefully, walked across to the right-hand wall of the stateroom, a section of which had been richly decorated with a mural. The painting showed the Emperor, ascendant above all, catching the spinning constellations in his outstretched hand. 'The stars,' Horus said. 'See, there? How he scoops them up? The zodiacs swirl into his grasp like fireflies. The stars are mankind's birthright. That's what he told me. That's one of the first things he told me when we met. I was like a child then, raised up from nothing. He set me at his side, and pointed to the heavens. Those points of light, he said, are what we have been waiting generations to master. Imagine, Horus, every one a human culture, every one a realm of beauty and magnificence, free from strife, free from war, free from bloodshed and the tyrannous oppression of alien overlords. Make no mistake, he said, and they will be ours.'

Horus slowly traced his fingers across the whorl of painted stars until his hand met the image of the Emperor's hand. He took his touch away and looked back at Aximand and Loken. 'As a found-ling, on Cthonia, I saw the stars very infrequently. The sky was so often thick with foundry smoke and ash, but you remember, of course.'

'Yes,' said Loken. Little Horus nodded.

'On those few nights when the stars were visible, I wondered at them. Wondered what they were and what they meant. Little, mysterious sparks of light, they had to have some purpose in being there. I wondered such things every day of my life until the Emperor came. I was not surprised when he told me how important they were.'

'I'll tell you a thing,' said Horus, walking back to them and resuming his seat. 'The first thing my father gave me was an astro-logical text. It was a simple thing, a child's primer. I have it here somewhere. He noted my wonder in the stars, and wished me to learn and understand.'

He paused. Loken was always captivated whenever Horus began to refer to the Emperor as 'my father'. It had happened a few times since Loken had been part of the inner circle, and on every occasion it had led to unguarded revelations.

'There were zodiac charts in it. In the text.' Horus took a sip of his wine and smiled at the memory. 'I learned them all. In one evening. Not just the names, but the patterns, the associations, the structure. All twenty signs. The next day, my father laughed at my appetite for knowledge. He told me the zodiac signs were old and unreliable models, now that the explorator fleets had begun detailed cosmological mapping. He told me that the twenty signs in the heavens would one day be matched by twenty sons like me. Each son would embody the character and notion of a particular zodiac group. He asked me which one I liked the best.'

'What did you answer?' Loken asked.

Horus sat back, and chuckled. 'I told him I liked all the patterns they made. I told him I was glad to finally have names for the sparks of light in the sky. I told him I liked Leos, naturally, for his regal fury, and Skorpos, for his armour and warlike blade. I told him that Tauromach appealed to my sense of stubbornness, and Arbitos to my sense of fairness and balance.' The Warmaster shook his head, sadly. 'My father said he admired my choices, but was surprised I had not picked another in particular. He showed me again the horseman with the bow, the galloping warrior. The dreadful Sagittary, he said. Most warlike of all. Strong, relentless, unbridled, swift and sure of his mark. In ancient times, he told me, this was the greatest sign of all. The centaur, the horse-man, the hunter-warrior, had been beloved in the old ages. In Anatoly, in his own childhood, the centaur had been a revered symbol. A rider upon a horse, so he said, armed with a bow. The most potent martial instrument of its age, conquering all before it. Over time, myth had blended horseman and steed into one form. The perfect synthesis of man and war machine. That is what you must learn to be, he told me. That is what you must master. One day, you must command my armies, my instruments of war, as if they were an extension of your own person. Man and horse, as one, galloping the heavens, submitting to no foe. At Ullanor, he gave me this.'

Horus set down his cup, and leaned forward to show them the weathered gold ring he wore on the smallest finger of his left hand. It was so eroded by age that the image was indistinct. Loken thought he could detect hooves, a man's arm, a bent bow.

'It was made in Persia, the year before the Emperor was born. The dreadful Sagittary. This is you now, he said to me. My Warmaster, my centaur. Half man, half army, embedded in the Legions of the Imperium. Where you turn, so the Legions turn.

Where you move, so they move. Where you strike, so they strike. Ride on without me, my son, and the armies will ride with you.'

There was a long silence. 'So you see,' Horus smiled. 'I am predisposed to like the dreadful Sagittary, now we meet him, face to face.'

His smile was infectious. Both Loken and Aximand nodded and laughed.

'Now tell them the real reason,' a voice said.

They turned. Sanguinius stood in an archway at the far end of the chamber, behind a veil of white silk. He had been listening. The Lord of Angels brushed the silk hanging aside, and stepped into the stateroom, the crests of his wings brushing the glossy material. He was dressed in a simple white robe, clasped at the waist with a girdle of gold links. He was eating fruit from a bowl.

Loken and Aximand stood up quickly.

'Sit down,' Sanguinius said. 'My brother's in the mood to open his heart, so you had better hear the truth.'

'I don't believe–' Horus began. Sanguinius scooped one of the small, red fruits from his bowl and threw it at Horus.

'Tell them the rest,' he sniggered.

Horus caught the thrown fruit, gazed at it, then bit into it. He wiped the juice off his chin with the back of his hand and looked across at Loken and Aximand.

'Remember the start of my story?' he asked. 'What the Emperor said to me about the stars? *Make no mistake, and they will be ours.'*

He took another two bites, threw the fruit stone away, and swallowed the flesh before he continued. 'Sanguinius, my dear brother, is right, for Sanguinius has always been my conscience.'

Sanguinius shrugged, an odd gesture for a giant with furled wings.

'*Make no mistake,*' Horus continued. 'Those three words. Make no mistake. I am Warmaster, by the Emperor's decree. I cannot fail him. I cannot make mistakes.'

'Sir?' Aximand ventured.

'Since Ullanor, little one, I have made two. Or been party to two, and that is enough, for the responsibility for all expedition mistakes falls to me in the final count.'

'What mistakes?' asked Loken.

'Mistakes. Misunderstandings.' Horus stroked his hand across his brow. 'Sixty-Three Nineteen. Our first endeavour. My first as Warmaster. How much blood was spilt there, blood from misunderstanding? We misread the signs and paid the price. Poor, dear Sejanus. I miss him still. That whole war, even that nightmare up on the mountains you had to endure, Garviel… a mistake. I could have handled it differently. Sixty-Three Nineteen could have been brought to compliance without bloodshed.'

'No, sir,' said Loken emphatically. 'They were too set in their ways, and their ways were set against us. We could not have made them compliant without a war.'

Horus shook his head. 'You are kind, Garviel, but you are mistaken. There were ways. There should have been ways. I should have been able to sway that civilisation without a shot being fired. The Emperor would have done so.'

'I don't believe he would,' Aximand said.

'Then there's Murder,' Horus continued, ignoring Little Horus's remark. 'Or Spiderland, as the interex has it. What is the way of their name for it again?'

'Urisarach,' Sanguinius said, helpfully. 'Though I think the word only works with the appropriate harmonic accompaniment.'

'Spiderland will suffice, then,' said Horus. 'What did we waste there? What misunderstandings did we make? The interex left us warnings to stay away, and we ignored them. An embargoed world, an asylum for the creatures they had bested in war, and we walked straight in.'

'We weren't to know,' Sanguinius said.

'We should have known!' Horus snapped.

'Therein lies the difference between our philosophy and that of the interex,' Aximand said. 'We cannot endure the existence of a malign alien race. They subjugate it, but refrain from annihilating it. Instead, they deprive it of space travel and exile it to a prison world.'

'We annihilate,' said Horus. 'They find a means around such drastic measures. Which of us is the most humane?'

Aximand rose to his feet. 'I find myself with Ezekyle on this. Tolerance is weakness. The interex is admirable, but it is forgiving and generous in its dealings with xenos breeds who deserve no quarter.'

'It has brought them to book, and learned to live in sympathy,' said Horus. 'It has trained the kinebrach to–'

'And that's the best example I can offer!' Aximand replied. 'The kinebrach. It embraces them as part of its culture.'

'I will not make another rash or premature decision,' Horus stated flatly. 'I have made too many, and my Warmastery is threatened by my mistakes. I will understand the interex, and learn from it, and parlay with it, and only then will I decide if it has strayed too far. They are a fine people. Perhaps we can learn from them for a change.'

THE MUSIC WAS hard to get used to. Sometimes it was magisterial and loud, especially when the meturge players struck up, and sometimes it was just a quiet whisper, like a buzz, like tinnitus, but it seldom went away. The people of the interex called it the aria, and it was a fundamental part of their communication. They still used language – indeed, their spoken language was an evolved human dialect closer in form to the prime language of Terra than Cthonic – but they had long ago formulated the aria as an accompaniment and enhancement of speech, and as a mode of translation.

Scrutinised by the iterators during the voyage, the aria proved to be hard to define. Essentially, it was a form of high mathematics, a universal constant that transcended linguistic barriers, but the mathematical structures were expressed through specific harmonic and melodic modes which, to the untrained ear, sounded like music. Strands of complex melody rang in the background of all the interex's vocal transmissions, and when one of their kind spoke face to face, it was usual to have one or more of the meturge players accompany his speech with their instruments. The meturge players were the translators and envoys.

Tall, like all the people of the interex, they wore long coats of a glossy, green fibre, laced with slender gold piping. The flesh of their ears was distended and splayed, by genetic and surgical enhancement, like the ears of bats or other nocturnal fliers. Comm technology, the equivalent of vox, was laced around the high collars of their coats, and each one carried an instrument strapped across his chest, a device with amplifiers and coiled pipes, and numerous digital keys on which the meturge player's nimble fingers constantly rested. A swan-necked mouthpiece rose from the top of each instrument, enabling the player to blow, hum, or vocalise into the device.

The first meeting between Imperium and interex had been formal and cautious. Envoys came aboard the *Vengeful Spirit*, escorted by meturge players and soldiers. The envoys were uniformly handsome and lean, with piercing eyes. Their hair was dressed short, and intricate dermatoglyphics – Loken suspected permanent tattoos – decorated either the left or right-hand sides of their faces. They wore knee-length robes of a soft, pale blue cloth, under which they were dressed in close-fitting clothing woven from the same, glossy fibre that composed the meturge players' coats.

The soldiers were impressive. Fifty of them, led by officers, had descended from their shuttle. Taller than the envoys, they were clad from crown to toe in metal armour of burnished silver and emerald green with aposematic chevrons of scarlet. The armour was of almost delicate design, and sheathed their bodies tightly; it was in no way as massive or heavy-set as the Astartes' plate. The soldiers – variously gleves or sagittars, Loken learned – were almost as tall as the Astartes, but with their far more slender build and more closely fitted armour, they seemed slight compared to the Imperial giants. Abaddon, at the first meeting, muttered that he doubted their fancy armour would stand even a slap.

Their weapons caused more remarks. Most of the soldiers had swords sheathed across their backs. Some, the gleves, carried long-bladed metal spears with heavy ball counterweights on the base ends. The others, the sagittars, carried recurve bows wrought from some dark metal. The sagittars had sheaves of long, flight-less darts laced to their right thighs.

'Bows?' Torgaddon whispered. 'Really? They stun us with the power and scale of their vessels, then come aboard carrying bows?'

'They're probably ceremonial,' Aximand murmured.

The soldier officers wore serrated half-discs across the skulls of their helmets. The visors of their close-fitting helms were all alike: the metal modelled to the lines of brow and cheekbone and nose, with simple oval eyeslits that were backlit blue. The mouth and chin area of each visor was built out, like a thrusting, pugnacious jaw, containing a communication module.

Behind the slender soldiers, as a further escort, came heavier forms. Shorter, and far more thick-set, these men were similarly armoured, though in browns and golds. Loken supposed them to be heavy troopers, their bodies gene-bred for bulk and muscle, designed for close combat, but they carried no weapons. There were twenty of them, and they flanked five robotic creatures, slender, silver quadrupeds of intricate and elegant design, made to resemble the finest Terra-stock horses, except that they possessed no heads or necks.

'Artificials,' Horus whispered aside to Maloghurst. 'Make sure Master Regulus is observing this via the pict feed. I'll want his notes later.'

One of the flagship's embarkation decks had been entirely cleared for the ceremonial meeting. Imperial banners had been hung along the vault, and the whole of First Company assembled in full plate as an honour guard. The Astartes formed two unwavering blocks of white figures, rigid and still, their front rows a glossy black line of Justaerin Terminators. In the aisle between the two formations, Horus stood with the Mournival, Maloghurst and other senior officials like Ing Mae Sing. The Warmaster and his lieutenants wore full armour and cloaks, though Horus's head was bare.

They watched the heavy interex shuttle move ponderously down the lighted runway of the deck, and settle on polished skids. Then hatch-ramps in its prow opened, the white metal unfolding like giant origami puzzles, and the envoys and their escorts disembarked. In total, with the soldiers and the meturge players, there were over one hundred of them. They came to a halt, with the envoys in a line at the front and the escort arranged in perfect symmetry behind. Forty-eight hours of intense inter-ship communication had preceded that cautious moment. Forty-eight hours of delicate diplomacy.

Horus gave a nod, and the men of First Company chested their weapons and bowed their heads in one, loud, unified motion. Horus himself stepped forward and walked alone down the aisle space, his cloak billowing behind him.

He came face to face with what seemed to be the senior envoy, made the sign of the aquila, and bowed.

'I greet you on–' he began.

The moment he started speaking, the meturge players began sounding their instruments softly. Horus stopped.

'Translation form,' the envoy said, his own words accompanied by meturge playing.

'It is disconcerting,' Horus smiled.

'For purposes of clarity and comprehension,' the envoy said.

'We appear to understand each other well enough,' Horus smiled.

The envoy nodded curtly. 'Then I will tell the players to stop,' he said.

'No,' said Horus. 'Let us be natural. If this is your way.'

Again, the envoy nodded. The exchange continued, surrounded by the oddly melodied playing.

'I greet you on behalf of the Emperor of Mankind, beloved by all, and in the name of the Imperium of Terra.'

'On behalf of the society of the interex, I accept your greetings and return them.'

'Thank you,' said Horus.

'Of the first thing,' the envoy said. 'You are from Terra?'

'Yes.'

'From old Terra, that was also called Earth?'

'Yes.'

'This can be verified?'

'By all means,' smiled Horus. 'You know of Terra?'

An odd expression, like a pang, crossed the envoy's face, and he glanced round at his colleagues. 'We are from Terra. Ancestrally. Genetically. It was our origin world, eons ago. If you are truly of Terra, then this is a momentous occasion. For the first time in thousands of years, the interex has established contact with its lost cousins.'

'It is our purpose in the stars,' Horus said, 'to find all the lost families of man, cast away so long ago.'

The envoy bowed his head. 'I am Diath Shehn, abbrocarius.'

'I am Horus, Warmaster.'

The music of the meturge players made a slight, but noticeably discordant sound as it expressed 'Warmaster'. Shehn frowned.

'Warmaster?' he repeated.

'The rank given to me personally by the Emperor of Mankind, so that I may act as his most senior lieutenant.'

'It is a robust title. Bellicose. Is your fleet a military undertaking?'

'It has a military component. Space is too dangerous for us to roam unarmed. But from the look of your fine soldiers, abbrocarius, so does yours.'

Shehn pursed his lips. 'You laid assault to Urisarach, with great aggression and vehemence, and in disregard to the advisory beacons we had positioned in the system. It would appear your military component is a considerable one.'

'We will discuss this in detail later, abbrocarius. If an apology needs to be made, you will hear it directly from me. First, let me welcome you in peace.'

Horus turned, and made a signal. The entire company of Astartes, and the plated officers, locked off their weapons and removed their helms. Human faces, row after row. Openness, not hostility.

Shehn and the other envoys bowed, and made a signal of their own, a signal supported by a musical sequence. The warriors of the interex removed their visors, displaying clean, hard-eyed faces.

Except for the squat figures, the heavy troops in brown and gold. When their helmets came off, they revealed faces that weren't human at all.

✠ ✠ ✠

THEY WERE CALLED the kinebrach. An advanced, mature species, they had been an interstellar culture for over fifteen thousand years. They had already founded a strong, multi-world civilisation in the local region of space before Terra had entered its First Age of Technology, an era when humanity was only just feeling its way beyond the Solar system in sub-light vehicles.

By the time the interex encountered them, their culture was aging and fading. A territorial war developed after initial contact, and lasted for a century. Despite the kinebrach's superior technology, the humans of the interex were victorious, but, in victory, they did not annihilate the aliens. Rapprochement was achieved, thanks in part to the interex's willingness to develop the aria to facilitate a more profound level of inter-species communication. Faced with options including further warfare and exile, the kinebrach elected to become client citizens of the expanding interex. It suited them to place their tired, flagging destiny in the charge of the vigorous and progressive humans. Culturally bonded as junior partners in society, the kinebrach shared their technological advances by way of exchange. For three thousand years, the interex humans had successfully co-existed with the kinebrach.

'Conflict with the kinebrach was our first significant alien war,' Diath Shehn explained. He was seated with the other envoys in the Warmaster's audience chamber. The Mournival was present, and meturge players lined the walls, gently accompanying the talks. 'It taught us a great deal. It taught us about our place in the cosmos, and certain values of compassion, understanding and empathy. The aria developed directly from it, as a tool for use in further dealings with non-human parties. The war made us realise that our very humanity, or at least our trenchant dependance on human traits, such as language, was an obstacle to mature relations with other species.'

'No matter how sophisticated the means, abbrocarius,' Abaddon

said, 'sometimes communication is not enough. In our experience, most xenos types are wilfully hostile. Communication and
bargaining is not an option.' The first captain, like many present,
was uncomfortable. The entire interex party had been permitted
to enter the audience chamber, and the kinebrach were attending
at the far end. Abaddon kept glancing at them. They were hefty,
simian things with eyes so oddly sunken beneath big brow ridges
that they were just sparks in shadows. Their flesh was blue-black,
and deeply creased, with fringes of russet hair, so fine it was
almost like feather-down, surrounding the bases of their heavy,
angular craniums. Mouth and nose was one organ, a trifold split
at the end of their blunt jaw-snouts, capable of peeling back, wet
and pink, to sniff, or opening laterally to reveal a comb of small,
sharp teeth like a dolphin's beak. There was a smell to them, a
distinctive earthy smell that wasn't exactly unpleasant, except
that it was entirely and completely not human.

'This we have found ourselves,' Shehn agreed, 'though it would
seem less frequently than you. Sometimes we have encountered
a species that has no wish to exchange with us, that approaches
us with predatory or invasive intent. Sometimes conflict is the
only option. Such was the case with the... What did you say you
called them again?'

'Megarachnid,' Horus smiled.

Shehn nodded and smiled. 'I see how that word is formed,
from the old roots. The megarachnid were highly advanced, but
not sentient in a way we could understand. They existed only
to reproduce and develop territory. When we first met them,
they infested eight systems along the Shartiel Edge of our provinces, and threatened to invade and choke two of our populated
worlds. We went to war, to safeguard our own interests. In the
end, we were victorious, but there was still no opportunity for
rapprochement or peace terms. We gathered all the megarachnid

remaining into captivity, and transported them to Urisarach. We also deprived them of all their interstellar technology, or the means to manufacture the same. Urisarach was created as a reservation for them, where they might exist without posing a threat to ourselves or others. The interdiction beacons were established to warn others away.'

'You did not consider exterminating them?' Maloghurst asked.

Shehn shook his head. 'What right do we have to make another species extinct? In most cases, an understanding can be reached. The megarachnid were an extreme example, where exile was the only humane option.'

'The approach you describe is a fascinating one,' Horus said quickly, seeing that Abaddon was about to speak again. 'I believe it is time for that apology, abbrocarius. We misunderstood your methods and purpose on Urisarach. We violated your reservation. The Imperium apologises for its transgression.'

TWO

Envoys and delegations
Xenobia
Hall of Devices

ABADDON WAS FURIOUS. Once the interex envoys had returned to their vessels, he withdrew with the others of the Mournival and vented his feelings.

'Six months! Six months warring on Murder! How many great deeds, how many brothers lost? And now he apologises? As if it was an error? A mistake? These xenos-loving bastards even admit themselves the spiders were so dangerous they had to lock them away!'

'It's a difficult situation,' Loken said.

'It's an insult to the honour of our Legion! And to the Angels too!'

'It takes a wise and strong man to know when to apologise,' remarked Aximand.

'And only a fool appeases aliens!' Abaddon snarled. 'What has this crusade taught us?'

'That we're very good at killing things that disagree with us?' suggested Torgaddon.

Abaddon glared at him. 'We know how brutal this cosmos is. How cruel. We must fight for our place in it. Name one species we have met that would not rejoice to see mankind vanished in a blink.'

None of them could answer that.

'Only a fool appeases aliens,' Abaddon repeated, 'or appeases those who seek such appeasement.'

'Are you calling the Warmaster a fool?' Loken asked.

Abaddon hesitated. 'No. No, I'm not. Of course. I serve at his will.'

'We have one duty,' Aximand said, 'as the Mournival, we must speak with one mind when we advise him.'

Torgaddon nodded.

'No,' said Loken. 'That's not why he values us. We must tell him what we think, each one of us, even if we disagree. And let him decide. That is our duty.'

MEETINGS WITH THE various interex envoys continued over a period of days. Sometimes the interex ships sent a mission to the *Vengeful Spirit*, sometimes an Imperial embassy crossed to their command ship and was entertained in glittering chambers of silver and glass where the aria filled the air.

The envoys were hard to read. Their behaviour often seemed superior or condescending, as if they regarded the Imperials as crude and unsophisticated. But still, clearly, they were fascinated. The legends of old Terra and the human bloodline had long been a central tenet of their myths and histories. However disappointing the reality, they could not bear to break off contact with their treasured ancestral past.

Eventually, a summit was proposed, whereby the Warmaster and his entourage would travel to the nearest interex outpost world, and conduct more detailed negotiations with higher representatives than the envoys.

The Warmaster took advice from all quarters, though Loken was sure he had already made up his mind. Some, like Abaddon, counselled that links should be broken, and the interex held at abeyance until sufficient forces could be assembled to annex their territories. There were other matters at hand that urgently demanded the Warmaster's attention, matters that had been postponed for too long while he indulged in the six-month spider-war on Murder. Petitions and salutations were being received on a daily basis. Five primarchs had requested his personal audience on matters of general crusade strategy or for councils of war. One, the Lion, had never made such an approach before, and it was a sign of a welcome thawing in relations, one that Horus could not afford to overlook. Thirty-six expedition fleets had sent signals asking for advice, tactical determination or outright martial assistance. Matters of state also mounted. There was now a vast body of bureaucratic material relayed from the Council of Terra that required the Warmaster's direct attention. He had been putting it off for too long, blaming the demands of the crusade.

Accompanying the Warmaster on most of his daily duties, Loken began to see plainly what a burden the Emperor had placed on Horus's broad shoulders. He was expected to be all things: a commander of armies, a mastermind of compliance, a judge, a decider, a tactician, and the most delicate of diplomats.

During the six-month war, more ships had arrived at high anchor above Murder, gathering around the flagship like supplicants. The rest of the 63rd Expedition had translated, under Varvarus's charge, Sixty-Three Nineteen having at last been left in the lonely hands of poor Rakris. Fourteen vessels of the 88th Expedition had also appeared, under the command of Trajus Boniface of the Alpha Legion. Boniface claimed they had come in response to the 140th's plight, and hoped to support the war

action on Murder, but it rapidly emerged he hoped to use the
opportunity to convince Horus to lend the 63rd's strengths to a
proposed offensive into ork-held territories in the Kayvas Belt.
This was a scheme his primarch, Alpharius, had long cherished
and, like the Lion's advances, was a sign that Alpharius sought
the approval and comradeship of the new Warmaster.

Horus studied the plans in private. The Kayvas Belt offensive
was a projected five-year operation, and required ten times the
manpower the Warmaster could currently muster.

'Alpharius is dreaming,' he muttered, showing the scheme to
Loken and Torgaddon. 'I cannot commit myself to this.'

One of Varvaras's ships had brought with it a delegation of eaxector tributi administrators from Terra. This was perhaps the most
galling of all the voices baying for the Warmaster's attention. On
the instruction of Malcador the Sigillite, and countersigned by
the Council of Terra, the eaxectors had been sent throughout the
spreading territories of the Imperium, in a programme of general
dispersal that made the mass deployment of the remembrancers
look like a modest operation.

The delegation was led by a high administrix called Aenid
Rathbone. She was a tall, slender, handsome woman with red
hair and pale, high-boned features, and her manner was exact-
ing. The Council of Terra had decreed that all expedition and
crusade forces, all primarchs, all commanders, and all governors
of compliant world-systems should begin raising and collecting
taxes from their subject planets in order to bolster the increasing
fiscal demands of the expanding Imperium. All she insisted on
talking about was the collection of tithes.

'One world cannot support and maintain such a gigantic undertaking singlehanded,' she explained to the Warmaster in slightly
over-shrill tones. 'Terra cannot shoulder this burden alone. We
are masters of a thousand worlds now, a thousand thousand. The

Imperium must begin to support itself.'

'Many worlds are barely in compliance, lady,' Horus said gently. 'They are recovering from the damage of war, rebuilding, reforming. Taxation is a blight they do not need.'

'The Emperor has insisted this be so.'

'Has he?'

'Malcador the Sigillite, beloved by all, has impressed this upon me and all of my rank. Tribute must be collected, and mechanisms established so that such tribute is routinely and automatically gathered.'

'The world governors we have put in place will find this too thankless a task,' Maloghurst said. 'They are still legitimising their rule and authority. This is premature.'

'The Emperor has insisted this be so,' she repeated.

'That's the Emperor, beloved by all?' Loken asked. His comment made Horus smile broadly.

Rathbone sniffed. 'I'm not sure what you're implying, captain,' she said. 'This is my duty, and this is what I must do.'

When she had retired from the room with her staff, Horus sat back, alone amongst his inner circle. 'I have often thought,' he remarked, 'that it might be the eldar who unseat us. Though fading, they are the most ingenious creatures, and if any could over-master mankind and break our Imperium apart, it would likely be them. At other times, I have fancied that it would be the greenskins. No end of numbers and no end of brute strength, but now, friends, I am certain it will be our own tax collectors who will do us in.'

There was general laughter. Loken thought of the poem in his pocket. Most of Karkasy's output he handed on to Sindermann for appraisal, but at their last meeting, Karkasy had introduced 'something of the doggerel'. Loken had read it. It had been a scurrilous and mordant stanza about tax collectors that even Loken could appreciate. He thought about bringing it out for general amusement, but Horus's face had darkened.

'I only half joke,' Horus said. 'Through the eaxectors, the Council places a burden on the fledgling worlds that is so great it might break us. It is too soon, too comprehensive, too stringent. Worlds will revolt. Uprisings will occur. Tell a conquered man he has a new master, and he'll shrug. Tell him his new master wants a fifth of his annual income, and he'll go and find his pitchfork. Aenid Rathbone, and administrators like her, will be the undoing of all we have achieved.'

More laughter echoed round the room.

'But it is the Emperor's will,' Torgaddon remarked.

Horus shook his head. 'It is not, for all she says. I know him as a son knows his father. He would not agree to this. Not now, not this early. He must be too bound up in his work to know of it. The Council is making decisions in his absence. The Emperor understands how fragile things are. Throne, this is what happens when an empire forged by warriors devolves executive power to civilians and clerics.'

They all looked at him.

'I'm serious,' he said. 'This could trigger civil war in certain regions. At the very least, it could undermine the continued work of our expeditions. The eaxectors need to be… sidelined for the moment. They should be given terrific weights of material to pore through to determine precise tribute levels, world by world, and bombarded with copious additional intelligence concerning each world's status.'

'It won't slow them down forever, lord,' Maloghurst said. 'The Administration of Terra has already determined systems and measures by which tribute should be calculated, pro rata, world by world.'

'Do your best, Mal,' Horus said. 'Delay that woman at least. Give me breathing space.'

'I'll get to it,' Maloghurst said. He rose and limped from the chamber.

Horus turned to the assembled circle and sighed. 'So…' he said. 'The Lion calls for me. Alpharius too.'

'And other brothers and numerous expeditions,' Sanguinius remarked.

'And it seems my wisest option is to return to Terra and confront the Council on the issue of taxation.'

Sanguinius sniggered.

'I was not wrought to do that,' Horus said.

'Then we should consider the interex, lord,' said Erebus.

EREBUS, OF THE Word Bearers Legion, the XVII, had joined them a fortnight earlier as part of the contingent brought by Varvaras. In his stone-grey Mark IV plate, inscribed with bas-relief legacies of his deeds, Erebus was a sombre, serious figure. His rank in the XVII was first chaplain, roughly equivalent to that of Abaddon or Eidolon. He was a senior commander of that Legion, close to Kor Phaeron and the primarch, Lorgar, himself. His quiet manner and soft, composed voice commanded instant respect from all who met him, but the Luna Wolves had embraced him anyway. The Wolves had historically enjoyed a relationship with the Bearers as close as the one they had formed with the Emperor's Children. It was no coincidence that Horus counted Lorgar amongst his most intimate brothers, alongside Fulgrim and Sanguinius.

Erebus, who time had fashioned as much into a statesman as a warrior, both of which duties he performed with superlative skill, had come to find the Warmaster at the behest of his Legion. Evidently, he had a favour to crave, a request to make. One did not send Erebus except to broker terms.

However, on his arrival, Erebus had understood immediately the pressure laid at Horus's door, the countless voices screaming for attention. He had shelved his reason for coming, wishing to add nothing to the Warmaster's already immense burden, and had instead acted as a solid counsel and advisor with no agenda of his own.

For this, the Mournival had admired him greatly, and welcomed him, like Raldorus, into the circle. Abaddon and Aximand had served alongside Erebus in numerous theatres. Torgaddon knew him of old. All three spoke in nothing but the highest terms of First Chaplain Erebus.

Loken had needed little convincing. From the outset, Erebus had made a particular effort to establish good terms with Loken. Erebus's record and heritage were such that he seemed to Loken to carry the weight of a primarch with him. He was, after all, Lorgar's chosen mouthpiece.

Erebus had dined with them, counselled with them, sat easy after hours and drunk with them, and, on occasions, had entered the practice cages and sparred with them. In one afternoon, he had bested Torgaddon and Aximand in quick bouts, then tallied long with Saul Tarvitz before dumping him on the mat. Tarvitz and his comrade Lucius had been brought along at Torgaddon's invitation.

Loken had wanted to test his hand against Erebus, but Lucius had insisted he was next. The Mournival had grown to like Tarvitz, their impression of him favourably influenced by Torgaddon's good opinions, but Lucius remained a separate entity, too much like Lord Eidolon for them to warm to him. He always appeared plaintive and demanding, like a spoilt child.

'You go, then,' Loken had waved, 'if it matters so much.' It was clear that Lucius strained to restore the honour of his Legion, an honour lost, as he saw it, the moment Erebus had dropped Tarvitz with a skillful slam of his sword.

Drawing his blade, Lucius had entered the practice cage facing

Erebus. The iron hemispheres closed around them. Lucius took up a straddled stance, his broadsword held high and close. Erebus kept his own blade extended low. They circled. Both Astartes were stripped to the waist, the musculature of their upper bodies rippling. This was play, but a wrong move could maim. Or kill.

The bout lasted sixteen minutes. That in itself would have made it one of the longest sparring sessions any of them had ever known. What made it more remarkable was the fact that in that time, there was no pause, no hesitation, no cessation. Erebus and Lucius flew at one another, and rang blows off one another's blades at a rate of three or four a second. It was relentless, extraordinary, a dizzying blur of dancing bodies and gleaming swords that rang on and on like a dream.

Abaddon, Tarvitz, Torgaddon, Loken and Aximand closed around the cage in fascination, beginning to clap and yell in thorough approval of the amazing skill on display.

'He'll kill him!' Tarvitz gasped. 'At that speed, unprotected. He'll kill him!'

'Who will?' asked Loken.

'I don't know, Garvi. Either one!' Tarvitz exclaimed.

'Too much, too much!' Aximand laughed.

'Loken fights the winner,' Torgaddon cried.

'I don't think so!' Loken rejoined. 'I've seen winner and loser!'

Still they duelled on. Erebus's style was defensive, low, repeating and changing each parry like a mechanism. Lucius's style was full of attack, furious, brilliant, dextrous. The play of them was hard to follow.

'If you think I'm taking on either of them after this,' Loken began.

'What? Can't you do it?' Torgaddon mocked.

'No.'

'You go in next,' chuckled Abaddon, clapping his hands. 'We'll give you a bolter to even it up.'

'How very humorous, Ezekyle.'

At the fifty-ninth second of the sixteenth minute, according to the practice cage chron, Lucius scored his winning blow. He hooked his broadsword under Erebus's guard and wrenched the Word Bearer's blade out of his grip. Erebus fell back against the bars of the practice cage, and found Lucius's blade edge at his throat.

'Whoa! Whoa now, Lucius!' Aximand cried, triggering the cage open.

'Sorry,' said Lucius, not sorry at all. He withdrew his broadsword and saluted Erebus, sweat beading his bare shoulders

'A good match. Thank you, sir.'

'My thanks to you,' Erebus smiled, breathing hard. He bent to pick up his blade. 'Your skill with a sword is second to none, Captain Lucius.'

'Out you come, Erebus,' Torgaddon called. 'It's Garvi's turn.'

'Oh no,' Loken said.

'You're the best of us with a blade,' Little Horus insisted. 'Show him how the Luna Wolves do it.'

'Skill with a blade isn't everything,' Loken protested.

'Just get in there and stop shaming us,' Aximand hissed. He looked over at Lucius, who was wiping his torso down with a cloth. 'You ready for another, Lucius?'

'Bring it on.'

'He's mad,' Loken whispered.

'Legion honour,' Abaddon muttered back, pushing Loken forward.

'That's right,' crowed Lucius. 'Anyway you want me. Show me how a Luna Wolf fights, Loken. Show me how you win.'

'It's not just about the blade,' Loken said.

'However you want it,' Lucius snorted.

Erebus stood up from the corner of the platform and tossed his blade to Loken. 'It sounds like it's your turn, Garviel,' he said.

Loken caught the sword, and tested it through the air, back and forth. He stepped up into the cage and nodded. The hemispheres of bars closed around him and Lucius.

Lucius spat and shook out his shoulders. He turned his sword and began to dance around Loken.

'I'm no swordsman,' Loken said.

'Then this will be over quickly.'

'If we spar, it won't be just about the blade.'

'Whatever, whatever,' Lucius called, jumping back and forth. 'Just get on and fight me.'

Loken sighed. 'I've been watching you, of course, the attacking strokes. I can read you.'

'You wish.'

'I can read you. Come for me.'

Lucius lunged at Loken. Loken side-stepped, blade down, and punched Lucius in the face. Lucius fell on his back, hard.

Loken dropped Erebus's sword onto the mat. 'I think I made my point. That's how a Luna Wolf fights. Understand your foe and do whatever is necessary to bring him down. Sorry, Lucius.'

Spitting blood, Lucius's response was incoherent.

'I SAID WE should consider the interex, sir,' Erebus pressed.

'We should,' Horus replied, 'and my mind is made up. All these voices calling for my attention, pulling me this way and that. They can't disguise the fact that the interex is a significant new culture, occupying a significant region of space. They're human. We can't ignore them. We can't deny their existence. We must deal with them directly. Either they are friends, potential allies, or they are enemies. We cannot turn our attention elsewhere and expect them to stay put. If they are enemies, if they are against us,

then they could pose a threat as great as the greenskins. I will go
to the summit and meet their leaders.'

XENOBIA WAS A provincial capital on the marches of interex territory. The envoys had been guarded in revelations of the precise
size and extent of the interex, but their cultural holdings evidently occupied in excess of thirty systems, with the heartworlds
some forty weeks from the advancing edge of Imperial influence.
Xenobia, a gateway world and a sentinel station on the edge of
interex space, was chosen as the site for the summit.

It was a place of considerable wonder. Escorted from mass
anchorage points in the orbit of the principal satellite, the
Warmaster and his representatives were conducted to Xenobia
Principis, a wealthy, regal city on the shores of a wide, ammo-
nia sea. The city was set into the slopes of a wide bay, so that it
shelved down the ramparts of the hills to sea level. The conti-
nental region behind it was sheathed in verdant rainforest, and
this lush growth spilled down through the city too, so that the
city structures – towers of pale grey stone and turrets of brass
and silver – rose up out of the thick canopy like hilltop peaks.
The vegetation was predominately dark green, indeed so dark in
colour it seemed almost black in the frail, yellow daylight. The
city was structured in descending tiers under the trees, where
arched stone viaducts and curved street galleries stepped down
to the shoreline in the quiet, mottled shadow of the greenery.
Where the grey towers and ornate campaniles rose above the forest, they were often capped in polished metal, and adorned with
high masts from which flags and standards hung in the warm air.

It was not a fortress city. There was little evidence of defences
either on the ground or in local orbit. Horus was in no doubt
that the place could protect itself if necessary. The interex did
not wear its martial power as obviously as the Imperium, but its

technology was not to be underestimated.

The Imperial party was over five hundred strong and included Astartes officers, escort troops and iterators, as well as a selection of remembrancers. Horus had authorised the latter's inclusion. This was a fact-finding mission, and the Warmaster thought the eager, inquisitive remembrancers might gather a great deal of supplementary material that would prove valuable. Loken believed that the Warmaster was also making an effort to establish a rather different impression than before. The envoys of the interex had seemed so disdainful of the expedition's military bias. Horus came to them now, surrounded as much by teachers, poets and artists as he was warriors.

They were provided with excellent accommodation in the western part of the city, in a quarter known as the *Extranus*, where, they were politely informed, all 'strangers and visitors' were reserved and hosted. Xenobia Principis was a place designed for trade delegations and diplomatic meetings, with the Extranus set aside to keep guests reserved in one place. They were handsomely provided with meturge players, household servants, and court officers to see to their every need and answer any questions.

Under the guided escort of abbrocarii, the Imperials were allowed beyond the shaded compound of the Extranus to visit the city. In small groups, they were shown the wonders of the place: halls of trade and industry, museums of art and music, archives and libraries. In the green twilight of the galleried streets, under the hissing canopy of the trees, they were guided along fine avenues, through splendid squares, and up and down endless flights of steps. The city was home to buildings of exquisite design, and it was clear the interex possessed great skill in both the old crafts of stonemasonry and metalwork, and the newer crafts of technology. Pavements abounded with gorgeous statuary and tranquil water fountains, but also with modernist public sculpture of light and sonics. Ancient lancet window slits were equipped with glass panels reactive to light and heat. Doors opened and closed via automatic body sensors. Interior light levels could be adjusted by a wave of the hand. Everywhere, the soft melody of the aria played.

The Imperium possessed many cities that were larger and grander and more cyclopean. The super-hives of Terra and the silver spires of Prospero both were stupendous monuments to cultural advancement that quite diminished Xenobia Principis. But the interex city was every bit as refined and sophisticated as any conurbation in Imperial space, and it was merely a border settlement.

On the day of their arrival, the Imperials were welcomed by a great parade, which culminated in their presentation to the senior royal officer of Xenobia, a 'general commander' named Jephta Naud. There were high-ranking civil officers in the interex party too, but they had decided to allow a military leader to oversee the summit. Just as Horus had diluted the martial composition of his embassy to impress the interex, so it had brought its military powers to the fore.

The parade was complex and colourful. Meturge players marched in great numbers, dressed in rich formal robes, and performed skirling anthems that were as much non-verbal messages of welcome as they were mood-setting music. Gleves and sagittars strode in long, uniform columns, their armour polished brightly and dressed with garlands of ribbons and leaves. Behind the human soldiery came the kinebrach auxiliaries, armoured and lumbering, and glittering formations of robotic cavalry. The cavalry was made up of hundreds of the headless artificial horses that had featured in the envoys' honour guard. They were headless no longer. Sagittars and gleves had mounted the quadruped frames, seating themselves where the base of the neck would have been. Warrior armour and robot technology had fused smoothly, locking the 'riders' in place, their legs folded into the breastbones of the steeds. They were centaurs now, man and device linked as one, myths given technological reality.

The citizenry of Xenobia Principis came out in force for the parade, and cheered and sang, and strewed the route of the procession with petals and strips of ribbon.

The parade's destination was a building called the Hall of Devices, a place which apparently had some military significance to the interex. Old, and of considerable size, the hall resembled a museum. Built into a steep section of the bay slopes, the hall enclosed many chambers that were more than two or three storeys high. Plunging display vaults, some of great size, showed off assemblies of weapons, from forests of ancient swords and halberds to modern motorised cannons, all suffused in the pale blue glow of the energy fields that secured them.

'The hall is both a museum of weapons and war devices, and an armoury,' Jephta Naud explained as he greeted them. Naud was a tall, noble creature with complicated dermatoglyphics on the right side of his face. His eyes were the colour of soft gold, and he wore silver armour and a cloak of scalloped red metal links that made a sound like distant chimes when he moved. An armoured officer walked at his side, carrying Naud's crested warhelm.

Though the Astartes had come armoured, the Warmaster had chosen to wear robes and furs rather than his battle-plate. He showed great and courteous interest as Naud led them through the deep vaults, commenting on certain devices, remarking with delight when archaic weapons revealed a shared ancestry.

'They're trying to impress us,' Aximand murmured to his brothers. 'A museum of weapons? They're as good as telling us they are so advanced... so beyond war... they've been able to retire it as a curiosity. They're mocking us.'

'No one mocks me,' Abaddon grunted.

They were entering a chamber where, in the chilly blue field light, the artifacts were a great deal stranger than before.

'We hold the weapons of the kinebrach here,' Naud said, to meturge accompaniment. 'Indeed, we preserve here, in careful stasis, examples of the weapons used by many of the alien species we have encountered. The kinebrach have, as a sign of service to us, foresworn the bearing of arms, unless under such circumstances as we grant them said use in time of war. Kinebrach technology is highly advanced, and many of their weapons are deemed too lethal to be left beyond securement.'

Naud introduced a hulking, robed kinebrach called Asherot, who held the rank of Keeper of Devices, and was the trusted curator of the hall. Asherot spoke the human tongue in a lisping manner, and for the first time, the Imperials were grateful for the meturge accompaniment. The baffling cadences of Asherot's speech were rendered crystal clear by the aria.

Most of the kinebrach weapons on display didn't resemble weapons at all. Boxes, odd trinkets, rings, hoops. Naud clearly expected the Imperials to ask questions about the devices, and betray their warmongering appetites, but Horus and his officers affected disinterest. In truth, they were uneasy in the society of the indentured alien.

Only Sindermann expressed curiosity. A very few of the kinebrach weapons looked like weapons: long daggers and swords of exotic design.

'Surely, general commander, a blade is just a blade?' Sindermann asked politely. 'These daggers here, for instance. How are these weapons "too lethal to be left beyond securement"?'

'They are tailored weapons,' Naud replied. 'Blades of sentient metal, crafted by the kinebrach metallurgists, a technique now utterly forbidden. We call them anathames. When such a blade is selected for use against a specific target, it becomes that target's nemesis, utterly inimical to the person or being chosen.'

'How?' Sindermann pressed.

Naud smiled. 'The kinebrach have never been able to explain it to us. It is a factor of the forging process that defies technical evaluation.'

'Like a curse?' prompted Sindermann. 'An enchantment?'

The aria generated by the meturge players around them hiccupped slightly over those words. To Sindermann's surprise, Naud replied, 'I suppose that is how you could describe it, iterator.'

The tour moved on. Sindermann drew close to Loken, and whispered, 'I was joking, Garviel, about the curse, I mean, but he took me seriously. They are enjoying treating us as unsophisticated cousins, but I wonder if their superiority is misplaced. Do we detect a hint of pagan superstition?'

THREE

Impasse
Illumination
The wolf and the moon

THEY ALL ROSE as the Warmaster entered the room. It was a large chamber in the Extranus compound where the Imperials met for their regular briefings. Large shield-glass windows overlooked the tumbling terraces of the forested city and the glittering ocean beyond.

Horus waited silently while six officers and servitors from the Master of Vox's company finished their routine sweep for spyware, and only spoke once they had activated the portable obscurement device in the corner of the room. The distant melodies of the aria were immediately blanked out.

'Two weeks without solid agreement,' Horus said, 'nor even a mutually acceptable scheme of how to continue. They regard us with a mixture of curiosity and caution, and hold us at arm's length. Any commentary?'

'We've exhausted all possibilities, lord,' Maloghurst said, 'to the extent that I fear we are wasting our time. They will admit to nothing but a willingness to open and pursue ambassadorial links, with a view to trade and some cultural exchange. They will not be led on the subject of alliance.'

'Or compliance,' Abaddon remarked quietly.

'An attempt to enforce our will here,' said Horus, 'would only confirm their worst opinions of us. We cannot force them into compliance.'

'We can,' Abaddon said.

'Then I'm saying we shouldn't,' Horus replied.

'Since when have we worried about hurting people's feelings, lord?' Abaddon asked. 'Whatever our differences, these are humans. It is their duty and their destiny to join with us and stand with us, for the primary glory of Terra. If they will not...'

He let the words hang. Horus frowned. 'Someone else?'

'It seems certain that the interex has no wish to join us in our work,' said Raldoron. 'They will not commit to a war, nor do they share our goals and ideals. They are content with pursuing their own destiny.'

Sanguinius said nothing. He allowed his Chapter Master to weigh in with the opinion of the Blood Angels, but kept his own considerable influence for Horus's ears alone.

'Maybe they fear we will try to conquer them,' Loken said.

'Maybe they're right,' said Abaddon. 'They are deviant in their ways. Too deviant for us to embrace them without forcing change.'

'We will not have war here,' Horus said. 'We cannot afford it. We cannot afford to open up a conflict on this front. Not at this time. Not on the vast scale subduing the interex would demand. If they even need subduing.'

'Ezekyle has a valid point,' said Erebus quietly. 'The interex, for good reasons, I'm sure, have built a society that is too greatly at variance to the model of human culture that the Emperor has proclaimed. Unless they show a willingness to adapt, they must by necessity be regarded as enemies to our cause.'

'Perhaps the Emperor's model is too stringent,' the Warmaster said flatly.

There was a pause. Several of those present glanced at each other in quiet unease.

'Oh, come on!' Sanguinius exclaimed, breaking the silence. 'I see those looks. Are you honestly nursing concerns that our War-master is contemplating defiance of the Emperor? His father?' He laughed aloud at the very notion, and forced a few smiles to surface.

Abaddon was not smiling. 'The Emperor, beloved of all,' he began, 'enfranchised us to do his bidding and make known space safe for human habitation. His edicts are unequivocal. We must suffer not the alien, nor the uncontrolled psyker, safe-guard against the darkness of the warp, and unify the dislocated pockets of mankind. That is our charge. Anything else is sacrilege against his wishes.'

'And one of his wishes,' said Horus, 'was that I should be War-master, his sole regent, and strive to make his dreams reality. The crusade was born out of the Age of Strife, Ezekyle. Born out of war. Our ruthless approach of conquest and cleansing was formulated in a time when every alien form we met was hostile, every fragment of humanity that was not with us was profoundly opposed to us. War was the only answer. There was no room for subtlety, but two centuries have passed, and different problems face us. The bulk of war is over. That is why the Emperor returned to Terra and left us to finish the work. Ezekyle, the people of the interex are clearly not monsters, nor resolute foes. I believe that if the Emperor were with us today, he would immediately embrace the need for adaptation. He would not want us to wan-tonly destroy that which there is no good reason to destroy. It is precisely to make such choices that he has placed his trust in me.'

He looked round at them all. 'He trusts me to make the

decisions he would make. He trusts me to make no mistakes. I must be allowed the freedom to interpret policy on his behalf. I will not be forced into violence simply to satisfy some slavish expectation.'

A CHILL EVENING had covered the tiers of the city, and under layers of foliage stirred by the ocean's breath, the walkways and pavements were lit with frosty white lamps.

Loken's duty for that part of the night was as perimeter bodyguard. The commander was dining with Jephta Naud and other worthies at the general commander's palatial house. Horus had confided to the Mournival that he hoped to use the occasion to informally press Naud for some more substantial commitments, including the possibility that the interex might, at least in principle for now, recognise the Emperor as the true human authority. Such a suggestion had not yet been risked in formal talks, for the iterators had predicted it would be rejected out of hand. The Warmaster wanted to test the general commander's feelings on the subject in an atmosphere where any offence could be smoothed over as conjecture. Loken didn't much like the idea, but trusted his commander to couch it delicately. It was an uneasy time, well into the third week of their increasingly fruitless visit. Two days earlier, Primarch Sanguinius had finally taken his leave and returned to Imperial territory with the Blood Angels contingents.

Horus clearly hated to see him go, but it was a prudent move, and one Sanguinius had chosen to make simply to buy his brother more time with the interex. Sanguinius was returning to deal directly with some of the matters most urgently requiring the Warmaster's attention, and thus mollify the many voices pleading for his immediate recall.

Naud's house was a conspicuously vast structure near the centre of the city. Six storeys high, it overhung one of the grander civic tiers and was formed from a great black-iron frame infilled with mosaics of varnished wood and coloured glass. The interex did not welcome armed foreigners abroad in their city, but a small detail of bodyguards was permitted for so august a personage as the Warmaster. Most of the substantial Imperial contingent was sequestered in the Extranus compound for the night. Torgaddon, and ten hand-picked men from his company, were inside the dining hall, acting as close guard, while Loken, with ten men of his own, roamed the environs of the house.

Loken had chosen Tenth Company's Sixth Squad, Walkure Tactical Squad, to stand duty with him. Through its veteran leader, Brother-Sergeant Kairus, he'd spread the men out around the entry areas of the hall, and formulated a simple period of patrol.

The house was quiet, the city too. There was the sound of the soft ocean breeze, the hissing of the overgrowth, the splash and bell-tinkle of ornamental fountains, and the background murmur of the aria. Loken strolled from chamber to chamber, from shadow to light. Most of the house's public spaces were lit from sources within the walls, so they played matrices of shade and colour across the interior, cast by the inset wall panels of rich wood and coloured gem-glass. Occasionally, he encountered one of Walkure on a patrol loop, and exchanged a nod and a few quiet words. Less frequently, he saw scurrying servants running courses to and from the closed dining hall, or crossed the path of Naud's own sentries, mostly armoured gleves, who said nothing, but saluted to acknowledge him.

Naud's house was a treasure trove of art, some of it mystifyingly alien to Loken's comprehension. The art was elegantly displayed in lit alcoves and on free-standing plinths with their own shimmering field protection. He understood some of it. Portraits and busts, paintings and light sculptures, pictures of interex nobles and their families, studies of animals or wildflowers, mountain scenes, elaborate and ingenious models of unnamed worlds opened in mechanical cross-section like the layers of an onion.

In one lower hallway in the eastern wing of the house, Loken came upon an artwork that especially arrested him. It was a book, an old book, large, rumpled, illuminated, and held within its own box field. The lurid woodcut illuminations caught his eye first, the images of devils and spectres, angels and cherubs. Then he saw it was written in the old text of Terra, the language and form that had survived from prehistory to *The Chronicles of Ursh* that lay, still unfinished, in his arming chamber. He peered at it. A wave of his hand across the field's static charge turned the pages. He turned them right back to the front and read the title page in its bold woodblock.

A Marvelous Historie of Eevil; Being a warninge to Man Kind on the Abuses of Sorcerie and the Seduction of the Daemon.

'That has taken your eye, has it?'

Loken rose and turned. A royal officer of the interex stood nearby, watching him. Loken knew the man, one of Naud's subordinate commanders, by the name of Mithras Tull. What he didn't know was how Tull had managed to come up on him without Loken noticing.

'It is a curious thing, commander,' he said.

Tull nodded and smiled. A gleve, his weighted spear was leant against a pillar behind him, and he had removed his visor to reveal his pleasant, honest face. 'A likeness,' he said.

'A what?'

'Forgive me, that is the word we have come to use to refer to things that are old enough to display our common heritage. A likeness. That book means as much to you as it does to us, I'm sure.'

'It is curious, certainly,' Loken admitted. He unclasped his helm and removed it, out of politeness. 'Is there a problem, commander?'

Tull made a dismissive gesture. 'No, not at all. My duties are akin to yours tonight, captain. Security. I'm in charge of the house patrols.'

Loken nodded. He gestured back at the ancient book on display. 'So tell me about this piece. If you've the time?'

'It's a quiet night,' Tull smiled again. He came forward, and brushed the field with his metal-sleeved fingers to flip the pages. 'My lord Jephta adores this book. It was composed during the early years of our history, before the interex was properly founded, during our outwards expansion from Terra. Very few copies remain. A treatise against the practice of sorcery.'

'Naud adores it?' Loken asked.

'As a… what was your word again? A curiosity?' There was something strange about Tull's voice, and Loken finally realised what it was. This was the first conversation he'd had with a representative of the interex without meturge players producing the aria in the background. 'It's such a woe-begotten, dark age piece,' Tull continued. 'So doomy and apocalyptic. Imagine, captain… men of Terra, voyaging out into the stars, equipped with great and wonderful technologies, and fearing the dark so much they have to compose treatises on daemons.'

'Daemons?'

'Indeed. This warns against witches, gross practices, familiars, and the arts by which a man might transform into a daemon and prey upon his own kind.'

Some became daemons and turned upon their own.

'So… you regard it as a joke? An odd throwback to unenlightened days?'

Tull shrugged. 'Not a joke, captain. Just an old-fashioned, alarmist approach. The interex is a mature society. We understand the threat of Kaos well enough, and set it in its place.'

'Chaos?'

Tull frowned. 'Yes, captain. *Kaos*. You say the word like you've never heard it before.'

'I know the word. You say it like it has a specific connotation.'

'Well, of course it has,' Tull said. 'No star-faring race in the cosmos can operate without understanding the nature of Kaos. We thank the eldar for teaching us the rudiments of it, but we would have recognised it soon enough without their help. Surely, one can't use the immaterium for any length of time without coming to terms with Kaos as a...' his voice trailed off. 'Great and holy heavens! You don't know, do you?'

'Don't know what?' Loken snapped.

Tull began to laugh, but it wasn't mocking. 'All this time, we've been pussyfooting around you and your great Warmaster, fearing the worst...'

Loken took a step forward. 'Commander,' he said, 'I will own up to ignorance and embrace illumination, but I will not be laughed at.'

'Forgive me.'

'Tell me why I should. Illuminate me.'

Tull stopped laughing and stared into Loken's face. His blue eyes were terribly cold and hard. 'Kaos is the damnation of all mankind, Loken. Kaos will outlive us and dance on our ashes. All we can do, all we can strive for, is to recognise its menace and keep it at bay, for as long as we persist.'

'Not enough,' said Loken.

Tull shook his head sadly. 'We were so wrong,' he said.

'About what?'

'About you. About the Imperium. I must go to Naud at once and explain this to him. If only the substance of this had come out earlier...'

'Explain it to me first. Now. Here.'

Tull gazed at Loken for a long, silent moment, as if judging his options. Finally, he shrugged and said, 'Kaos is a primal force of the cosmos. It resides within the immaterium... what you call the warp. It is a source of the most malevolent and complete corruption and evil. It is the greatest enemy of mankind – both interex and Imperial, I mean – because it destroys from within, like a canker. It is insidious. It is not like a hostile alien form to be defeated or expunged. It spreads like a disease. It is at the root of all sorcery and magic. It is...'

He hesitated and looked at Loken with a pained expression. 'It is the reason we have kept you at arm's length. You have to understand that when we first made contact, we were exhilarated, overjoyed. At last. At last! Contact with our lost kin, contact with Terra, after so many generations. It was a dream we had all cherished, but we knew we had to be careful. In the ages since we last had contact with Terra, things might have changed. An age of strife and damnation had passed. There was no guarantee that the men, who looked like men, and claimed to come from Terra in the name of a new Terran Emperor, might not be agents of Kaos in seemly guise. There was no guarantee that while the men of the interex remained pure, the men of Terra might have become polluted and transformed by the ways of Kaos.'

'We are not–'

'Let me finish, Loken. Kaos, when it manifests, is brutal, rapacious, warlike. It is a force of unquenchable destruction. So the eldar have taught us, and the kinebrach, and so the pure men of the interex have stood to check Kaos wherever it rears its warlike visage. Tell me, captain, how warlike do you appear? Vast and bulky, bred for battle, driven to destroy, led by a man you happily title Warmaster? *War* master? What manner of rank is that? Not Emperor, not commander, not general, but Warmaster.

The bluntness of the term reeks of Kaos. We want to embrace you, yearn to embrace you, to join with you, to stand shoulder to shoulder with you, but we fear you, Loken. You resemble the enemy we have been raised from birth to anticipate. The all-conquering, unrelenting daemon of Kaos-war. The bloody-handed god of annihilation.'

'That is not us,' said Loken, aghast.

Tull nodded eagerly. 'I know it. I see it now. Truly. We have made a mistake in our delays. There is no taint in you. There is only the most surprising innocence.'

'I'll try not to be offended.'

Tull laughed and clasped his hands around Loken's right fist. 'No need, no need. We can show you the dangers to watch for. We can be brothers and–'

He paused suddenly, and took his hands away.

'What is it?' Loken asked.

Tull was listening to his comm-relay. His face darkened. 'Understood,' he said to his collar mic. 'Action at once.'

He looked back at Loken. 'Security lock-down, captain. Would... I'm sorry, this seems very blunt after what we've just been saying... but would you surrender your weapons to me?'

'My weapons?'

'Yes, captain.'

'I'm sorry, commander. I can't do that. Not while my commander is in the building.'

Tull cleared his throat and carefully fitted his visor plate to his armour. He reached out and carefully took hold of his spear. 'Captain Loken,' he said, his voice now gusting from his audio relays, 'I demand you turn your weapons over to me at this time.'

Loken took a step back. 'For what reason?'

'I don't have to give a reason, dammit! I'm officer of the watch, on interex territory. Hand over your weapons!'

Loken clamped his own helm in place. The visor screens were alarmingly blank. He checked sub-vox and security channels, trying to reach Kairus, Torgaddon or any of the bodyguard detail. His suit systems were being comprehensively blocked.

'Are you damping me?' he asked.

'City systems are damping you. Hand me your sidearm, Loken.'

'I'm afraid I can't. My priority is to safeguard my commander.'

Tull shook his armoured head. 'Oh, you're clever. Very clever. You almost had me there. You almost had me believing you were innocent.'

'Tull, I don't know what's going on.'

'Naturally you don't.'

'Commander Tull, we had reached an understanding, man to man. Why are you doing this?'

'Seduction. You almost had me. It was very good, but you got the timing off. You showed your hand too soon.'

'Hand? What hand?'

'Don't pretend. The Hall of Devices is burning. You've made your move. Now the interex replies.'

'Tull,' Loken warned, placing his hand firmly on the pommel of his blade. 'Don't make me fight you.'

With a snarl of disappointed rage, Tull swung his spear at Loken.

The interex officer moved with astounding speed. Even with his hand on his blade, Loken had no time to draw it. He managed to snatch up his plated arms to fend off the blow, and the two that followed it. The lightweight armour of the interex soldiery seemed to facilitate the most dazzling motion and dexterity, perhaps even augmenting the user's natural abilities. Tull's attack was fluent and professional, slicing in blows with the long spear blade designed to force Loken back and down into submission. The microfine edge of the blade hacked several deep gouges into Loken's plating.

'Tull! Stop!'

'Surrender to me now!'

Loken had no wish to fight, and scarcely any clue as to what had turned Tull so suddenly and completely, but he had no intention of surrendering. The Warmaster was on site, exposed. As far as Loken knew, all Imperial agents in the area had been deprived of vox and sensor links. There was no cue to the Warmaster's party, or to the Extranus compound, and certainly none to the fleet. He knew his priority was simple. He was a weapon, an instrument, and he had one simply defined purpose: protect the life of the Warmaster. All other issues were entirely secondary and moot.

Loken focussed. He felt the power in his limbs, in the suddenly warming, suddenly active flex of the polymer muscles in his suit's inner skin. He felt the throb of the power unit against the small of his back as it obeyed his instincts and yielded full power. He'd been swatting away the spear blows, allowing Tull to disfigure his plate.

No more.

He swung out, met the next blow, and smashed the blade aside with the ball of his fist. Tull travelled with the recoil expertly, spinning and using the momentum to drive a thrust directly at Loken's chest. It never landed. Loken caught the spear at the base of the blade with his left hand, moving as quickly and dazzlingly as the interex officer, and stopped it dead. Before Tull could pull free, Loken punched with his right fist against the flat of the blade and broke the entire blade-tip off the spear. It spun away, end over end.

Tull rallied, and rotated the broken weapon to drive the weighted base-end at Loken like a long club. Loken guarded off two heavy blows from the ball-end with the edges of his gauntlets. Tull twisted his grip, and the spear suddenly became charged with dancing blue sparks of electrical charge. He slammed the crackling ball at Loken again and there was a loud bang. The discharging force of the spear was so powerful that Loken was thrown bodily across the chamber. He landed on the polished floor and slid a few metres, dying webs of charge flickering across his chestplate. He tasted blood in his mouth, and felt the brief, quickly-occluded pain of serious bruising to his torso.

Loken scissored his back and legs, and sprang up on to his feet as Tull closed in. Now he brought his sword out. In the multi-coloured light, the white-steel blade of his combat sword shone like a spike of ice in his fist.

He offered Tull no opportunity to renew the bout as aggressor. Loken launched forward at the charging man and swung hammer blows with his sword. Tull recoiled, forced to use the remains of the spear as a parrying tool, the Imperial blade biting chips out of its haft.

Tull leapt back, and drew his own sword over his shoulder from the scabbard over his back. He clutched the long, silver sword – a good ten fingers longer than Loken's utilitarian blade – in his right hand, and the spear/club in his left. When he came in again, he was swinging blows with both.

Loken's Astartes-born senses predicted and matched all of the strikes. His blade flicked left and right, spinning the club back and parrying the sword with two loud chimes of metal. He forced his way into Tull's bodyline guard and pressed his sword aside long enough to shoulder-barge the royal officer in the chest. Tull staggered back. Loken gave him no respite. He swung again and tore the club out of Tull's left hand. It bounced across the floor, sparking and firing.

Then they closed, blade on blade, The exchange was furious. Loken had no doubts about his own ability: he'd been tested too many times of late, and not found wanting. But Tull was evidently a master swordsman and, more significantly, had learned his art via some entirely different school of bladesmanship. There was no common language in their fight, no shared basis of technique. Every blow and parry and riposte, each one essayed was inexplicable and foreign to the other. Every millisecond of the exchange was a potentially lethal learning curve.

It was almost enjoyable. Fascinating. Inventive. Illuminating. Loken believed Lucius would have enjoyed such a match, so many new techniques to delight at.

But it was wasting time. Loken parried Tull's next quicksilver slice, captured his right wrist firmly in his left hand, and struck off Tull's sword-arm at the elbow with a neat and deliberate chop.

Tull rocked backwards, blood venting from his stump. Loken tossed the sword and severed limb aside. He grabbed Tull by the face and was about to perform the mercy stroke, the quick, down-up decapitation, then thought better of it. He smashed Tull in the side of the head with his sword instead, using the flat.

Tull went flying. His body cartwheeled clumsily across the floor and came to rest against the foot of one of the display plinths. Blood leaked out of it in a wide pool.

'This is Loken, Loken, Loken!' Loken yelled in this link. Nothing but dead patterns and static. Switching his blade to his left hand, he drew his bolter and ran forward. He'd gone three steps when the two sagittars bounded into the chamber. They saw him, and their bows were already drawn to fire.

Loken put a bolt round into the wall behind them and made them flinch.

'Drop the bows!' he ordered via his helmet speakers. The bolter in his hand told them not to argue. They threw aside the bows and shafts with a clatter. Loken nodded his head at Tull, his gun still covering them both. 'I've no wish to see him die,' he said. 'Bind his arm quickly before he bleeds out.'

They wavered and then ran to Tull's side. When they looked up again, Loken had gone.

HE RAN DOWN a hallway into an adjoining colonnade, hearing what was certainly bolter firing in the distance. Another sagittar appeared ahead, and fired what seemed like a laser bolt at him. The shot went wide past his left shoulder. Loken aimed his bolter and put the warrior on his back, hard.

No room for compassion now.

Two more interex soldiers came into view, another sagittar and a gleve. Loken, still running, shot them both before they could react. The force of his bolts, both torso-shots, threw the soldiers back against the wall, where they slithered to the ground. Abaddon had been wrong. The armour of the interex warriors was masterful, not weak. His rounds hadn't penetrated the chestplates of either of the men, but the sheer, concussive force of the impacts had taken them out of the fight, probably pulping their innards.

He heard footsteps and turned. It was Kairus and one of his men, Oltrentz. Both had weapons drawn.

'What the hell's happening, captain?' Kairus yelled.

'With me!' Loken demanded. 'Where's the rest of the detail?'

'I have no idea,' Kairus complained. 'The vox is dead!'

'We're being damped,' Oltrentz added.

'Priority is the Warmaster,' Loken assured them. 'Follow me and–'

More flashes, like laser fire. Projectiles, moving so fast they were just lines of light, zipped down the colonnade, faster than Loken could track. Oltrentz dropped onto his knees with a heavy clang, transfixed by two flightless arrows that had cut clean through his Mark IV plate.

Clean through. Loken could still remember Torgaddon's amusement and Aximand's assurance… *They're probably ceremonial.*

Oltrentz fell onto his face. He was dead, and there was no time, and no Apothecary, to make his death fruitful.

Further shafts flashed by. Loken felt an impact. Kairus staggered as a sagittar's dart punched entirely through his torso and embedded itself in the wall behind him.

'Kairus!'

'Keep on, captain!' Kairus drawled, in pain. 'Too clean a shot. I'll heal!'

Kairus rose and opened up with his storm bolter, firing on auto. He hosed the colonnade ahead of them, and Loken saw three sagittars crumble and explode under the thunderous pummel of the weapon. Now their armour broke. Under six of seven consecutive explosive penetrators, *now* their armour broke.

How we have underestimated them, Loken thought. He moved on, with Kairus limping behind him. Already Kairus had stopped bleeding. His genhanced body had self-healed the entry and exit wounds, and whatever the sagittar dart had skewered between those two points was undoubtedly being compensated for by the built-in redundancies of the Astartes's anatomy.

Together, they kicked their way into the main dining hall. The room was chaotic. Torgaddon and the rest of his detail were covering the Warmaster as they led him towards the south exit. There was no sign of Naud, but interex soldiers were firing at Torgaddon's group from a doorway on the far side of the chamber. Bolter fire lit up the air. Several bodies, including that of a Luna Wolf, lay twisted amongst the overturned chairs and banquet tables. Loken and Kairus trained their fire on the far doorway.

'Tarik!'

'Good to see you, Garvi!'

'What the hell is this?'

'A mistake,' Horus roared, his voice cracking with despair. 'This is wrong! Wrong!'

Brilliant shafts of light stung into the wall alongside them. Sagittar darts sliced through the smoky air. One of Torgaddon's men buckled and fell, a dart speared through his helm.

'Mistake or not, we have to get clear. Now!' Loken yelled.

'Zakes! Cyclos! Regold!' Torgaddon yelled, firing. 'Close with Captain Loken and see us out!'

'With me!' Loken shouted.

'No!' bellowed the Warmaster. 'Not like this! We can't–'

'Go!' Loken screamed at his commander.

The fight to extricate themselves from Naud's house lasted ten furious minutes. Loken and Kairus led the rearguard with the brothers Torgaddon had appointed to them, while Torgaddon himself ferried the Warmaster out through the basement loading docks onto the street. Twice, Horus insisted on going back in, not wanting to leave anyone, especially not Loken, behind. Somehow, using words Torgaddon never shared with Loken, Torgaddon persuaded him otherwise.

By the time they had come out into the street, the remainder of Loken's outer guard had formed up with them, adding to the armour wall around the Warmaster, all except Jaeldon, whose fate they never learned.

The rearguard was a savage action. Backing metre by metre through the exit hall and the loading dock, Loken's group came under immense fire, most of it dart-shot from sagittars, but also some energised beams from heavy weapons. Bells and sirens were ringing everywhere. Zakes fell in the loading dock, his head shorn away by a blue-white beam of destruction that scorched the walls. Cyclos, his body a pincushion of darts, dropped at the doors of the exit hall. Prone, bleeding furiously, he tried to fire again, but two more shafts impaled his skull and nailed him to the door. Kairus took another dart through the left thigh as he gave Loken cover. Regold was felled by an arrow that pierced his right eyeslit, and got up in time to be finished by another through the neck.

Firing behind him, Loken dragged Kairus out through the dock area onto the street.

They were out into the city evening, the dark canopy hissing in the breeze over their heads. Lamps twinkled. In the distance, a ruddy glow backlit the clouds, spilling up from a building in the lower depths of the tiered city. Sirens wailed around them.

'I'm all right,' Kairus said, though it was clear he was having trouble standing. 'Close, that one, captain.'

He reached up and plucked out a sagittar shaft that had stuck through Loken's right shoulder plate. In the colonnade, the impact he'd felt.

'Not close enough, brother,' Loken said.

'Come on, if you're coming!' Torgaddon yelled, approaching them and spraying bolter fire back down the dock.

'This is a mess,' Loken said.

'As if I hadn't noticed!' Torgaddon spat. He uncoupled a charge pack from his belt and hurled it down the dockway.

The blast sent smoke and debris tumbling out at them.

'We have to get the Warmaster to safety,' Torgaddon said. 'To the Extranus.'

Loken nodded. 'We have to–'

'No,' said a voice.

They looked round. Horus stood beside them. His face was sidelit by the burning dock. His wide-set eyes were fierce. He had dressed for dinner that night, not for war. He was wearing a robe and a wolf-pelt. It was clear from his manner that he itched for armour plate and a good sword.

'With respect, sir,' Torgaddon said. 'We are drawn bodyguard. You are our responsibility.'

'No,' Horus said again. 'Protect me by all means, but I will not go quietly. Some terrible mistake has been made tonight. All we have worked for is overthrown.'

'And so, we must get you out alive,' Torgaddon said.

'Tarik's right, lord,' Loken added. 'This is not a situation that–'

'Enough, enough, my son,' Horus said. He looked up at the sighing black branches above them. 'What has gone so wrong? Naud took such great and sudden offence. He said we had transgressed.'

'I spoke with a man,' Loken said. 'Just when things turned sour. He was telling me of Chaos.'

'What?'

'Of Chaos, and how it is our greatest common foe. He feared it was in us. He said that is why they had been so careful with us, because they feared we had brought Chaos with us. Lord, what did he mean?'

Horus looked at Loken. 'He meant Jubal. He meant the Whisperheads. He meant the warp. Have you brought the warp here, Garviel Loken?'

'No, sir.'

'Then the fault is within them. The great, great fault that the Emperor himself, beloved by all, told me to watch for, foremost of all things. Oh gods, I wished this place to be free of it. To be clean. To be cousins we could hug to our chests. Now we know the truth.'

Loken shook his head. 'Sir, no. I don't think that's what was meant. I think these people despise Chaos… the warp… as much as we do. I think they only fear it in us, and tonight, something has proved that fear right.'

'Like what?' Torgaddon snapped.

'Tull said the Hall of Devices was on fire.'

Horus nodded. 'This is what they accused us of. Robbery. Deceit. Murder. Apparently someone raided the Hall of Devices tonight and slew the curator. Weapons were stolen.'

'What weapons, sir?' Loken asked.

Horus shook his head. 'Naud didn't say. He was too busy accusing me over the dinner table. That's where we should go now.'

Torgaddon laughed derisively. 'Not at all. We have to get you to safety, sir. That is our priority.'

The Warmaster looked at Loken. 'Do you think this also?'

'Yes, lord.'

'Then I am troubled that I will have to countermand you both. I respect your efforts to safeguard me. Your strenuous loyalty is noted. Now take me to the Hall of Devices.'

THE HALL WAS on fire. Bursting fields exploded through the lower depths of the placer and cascaded flames up into the higher galleries. A meturge player, blackened by smoke, limped out to greet them.

'Have you not sinned enough?' he asked, venomously.

'What is it you think we have done?' Horus asked.

'Petty murder. Asherot is dead. The hall is burning. You could have asked to know of our weapons. You had no need to kill to win them.'

Horus shook his head. 'We have done nothing.'

The meturge player laughed, then fell.

'Help him,' Horus said.

Scads of ash were falling on them, drizzling from a choking black sky. The blaze had spread to the oversweeping forest, and the street was flame lit. There was a rank smell of burning vegetation. On lower street tiers, hundreds of figures gathered, looking up at the fire. A great panic, a horror was spreading through Xenobia Principis.

'They feared us from the start,' the Warmaster said. 'Suspected us. Now this. They will believe they were right to do so.'

'Enemy warriors are gathering on the approach steps,' Kairus called out.

'Enemy?' Horus laughed. 'When did they become the enemy? They are men like us.' He glared up at the night sky, threw back his head and screamed a curse at the stars. Then his voice fell to a whisper. Loken was close enough to hear his words.

'Why have you tasked me with this, father? Why have you forsaken me? Why? It is too hard. It is too much. Why did you leave me to do this on my own?'

Interex formations were approaching. Loken heard hooves clatter-ing on the flagstones, and saw the shapes of mounted sagittars bobbing black against the fires. Darts, like bright tears, began to drizzle through the night. They struck the ground and the walls nearby.

'My lord, no more delays,' Torgaddon urged. Gleves were massing too, their moving spears black stalks against the orange glow. Sparks flew up like lost prayers into the sky.

'Hold!' Horus bellowed at the advancing soldiers. 'In the name of the Emperor of Mankind! I demand to speak to Naud. Fetch him now!'

The only reply was another flurry of shafts. The Luna Wolf beside Torgaddon fell dead, and another staggered back, wounded. An arrow had embedded itself in the Warmaster's left arm. Without wincing, he dragged it out, and watched his blood spatter the flagstones at his feet. He walked to the fallen Astartes, bent down, and gathered up the man's bolter and sword.

'Their mistake,' he said to Loken and Torgaddon. 'Their damn mistake. Not ours. If they're going to fear us, let us give them good reason.' He raised the sword in his fist.

'For the Emperor!' he yelled in Cthonic. 'Illuminate them!'

'Lupercal! Lupercal!' answered the handful of warriors around him.

They met the charging sagittars head on, bolter fire strobing the narrow street. Robot steeds shattered and tumbled, men falling from them, arms spread wide. Horus was already moving to meet them, ripping his sword into steel flanks and armoured chests. His first blow knocked a man-horse clear into the air, hooves kicking, crashing it back over onto the ranks behind it.

'Lupercal!' Loken yelled, coming to the Warmaster's right side, and swinging his sword double-handed. Torgaddon covered the left, striking down a trio of gleves, then using a lance taken from one of them to smite the pack that followed. Interex soldiers, some screaming, were forced back down the steps, or toppled over the stone railing of the street to plunge onto the tier beneath.

Of all the battles Loken had fought at his commander's side, that was the fiercest, the saddest, the most vicious. Teeth bared in the firelight, swinging his blade at the foe on all sides, Horus seemed more noble than Loken had ever known. He would remember that moment, years later, when fate had played its cruel trick and sense had turned upside down. He would remember Horus, Warmaster, in that narrow firelit street, defining the honour and unyielding courage of the Imperium of Man.

There should have been frescoes painted, poems written, symphonies composed, all to celebrate that instant when Horus made his most absolute statement of devotion to the Throne.

And to his father.

There would be none. The hateful future swallowed up such poss-ibilities, swallowed the memories too, until the very fact of that nobility became impossible to believe.

The enemy warriors, and they were enemy warriors now, choked the street, driving the Warmaster and his few remaining bodyguards into a tight ring. A last stand. It was oddly as he had imagined it, that night in the garden, making his oath. Some great, last stand against an unknown foe, fighting at Horus's side.

He was covered in blood, his suit gouged and dented in a hundred places. He did not falter. Through the smoke above, Loken glimpsed a moon, a small moon glowing in the corner of the alien sky.

Appropriately, it was reflected in the glimmering mirror of ocean out in the bay.

'Lupercal!' screamed Loken.

FOUR

Parting shots
The Sons of Horus
Anathame

'WHAT WAS TAKEN?' Mersadie Oliton asked.

'A weapon, so they claim.'

'One weapon?'

'We didn't take it,' Loken said, stripping off the last of his battered armour. 'We took nothing. The killing was for nothing.'

She shrugged. She took a sheaf of papers from her gown. They were Karkasy's latest offerings, and she had come to the arming chamber on the pretence of delivering them. In truth, she was hoping to learn what had befallen on Xenobia.

'Will you tell me?' she asked. He looked up. There was dried blood on his face and hands.

'Yes,' he said.

THE BATTLE OF Xenobia Principis lasted until dawn, and engulfed much of the city. At the first sign of commotion, unable to establish contact with either the Warmaster or the fleet, Abaddon and

Aximand had mobilised the two companies of Luna Wolves gar-
risoned at the Extranus. In the streets surrounding the compound
area, the people of the interex got their first taste of the power
of the Imperial Astartes. In the years to come, they would experience a good deal more. Abaddon was in wrathful mood, so much
so that Aximand had to rein him back on several occasions.

It was Aximand's units that first reached the embattled Warmaster on the upper tier near the Hall of Devices, and fought a route
to him through the cream of Naud's army. Abaddon's forces had
struck at several of the city's control stations, and restored communications. The fleet was already moving in, in response to the
apparent threat to the Warmaster and the Imperial parties on the
ground. As interex warships moved to engage, landing assaults
began, led by Sedirae and Targost.

With communications restored, a fullscale extraction was coor-
dinated, drawing all Imperial personnel from the Extranus, and
from fighting zones in the streets.

Horus sent one final communiqué to the interex. He expected no
response, and received none. Far too much blood had been spilled
and destruction wrought for relations to be soothed by diplomacy.
Nevertheless, Horus expressed his bitter regret at the turn of events,
lamented the interex for acting with such a heavy hand, and
repeated once again his unequivocal denial that the Imperium had
committed any of the crimes of which it stood accused.

WHEN THE SHIPS of the expedition returned to Imperial space,
some weeks later, the Warmaster had a decree proclaimed. He
told the Mournival that, upon reflection, he had reconsidered
the importance of defining his role, and the relationship of the
XVI Legion to that role. Henceforth, the Luna Wolves would be
known as the Sons of Horus.

The news was well-received. In the quiet corners of the flagship archives, Kyril Sindermann was told by some of his iterators, and approved the decision, before turning back to books that he was the first person to read in a thousand years. In the bustle of the Retreat, the remembrancers – many of whom had been extracted from the Extranus by the Astartes efforts – cheered and drank to the new name. Ignace Karkasy sank a drink to the honour of the Legion, and Captain Loken in particular, and then had another one just to be sure.

In her private room, Euphrati Keeler knelt by her secret shrine and thanked her god, the Emperor of Mankind, in the simple terms of the Lectitio Divinitatus, praising him for giving strong and honourable men to protect them. Sons of Horus, all.

AIR HUMMED DOWN rusting ducts and flues. Darkness pooled in the belly vaults of the *Vengeful Spirit*, in the bilges where even the lowliest ratings and proto-servitors seldom strayed. Only vermin lived here, insect lice and rats, gnawing a putrid existence in the corroded bowels of the ancient ship.

By the light of a single candle, he held the strange blade up and watched how the glow coruscated off its edge. The blade was rippled along its length, grey like napped flint, and caught the light with a glitter like diamond. A fine thing. A beautiful thing. A cosmos-changing thing.

He could feel the promise within it breathing. The promise and the curse.

Slowly, Erebus lowered the anathame, placed it in its casket, and closed the lid.

'AND THAT IS all?'

'We tried,' said Loken. 'We tried to bond with them. It was a brave thing, a noble thing to attempt. War would have been easier. But it failed.'

'Yes,' he said. Loken had taken up the lapping powder and a cloth, and was working at the scratches and gouges on his breast-plate, knowing full well the scars were too deep this time. He'd have to fetch the armourers.

'So it was a tragedy?' she asked.

'Yes,' he nodded, 'but not of our making. I've never... I've never felt so sure.'

'Of what?' she asked.

'Horus, as Warmaster. As the Emperor's proxy. I've never questioned it. But seeing him there, seeing what he was trying to do. I've never felt so sure the Emperor made the right choice.'

'What happens now?'

'With the interex? I imagine attempts will be made to broker peace. The priority will be low, for the interex are marginal and show no inclination to get involved in our affairs. If peace fails, then, in time, a military expedition will be drawn up.'

'And for us? Are you allowed to tell me the expedition's orders?'

Loken smiled and shrugged. 'We're due to rendezvous with the 203rd Fleet in a month, at Sardis, prior to a campaign of compliance in the Caiades Cluster, but on the way, a brief detour. We're to settle a minor dispute. An old tally, if you will. First Chaplain Erebus has asked the Warmaster to intercede. We'll be there and gone again in a week or so.'

'Intercede where?' she asked.

'A little moon,' Loken said, 'in the Davin System.'

ABOUT THE AUTHOR

Dan Abnett is a multiple *New York Times* bestselling author and an award-winning comic book writer. He has written almost fifty novels, including the acclaimed Gaunt's Ghosts series, and the Eisenhorn and Ravenor trilogies. His Horus Heresy novel *Prospero Burns* topped the SF charts in the UK and the US. In addition to writing for Black Library, Dan scripts audio dramas, movies, games, comics and bestselling novels for major publishers in Britain and America. He lives and works in Maidstone, Kent.

THE HORUS HERESY®

Graham McNeill

FALSE GODS

The heresy takes root

An extract from False Gods
by Graham McNeill

A REVERED HUSH fell on the assemblage and every person present
dropped to one knee as the Emperor's chosen proxy made his
entrance. Karkasy felt faint at the sight of the living god, arrayed
as he was in a magnificent suit of plate armour the colour of a
distant ocean and a cloak of deepest purple. The eye of Terra
shone on his breast, and Karkasy was overcome by the magisterial beauty of the Warmaster.

To have spent so long in the 63rd Expedition and only now to
lay eyes upon the Warmaster seemed the grossest waste of his
time, and Karkasy resolved to tear out the pages he'd written in
the Bondsman Number 7 this week and compose an epic solilo-
quy on the nobility of the commander.

The Mournival followed him, together with a tall, statuesque
woman in a crimson velveteen gown with high collars and
puffed sleeves, her long hair worn in an impractical looking

coiffure. He felt his indignation rise as he realised this must be Vivar, the remembrancer from Terra that they had heard about.

Horus raised his arms and said, 'Friends, I keep telling you that no one need kneel in my presence. Only the Emperor is deserving of such an honour.'

Slowly, as though reluctant to cease their veneration of this living god, the crowd rose to its feet as Horus passed amongst those closest to him, shaking hands and dazzling them with his easy charm and spontaneous wit. Karkasy watched the faces of those the Warmaster spoke to, feeling intense jealousy swell within his breast at the thought of not being so favoured.

Without thinking, he began pushing his way through the crowd towards the front, receiving hostile glares and the odd elbow to the gut for his troubles. He felt a tug on the collar of his robe and craned his neck to rebuke whoever had thought to handle his expensive garments so roughly. He saw Euphrati Keeler behind him and, at first, thought she was attempting to pull him back, but then he saw her face and smiled as he realised that she was coming with him, using his bulk like a plough.

He managed to get within six or seven people of the front, when he remembered why he had been allowed within this august body in the first place. He tore his eyes from the Warmaster to watch Erebus of the Word Bearers.

Karkasy knew little of the XVII Legion, save that its primarch, Lorgar, was a close and trusted brother of Horus. Both Legions had fought and shed their blood together many times for the glory of the Imperium. The members of the Mournival came forward and, one by one, embraced Erebus as a long lost brother. They laughed and slapped each other's armour in welcome, though Karkasy saw a measure of reticence in the embrace between Loken and Erebus.

'Focus, Ignace, focus…' he whispered to himself as he found his gaze straying once again to the glory of the Warmaster. He tore his eyes from Horus in time to see Abaddon and Erebus shake hands one last time and saw a gleam of silver pass between their palms. He couldn't be sure, it had happened so fast, but it had looked like a coin or medal of some sort.

The Mournival and Vivar then took up positions a respectful distance behind the Warmaster, as Maloghurst assumed his place at his master's side. Horus lifted his arms and said, 'You must bear with me once again, my friends, as we gather to discuss our plans to bring truth and light to the dark places.'

Polite laughter and clapping spread towards the edges of the yurt as Horus continued. 'Once again we return to Davin, site of a great triumph and the eighth world brought into compliance. Truly it is–'

'Warmaster,' came a voice from the centre of the yurt.

The word was spoken softly, and the audience let out a collective gasp at such a flagrant breach of etiquette.

Karkasy saw the Warmaster's expression turn thunderous, understanding that he was obviously unused to being interrupted, before switching his scrutiny back to the speaker.

The crowd drew back from Erebus, as though afraid that mere proximity to him might somehow taint them with his temerity.

'Erebus,' said Maloghurst. 'You have something to say.'

'Merely a correction, equerry,' explained the Word Bearer.

Karkasy saw Maloghurst give the Warmaster a wary sidelong glance. 'A correction you say. What would you have corrected?'

'The Warmaster said that this world is compliant,' said Erebus.

'Davin is compliant,' growled Horus.

Erebus shook his head sadly and, for the briefest instant,

Karkasy detected a trace of dark amusement in his next pronouncement.

'No,' said Erebus. 'It is not.'